INK'S DEVIL

MANDA MELLETT

COPYRIGHT

CAST OF CHARACTERS

Officers

Demon – President

Beef - Vice President

Buzzard – Secretary/Treasurer

Thunder – Sergeant-At-Arms

Mace – Enforcer

Sparky – Road Captain

Patched Members

Hellfire

Bomber

Cad

Ink

Lizard

Pyro

Paladin

Rusty

Skull

Judge

Wills

Prospects
Karl
Beaver
Smithy – Failed Prospect

Old Ladies & Children
Violet (Demon's): Theo
Steph (Beef's)
Sindy (Buzzard's)
Moira (Hellfire's): Demon, Kennedy, Samuel
Jeannie (Bomber's)
Jayden (Paladin's)
Mel (Pyro's)

Sweet Butts
Bella
Breezy
Sheila
Titsy
Tulia

Deceased Members
Blackie – Previous President
Furnace – Previous VP
Ingot – Previous Enforcer
Taser

SATAN'S DEVILS MC

CHAPTER ONE

Ink

"So, Pyro's married. Got the ball and chain well and truly attached now." Lizard, my MC brother and manager of the Satan's Devil's tattoo parlour, chuckles raising what must be his sixth beer of the night as if in salute.

"Yeah. How about that?" Mace, our enforcer replies, his brow furrowing. "It was obvious what he thought about her from the start, but he had to stay clear as Skull, *God damn his soul*, had claimed her." His face twists and then relaxes into an approximation of a smile. "But never believed Ro would end up married."

"Kid coming along too," I say, pressing my lips together. "He seems fuckin' happy about it. Me? Nah. I prefer being single." I glance around the posh banqueting hall where the wedding reception is being held. Breezy, Titsy, Sheila, Tulia, and Bella, our sweet butts, have all been invited and seem to scrub up well. Today, they're wearing clothes more suitable to the occasion rather than the barely nothing that's their usual attire. My cock twitches as I wonder which I'll go with tonight. One, that's for certain. Maybe two if I get my chance. I'll have to get in quick though. Weddings make everyone horny and they'll be in high demand.

Club girls know the score and exactly what they are there for, which is to satisfy the members in any way they want their appetites met. No courtship necessary or even foreplay if you're not in the mood, but usually I am, ensuring both partners have fun and get off. I don't need a woman to be faithful to me, nor me to them.

Stick with one woman like Pyro? Nah. Though, if the proud beam on his face is anything to go by, it seems to suit my brother well enough.

Mace stares down into his bottle of beer, then glances up and gives me a nudge. "Well will you take a look at that? Mel's coming over. That bitch with her looks hot."

She looks fucking huge. My eyes widen as I watch what must be the tallest woman I've ever seen crossing the room. Mel is looking like a little kid at her side. As my eyes soak her in, I notice her hair is bright blue, matching the shade of the brides-maid's dress she's wearing. Definitely not a sign suggesting she's shy.

Lizard has overheard Mace's comment and leans in, uttering confidentially, "I could definitely do her." Then, louder, he calls out, "Hey, Mel. Are you going to introduce us?" He doesn't try to hide the leer in his eyes as his gaze takes in her friend, a process that uses more than a moment, as there's a lot of her to observe. Liz is right to take his time. Christ, that woman's nearly as tall as I am, and I'm six-foot-six.

Mel's smiling which is nothing new. She's not stopped beaming since Pyro slid his ring on her finger a few hours ago. "Sorry Liz," she says bluntly, "it's not you she's interested in."

Mace straightens beside me.

"Or you," she chuckles.

In a mock show of hurt he places his hand over his heart.

There are only three of us propping up this part of the bar. I raise my eyebrow.

"Yeah, Ink. It's you. Ink, this is Beth. Beth, this is Ink. The rest is up to you."

Fuck me. With that Mel turns and strides off heading toward

her husband as though she can't bear being parted with him for long, leaving me with her friend.

Beth glances after Mel in surprise at having been so abruptly abandoned, and while she'd looked confident walking over, now she shifts awkwardly, balancing her weight first on one foot and then the other, sending sly appraising glances my way through her eyelashes.

Lizard had been right. She's a good-looking bitch. A bit younger than Mel, mid-to-late-twenties would be my guess. The startling colour of her hair is so vivid, it suggests she's only just dyed it. It hangs down past her shoulders in waves and perfectly matches the colour of her eyes. Her skin is fair, as is most of ours. After all, it's winter. Her midnight-blue dress hugs her figure showing she's slender, not much to offer in the tits department, but with a shapely ass. Intriguingly, she's looking me straight in the face. Bitches normally have to crane their necks to look up at me.

Interesting as she is, I don't do citizens.

The silence stretches out. Liz and Mace have started a discussion about the new model Harley is bringing out, and while I'm eager to join in and offer my opinion, I'd be rude to ignore Mel's friend. But I don't have anything to say to her, any small talk would have to involve bikes or sport.

In the end, it's her who breaks the silence. "Why, Ink?" Her hand indicates my skin, left bare as nature intended.

Knowing exactly what she's asking, it's not the first time the question has been posed. I shrug. "I don't like needles. No fuckin' way am I getting a tattoo."

"Fuckin' pussy," Liz overhears and mutters out of the side of his mouth.

Reaching around Mace, I clip Lizard's ear.

Our interaction makes Beth give a nervous laugh, before saying, "I don't have any either."

I don't give a fuck one way or another. Caught by movement out of the corner of my eye, my gaze shifts behind her. It's Tulia, and she's gesturing at me. I give her a nod, and Beth turns to see what I'm looking at. Her face falls when she sees it's another girl. Her expression suggests she already knows about the club whores and interprets my non-verbal communication with Tulia correctly.

I know I'm being a bastard, and with the club girl hovering in the background, feel strangely compelled to offer an explanation. "Look, Beth, I'm not in the market for a civilian." As her head tilts in confusion, I try again. "You're obviously a nice girl, Beth. I'm a biker. I stick with my own kind, if you get my drift." Another glance behind her shows Tulia's now been joined by Breezy. Judge is openly fondling Breezy's tits as he pulls her back against him, and from the movement of his hips and the dilation of her eyes it's not hard to guess he's rubbing his cock against her.

Beth swallows hard, then offers, "I could walk on the wild side."

"Nah, sorry, darlin', but I'm not interested." I'm direct and to the point. Nothing to gain by leading her on and trying to let her down gently.

"You want biker cock, sweetheart? I'll give it to you." Mace is equally candid.

She gasps at his bluntness. Her shocked reaction shows that my gut feeling is right. Beth wants some of what Mel's got, a ring on her finger, not a quick roll in the hay.

Weddings. The worst possible place to hook up. Girls get stars in their eyes and start dreaming of a happy forever. The bride's joy in her new status is infectious. If I was ever going to pick up a civilian, a place where a husband and wife have just spoken vows is the very last location I'd choose.

"I, er…"

Belatedly, I realise Beth is trying to find a suitable response to Mace. I help her out, chuckling, "Just tell him to get lost, babe."

But she doesn't. Instead she pushes past me and puts a hand

on the enforcer's arm. "You offering?" she asks, her voice having taken on a huskiness that goes straight to my cock.

I don't know the reason, but all of a sudden my jaw tightens. *If anyone's cock is going to see some action with Beth, it's going to be mine.* Hastily, I revise my opinion of her. Perhaps she's not such a 'nice' girl as I first thought. Maybe she does know the score and is willing to bed a man with no promises of anything more.

"He's not," I tell her sharply, lifting the hand that she placed on Mace's arm, and tightening my fingers around hers. Giving a head shake of warning to my companions, I pull her away from the bar, to a corner where we won't be overheard. Purposefully, I back her up until her spine is against the wall and there's nowhere for her to go. I crowd her, my body right up in her personal space, and brace one hand against the fancy brickwork. The other, I use to tilt her chin toward me. With her height, she's looking me straight in the eyes.

"One offer. One chance to turn it down. You say yes, little girl, and you're going to get what you think you're after, biker cock. But there's not going to be any happily ever after, you got it? Okay? Yeah, you're a good-looking bitch and I..." I don't have to shift my hips much to rub my rock-hard cock against her, "I'm in the mood to fuck. That's all I'm offering." I'd called her little, she's anything but that. Slender, but so tall, I'm already wondering if she's going to feel different than girls I've had in the past. The novelty of her parts fitting exactly against mine makes me hope she'll say yes. I'm all up for variety, and Beth would make a great notch on my bed post.

Her eyes flare. *With interest? Anger? Disgust?*

But it seems it's the former when she places her hand against my chest. "One night. But not one fuck. Unless," it's her turn to break off and give an impudent grin, "you can only get it up once."

She's taunting the fucking beast here.

"Only once? I'll fuck you so many times your cunt will be sore, and you won't be able to walk straight for days."

"Yeah?" Her eyes dilate. "Well I'll want it so much your dick might fall off."

I bark a strangled laugh at the way she's trying to come back at me with dirty talk that sounds alien coming out of her pretty civilian mouth. A doubt remains in my head.

"Whether or not you can break my dick, this is just one night, little girl. When you leave my bed, you won't be coming back. Fuckin' is all I'm offering, okay? I don't do sweet talk, I won't be murmuring sweet little nothings into your ear. My cock, your cunt. That's all I want."

I'm describing an interaction with a whore, but I need her to know what she's getting into. Don't want her feeling hurt and used afterward, she's got to understand the little she's going to get.

The sounds of the wedding are continuing all around us. People's laughter and upbeat conversations can be heard even over the music which is playing loudly, but we seem to be in an oasis apart from everything else. I give her one last chance. "If you've got any ideas in your head about trying to change my mind, you can drop them now. Never had a cunt that tempted me back for more."

She's the one now thrusting her hips against me, her bravado causing my cock to swell further. "What makes you think your dick is so good, I'll want a second time?"

Oh, she will. She'll be begging me for it. But I've told her the score.

"You sure?" One final check. "This is for tonight only."

A little nod.

"Words, babe."

"I'm sure. Just one night."

I give her one more moment, then push myself upright. Taking a firm hold of her hand, I stride across the ballroom and out the door, fleetingly observing she doesn't need to run to keep up.

As I pass by the windows, I see snow falling outside, and I'm fucking glad we've all got rooms in this swanky hotel tonight. Satan's Devils are perhaps not the clientele they usually have staying, but hell, I've drunk too much to ride. Not that I'd even ride sober with the amount of white shit I can see on the ground.

It also means we don't have far to go, and the elevator only has to rise a couple of floors. Long enough for me to turn her, her back to my front, and I cover those small tits with my hands. They might not be large, but as I slide my fingers underneath that plunging neckline of her dress and tweak her nipples, I can immediately tell they're sensitive, if her gasp and the way her ass drives into my cock is any indication.

Tits. What can I say? I like them. Bigger is best, but hey, any port in a storm, and I'll be able to make this work.

A ding and a mechanical *door opening* announcement and we've arrived at my floor. I pull up her dress so she's decent again, then taking her by the arm, drag her out of the elevator and along to the correct door. Having presented the key card, I give her access to my room.

Impersonal, of course. I won't be able to be too inventive. If I were back at the compound, I'd have far more options. But hey, never let it be said I'm at a loss for ideas.

If she wants biker cock, she'll get it. Just this once. I was honest when I warned her, where civilians are concerned, I never do them twice.

"Clothes off, babe," I instruct as I turn to close the door, hanging the 'do not disturb' sign outside.

"No kiss?"

I don't even reply. I'm not going to bother to go through some slow seduction routine. She told me she was sure, and I'd told her my cock was the only thing on offer. For as long as I can remember, I've only been with the whores, or women who know the score. If she wants more, well, she knows where to find the door.

I turn away again, wondering whether she's going to run. Instead, from behind me I hear the rustling of the satin of that bridesmaid's dress which indicates she's obeying. Taking off my cut, I reverently place it over the back of the chair, then unbutton the dress shirt I'd worn in deference to the occasion. My top half bare, I place one foot on the same chair that's holding my leather, undo one boot and remove my sock, then I do the same to the other. Finally, I undo my pants and pushing them down over my hips, take them off.

My cock's already standing at attention as I turn, pleased to find Beth has done exactly as I asked, and is lying naked on the bed, her head propped on the pillows, her feet stretched right out almost touching the end. One arm lies across her breasts. Her body is slightly twisted, weight on one hip and her legs pressed tightly together so her sex is hidden to my eyes.

She's shy. I grin, it's been a long time since I've seen a sight like that. The club girls would have left nothing to the imagination and probably would be playing with themselves by now. Strangely I find I like the change.

I grin as I see where her eyes are focused. "Like what you see?"

Not too shy, I have to quickly amend, when I hear her reply, "Is that all you've got?"

Is that all I've fucking got? But fuck me if I don't look down to check my cock hasn't shrunk in the wash. Nope, it's all there in its impressive glory. *Has she been with bigger men before? Or is she just yanking my chain?* I suspect it's the latter, but if not, she's going to learn size doesn't matter, it's what you do with it that counts. I've no doubt I can impress her on that account. All she's doing is racking up punishments. First one, I start counting in my head.

Her casual words are at odds with her behaviour. Even from here I can tell she's turned on. Her state betrayed by the red flush on her face which extends down her neck to the top of her breasts hidden under that arm. Her pupils are large, and the air has that faint tinge of sex, making my nostrils flare.

"Move your arm, babe. Put your hands over your head. And

open your legs. Fair's fair. You've seen my goods, now let me see what you've got."

I'm used to the club girls immediately doing exactly what I say. She doesn't. I grin, again. She's going to find out what happens to disobedient little girls. First, though, I need to take the edge off. Time for fun later.

Challenge accepted.

I move fast, throwing myself on the bed, my weight making her bounce, then I take first one hand then the other, imprisoning both in one of mine and forcing them up and over her head. Working in tandem, one of my knees comes between hers, forcing her legs to part. A quick glance down shows me she's shaved, waxed… fuck, I don't care, except that I'm pleased she's bare. One of my pet peeves is getting pubes in my mouth.

She tries to move, but I've got her pinned in place.

"Didn't think this through, did you, little girl?" I rasp against her ear. "You wanted a biker to fuck you, and that's exactly what you're going to get."

There's a sharp intake of breath and her skin flushes more as I feast my eyes on her tits. They're small, but perky, and the areolas are a lovely shade of light brown. Her nipples harden with just my gaze on them. Yeah, there can be no doubt she's already aroused.

Unable to resist any longer, I lower my head and suck one of those peaks right into my mouth and using my teeth, nip it gently. Her back arches as she gasps. Yup, she's sensitive alright, and for the second time I wish I was back in my own room, so I could decorate those nipples with clamps decked out in blue jewels to match her stunning hair.

I pinch the other nipple that I've neglected between the first finger and thumb of my free hand. Again, she makes a sound and squirms, but the effect is to grind her pelvis against my cock. I'm pushing her, pleased she's making no complaint, that little moan can only be interpreted as one of encouragement.

After spending a couple of minutes torturing her nipples, I

glance at her face. Her head is thrown back, her eyes are closed, and her lips are firmly pressed together as she concentrates on taking all the pleasure I'm so clearly giving her.

"Don't move your arms," I instruct.

Removing the hand I've used as a makeshift restraint, I pause a second to see if she obeys. I'm not even sure she's aware that I've released her as I nibble my way down her stomach and to that nirvana between her legs.

But my first lick of her moisture from slit to clit has her bowing up from the bed, and her hands fluttering in the air.

"Babe," I warn, raising my head, "that's the third."

Her mouth forms an O and her arms go back to where I want them.

CHAPTER TWO

Beth

I *'d asked for this.* I'd asked for meaningless sex with a biker just to see what it was like. Had I not had a few drinks to give me Dutch courage, I'd never have had the nerve to go after him so blatantly, but I had. Not enough to be drunk and not know what I was doing, but sufficient for me to suppress the shy introvert inside, and for once, actually ask for what I wanted.

I'd been eyeing him up all day. The first thing I'd noticed was how tall he was. His handsome face was the second. Next, it was just the way that he was. I'd heard him talk and joke with his friends, seen him firmly move one of the bikers out of the way when a waiter was passing with drinks. When Violet got the clasp of her necklace caught in her hair, it was he who saw what was wrong and quickly had it sorted. His behaviour seemed to show he was a take charge dominant man, just the sort of man I dreamed of, but never expected to meet. I wasn't going to pass up this opportunity.

I hadn't needed the words to know this was just once, but something told me that it would be worth it. As long as I kept telling myself I didn't need a repeat, the experience would be something to remember.

So far this encounter with the tattoo-less biker so inappropriately called Ink is already nothing like any sex I've ever had before. My prior experiences have involved flirting, the polite telegraphing that both parties are interested, then a kiss which becomes increasingly sensual, with hands gradually coming into play, mutually commencing and taking liberties with a hesitant exploration of each other's bodies.

Then, if it progresses and moves into the bedroom, a polite and slow removal of clothes, with glances and sighs of appreciation as the usually hidden areas of skin are exposed.

To be told to undress, and then not even be able to offer a tantalising striptease—*he'd turned his back*—had put me on edge.

His commands continue. Do this, do that. So far out of my comfort zone, I'm surprised to discover I'm enjoying it.

Ink's by far the tallest man I've ever been with, every other partner has been shorter. While I've had a couple of relationships that have worked for a while, most times my height has been, or has quickly become a factor. I've even been at the mercy of men who simply wanted to parade me around like a trophy they've won, or then there are those who expected me to be the dominant partner and were disappointed to find I was no dominatrix.

I view relationships like Mel has with Pyro as being far out of my reach. In my experience, men just aren't protective of me, rather seeing me in the role of protector.

Ink, well, he's a million miles away from any other man I've ever had in my bed.

If I were asked, I'd say my preference is to be an equal player, to give tit for tat. When I'm touched, to touch back. Ink's not giving me a chance to do that. He's keeping me off kilter, but any complaint dies on my lips as I discover I don't hate what he's doing.

He isn't polite, he's taking what he wants, and I'm fast discovering that's exactly how I want it too.

He'd wasted no time homing in on my nipples. Instead of gradually increasing the pressure to what I enjoy, exploring to find out what I might like, he applied it immediately. My breasts have always been sensitive, they might be small, but someone playing with them always turns me on. Ink's roughness was just what I needed. It just wasn't what I'd expected.

He expects me to take what he gives without being an active participant myself, it's something I'd never have said I'd enjoy. But, oh boy, when he starts licking me *there*, his pressure is just right, and he seems to know where everything is and exactly how to find it. *Jeez*. He's found my G-spot now, when other men I'd been with would have been unable to find it with Siri's help and a map.

His mouth is on my clit, his fingers inside me. With my tits still throbbing from the pinches he'd administered, I'm not going to last long.

How many women must he have pleasured to know exactly what to do?

A lot. But I knew what I was getting in to when I asked for sex with a biker. My friend Mel doesn't come into work every day with a huge satisfied smile on her face for no reason. Now, I suspect I'm finding out why.

My brain switches off as my muscles start clenching, little ripples across my stomach until *oh, yeah, there*. I scream. I can't help it.

As I try to get my breath back, I feel cooler air on my skin as he lifts his body away. Cracking open my eyes, I watch as he takes the couple of steps he requires to get to his pants and delves into a pocket. Then he comes back carrying a handful of condoms, they flutter down on to the bed. I try to count them. Six? Seven? *Really?*

He sees my eyes widen and grins. "Promised you wouldn't be able to walk."

Disobeying him, I lower my hand and wave toward the packs on the bed. "Prove it."

"That's four. Five unless you put your hand back."

My brow furrows as I've no idea what he's talking about, but as he's ceased all movement and is just waiting, I do what he says, and once again have my hands clasped behind my head. Then I watch entranced as he tugs at his dick before swiftly opening the first packet, and covering himself with latex.

Jeez. This man can move fast. Next thing I know, he's between my thighs, my ass slightly raised and my legs up over his shoulders. Then… Oh, he's pushing in.

I was teasing him about his size. He's by far the biggest man I've been with, a cock in proportion to his even taller-than-me height and muscular body. It's thick and long and there's a burn as he pushes inside, even though he'd prepared me, and I am dripping wet.

I gasp, he stills, then pushes again.

"Relax," he instructs, then leans forward so I feel the chuckling vibration of his voice. "This won't hurt a bit."

I bite back a scoff. *Easy for him to say.*

But despite his comment, he's as gentle as a man his size can be and takes his time slowly working himself in. When I reopen my eyes, I see him gazing at me intently and know he's keeping track of all my expressions.

At last he's fully seated inside me, and he pauses, giving me a moment to adjust.

I can't resist. "Are you in?"

He barks a startled laugh. "Oh, pretty Beth, that's six."

Why does he keep spitting numbers at me?

Then I couldn't give a damn. My brain turns to mush as he starts moving.

Christ, this man knows what to do. That swivel of his hips makes his cock touch all the right places. Then he does it again. And again. Oh God, am I going to survive this?

Like many tall girls I was a late bloomer. Even my first self-administered orgasm was so late in putting in an appearance, I'd begun to fear I was asexual. But a study had reassured me my late development was normal due to the excessive hormones responsible for my height. In addition, I've only been able to come from oral fairly recently. Until tonight, I'd given up on the hope I might be capable of coming from internal stimulation alone, but as my body tenses and reacts to his, I start to wonder if Ink might prove me wrong.

I've never felt anything like this in my life. He's not rough but forceful, hammering in until the bed's bouncing against the wall and my last conscious thought is that anyone in the next room must hear the knocking and will be left in no doubt as to what we're doing in here. But I don't give a damn as my muscles tighten in the telltale signs that I'm coming. I couldn't stop it if I tried. My pussy clamps on his cock and my hands move again, this time to shove my fist in my mouth to muffle my scream.

"Seven," he announces. "Want to hear you, babe."

"Did you…?"

After giving me just a few seconds to recover, he resumes thrusting. "No."

"God!" I cry out a minute later, when he brings me to the peak and I go over again.

I have three orgasms before he finally lets himself go. I feel him swell, feel his body leaning on mine, feel him press in, pull out slightly, then repeats his action twice more. The third time he holds himself in groaning, "Fuck, babe, fuck."

As I slowly recover my senses, I open my eyes to see him, his lungs heaving and his head bowed.

Hmm. He said he had stamina. I'm just about to make a snide comment, when he suddenly raises his head, looks at me and grins widely. "Not bad, little girl. Not bad at all."

Will he be giving me marks out of ten next? Or was that his weird number counting? If I've only earned a seven, is that disappointing or good?

He pulls out, and holding the condom securely, disappears into the bathroom. Shortly after, I hear a toilet flush and the sound of water running in a sink.

When he reappears, he looks serious for a second, eyeing the room. Then he breathes out unexpected words.

"Ah, that will do. Come here, babe."

Instead of returning to the bed, he sits in the armchair that the hotel provided.

My eyes crease as I watch him pat his lap. If he wants to cuddle, why hasn't he joined me on the comfortable mattress? But yeah, well, I could do with being held for a moment. After how he's treated our encounter, it's something I didn't expect.

I groan slightly as I pull my overworked body up, and naked, cross the room to him, my lips curving in anticipation of his arms encircling me. But as I turn to place my ass on his lap, he instructs again.

"Nah, babe. Lie over my legs."

What? "What?" I ask out loud.

He pats his lap.

I don't move.

"Christ, woman, that's eight. Do as you're fuckin' told."

Proving once again how fast he can move, he strikes like a snake, standing and manhandling me until he's sitting back down and I'm lying with my stomach on his thighs, my legs trapped by one of his strong muscled calves, and his hand pushing hard on my back to keep me down. "You're going to have to learn to do as I say," he murmurs.

"Ow!" The sharp slap to my ass startles the cry out of me, as much from the shock as the pain. *He hit me.* Oh no, I'm not putting up with that. But as I struggle, I feel his palm rubbing my buttock until the sting becomes a warm flush that heats my skin, and I'll be damned if my clit doesn't tingle.

The heat of his hand disappears, and another hard smack comes on my opposite flank.

Jeez. That hurt. That…

He rubs again, and this time I can feel myself growing wet.

"You smell good," he says softly in an amused voice. "Your sex. Sweet."

I've tensed slightly, in case there is more to come. "Relax, it will hurt more if you tighten your muscles."

"It won't hurt at all if you stop." I wriggle, but he's got me locked down.

"Nah." He chuckles. "You've more to come. One, you insulted my cock. Two, you were too slow to do what I said. Three, you disobeyed me when you lowered your arms. You're a disobedient little thing, aren't you?" He carries on listing the infractions I'd supposedly committed, punctuating each one with a sharp slap to my ass, until he gets to the final numbers. "Seven, you critiqued my performance, and eight, you refused to lie on my lap."

My skin burns and I'm sure my backside is bright red, but instead of being furious and angry, I feel languid, and slightly disappointed he's stopped. My clit throbs and I swear I'm as aroused as I've ever been. Me, who always wondered why some women, and men come to that, like being spanked so much. One thing's for certain, Ink's making me re-evaluate a lot of my assumptions about myself tonight.

His hands gently stroke my back and my ass. "You're a lovely shade of pink, little girl. You mark well. I can even see my handprint."

Is it so wrong that there's something about him having marked me that I like? Mentally, I shake myself. *You wanted the biker loving experience, this is what you got.* Idly I wonder if Pyro spanks Mel, and whether she likes it.

"I think you enjoyed that," he chuckles.

"How do you come to that conclusion?" I summon the strength to respond.

"Because you're making no effort to move."

"I happen to like staring at the floor," I indignantly respond.

Now he's outright laughing. "You enjoyed it so much, babe, think you ought to thank me." His arms gently straighten me. "Now get on your knees and show me how grateful you are."

My eyes widen. As if making sure I'm left in no doubt of what he wants, he strokes his hard again cock, and stares at my mouth.

He wants me to suck him.

One of his eyebrows is raised in challenge. *He thinks I'm going to refuse.* I might have, it's not exactly something that I enjoy, but I'll be damned if I'm going to give the satisfaction of proving him right that I can't handle the needs of a biker.

As sexily as I can, I slide down to my knees, relieved that the floor is carpet and not tile, place my hands on his thighs and pull myself in between his parted legs. His cock is clean, he must have washed himself after removing the condom, but as it bobs in front of my eyes, a drop of pre-cum leaks from the tip.

First, I lick my lips, then stretch out my tongue and lick that tempting drop off. It tastes salty, and not too unpleasant.

He growls, as I proceed to circle my tongue around the head of his dick. *Oh, the power.* Relishing that the tables are turned, I take him inside my mouth, my hands circling the length I can't take in. He might have issued the demand, but it's me who's now in control as I proceed to try to drive him out of his mind, spurred on by the sounds he's making.

Can I swallow? The thought makes me gag, and I pull away for a second but refuse to give up. *He issued a challenge to me when he intimated he'd be too much for me to handle.* It's not like me to back down from a dare. My competitive side coming out, I'm determined to prove him wrong.

I feel his dick thickening and prepare myself, but he pulls me away with a roar.

"On the bed. Hands and knees."

This time I'm quick to oblige, my willingness partly due to relief.

A tearing sound of foil ripping then unbelievably fast, I feel his cock pressing into me. I'm already stretched and wet, so this time my body welcomes him home with none of the discomfort of before.

He holds me to him, one strong arm across my stomach, trapping me so I'm imprisoned against him. He's already close, already aroused by my mouth. There's no finesse now as he reaches down and rubs at my clit.

"You gonna come for me, babe?"

I try to answer, but he's touching all the right spots. My body does my talking for me. As my muscles tense and I reach my peak, he releases into the condom.

When he gently lets me go, I fall forehead first onto the soft bed, but he doesn't pull out immediately. Instead, with his dick softening inside me, he gathers up some of my wetness and rims my asshole.

I tense.

"Ever had a cock in there?"

"No," I say with determination. I never will either.

"Should try it babe," he encourages, as if realising my reluctance. "Hmm, the things you're missing out on. Ever thought of having two cocks inside you? One where my cock is now, and another… here?" As he speaks, he pushes his finger more firmly against me.

Two cocks filling me? There's not enough room.

"I think you're enough by yourself."

"Never say never," he says, at last pulling out. "Life's too short to be missing out on all those experiences. If you change your mind, I'm sure I can find one of my brothers who's up for double-teaming. Hmm, Mace, perhaps?"

He'd fuck me with one of his brothers? Perhaps that doesn't count as going back twice. For a moment I even give it consideration, then shake the idea out of my head. One biker's a lot to handle. Two? Far too much.

He gives me a little longer to recover this time, then he's up for more. Slowly those condoms on the bed do indeed disappear. It must be the early hours of the morning when at last he flops over and lies on his back.

"Think you've totally drained me, little girl. Hope you got what you were looking for."

I did. Boy, did I. And more. "It wasn't too much of a disappointment." I try to make my voice nonchalant.

He laughs. "Fuck, babe. I think more would have killed you. Not that it would be a bad way to go. Talking about going, you got your own room here?"

He knows that I have. It's a not too subtle hint I'm no longer welcome.

I turn on my side and run my hand over his chest. He traps it in his and stops me. His eyes harden slightly. "Told you how this was going to go. I'm not one for cuddling, and I always sleep alone."

I knew what I was walking into, I can't pretend I didn't. This was nothing more than a biker fucking, something he's done many times before, even if it's my first such encounter. I can't act disappointed, he'd set out the terms and I agreed to them.

I got what I wanted and more. No regrets, I tell myself fiercely. I can't complain, he certainly delivered on his promise, and I'd had the night I'd hoped for.

I try to sound casual. "Something to be said about doing the walk of shame in the night, rather than in the morning." I gaze at his handsome face for one last moment, then slide off the bed. I put on my panties and bra, then pull my dress over my head. "Zip me up?"

"Come here." I perch on the edge of the bed as he performs the action I'd requested. I feel a feather light touch to my neck. A caress of his lips, and his warm breath touches me.

Play on it? Turn around and try to kiss him?

I harden my resolve and stand. "Thank you, Ink," I tell him, without turning around.

As I collect my purse and walk to the door, I hear him say, "The pleasure was all mine, little girl."

He's got that wrong.

CHAPTER THREE

Beth

Back in my room, I awkwardly twist to reach the tricky zipper and remove my dress once again, then slip into the PJs I'd brought to sleep in. It's after four am, I notice, seeing the digital numbers on the radio by the side of the bed.

Climbing on top of the covers, I pull up my knees, folding my arms around them.

Well, I've done it. For months I'd badgered Mel to introduce me to her biker friends, and today—yesterday, I correct—I'd met them.

Will I come to look back on last night with regret?

That's one question that's hard to answer with my body still humming from the pleasure he gave me. One thing for certain is I'll never forget how good sex with Ink was.

I snuggle down, hugging the pillow to me. *Did I make him feel good too? Or was it just another fuck to him?* Had there been nothing to distinguish me from the hundreds of women he'd probably been with?

Mentally I slap myself around the head. Of course, there wasn't. He took what I offered without making any promises. That's it, it's over. The sooner I come to terms with that the better.

I went into this with my eyes open. If my eyes are watering, it's just because I'm tired.

Turning over, I try to sleep. After tossing and turning, finally my exhausted and well-used body drags me into slumber.

I wake with tender ass cheeks and aches in muscles I couldn't remember having felt before. Ink had made good on his promise that I'd have trouble moving this morning. A hot shower eases the worst of the aching and helps in my effort to not walk bowlegged.

Carefully, I pick my discarded bridesmaid's dress up off the floor and fold it reverently even though it will have to go for dry cleaning. Mel was thoughtful, letting us choose styles which meant we could get more than one use out of our dresses. Though, when I'll wear it again, I'm not sure. I'll treasure it, knowing whenever I see it hanging in my closet it will remind me of the night I took my chances to have sex with a biker. Even if the only result is having made some memories to fuel my time alone with my vibrator.

Pulling on my comfortable jeans and a light sweater, I open the curtains and look out of the window. Last night it had been snowing, but now the weather has warmed, and already the ice is melting. Traffic is moving freely, and as I look out, I hear engines roar and see half a dozen motorcycles heading out.

Is Ink one of the riders? I can't be sure, they're too far away and any of them could be him or not.

After I watch them disappear from sight, I continue to put away clothing and cosmetics I'd brought for my overnight stay and check around to make sure I haven't left anything while musing I'd gotten exactly what I'd come looking for.

Or, had I?

I sit back down on the bed, putting my head in my hands.

In the sober light of day, my rash decision last night doesn't seem so sensible. Had I been swept away by the emotional environment of Mel's wedding?

I'd been shocked as hell when my sensible friend had first hooked up with a biker, having heard rumours the Satan's Devils were criminals and walked on the wrong side of the law. Mel had had the same concerns at first, but she'd taken time to learn about the club. I look up to Mel and respect her views. When she said, far from being into illegal things, they were a band of men who loved the freedom of riding motorcycles and the camaraderie of their club, I'd believed her. That they kept to themselves and lived by their own rules rather than the laws of the state, well, who could blame them as long as they stayed clear of breaking citizen ones.

If Mel saw no problem with her association with the Devils, then who was I to argue? Then I'd seen with my own eyes just how they were when I met both of her boyfriends.

Mel's first biker was Skull. That had been bad business. I bite my lip as I remember, still feeling guilty for how that had turned out. Skull was so protective of Mel and so demonstrably loving of her, it was hard to believe he had been lying the whole time. But rather than being a criminal, he'd turned out to have been an undercover cop. It was actually his failure to find any evidence of illegal activity that confirmed my view the Satan's Devils weren't into that kind of thing. No drug running, no guns, and no prostitution.

Skull had been the epitome of a handsome, caring, strong and protective lover. Despite him being half a foot shorter than myself, I had, briefly, wished his handsome and attentive eyes had fallen on me instead of Mel. But he'd known what he was after, a woman who'd be accepted by the club and who could gather information he hadn't been able to find out himself. When he'd disappeared and was thought dead, she was left devastated and pregnant. She lost the baby after I had seen Skull very much alive in Vegas.

Pyro stood by Mel when Skull vanished, supported her when he reappeared. They'd grown close and it had come as a surprise to no one when they ended up married.

Two bikers and one woman. I had lived vicariously through her.

I shake my head as I compare my past boyfriends to Mel's. The men I tend to meet are decidedly boring. Accountants, government workers like myself, and even one disastrous date with a lawyer whose favourite topic was himself. None of them looked at life in the same way as Mel's men. None of them were *exciting*.

Mel tried to protect me from her new family. She didn't think I could handle a biker of my own. Perhaps she was right, I muse. After last night, it's hard not to feel used and dirty.

Mel had tried to explain that most of the bikers enjoy their single status, that the club even keeps whores for them to use. It would take a special woman to tempt them away from the life they had chosen and get them to see the merits of being faithful. Had I thought one night with me and then Ink would see me as someone he couldn't get enough of? Hell, maybe. Doesn't every woman think she can change a man, when really, I just gave him exactly what he wanted? A chance to get his dick wet.

It's hard to believe there's a someone anywhere out there for me.

It's not self-pity, it's fact. I'm an introvert hiding in an extrovert's body. I look confident because of my height. Because I tower over most people, they expect me to take charge, expect me not to be scared, when underneath there's an insecure woman inside. That's why I needed alcohol to push me to take what I wanted last night. If I was sober, I'd have waited for a non-existent man to come over. Ink liked my confidence, that I appeared to be a woman who went after what they wanted.

But I'm not her.

He wouldn't like the real me once he got to know her.

I've never known what it was like to feel protected, loved, safe and coveted, but for a moment last night, I had felt like I was.

A dream, that's all. I give myself a shake. Good while it lasted, but now I have to put it behind me.

I stand. I close the zip on my bag and give the room one last look over. There's nothing left of me here. As for Ink, the aches and soreness will soon go, and his loving will be a memory I'll replay on those long, lonely nights.

I'd found myself a biker and enjoyed the experience. Any admission I'd lied when I said that was all I was after will never be spoken out loud.

Mel warned me Ink would take if I offered.

But he'd given as well. I had had the best sex ever. I had found that I enjoyed being bossed around in the bedroom; Ink had been so different from men who politely ask what I need, or worse, and fumble until they get it right. I grin to myself. I hadn't needed to fake anything. Yes, Ink's kind of loving was just what I was looking for, but doubted I'd ever find. That's what I'm missing, that's why there's an emptiness inside me. It wasn't the man, it was the experience itself.

But it hadn't been just sex. No, there was more, there was easy laughter and joking.

Don't go there. We fucked, or in his words, Ink gave me his cock several times. That's all it was.

Picking up my bag I walk to the door. *Little girl.* My lips curve slightly as his words echo in my head. Little, I'm most certainly not, but for just one night, I enjoyed being ordered around, and being made to feel small and protected.

I want more. I want more with Ink.

No. I don't, *can't,* want what's impossible to have.

Making a concerted effort to leave any regrets behind in this room, I pull open the door and step out.

Although I know there will be breakfast provided, I'm really not in the mood. Mel will want to know how I got on with Ink, and it's far too soon to share or even decide whether I'll be revealing any details at all. I need time to process last night on my own without dissecting it with anyone else. One day I'll tell her, and we'll laugh about it. The spanking and how much I enjoyed it, I'll keep to myself. But I'll probably let her know I did indeed get the full biker experience.

I also want to sneak out unseen just in case Ink's still around. How do I face him today? Not without blushing, that's for certain. And how will his biker companions react? Will there be sniggers, laughs and pointed remarks? That wouldn't surprise me.

So, I wheel my little carry-on case down the hallway, then hold my breath when the elevator dings and the door opens on the ground floor. I can hear raucous laughter from the restaurant, but thankfully there's no one I recognise in the lobby. Handing in my key card, I tap my fingers impatiently on the desk while they check me out and print my receipt.

At last I'm free to escape, letting out a heartfelt sigh when I reach my car unimpeded.

After that, my drive home seems anti-climactic.

"You looked beautiful yesterday." Mom comes and hugs me when I walk in the front door. "I was so proud of you." She'd been one of the wedding guests, but since she wasn't part of the bridal party, she hadn't stayed at the hotel.

I shrug her comment off with an embarrassed grin. "I don't know why. All I did was stand there and look pretty."

"You did that so well. I'm proud of what I made."

I giggle. But I suppose she did have a part in making me and how I turned out.

"Hey, Sis. That you?" a voice booms from the living room, shortly followed by the man himself. It's my little brother, Connor. Well little refers to age, not size. He's an inch taller than me, both of us towering over our parents.

"Con!" I tell him, genuinely delighted. "I've not seen you for ages. What have you been up to?"

His shoulders rise and fall, while I eye him intently. He's lost a bit of weight since I last saw him; his face no longer has its baby roundness and is now angular like a man's. He looks harder too. Connor lives with our dad up in Denver.

Patsy, our mom, and our father had separated when we were young, she ended up with sole custody of Connor and me. Dad hadn't bothered to have anything to do with us, never remembered our birthdays or Christmas. It was only six years ago when Connor turned sixteen that my brother wanted to know more about the man who sired him. Apparently, when he'd tracked him down, it turned out they'd gotten on, and Connor moved out to live in Denver with him when he was eighteen. Mom had protested, but as he was then an adult, she could do nothing to stop him.

That was four years ago. My doubts that my father has been a good influence, possibly going so far as to turn Connor against our mom, seem to be spot on, though he and I still get along. It's rare he comes to visit. I can't remember seeing him for almost twelve months. I'm delighted he's here, but also, suspicious.

"To what do we owe this pleasure?" I ask him.

Another raise and dip of his shoulders. "Had some business in town, thought I'd say hello while I was here."

"You going back to Denver later, or do you want to stay?" my mom asks with a tinge of optimism. "I can get a pot roast or something going."

"Nah, I'll get back." His face tightens. "Wouldn't want to put you out, Mom."

He turns away when she brushes off his comment, almost cutting her off when she says it's no trouble. He addresses me instead, "So where were you yesterday that you stayed out all night?" He looks pointedly at the overnight bag I've let drop to the floor.

"At Mel's wedding." I gratefully take the cup of coffee Mom's just poured for me and blow on it to cool it down. "A friend from work," I add, in case he doesn't remember.

"So, did you hook up with someone? Is that why you stayed

out? No thanks." The last is to my mom offering to fill a cup for him.

"No," I deny fast, shocked that he thinks he can walk back in after months away and start questioning what I get up to. "They booked rooms for the bridesmaids and bridal party." *As if it's any of his business,* I think to myself. I also keep quiet that the whole of the Satan's Devils MC also stayed. I decide to get the conversation away from me before any thought of last night can show on my face and betray that I've just skirted around the truth. "So, do you still work with our dad? What business are you in now, Con?"

He seems as eager to talk about what he does as I am to discuss the details of last night. "This and that," he says dismissively. Then glances at the clock on the wall. "Well, I best be off. More snow is forecasted for later and I don't want to get caught in a storm. Nah, Mom, I'll see myself out. Oh, and I'll be down here more often, and I'll pop in again."

"That will be nice, Connor," Mom replies eagerly, but she's speaking to his back and the dismissive wave of his hand.

The front door closes behind him with a bang.

Mom needs a hug, I can see that. "Mom…"

"No, don't make excuses for him, Bethany. We all know what went wrong."

Yes, we do. Connor discovered his father, and from that point on, he'd changed.

Growing up, I hadn't been very curious about the man who's responsible for giving me life. I was more angry that he'd abandoned me and that I had never heard from him. It was only later I'd begun to ask questions. Getting the details out of Mom had been difficult, as they came in bits and pieces. The older I became, the more information she thought I could handle. Eventually she'd told me everything.

Phil, my dad, had been an accountant when he and Mom married. He'd been caught cooking the books but was let off with a slap on the hand. Lost his job though. From then on, he started wheeling and dealing. Mom never knew what he was up to, but she thought it had to be shady, the amount of money he was bringing home. Having prepared herself for him to go to jail once, she was just waiting for him to be arrested again. She decided, in her own words, if she was going to be left alone, she'd rather be so on her own terms. So, she left him, or, rather, asked him to leave. Without needing much persuasion, eighteen years ago, he did.

From then on, she brought Connor and me up by herself, and I might be biased, but if you ask me, she'd made a good job of it. Until Connor set out to discover his sperm donor, that is.

"Well it sounds like we might be seeing more of him," I tell her, hoping I sound optimistic as I add, "Maybe we can turn him back around."

Another glance toward the front door. "It could be a good sign that he dropped in. Maybe he doesn't want to be such a stranger?" Then she turns back to me, and she's smiling instead of frowning. "Now do you want to go unpack and then help me decide what to cook for dinner?"

After telling her she'd gotten my mouth watering with the mention of the pot roast, I take my bag up the stairs and step back into my real life. As I unpack my clothes and put them away, I try to empty my head of a certain biker.

Shut him in the closet and turn the key.

Moments later I'm descending the stairs and offering cheerfully, "What can I do to help, Mom?"

CHAPTER FOUR

Ink

S lowly waking, I groan, then stretch, then placing my hand on my morning wood, realise my cock is slightly sore. I grin, if I can feel it the next day, fuck me, I doubt Beth can walk.

Beth. I hadn't expected to enjoy her so much, nor fuck her so many times. Nor utilise almost every position in my repertoire and hadn't had a thought in my head about spanking her when we'd first come to my room. A quick fuck, a release, then I'd have patted her ass and chased her out. Only, it hadn't happened quite that way.

She intrigued me. She'd approached me, I hadn't targeted her, nor would I have done, she's a civilian. What I saw was a confident woman going after what she wanted, and she got my respect and the promise to provide what she was after.

At six-feet-six, I know my height gives me an advantage which I milk the hell out of. With muscles to boot, not many men challenge me. I expected the same would be true of Beth, but once she was in my room, I began to think, what I saw as a benefit to her could be a drawback. One by one my assumptions were proved wrong, and I began to see her confidence was an act.

I'm now full of admiration that she actually came on to me.

Thank fuck she had, I'd have missed out had she lost her nerve. I'd ended up with a night to remember, and one that I'll certainly put in my spank bank.

I hadn't expected Beth to be a virgin, but I had expected her to be more experienced than she clearly was. Turns out, I'd enjoyed introducing her to new things. My lips curve as I remember marking her ass. She'd been shocked, but thoroughly enjoyed it. *If I'd been in my own space, I'd have had more things to teach her.*

She'd been assertive enough to joke with me though. Laughing at my cock? I growl as I remember. Well, I'd certainly shown her it was no joking matter. I'd laid out six condoms to shock her, I'd expected to use one. Then when that turned into two, I thought we may use four. But when I'd finally run out of stamina, I realised we'd used the lot.

I'm thirty, not old, but hell, six times in one night? I grin in the mirror as I shave. Beth certainly kept my engine revving. Even the memory of how she responded has my cock perking up. Time to find a club whore later.

I wonder what Beth would look like handcuffed to my bed wearing nipple clamps?

No, I've got to get that thought right out of my head. Nice girls like her could easily get the wrong idea if I asked to see her again, and I'm not in the market for more than a casual hookup. But the image stays lodged in my mind as I pull on my clothes, the same ones as I wore yesterday. I'll change into a clean pair of jeans and a fresh shirt when I get back to the clubhouse, there was no point bringing spare clothes.

Last night with Beth was different from going with one of the sweet butts, I muse as I pack my toiletries away and slip into my cut. *Only because she wasn't like them,* I tell myself. I hadn't known what to expect. Once again, I grin as I go over the events of last night in my head. Half of me thought she'd run away screaming as I hadn't gone through anything close to a seduction. I'd just told her to strip. Well, what's the point of making a big deal out of removing clothes? Most of the activity takes place naked, why waste time? I'm all for efficiency.

Christ, I'm making wood just thinking about her.

A loud knock comes on my door, and a voice floats through it. "You awake, Bro?"

Adjusting my cock so it's comfortable, I go to open up. "Yo, Mace."

The enforcer pokes his head around the door. "You alone?"

Shaking my head, I chuckle. "Of course, I am."

"She lost her nerve then?"

"Six condom wrappers in the bin shows that she didn't." I smirk.

"Oh, you tore a few, that happens. Overeager I expect."

I go to belt him around the side of his head, but he jumps out of reach, laughing.

"She worth giving a try?"

I make a seesaw gesture with my hands, while trying to hide the fact I'm gritting my teeth. "Wouldn't say that. She was pretty vanilla."

Mace's way of fucking is very similar to my own, so his face falls. Then his eyes narrow. "But six condoms, man?"

"Nah, fuckin' with ya, Bro," I contradict myself. "Once was enough. It was marginally better than using my hand."

He doesn't seem to know which of my statements to believe. As he eyes the waste bin the other side of the room and makes as though to enter, I place my hand firmly against his chest and push him out the door, pausing only to grab my saddlebag and my thick leather jacket which I'll surely need. Outside, it will be fucking cold.

He chortles. I'm transparent it would seem. "You staying to eat here?"

"Nah. Had enough mixing with civilians last night. Want to take my chance riding home while the snow is still melted. There's more forecasted for later."

"Not until tonight, thank fuck. Hey, you just don't want to face her today, do you?"

Yes and no. Yes, because my evil side wants to make her uncomfortable with knowing looks and winks, maybe a comment about the stiff way she's walking. No, because the sooner she's out of sight, she'll be out of mind. But of course, I don't make that admission. "Don't give a damn one way or another, Ground Pounder."

"Bet you do, you fuckin' Leatherneck."

Mace was in the United States Army, I'm an ex-Marine. We often trade insults. Well, he invites it as he still wears his hair military short, mine I've allowed to grow out. We continue verbally sniping at each other and exchanging playful punches while waiting for the elevator to arrive.

"Christ, this is a fuckin' fancy hotel. Should have known it was too good for rabble like you two."

"Hey, VP." I move aside to make way for Steph, Beef's blind wife, to step inside the elevator that's just arrived, her guide dog Max competently leading her into it. "How you doing today?"

"I'm tired," Steph says, turning toward me. If it wasn't for my knowledge of her and that she's not quite looking high enough to meet my eyes, you'd never know she couldn't see out of them.

"Yeah," the VP takes over, "some asshole in the room next to ours kept us awake until the early hours. Fuckin' headboard knocking against the fuckin' wall. And screams, of 'fuck yeah, just like that, right there,'" he mimics in a falsetto.

Mace chokes back a laugh.

Seeing Beef's arched brow, I know he knows fucking well, he wasn't in the room next to mine.

"Asshole," I tell him.

Mace slaps my back. "Probably had a knock-on effect through the rooms." He pauses and considers his words. "Knock-on effect. Literally." He cracks up.

I try to glare but can't keep the stern expression on my face. Fucking assholes, the lot of them, these brothers that I profess to love. By the time we exit the hotel, I'm chuckling myself as I do up the zip of my jacket right to the neck, pull on my winter riding gloves and place a beanie on my head, then take out my bandana. Before I wrap it around my mouth and nose, I nod to Beef's bike.

"Those heated grips work?"

"Yeah. Keep my palms warm, anyway," Beef replies as he waits for Steph to steady herself and put her arms around him. I notice him watching the prospect he must have summoned as Karl opens the door of the truck and Max hops inside. That's our VP, making sure everyone's accounted for, whether canine or human.

As Steph rests her head against his back, I wonder what it's like to have a bitch up behind you. I wouldn't know, I've never taken anyone on my bike before, never wanted to, which is why I only have a single seat on mine. But their closeness, their love is almost palpable. Just for one teeny second, I'm jealous. The alien sensation proves the thought I had yesterday is right. Weddings really do fuck with your mind.

But hey, there's a cure for that. By now all the sweet butts will have returned to the compound, and I can take my choice. Unless they're in high demand, which they might well be. It wouldn't surprise me if everyone was like me, and Pyro and Mel's nuptials will have made them horny.

The ride to the compound is a chilly one, but the roads have been gritted and cleared, just needing a little extra care to be taken, and one eye kept out for black ice. As the weather determines how often we can ride now, I enjoy the cold air rushing past, relishing in the freedom of the road. The VP's in front as he should be, Mace and I ride alongside each other.

This is the life. Whatever the elements throw at us.

Nevertheless, I rub my hands together briskly then blow on them once I enter the warmth inside the clubhouse.

"Need someone to warm you up, Ink?" a voice full of seduction murmurs into my ear. It's easily recognisable as Sheila.

Now that would definitely melt the cold that seems to have seeped into my bones. "Sure, doll. Why not?"

Detouring only to grab a bottle of beer from the bar, I head on up to my room, confident the sweet butt will be following.

Maybe I overworked my cock last night, I muse sometime later when Sheila's left to move on to the next brother who wants his needs seen to. Oh, it perked up and did its job, but the release didn't feel the same. Not as satisfying. Strange.

The rest of the day passes like any other Sunday, drinking and playing pool or cards with anyone who wanted a game. For once I go to bed fairly early. Well, last night I didn't get much sleep.

I've been a member of the Satan's Devils MC for four years. I'd joined the Marines when I was eighteen, did a few tours, saw shit no man should ever see, and left after eight years feeling I've given enough to my country. Before I joined up, I used to see the Satan's Devils riding around my hometown of Pueblo, knew of their reputation, or enough to steer clear. But my view of them changed when I'd bumped into Mace in a bar while home on leave, got talking to him, and made a connection. After that, I sought him out after every tour, and from our chats, began to revise my opinion of the bike-loving Devils.

When I received my discharge papers, I became a prospect. Hellfire patched me in after a year. I quickly found my place working alongside Pyro and Mace in the auto-shop, which is where I spend the working week. As it's now Monday morning, that's where I can be found.

"Got a job for you, Ink."

I stand and wait for Pyro's instruction. He's the manager here and I look to him to allocate work.

He hands some paperwork to me. "Man wants Marilyn Monroe air brushed onto the tank of his bike."

"Yeah?" I glance down at the iconic photo. No wonder he's

given this to me. As well as being a mechanic, I've found I'm quite a good artist too. "No problem. I'll start immediately."

"Why does he get all the cushy jobs?" grumbles Mace.

Pyro mock punches his arm. "'Cause you can't paint for shit," he replies.

"You not taking a honeymoon, Ro?" I ask, finding it strange he's back to work so soon after getting hitched.

"Nah. Got too many expenses with the new house."

"Then you'll have to save up for shit for the kid." Money, the root of everything.

The reminder that his wife is pregnant makes Pyro beam. Then his face falls. "Early days, Brothers. We won't be getting shit together for months yet."

Mace and I exchange glances. We're all convinced Mel miscarried last time due to the stress caused by Skull. But there's always a chance it had nothing to do with that, and her body could have just rejected the baby. Christ, it's understandable they must be worried.

I slap his back. "You need anything to stop her getting stressed, you ask, Brother. If it's money you need, I've got some saved, which is yours if you want." I have too, a few grand, not a huge amount, but I'd not hesitate about giving it up to help a brother.

Pyro nods. "Appreciate that, Ink."

"Count me in, Bro. If you ever need to cut back your hours to be there for her, I'll pick up the slack." Mace isn't going to be left out.

It didn't really need to be said. We're family, we step up to support each other. Whatever it takes. Once a brother takes an old lady, she becomes one of ours as well.

I settle down to work, and the next couple of days pass like any other. I do my job, go back to the compound, drink, eat and fuck. Wash, rinse and repeat. A routine, but not one that leaves me bored.

On Wednesday, I take my seat in church alongside my brothers.

Buzzard runs through the finances. Pyro raises his chin toward me when the reports from the auto-shop are favourable. Much of it down to the publicity we've had going out for our set-price winter checks on cars, for supplying chains and snow tyres, and keeping a good stock of new batteries for when the old ones just don't cope with the cold. It makes up for the lack of servicing and custom jobs on bikes which tend to drop off this time of year. Weekend warriors tend to avoid winter riding.

Devil's Ink, the tattoo parlour which is Lizard's baby, is also doing well, and Vi, Demon's wife, has completed her apprenticeship and become an artist herself now. Piercings, it seems, are proving a roaring trade, and of course, there's repartee when Sparky asks Lizard exactly how many cocks he's held in his hands.

Once Prez brings the meeting back to order, we learn takings are also up at the bowling alley, and Rusty grins, adding the explanation himself.

"People tend to look for indoor activities in the winter," he explains. "And Steph's idea about promoting children's and adults' birthday parties has taken off. Almost more bookings than we can cater for."

"Sparky, how's Tits Up?" Demon asks.

Sparky's a mechanic, but brothers have been rotating the management of our strip club since Taser betrayed us and was put down.

"Good. Held auditions for a new dancer. Settled on one. She's got some great moves. I think the customers will like her."

Demon nods. It looks like he thinks Sparky's doing a good job. My thought confirmed by his next words. "You want to take the management on permanently?"

Sparky grimaces. Unlike our other businesses, Tits Up opens late and stays open until the small hours. A manager's free time is curtailed.

"I've got an idea," Beef puts in. "Why not have two managers? Week on, week off. Day on, day off, or however they work that shit. That way the burden is shared."

Wills raises his hand. "I know I'm still green, but I don't mind stepping up if Sparky shows me the ropes."

"Hey, boy, you old enough to know tits from ass?" Bomber slaps his palm down on the table chuckling loudly at his own humour.

"Yeah, will you be able to stop shooting your load when you see the dancers wrapped round that pole?" Rusty adds.

"He'll wish they were wrapped around his pole." Thunder chortles with the rest.

Wills, twenty-three if I remember right and quite old enough to work in an adult club, lets the witticisms flood over him, and with only a slight twitch to his lips replies in a serious tone, "I'll have to try now, won't I?"

Wills has only sat around the table for a year, but he's got a sensible enough head for the job. I raise my hand in support when Demon asks.

"Any objections?"

There are none. Wills has a new job. Sparky looks relieved he'll be getting more time off.

"Pal? Cad? How's the security business?"

That too, it would appear, is coming along fine.

It's a routine meeting, nothing out of the ordinary until other business comes around. Demon suddenly frowns. At this point in the meeting it's unusual, and I'm not the only one to sit forward.

"Got something we need to keep a look out for. Had word from both the Wretched Soulz and the Silvestri." As he mentions the dominant MC and the local Mafia, everyone sits up straighter. "There are drugs coming into town, and it's not them controlling it."

We don't allow dealing on or near our premises. We like Devil's Ink, Devil's Pins, and Tits Up to have a good reputation, and have an agreement with both organisations that they deal in other parts of town.

"I haven't seen anything," says Sparky, frowning. "I'll start keeping an eye out." He raises his chin toward Wills, who gives him a sharp nod.

Prez continues, "That's what I'm asking everyone to do. We don't know who the asshole is. RIP thinks it could be organised crime stepping on everyone's toes." If RIP, the prez of the Wretched Soulz sees fit to issue a warning, it's something we should heed.

"What do you want us to do if we catch someone dealing?"

"Bring them in, if you can. We'll question them ourselves, then pass what's left off onto the dominant. RIP would be grateful."

Doing a favour for the prez of the Wretched Soulz would gain us some bonus points.

That agreed, the gavel comes down.

CHAPTER FIVE

Beth

I beam when I see Mel walking into the office on Monday morning. She's smiling and looking relaxed and happy. Well, she tied the knot with Pyro two days ago, and discovered she was having his baby. Certainly, a lot to be happy about.

Although it's silly after such a short time, and she was living with him already, I can't help the inane enquiry spilling out of my mouth, "What does it feel like to be married?" There's a glow on her face which suggests she and Pyro have continued their celebrations all weekend.

She could just have answered briefly, but to my surprise, she pulls up a chair. "Skull did a number on me," she starts. She doesn't need to tell me that, I already know. "When he walked out and never came back, it was hard, but I could accept he was dead. When I found he was alive, well, that broke me. It proved I wasn't woman enough to keep him."

"He was already married," I point out, gutted Mel thought she wasn't good enough for the bastard.

"I know, but still. It shook me, you know? It affected my relationship with Pyro."

"You didn't expect he'd do the same thing and disappear, did you?" I hadn't considered that. Anyone could see leaving Mel was the last thing Pyro would voluntarily do. He was devoted to her, even when he thought she'd never be his. Had Mel not seen that?

"Stupid, I know. He proves how much he loves me every day. But yes, I'd lost all confidence in myself. But being married to him? Again, it doesn't make sense, marriages fail all the time, but it shows a commitment in the eyes of the world. So, to answer your question, marriage has made me more sure of myself."

I smile broadly at her. "Being pregnant probably helps too. Jeez, Mel, Pyro was possessive even when the child you were carrying wasn't his. He must be over the moon with your news."

"We both are." But there's a hesitancy in her voice.

"You're worried something will happen?"

Her head bobs up and down. "If I had a reason for why I miscarried last time, if I could be certain it was stress that had caused it, then I'd feel more relaxed. But I don't. Yes, I'm worried."

"If I can do anything to help…" I don't know what I could do, but Mel's my friend and I want to support her. "Anything," I stress, genuinely wishing I could ease some of her burden.

She waves her hand dismissively. "Enough about me. Now I want the dirt on you and Ink. I saw you going off with him." She winks. "Did you get the biker-loving you wanted, or did you chicken out?"

I've been thinking about that night all weekend. "I can't deny it, can I, Mel?" My mouth curves up, then down. "Turns out you were right. He was only after a good time. But," I say fast, "I'm totally alright with that."

Her lips press together as though it was what she'd expected, and indeed, how she'd warned me, but still she asks, "Did you make any plans to see him again?"

I shake my head. "No, he made it clear from the start it was only going to be one night."

She narrows her eyes as she looks at me. "Are you sure you're okay with how it turned out?"

She'd call me out if I try to lie. I sigh. "Mel, you've known me for years. Ink caught my eye, and you did your part introducing me. But all Ink wanted was sex, he was quite clear on that. I accepted his terms. Maybe I did have thoughts I might change his mind, but he left me in no doubt there was no chance. If we did get together again, it would only be a repeat, no emotions involved." Well, not on Ink's part at least. "It is what it is, Mel. Ink is a once only man. He's been there, done that. I can't complain, the experience was worth it. He left me satisfied, and I've got memories to use when, well…"

Mel lightly slaps at my arm and I don't need to complete the sentence.

Then she gives me a long calculating look. "It's harder for women not to think with their hearts."

My shoulders rise and fall. "What can I say? We see the whole package, they don't. Ink only slept with me as I told him he could with no demands, to push for more now would only prove me a liar."

"You know," she says after a moment, "I was surprised you went through with it. After I took you over to him, I expected to find you hot on my heels demanding to know why I just left you."

"You know me too well," I grin. "Let's just say tequila had a lot to do with it."

"You weren't drunk," she says, sharply. "I'd never have…"

"No," I touch her arm lightly. "We'd been steadily drinking all day, but eating too, so I was buzzed, but not falling on my face out of it. I was sober enough to make decisions."

Mel looks relieved. "A confidence boost?" She doesn't need my nod to confirm it. "People get you all wrong, don't they, Beth?"

My lips press together. Even when I was a kid I was ridiculed; Christ knows how cruel children can be to someone who's different. Boys didn't like me towering over them, girls thought I was odd. Kids pick on the weakest, and though I was big, I was far from strong, and my rapid growth caused problems with my health. Grown folks expected me to be the adult in the room, even when I was with kids my own age. I've always felt a misfit, never rush to try and fit in, instead biding my time finding out who to trust. Approaching a stranger is so far out of my comfort zone, I'm not surprised Mel thought it strange.

Mel stands. "I suppose I better get back to my own desk and start work. Oh, by the way, it's Demon's birthday next weekend. Vi's throwing a surprise party for him. She's asked me to bake a cake and other goodies. Why don't you come along?"

Her invitation surprises me, so much so I narrow my eyes. "You've always kept me away from the compound before."

She exhales air loudly. "Only because I know what they're like. Pyro's brothers are set in their bachelor ways. I knew if you offered, they'd take. I didn't want you to be hurt. But now, after Ink, you understand that and know what they're like. And in at least one case, intimately." She waggles her eyebrows, making me giggle. "So, keeping you from them is a lost cause. You never know, Ink might see what he's missing."

Hmm. I thought that might be behind it. "You're barking up the wrong tree there, Mel."

She nudges my arm with her elbow. "Oh, come on. It's worth a try."

Might he see me and realise he fell madly in love with me after one night? No, don't go there. There's no chance and anyway, I'd be a fool to go back again when it would only be sex. Once I might escape with my heart, but twice? No chance.

"It's the prez's birthday," I start, hesitantly, looking for an excuse which won't betray my thoughts. "They won't want a stranger there."

She nudges me again. "Hardly a stranger. You got to know the girls well at my wedding. I know Vi, Steph and Jay all like you. I can check with Vi if you want, but I don't see a problem inviting you."

I did get on fine with the women who were Mel's other bridesmaids and had a few good laughs along the way, especially when I'd gotten to my knees so I wouldn't stand out in the photographs. It's not as though I'd be among people I don't know. I bite my lip. "Okay," I say at last. "But talk to Vi. If she's onboard with the idea, I'd love to come."

"Beth, that would be great." She sounds really excited as she bends down and kisses me on my cheek. "I love my two worlds mixing."

I suppose she would rather than having friends at work and a completely separate life with Pyro and his brothers. But after Mel had gone to her own desk, I quickly change my mind. *Damn, why did I say yes? Now I can't let Mel down.* Though Mel, herself, asked me to go, what if Ink thinks I've wrangled an invite so I can chase him? I start hoping Vi will say that she wants Demon's party to be club and family only.

If I hadn't gone with Ink at the wedding, I'd have leapt at the chance of going to the compound to get a deeper insight into the biker life. But I had gone with Ink and seeing him again is going to be awkward. Isn't it? *Only if I make it so.*

I stare over at Mel who's already got her head down hard at work. Between now and then I've got to put thoughts of Ink right out of my mind. If I go to the party and he's there, I'll greet him politely, of course, but will make no reference to how we got together on the night of Mel and Pyro's wedding. Most of all, I won't show for a moment I've got any regrets.

Maybe another biker would catch my eye? Do they all make love—*fuck*—like Ink? Perhaps taking another for a test drive would get Ink out of that rather annoying place he seems to have cornered for himself in my head.

Just for a moment I let myself imagine being a girl like that. A girl who could divorce her heart and jump from one bed to the other just for sex. Oh, yeah, I know Ink's very familiar with those, his club calls them sweet butts.

Problem is, I'm not sweet butt material, and there's only one biker I want. Damn it. I wish Ink had never caught my eye at Mel's wedding. Maybe I'd be better off dreaming what he'd be like, rather than knowing. However much I try to fool myself, there was more to our encounter than sex. I felt we had a connection. If it hadn't been on one side only, it would have been Ink inviting me to the club and not my friend.

I start to wish Mel had never suggested the party, because there's a devil on my shoulder whispering in my ear that perhaps if Ink sees me again, he'll want a repeat of that night. Huh, the angel on my other shoulder replies, more likely, he'll simply give me one of those chin lifts the men do, and then ignore me.

Far worse, Mel warned me bikers aren't shy, and I'm likely to see them fucking in public. How would I feel if I saw Ink with one of their club girls?

Maybe that's just what I need to stop thinking about him, I even dreamed of Ink last night.

It would break my heart to see him with someone else.

One minute I want to go, the next I don't. When Thursday comes around, and I see Mel approaching my desk, I know I've made up my mind. I'm not going. I'm just opening my mouth to tell her when she gets in first.

"I was right. Vi said she'd love you to come along. She took a liking to you, Beth. She said she can't wait to see you again. Steph's looking forward to seeing you again too." She falters. "Well, hear you in her case I suppose. And Jay said to tell you hi." She stops at last, her face beaming.

How can I get out of this now?

"I don't know," I start. "I've been rethinking this."

"Overthinking it," she says sharply and intuitively. "Look, forget about Ink. Just come and have a good time with friends. Vi will be so disappointed if you don't turn up." She then turns on the guilt. "Pyro's keeping Demon out of the way, so we can set up the party as his surprise. I was banking on you to help me carry the stuff that I'll have baked." And then, I swear, she turns on her puppy dog eyes. "Please?"

How can I refuse? I'll never turn down a request for help from family or friends.

I can't. "I'll come."

She hugs me tight.

That's how I find myself Saturday afternoon helping Mel load enough cakes and desserts to feed an army into her car. As my eyes widen when she brings out tub after tub, she laughs.

"This will all disappear. They're hungry men."

"They must be," I mutter under my breath, helping her carry out another load.

When we arrive at the compound, I don't see many bikes and wonder where they're stored, until Mel enlightens me. It's luckily a mild day for once, and the men are all out on a run taking advantage of the weather. It's just the women and prospects inside.

I feel relieved at my slight reprieve, so follow her in. Vi organises the men wearing cuts with the word prospect on the back and who I discover are called Beaver and Karl, to bring in the stuff Mel's brought. The clubhouse is already decorated with balloons, and a banner's waiting to be put up.

Having exchanged hugs with Vi, Steph and Jay, I point to the banner. "Where do you want that?"

"I thought above the bar."

No sooner are the words out of Vi's mouth, I'm pulling up a step stool that's already been brought in and pinning up one end of the 'Happy Birthday' sign.

"Be careful," says Mel.

"No worries, I got this." I don't mind heights, nor balancing precariously on rickety old steps.

Once they know I'm happy to pitch in, I'm given other tasks as they take advantage of my height, and soon the room starts to take shape. In the centre of it all is the amazing birthday cake that Mel has made.

"Oh, no, you don't!" I catch hold of Theo as he toddles toward it with his hands outstretched, and I chuckle as I swing him up in my arms. "Rascal."

"Thank you." Vi's grateful comment is heartfelt.

Mel sighs with relief that the toddler hasn't managed to swipe his fingers through the lush chocolate icing. I understand his thwarted desire, having to restrain from doing the same thing myself.

Theo's wriggling in my arms, trying to get down, obviously having figured out he's got a woman with no experience of children holding him.

"I'll take him," Mo, Demon's mom and Vi's mother-in-law, calls out. "Come to Gramma, Theo."

"You need eyes in the back of your head," Sindy says. I remember she's married to Buzzard, their treasurer.

"Now I'm glad I never had any," Jeannie remarks, shaking her head as Theo starts having a tantrum at being denied cake. Bomber's her man I recall.

As I look around at the room, which does and doesn't fit what my imagination had conjured up—yes, there's a bar, a pool table as I'd seen in my head—but the tables and chairs and comfortable looking sofas are matching and not that old if I'm any judge. The walls look freshly painted too.

"It's not bad," I remark to Mel. "I must admit I expected it to be rougher."

"They had some trouble about a year back. Had to rebuild some of the walls and replace stuff and redecorate. Jay will tell you all about it, I wasn't here then. Apparently, it wasn't as nice as this before."

That explains why the decoration and furniture still looks clean and fairly new.

I find I'm having fun, pitching in and working alongside these friendly women. It's light work and we have a few laughs.

The club whores don't appear to be here. I begin to hope they're not invited, and perhaps after all, I won't have to watch Ink fooling around.

We've just finished setting out all the food when from outside there's a loud roar of bikes. I go to stand by Mel as we look expectantly toward the door. After helping with the preparations, I'm anticipating seeing the surprise on their prez's face.

Men flood in, but the star of the show is missing, as is Mel's man. I realise fast that this was planned, and Pyro is probably delaying him outside as the other men quickly divest themselves of their winter riding clothes and gather around in a circle.

They've just got themselves organised when the door opens again.

"Happy fuckin' birthday, Prez," rings out all around me, a deafening roar from the men.

"What the fuck?" Demon stops dead. Then rounds on Pyro, his eyes narrowing as he spits out, "There's nothing fuckin' wrong with your bike, is there?"

Pyro grins and shrugs, then makes a beeline toward the woman standing by my side.

"Jeez." Demon's still stunned. "Brothers. Ladies. What can I say? I didn't expect this. Where's my ol' lady?"

Vi has a big grin on her face as she walks over to her man. He takes her lips in a way that makes me swoon.

Having been made to feel welcome, having worked alongside the other women, I feel comfortable and relaxed enough to put my fingers to my lips and let out a loud whistle in appreciation.

I shouldn't have done that.

I've never been able to hide in a crowd. The eyes of an even taller Ink catch mine from the other side of the room.

CHAPTER SIX

Ink

I've spent this whole week fucking the whores, but none of them have left me satisfied. When they go from my bed, I have an unfilled hole inside me. Oh, they relieve my cock, but something is missing.

I tried nipple clamps on Bella when I was fucking her over the pool table, they didn't look right, and she complained they hurt her, so I'd quickly taken them off. Double-teamed Breezy and Sheila with Mace, but what was usually exciting had me feeling bored. Even their mouths didn't seem right around my cock. Titsy, well, when she was discarding her clothes, I almost told her not to bother. When I brought Tulia back to my room, I went through the motions but wasn't into it.

Though I didn't want to admit it, I couldn't get a certain woman out of my fucking head.

What I can't understand is why. I may have had off days in the past, but it's been a week now. Why aren't the whores providing me with what I want?

I only come when whoever's face under me morphs into the one of the girl I fucked in the hotel last Saturday night.

Time, I tell myself over and over again. I just need time. Memories fade, and so will my obsession with the woman I don't want. If there's one lesson I've learned, it's never go back for more. Not with a woman who doesn't understand that while I like to fuck, I've nothing else to offer. I don't want an old lady, can't ever see myself settling down. I live the life of a biker for a reason—I enjoy the freedom.

The ride out was good today, a chance to clear my head, to let the wind blow the cobwebs away. Still cold as hell, yes, but nowhere near freezing and the day was dry at least. What I knew was an excuse to get Demon away from the club was welcomed by us all. Hopefully now we're coming out of the other side of winter, we'll be able to ride more.

I, of course, knew what to expect when we arrived back at the clubhouse. The only person who didn't had been Demon. I felt pleased for Vi, her plans had gone like clockwork. I'd had to smother my laughter when Pyro asked the prez's advice about a non-existent rattle on his ride.

Vi and Demon's heated kiss hadn't been PG, but someone had clearly been impressed. Someone who's loud whistle had caught my attention from across the room. Not a someone I'd expected to see, not in the place I call home.

Beth's here. Be fucking hard to miss her given the way she towers over all the girls and even some of my brothers.

As our eyes lock, my cock immediately begins to swell.

I can only see two options. March over to her, take her hand, her hair, fuck I don't care which and drag her up to my room and sink my thickening cock into her sweet depths, or, I can run upstairs and take care of this shit myself.

For more time than I should, I stand staring as our eyes lock. I've heard the term rooted to the spot, but I have never experienced the feeling before. It's like I'm resisting a magnetic force that's trying to draw me across the room. This hold, this thrall she has me in, there's no other term for it. *It's dangerous.*

She breaks eye contact first, but not of her own volition. No, because Judge has come up behind her and caught her attention.

Well I'll be fucked if Sparky's not heading toward her as well. My hands curl at my sides.

"Good ride that, Brother."

My eyes are fixed on what's happening across the room.

"Hey, I said that was a fuckin' good ride. Needed that."

Rapidly I shake my head. "What?"

Mace stares at me, his brow creasing. "You feeling alright? I didn't see you come off and knock your head, still, might have missed it."

"I haven't banged my fuckin' head," I growl and turn away, as my eyes are drawn back to Beth again. *Has Judge dared to put his hand on her?*

Mace turns to see where I'm looking. His eyes widen. "Hey, that's that bitch from the wedding, isn't it? Mel's friend. Christ, those jeans hug that ass nicely. Thought she looked pretty in that dress last week, but those tight-fitting pants?" He lets out a low whistle. "Those legs go on for miles, they'd feel great wrapped around my waist. She's fuckin' hot, Brother. Think I might need to go and chase those youngsters off."

"Sparky's my age," I rasp.

His elbow bumps my arm. "Yeah, I was talking about Judge. We can teach her something those youngsters can't, eh, Brother?"

We? Sure, the enforcer and I have shared women before, even as recently as this past week, but the thought of watching him and Beth turns my stomach. Nah, can't be that making me suddenly feel sick. Maybe I downed my beer too fast. Drank on a too-empty stomach, must be what it is.

"She doesn't want anyone pawing at her," I warn him.

His eyes narrow as he observes, "Well, she doesn't seem to be pushing anyone away. Judge has his arm around her now. And fuck me," he laughs as he continues to describe the scene, "Judge is staring *up* into her face. He'd have to go on tippy-toe to kiss her. Now that I've gotta see."

I've got eyes in my fucking head. There's only an inch or two height difference, so tiptoe's stretching it a bit. And there's no need for a fuckin' running commentary. "He should leave her the fuck alone."

Mace turns back to me, shaking his head in confusion. "You've already tapped that. You never do a civilian more than once. Surely, you're not getting jealous?"

Jealous? Not fucking likely. "Of course, I'm fuckin' not," I bark. "You know me better than that, Ground Pounder."

"Thought I did, Leatherneck," he half says, half mumbles. Then he looks again at my face. "Look, Ink, I'll be fuckin' straight with you. There are girls you fuck and forget, and girls you fuck then can't get out of your head. If she's the latter, nothing's stopping you going in for a repeat."

Fuck knows, right now I'm tempted. If only to get those assholes off her back. There's one good reason I can't. "It will give her ideas."

"Might, might not." A burst of feminine laughter reaches my ears. "But if you don't move in now, you could lose your chance. Looks like Judge is getting pretty... no, I was wrong. Sparky seems to have caught her interest now."

"I don't want a bitch," I say, unsure whether I'm trying to convince myself or him. *Is she really thinking of going with one of my brothers? Is she so shallow to jump from my bed into one of theirs?* I slam the heel of my hand against my forehead as I remember that's exactly what I've been doing all week, trying to fuck her out of my mind.

"She might not want a man." He jerks his head in her direction. "She might turn you down, might prefer Judge who's not got so many miles under his belt."

"I'm thirty for fuck's sake, not over-the-hill. And it doesn't matter whether or not she prefers a younger man, they're not getting the chance."

Mace eyes me from head to toe, then grins. "Get the fuck over there and talk to her. Your face is red as though you're going to blow a gasket, and you're sporting one hell of a chubby in your pants. If she turns you down, reckon you're going to need a very cold shower."

I shift my stance, hoping to make my swollen cock less noticeable, but all I do is press it harder against my zipper, and wince.

He throws up his hands. "I'm going to get a beer. Go see her, talk to her, fuck her, but do something, or else I might have to take away your gun. You look like you could kill someone right now."

He's the enforcer. He's allowed. But hey, disarming me at the prez's birthday party would be embarrassing.

I wait maybe five seconds after he's walked away, then as if there's an invisible piece of string pulling me across the room, I close the gap between us.

"Get out of here." I glare at Judge, then turn the force of my stare onto Sparky. Judge raises his hands and steps back.

Sparky, though, he unwisely decides to taunt the beast as he puts an arm around Beth. "We were just getting acquainted."

"Well you can get un-fuckin'-acquainted fast. And unless you want to lose that arm, take it a-fuckin'-way from her."

Beth's eyes meet mine, she looks shocked, which probably matches the way I'm feeling. *What the fuck am I doing?*

The room is crowded and busy. People are jostling around us making their way to the bar and returning with plates laden with food. Automatically, I move Beth out of the way when a brother steps back and nearly bumps into her.

For the first time in my life, I don't know what to say. I know how to fuck, but not how to speak to a bitch. If she asks me why I chased the others off, what could I tell her? My mouth has gone dry, and I swallow, trying to find some justification for sending my brothers away. Christ, I may as well have peed on her. All I can think to express is, *Let's go fuck.*

But she's different today. Last week, it had been clear what was on her mind, today she looks nervous, unsure. Like the little girl I'd come to know her for, not the put-it-all-out-there woman who had brazenly approached. Suddenly it's me who's uncertain. Would she even want a repeat if I made the suggestion?

Could she be thinking, *been there, done that?* Would she prefer me to step away? Would she really have liked to see what Sparky or Judge could offer? It dawns on me I don't like it when the tables are turned.

As her mouth opens, I only need to incline my head slightly to hear her words.

"I, er, I was just going to get some food."

Food. Fill a plate, find a table. Sit down and talk. Conversation with a bitch? Not what I normally do. I know fuck all about girly shit and stuff she'd probably want to talk about. I don't watch TV apart from the odd game or that show where they customise motorcycles. I glance at her again, noticing she's not meeting my eyes, and she's shifting from one foot to the other.

I could shrug, walk away, leave her to her own devices. "Sure, let's fill a couple of plates," I find myself saying, telling my cock it will have to behave while I feed a different appetite instead. *She's here for a birthday party, fuckface.*

The old ladies have done us justice. Before Vi, Jay, and Steph came along, the sweet butts reluctantly prepared food under the direction of Jeannie. Now Steph and Vi have taken charge of the kitchen, the quality of what they make has definitely taken an upturn. Add in Mel and her offering of cakes and desserts and we're set. Of course, the women don't spend all their time cooking for us men, even we're not as cavemen as to expect that. But on a day like today, they've gone to town.

I grab a few items then look around, most people are eating standing around the laden bar-top as though not wanting to step away and miss anything. So there are a couple of tables empty. Pointing out one and signalling my intention with a jerk of my head, I'm pleased when Beth steps in line behind me.

We sit, and for a moment all we do is stuff our faces. What can I say? This is good shit and eating it hides that neither of us seem to know how to kick off a conversation.

"You work with Mel?" I say lamely, once my plate is clean. I already know that.

"I do." She smiles. "And do you work?"

She clearly doesn't know much about the club. "I do." I throw her simple reply back at her. But rather than letting the conversation run dry, I give her more. "I work at our auto-shop. All the brothers have jobs. It's not all riding around and having fun."

"Is your shop busy?" she asks with genuine interest. "Don't people worry about bikers working on their cars?"

"I'm an ex-Marine, Pyro and Mace are ex-Army. We learned our trade when we served." Among other things, but no need to go into that. "Got all the certificates and qualifications. We do fuckin' good work. Many of our customers are regulars and wouldn't go anywhere else. Got enough going on, we employ civilians as well." We've got a good reputation which we deserve. As she looks interested, I continue, "As for bikes, doesn't matter whether men wear a cut or not. There's nothing a man with a motorcycle likes more than chatting with like-minded folks. We get people riding out just to talk about customisation and shit like that. Even get a few come down regularly from Denver and other surrounding towns and cities."

She nods, and it would appear she's impressed. "You live here? At the club?"

I jerk my chin in an upward direction. "Yeah, I've got a room here. Most brothers have. Well, Hell, Bomber, and Buzz have lived in town for years, Demon moved out a year back, and now Beef and Steph have got a house too. And of course, Pyro and Mel, but you know that. The rest of us live here."

"I live with my mom." Without me asking for an explanation, she tells me why. "It's cheap and convenient. Oh, I pay rent, but not as much as I would with my own place."

"You must get on well with your mom."

"Yes." She grins. "She's just turned fifty but looks much younger, people often think we're sisters. She's got a young outlook on life. She's also become a good seamstress over the years, so she can do my clothes. She's branched out and made it into a small business."

My eyes crease. "Clothes?"

Her hand waves toward herself. "If you hadn't noticed, I'm a bit taller than most girls. These skinny jeans are a man's size and fit alright, but tops they make for big girls assume they're large everywhere." She indicates her breasts and holds her hands a few inches away from them. In doing so she draws my attention to her body, and I can't help but focus on her tits. The memory of how they felt under my hands and mouth makes my cock start to misbehave once more. I try to focus on what she's saying. "Mom alters tees and stuff that's long enough but too wide. And some things she makes completely from scratch. She had to start altering my clothes when I started my growth spurt and didn't stop, so she's had plenty of practice."

"How tall are you?"

"I was six-foot-one when I was twenty, I'm six-foot-one and three-quarters now I've reached twenty-seven."

I almost spit out the mouthful of beer I've just taken. "You're still growing?"

She gives a twisted grin. "It's slowing down, hopefully stopped."

An image comes into my mind and I spit out a mouthful of beer as I laugh.

"What?" Her brow furrows.

"I just thought of a scene from *Alice in Wonderland*."

She rolls her eyes. "You mean the 'drink me' potion where she grows too big? I may have heard that before."

I chuckle. "That's it. Perhaps we can find you a magic mushroom to munch on to reverse the effects."

"I wish we could," she says, glumly.

Hmm. Have I hit a sore spot? "Do you mind being so tall?"

"Do you?"

I shrug. "It's different for a man. I'd rather be tall than short, but I suspect it's not the same for a girl."

"You're taller than most, though."

My shoulders rise and fall for a second time. "I used to get asked if I was a basketball player, but that stopped when I started wearing a cut."

"And what's the weather like up there?" She chuckles.

We share a moment. Yeah, tall people can be the butt of many jokes. It's almost a way to cut us down to size.

"I like you being tall," I tell her, my mouth running without my brain being in control. "Nice not to get a crick in my neck or need to bend myself in two to fuck you." I change the subject quickly before she can read too much into it. "So, sports. You do any?"

"I run."

Yeah, she looks fairly athletic. I imagine her running around the block a couple of times when the weather is warm enough. "Often?" I ask, while trying to get the thought of her in tiny running shorts out of my head.

"Every day. Either outside or in the gym if the weather is against me. I like entering half-marathons."

I eye her with a new respect. All the sweet butts ever do is sit around on their asses, the most energy they use outside of bed is doing their hair, donning their makeup or painting their nails. "Anything other than running?"

"That basketball joke?" I nod as it seems to be expected. "Well, yes, I was on a team at school for a while."

My brow creases as it looks like a painful memory. "What happened?"

"I sprouted early, so I was taller than the girls on most other teams."

An ideal player in my opinion. "You get hurt?"

Her chin rises and falls. "But not in the way you're thinking. I got more baskets than anyone else, and it was hard for anyone to take the ball from me. So, there was jealousy on my own team.

Our opponents? They'd accuse us of cheating. Oh, not on the field, but in the locker rooms. I left the team."

"You were bullied?"

"I was the odd one out. So, yeah. That's when I learned it was better to try to hide, than be seen."

Seems anyone who doesn't fit the norm is fair game. Fuck, I know that as I wear my cut, but as an adult I can handle it. Not so much so for a kid. Boys tend to settle their fights with fists, girls use spiteful words. I wouldn't be surprised if the latter caused more hurt. I reach over the table and squeeze her fingers, before drawing back my hand. While she's with me, no one is going to be picking on her. If they do, they'll have to answer to me. My sudden desire to be there to protect her is surprising.

Again, I move on to another topic. "Your mom okay with you coming here tonight?"

Once again, her eyes meet the ceiling before looking back. "I'm twenty-seven, Ink, not a kid. Wouldn't matter if she did, but to answer you properly, no. She's always respected Mel's judgement. She was at the wedding. I don't know if you remember?"

Probably not. I didn't take much notice of citizen guests. Replaying her words in my head, I snort. "Seems like we've got to up our game if we're becoming respectable."

I've made her giggle. "I don't know about that. People who don't know you're big softies are still scared when they see your motorcycles coming along the road."

My eyebrows rise, and I lean in. "Softie? You reckon I'm *soft?*" There's more than a hint of suggestion in what I'm saying.

She doesn't miss it. She swallows, then those blue eyes land on me, focused and not looking anywhere else. "I thought you didn't do repeats."

I don't, but I'm realising that for her, I might make an exception.

I'm trying to formulate an answer that won't raise her expectations too far but would allow us to end this party with us both getting some satisfaction, when a shadow looms over me.

"Ink," Mace's unwelcome voice interrupts me just as I'm opening my mouth. "Got trouble at Tits Up. Few of us are riding out. Beef wants you along."

My eyes close briefly as I sigh. "Sorry Beth," I tell her, already getting to my feet. "Duty calls. If you're still around when I return, we'll continue this, er, conversation."

The flare in her eyes shows she knows exactly where our discussion was leading, and the crestfallen look on her face must mimic my own disappointment.

Fuck.

"What is it?" I snap at Mace, once we're headed to the bikes, earning myself a quick glance and a raised brow at my unusual impatience. Luckily for him, he leaves it alone.

"Looks like someone might be dealing behind the strip club. Beef thinks it might be the asshole who was mentioned in church. Need to see whether we can catch up with him."

CHAPTER SEVEN

Beth

Bad timing or what? I stare after Ink's retreating form, not missing the tension in his shoulders, his shortness with Mace signalling he's not happy at being called away. I'm part relieved, part disappointed. After our conversation which I certainly hadn't come here today expecting would take place, I thought Ink was going to ask me to go up to his room. I couldn't have refused. Couldn't, because this controlling man wakes something inside me. Shouldn't, because to go back for a second time would surely be a mistake.

Damn him. Why had he come over and stolen me away when I'd been sharing light-hearted jokes with his friends? Why had he taken time to eat and talk with me? Surprisingly I'd enjoyed our conversation and liked what I'd learned about him. He'd been focused completely on me, not looking for an escape, or, until the final few minutes, making any suggestion we'd do more than use words. His good looks, his masculinity, are a dangerous combination. He's exactly the man I've been looking for all my life and spending more time with him will only set me up for disappointment.

When the men had arrived back from their ride, Mel had become glued to Pyro's side. I'd grinned, seeing she hadn't had much choice in the matter, her husband's arm kept her there as though he couldn't bear to be away from her. She'd sent me an apologetic smile, but I waved her off. If it was a room full of strangers maybe I'd be more nervous of being left to my own devices, but surprisingly, after the wedding and reception last week, I feel as though I'm among friends. I've been greeted and said hello to by name by everyone who's come close. Maybe it's down to Vi's approval, she's certainly not held back in telling how much I'd helped get things ready.

So, I'd stood, sipping my soda, feeling relaxed simply soaking up the general vibe. Pyro was far from the only one to show his greed for the company of his woman. Paladin quickly seated himself with Jay on his lap, Demon held on to Vi as if afraid she could disappear any moment, and Beef and Steph were joined like Siamese twins. Even Hellfire and Mo looked like they've been parted for days rather than a few hours. Buzzard and Bomber had quickly commandeered the presence of their women. When these men love, they love hard. I couldn't help but wonder what such devoted attention would feel like.

I was well aware I was a single woman stood in a room which, apart from the aforementioned, is packed with otherwise single men. Unless I find somewhere to sit, it's impossible for me to disappear into the background. I wasn't left alone with my thoughts for long, and I was grateful for the interruption, and a chance to take my mind off my envy of the happy couples.

Judge had made me laugh, Sparky trying to outdo him as they both related tales of the ride they'd just been on. At first, I listened in awe, then realised some of the embellishments were just too ridiculous to be believable. I was soon cracking up with some of the outlandish tales.

Neither man had been anything but gentlemanly. Though their closeness and the way their hands would brush my arms gave me the impression that I could have gone with either of them had I given the slightest indication that I wanted to. They'd made me feel attractive and desired.

But they hadn't made any part of me tingle.

They weren't Ink.

He knew I was here. Stupidly, I'd drawn attention to myself when I'd gotten carried away in the heat of the moment, or more accurately, by that kiss that Demon and Vi had shared. For a second, I'd wondered whether he was going to come over. He didn't.

Move on girl, I'd lectured myself. *If you want a biker, there're plenty of others here.*

But it's not another biker I want. When I'd carried on talking to the two men, I knew words were the only thing we'd be sharing. Only half listening at times, I'd decided I'd stay long enough to be polite, then slip away. Seeing Ink so disinterested had been painful.

Until he'd stormed over.

His dismissal of Judge and Sparky had been abrupt, and for a moment I was stumped to find an explanation. The one that occurred to me seemed ridiculous, but I could think of no other. Could he be jealous of their attentions toward me?

The two bikers I'd been speaking to were pleasant but hadn't stirred me at all. As soon as Ink stepped close, it had been different. His smell of leather and man was dissimilar to theirs in a way I couldn't explain, and a delightful shiver had gone through me, as though my body had already been programmed to react to him. It wasn't a welcome revelation. However much I'd tried to dismiss that night from my head, Ink had apparently gotten under my skin.

I'd been surprised when he'd approached, and nervous. Conscious of the mistake I'd probably be making if he offered and I'd gone with him again. It would just be sex, and a repeat of that amazing night would make moving on that much harder.

While I could at least partly blame alcohol for what happened last week, it would compound my mistake to take up any offer made in the cold light of day and both of us completely sober. So rather than hear him make a suggestion I might find hard to resist, I'd fumbled my way through the insinuation my appetite was for food, and to my surprise, he'd allowed the distraction.

I hadn't expected we'd talk, that he'd open up about what he did for the club, which in light of their reputation sounded boring, yet also, reassuring. He did a job he was trained for. He even asked a little about my life. Yes, we'd gone through some social niceties, and even made a few jokes. We hadn't discussed what happened last week, well, not using words. The heat in his eyes, the flare in his cheeks, the answering flush on mine—our mouths might be saying one thing, our bodies another. Physical reactions didn't lie. *You turn me on*, I'd signalled, *I want you*, came back.

I knew what he was going to suggest. However much I want to deny it, my answer would not have been a refusal.

I'm frustrated that he's been called away, discreetly squeezing my thighs together in a vain attempt to ease the arousal which had been building while we'd been talking, knowing I won't be getting any other relief now and trying to tell myself it's all for the best.

"You okay, Beth? Sorry I've been ignoring you, but Pyro wanted me close and then I had to sort out more food. Christ, these bikers can eat." Mel flops down in the chair Ink had so recently vacated.

"Hi Mel." I give myself a little shake. So caught up in my thoughts, I hadn't seen her approaching. "No worries. You've been stocking and restocking the plates. And there I'd been thinking you'd brought far too much with you."

"Not enough," she laughs. "We've almost run out." Her breath huffs out as though she's exhausted. She probably is, she'd been cooking all morning and then running around.

"As normal, Mel, you've outdone yourself." I rub my stomach as if to show where some of her food went, and that her efforts hadn't been wasted.

But she's not here to discuss the spread she helped put on.

"Saw you talking to Ink." Her brows rise. "You getting along with him?"

I shrug. I had been ready to jump into his bed if that means anything, but that I keep to myself. "We were having a decent enough conversation before he was called out."

"Hmm." Her sharp eyes flick to me, then move to the doorway which the bikers had so recently disappeared out of. "No idea what that's all about. But they could return soon. You going to hang around and wait to see if he comes back? To continue your conversation?" She puts the final word in air quotes as if she's not at all fooled and had known exactly where our talk would have been leading.

Am I that transparent? Or, is Mel just used to living around bikers who are used to easy women. *Is that what I am?* Suddenly him going out on a job seems a welcome intervention to stop me from making a mistake. Sure, the night with him was worth repeating, but was it worth risking me getting more involved with him? Would it make it harder to walk away at the end of the evening? I purse my lips, thinking how different it is for men, how sex is so much simpler for them, reduced to a bodily function. Today, I've seen another side of Ink which has made me like him more.

"He's not going to want to get involved with me, is he, Mel? I think it's best if I go."

Her eyes fill with sympathy, and her lips thin. "I wish I could, but I can't tell you you're wrong, Beth. These men, honey, they live this life because of the freedom. Some, like Pyro, come to realise in time it's not everything. But Ink? Whether he will or not in the future, I'm not sure he's there now."

I nod. She's right. Maybe in time a good woman will sweep Ink off his feet, but whether or not I'm that woman, the timing is wrong. I won't be able to change him. Best not to try.

There's a scraping of chairs as Steph and Jay join us. Once released from his harness, Max, Steph's adorable guide dog comes over to me, sniffing at my hands. I let him, realising he's reacquainting himself with the scent of the woman he met briefly last week. When he's satisfied, I pat his head, give him a quick scratch behind his ear, then he lies down resting his muzzle on my feet.

"How have you been, Beth? Recovered from last weekend? That was a blast, wasn't it?"

I shrug, then realise Steph can't see me. "The wedding was fun," I tell her, honestly. "I don't think I stopped laughing all day. My face hurt from smiling."

"Fun?" Jay lets off a peel of laughter. "I'd say you had fun, girl." She accompanies her words with an exaggerated wink.

My eyes narrow fast as I glare at her. "What has Ink said?" I ask tightly.

"Uh uh," Mel gets in quickly. "These men don't gossip, well, maybe amongst themselves, but definitely not to us. It was kinda hard to miss when Ink dragged you off." She waves around the table. "We all saw you."

"I heard." Steph laughs. "I think Vi's exclamation and laugh drew everyone's attention to the two of you."

"Well?" Vi looks unrepentant. "Beth had scored."

Well hell, looks like I can't keep anything private. No point in denying it, though anything other than Ink and I getting it on together is just conjecture. I'm not going to share what a revelation it was. I turn the tables on Mel.

"And what about you?" I add an exaggerated wink. "Pyro taking good care of you?"

She reddens, leading me to believe Pyro's been very attentive to her needs over the past week, but she like me, she doesn't elaborate. "Much like it was before we got hitched. I definitely haven't got any complaints."

"How's the pregnancy going?" Jay asks. "Any sickness?"

"Fine at the moment and no, but it's early days." Her mouth twists. "We probably shouldn't have said anything yet, but Ro thought we needed support should things go south."

"They won't." I reach over the table and take her hand. "This time you've got a good man beside you, not that bastard."

"We've all got good men," Steph observes, and Jay nods.

"Stop," I tell them, my smile hiding the truth of what I'm saying. "You're making me jealous."

"Beth might have Ink from what I just saw," says Vi. "You and he seemed to be getting on well. I think that's the first time I've seen him actually talking to a woman."

But Jay's shaking her head. I tilt my head toward her, seeing she's looking at me sadly. Then she warns, "Don't pin your hopes on him, Beth."

I raise an eyebrow.

She shifts, seeming uncomfortable. "Look, I've been around bikers for the past five years. Sure, I saw lots of the men hook up with girls in the Tucson club, take them as their old ladies. I saw brothers you thought would be single for life find their one and end up loyal. But," she pauses, "I've also seen men who you knew would never make a commitment or weren't ready to do so now."

She's the youngest old lady, but she's the one who's giving it to me straight. It's no different from what Mel was just telling me, but blunter. "You're saying Ink's one of the latter?"

"If this week is anything to go by, yes." She tosses me a look of compassion. "I'd want to know, if I were you, so I'm going to tell you. Since the wedding, Ink's been with every whore that's here, and has even gone back for seconds."

"Pal!" a deep and very pissed off voice barks. "Get the fuck over here, now."

We all jump, swinging around to see a furious Ink standing behind us. His face is bright red.

"What?" Pal's there in an instant, his eyes widening in concern as he examines Jay closely to see if there's anything wrong.

"Teach your woman a fuckin' lesson about keeping her mouth shut about brothers' business."

Pal studies Ink for a second, registering his set expression, then glares at Jay. Jay flushes as she looks between her man and Ink who I swear is shaking with rage. "I'd want to know," she says angrily, standing and pointing a finger at Ink. "It's not fair to lead someone on…"

"Come on, Jay." Pal's expression threatens Ink and he puts himself between Jay and the man she's told tales on.

"Leave us, Mel, Vi," Ink instructs.

"I'm going," says Steph, tapping her thigh to get Max to her side.

"We gotta problem?" Beef's stepped up and is already helping his wife out of her seat.

"Only as far as these bitches can't keep their mouths shut," Ink spits out.

Beef growls and reaches forward, grabbing Ink by the neck and pushing him back. "Never call my woman a bitch again. You got it?"

CHAPTER EIGHT

Beth

Ink's glaring at Beef, both men look ready to throw down.

I stand, grab my purse, and start to head for the exit. Until Jay's revelation I'd been enjoying myself. Now a fight's going to break out, and it's partially my fault. I should never have come. Jay hadn't told me anything other than what I'd already suspected. Of course, Ink hadn't spent the week pining for me, he'd been fucking everything in sight.

I'm almost at the door when suddenly I'm lifted in the air, thrown over a shoulder, and while I struggle and beat my fists on Ink's back, he's got a tight hold of me and is heading toward a stairway.

"Put me down!" I shout at him, then, from my upside-down view, catch sight of Pyro. Mel's frantically pushing at his arm, but he wraps it tighter around her, holding her back.

Then the fucker gives Ink a thumbs-up. *Well he's no freaking help.*

"Mace!" I scream as I see the enforcer, but my plea gets Ink's hand slapping me on my ass.

"We're going to fuckin' talk," Ink snarls at last.

"I've got nothing to say to you," I cry out. "Put me down. I want to go home."

We're at the top of the stairs and starting off down a hallway with doors to the right and the left. Ink stops at one and opens it.

He doesn't let me down when we're inside, instead, he twists so I fall on my back on the bed, then immediately his body comes down over mine pinning me to the mattress.

He's got the muscles I don't, so has no problem overpowering me. He yanks on one of my hands, raising it over my head, then there's a snick. Then he does the same to the other and a second similar noise sounds. I pull on my arms, but they've been secured. I'm enraged.

I buck, he moves off. *Yes!* But it's only to fasten my left ankle to the foot of the bed before I realise what he's doing. Now knowing, I kick out my last free limb, uncaring whether I catch him in the balls. But he jumps out of reach, then comes back in, easily catching it and seconds later, that leg's captive as well.

"Handcuffs and leg restraints? Really?" I rattle the chains securing my wrists and feet. Yanking on them so hard they hurt, but they don't budge an inch. I try again, I'm going nowhere. So, I open my mouth and scream, "Help!" as loud as I can.

"Fuck it, woman." Ink opens a drawer by the side of the bed and takes something out. He waves it threateningly in front of me. My eyes widen as I recognise from books I've read, *a ball gag.* "I want to talk to you, want you to listen. You gonna shut up and let me? Or do I use this?"

"Let me go, Ink. Damn you to hell and back." I feel sparks fly from my eyes. "Untie me now. You can't keep me prisoner on the bed where you had God knows how many women over this past week." Then I increase the volume. "Help! Help me someone!"

He leans in menacingly close, that implement he's holding approaching my face.

"You can't gag me—"

He proves that can't doesn't appear to be in his vocabulary.

"Mmm humph." I try to speak but can't form words, or scream for help. Unease goes through me; my rage subsides to be replaced by fear.

"Oh, fuck, Beth." His eyes soften, picking up my anger has turned to something else. "I'm not going to hurt you. I just need you to listen for a moment, okay?" He brushes his hands back through his hair and interlocks them behind his head. "Yeah, you heard right. I fucked the whores. Bella, I fucked over the pool table. Titsy in the kitchen but that stays between us, Jeannie would have my hide if she knew. Breezy and Sheila with Mace in his room. Perhaps I did Tulia in here, but it's not what you think."

With each name he mentions, my eyes open wider. With every admission, tears start to leak. I knew I could easily give this man the power to hurt me, what I hadn't realised is that I already had. I'd told myself over and over that there was no point daring to hope that Ink hadn't really meant the words he'd said to me, but deep down I'd held on to the foolish dream. I thought I came here with little expectation, but I admit now that I had, deep down, hoped I hadn't been the only one to remember how special the night of Mel's wedding had been.

Our interaction last weekend which had been such a revelation to me had meant nothing to him.

Perhaps it's lucky I can't talk. I'm torn between spitting fire at him and accusing him of being a manwhore, but they would be wasted words. I knew what he was, it's not his fault I'm upset. It's no one's fault but my own, thinking he was different.

But it's hard to keep quiet. "Mmm mumph." Though my indignance is muffled by the gag.

He shakes his head. "I know, I've upset you. Beth, I don't know, fuck. This is new to me." His eyes settle on mine. "Seems I care. I fuckin' care that I've hurt you. Why?" He barks a laugh. "I don't have fuck all idea why. I told you exactly what I wanted last week. I told you what I do and who I am. I hit it and beat it. And I don't fuckin' lie or hide shit." Now he sits on the bed and puts his head in his hands, his palms rubbing against his cheeks. "I had no expectations of seeing you again, but you had to walk into my fuckin' club, didn't you? Had to taunt me with your delectable fuckin' curves, legs which go on for weeks. Had to get my cock as hard as steel with just one look at you."

I try and make another sound.

He's not finished. "When I saw you, saw my brothers sniffing around, I knew I wanted another chance. I swear, I wouldn't have lied to you. I would have told you myself what I'd been doing. Would have tried to explain, but Jay took that chance out of my hands. I knew you wouldn't listen, so that's why..." He waves his hands to where I'm lying trussed like a Thanksgiving turkey.

I shake my head vigorously trying to dislodge the gag. I can't.

"Fuck, how can I explain if I don't understand it myself." His head moves slowly side to side. "I've been here four years, babe. For three of them I've been fucking the whores. Even before then when I fucked civilians, it was only ever once then I moved on. A fuck was a fuck, nothing more nothing less, I didn't get attached to them, and didn't want anyone to latch onto me. But when I fucked you?" A look of disbelief covers his face. "Fuckin' amazing. Never came like that before, not so many times nor so hard. Fluke? The wedding? I didn't know what it was. So yeah, I fucked the whores. Trying to get back the satisfaction I'd always felt before. But it's gone. Seems there's only one woman my cock wants." He touches his length in case I hadn't understood. "Hell, woman, you're angry and rightfully so. But seeing you like this? Tied up on my bed? Fuckin' incredible. I've dreamed about this all week and thinking of you was the only way I was able to get off. I'm going to take the gag out now. You gonna scream?"

Scream for help? No. Rant and rage? Yes. *He tried to fuck me out of his head?* I suppose the only comfort I can take is that that strategy seems to have been a failure. Maybe in his twisted biker way his rationalisation makes sense.

He's explained. Now it really is over. I'll find my purse —*where the hell did I leave it?*—gather my dignity and go. I'm not staying in someone's bed which should rightly have a turnstile on it.

Resignation must show on my face, as he reaches for the ball gag and unbuckles the strap. I have to swallow back the saliva that's pooled around it. Gently, Ink takes a tissue and wipes off some that's trickled out.

I wait for him to undo the restraints, but he makes no move to do so.

"Untie me, Ink."

"Babe."

"Ink, don't babe me," I try to snap, but there's a catch in my voice.

Abruptly he stands, giving me his back. "I hurt you, Beth. That's the last fuckin' thing I wanted to do. That's why I don't do this." Going to the door, he leans his head against it, knocking his forehead gently against the wood. "I have no fuckin' idea what I'm doing. Censure me all you like, but this past week, I was doing what I always do. I couldn't stop thinking about you, so I fucked hoping it would help. Didn't know any better."

I wouldn't have known if Jay hadn't opened her mouth, unless he's being truthful when he says he would have told me. I close my eyes and think. He'd made me no promises; how can I criticise how he spent his time? Why should I worry about what coping mechanism he used? Though maybe it's important he had to employ one.

"If I hadn't come here today, would you have sought me out?"

He tenses at my question. After a moment, he shakes his head. "I can't answer that, babe." Then he spins and comes back over to me. "I can't fuckin' answer as I don't know what the fuck I'd have done. All I know is you're in here," he taps his head, "and try as I might, I can't get you out. So yeah, I might have come to find you."

"Or your strategy might eventually have worked."

He barks a loud laugh. "Well, it hasn't as yet."

I hate the thought of him going with the whores and doubt he'd ever be able to give up the free sex. I certainly wouldn't want to share. "Untie me, Ink. I'd like to leave now."

"What if I don't want to?" His eyes darken. "Oh, hell, Beth. You ask me again, and I'll free you faster than you can blink. Know this though, I don't want you to go."

"Why not?" I should give him the words, get up and leave. Go home and forget him. But there's a part of me, a big part, that wants to grab any chance with both hands.

"I don't fuckin' know," he complains, seeming frustrated. "All I know is I want you to stay. I'll tell you this, you, cuffed to my bed? Best fuckin' thing I've ever seen in my life. Let me fuck you, *little girl*. Let's see whether last week can be repeated. Let's see if there is something special between us."

Little girl. His voice, deepening on the words, sets parts of me alight. The traitorous bits.

"What happens if there is something?" My voice sounds weak, almost a whisper. "What if it is special?"

His lips press together, then he replies probably as honestly as he can, "Fuck knows, babe. Uncharted territory for me. But if you're up for it, and we want to fuck again, then we will. We'll see where this leads us."

He's been honest with me, I have to be truthful back. "I thought I could do this. I thought I could accept your terms. One night and walk away. I tried Ink, I tried so hard to forget you. I tried to chalk it up to one of the best nights I've ever had and be content with that. If I stay now, I can't promise I'll walk away tomorrow and not look back. That's not who I am."

His lips press together. Then a fleeting grin crosses his face. "Knew I was right to avoid civilians." When I start to bristle, his hand lightly covers my mouth. "What I didn't know was the reason. Turns out I was protecting myself as well as them. I've spent a week holding back, not making contact, not coming after what I wanted. All I can suggest is we take this one step at a time, Beth. I can't make you any promises, except to tell you the truth. I've never felt this way before."

"I can't fuck you, not when you're fucking the whores." I'm not certain I trust him.

"Don't want the whores, babe. Not when it's you that I'm fantasising about. I'll make you that promise, and once my word's given, I keep it." He breaks off and chuckles. "And if I didn't? Seems like your friends would tell on me."

"You were angry at Jay."

"Fuck yeah. Wouldn't have kept that from you, babe, but I should have been the one to tell you, not her."

"You'd never have admitted it," I tell him, my eyes flashing scorn. "Men never do."

He climbs onto the bed and grasps my chin. "Don't make out that you know me, little girl. I've got nothing to apologise for. You and me? We didn't make a commitment. We weren't even supposed to see each other again. If you'd stepped out with another man? Fuck, wouldn't like the idea, but wouldn't blame you."

Let me get this right. "You're saying you'll stay away from the whores?"

His look is earnest. "Hell yeah, while we're fucking, I'll be faithful, as no other cunt matches up."

My lips curve at his phrasing. Bikers are definitely a different breed of men.

Can I forgive him for being unfaithful when we weren't even together? When, as he said, we'd made no commitment? Would I think more of him if he'd said he'd been pining for me all week long? Probably, yes, but unrealistic given his lifestyle. The fact I should bank is that other women couldn't satisfy him.

"Did you use condoms?" I suddenly blurt out.

"Fuck yes." His eyes widen at just the suggestion he maybe hadn't. "Girls are clean, Beth, as am I. We all get regularly tested."

Do I trust him on that? I've no option but to take his word for it. Asking to see his results seems a bit much and would display a lack of trust. I decide to accept it.

But he sees the doubt in my eyes. Crossing to his desk, he opens the drawer, fusses around in it, then pulls out an envelope. Coming back to me, he slides a piece of paper out and shows it to me. It's ten days old, but a clear result.

"I've not gone without a condom," he stresses. "Wouldn't put any woman at risk, and," he chuckles, "not too keen on picking up something myself."

Healthwise, I'm satisfied, or as much as I can be. I dither between insisting he untie me and walking out of his life, this time to stay away completely, or... I pull on the restraints once again, unable to deny being at this handsome man's mercy is doing something to me. Heaven help me, but I want to give in. I want his hands on me.

But this time, I want more. Possibly more than he wants to give. "Kiss me," I demand, pushing him, remembering he'd given his cock freely, but not his mouth.

"You issuing the orders now? Pretty damn brave, little girl, when I've got you tied to my bed." But instead of backing away, he comes closer.

Damn, he's lowering his face to mine as he mumbles, "Been so fuckin' long, don't know if I remember how to do this."

Then, our lips meet. Soon, his tongue is demanding entry into my mouth. I reciprocate as best I'm able without the ability to hold him tight.

Jeez, he might have thought he's forgotten the mechanics, but he's perfect. I moan, the meeting of tongues not satisfying the urges rising within me. He murmurs against my lips, "You, too, huh, babe?"

As much as I can with our mouths once again fused like limpets, I try to nod.

Gradually he retreats, placing a gentle kiss to each corner of my lips. His eyes have darkened, and his pupils are dilated.

Then, with his gaze fixed firmly on mine, he moves down the

bed and undoes the button, then the zipper of my jeans. A puzzle to be solved, but he undoes my leg restraints, then slides my shoes, then my jeans and panties off. My legs are free, I have no impulsion to hurt him, not like I would have done only moments before.

He eyes my long-sleeved tee. "Is this a favourite?"

I make a negative gesture. It's fairly plain. I hadn't known what I was coming into and was slightly nervous of wearing anything with a decal on it in case it offended someone. There's only one problem. "It's all I've got with me."

Before the last word is out of my mouth, he's taken a wicked-looking knife out of his belt and is slicing my tee up the middle. As I gasp, he offers, "I'll give you one of mine to wear home."

I'm a grown woman, I'm sure my mom will understand.

As the cold steel of his blade whispers against my skin and the material parts baring me, I feel the rush of wetness that unexpectedly accompanies his action. My cheeks redden, and his eyes flare.

CHAPTER NINE

Ink

The outing to Tits Up had been a bust. Whether Cad had seen something on the cameras or not, when we'd arrived, there'd been no one there and no point hanging around. So, having checked it all out we came back to the party, me already in a bad mood thinking Beth would have left while I'd been out wasting my time.

I had no idea what this woman was doing to me. I'd actually enjoyed sitting and just getting to know her, whereas normally, I'd think talking with a bitch was a waste of good time. I'd been semi-hard since seeing her in the clubhouse but had managed to put my needs to the back of my mind, waiting until we'd got to the point where we were on the same wavelength. Then, I'd been called away.

If she's gone, I'll get her address from Mel and track her down. Fuck knows why, but something tells me she's worth running after.

My mood started to improve as I realised our next encounter is only delayed and not abandoned. I started to plan how to get her into my bed once again, knowing I'd need to try to explain why it's her I'm making an exception for, breaking my own rules of never returning for more.

I'd been pleased to walk in the door and see the group of women, something lightened inside as I realised, she'd stayed after all.

I can move quietly, I was in the Marines after all. I crept up to surprise her…

I'd been beyond angry to hear Jay telling her what I'd been up to over the past seven days. It hadn't been her place to tell Beth.

Now I had to think fast as she abruptly stood, picked up her purse and was going to walk out.

No, little girl, you're not escaping me so fast. I'd done nothing wrong, we'd made no promises, nor even planned to see each other again. But I don't hide shit like that, I'd have told her, but gently. Probably during an orgasmic haze when she'd forgive me anything.

But Jay had to blurt it out, and fuck, I might be an unfeeling asshole myself, but I knew that would have hurt. If I wasn't going to lose her, I had to think fast. Had to take her somewhere and make her listen to me. Words weren't going to do it, actions might.

I don't talk to bitches, well, I usually leave that up to my cock, but Beth had deserved words. More by accident than desire, I'd found ones which worked. I'd resorted to the truth as I didn't have anything to hide.

I'd calmed her down, with the result she's now lying hand-cuffed to my headboard. She'd be lying if she tried to tell me my dominance wasn't turning her on. Each time I inhale, I smell the delicious perfume of her arousal, there's something different about hers, it's a scent that goes straight to my already throbbing dick.

There's expectation in her eyes, intrigue as to what I'm going to do next. She's fully into this and not simply going through the motions that I've become used to with the whores. My actions are new and exciting to her, and while I may have tied up a woman more than a time or two before, her reactions are making it fresh for me too.

Gazing down at her ruined shirt, I allow myself a moment to caress her with just my eyes. Her skin reddens as though I was touching her. *Fuck, she's beautiful.*

I may have had to fight to hold myself back, and not give in too fast, but as soon as I'd seen her across the room earlier, I'd thanked fuck I'd been given an opportunity to rectify the mistake I'd made in thinking I could let her go. I'll be honest with myself and with her. I have no idea what I'm doing here, don't even know if I can make it work. But if anyone's worth giving this relationship shit a try, it's going to be her.

She moans and squirms under my examination.

"Need something, little girl?"

"Need your hands on me."

And I need to touch her. Pushing the remnants of her tee to either side of her body, I'm tempted to slice up the sleeves and remove it entirely, but the material hugs her biceps tightly, and I don't want to risk nicking her perfect skin, I can make this work. Thank fuck, her bra is front fastening. With just a flick of my wrist I have that undone, leaving her breasts naked to my eyes. My memory hasn't failed me, they're not much more than a handful but provide greater temptation to my cock than the fake or even the naturally more voluptuous ones I've sampled over the past few days.

I grin evilly.

Her breath hitches. "What?"

Leaning across her, I open the drawer where I keep my shit, and take out a packet. Fuck knows what made me make this purchase. I tell myself it was an impulse buy and nothing to do with the woman I was with last weekend, but the colour blue of the jewels perfectly matches her hair even though the brilliance of it has dulled some since the wedding.

The thought of seeing her wearing nipple clamps, her whole body flushing, a wave of red moving down her skin as though illuminating the path to the heaven that's hidden between her legs, is something that has my cock once again painfully pressing against the material of my jeans. So much so, I leap away from her, shrugging out of my clothes as if I was ridding myself of acid instead of denim.

Then I get down to business. Fastening my lips over one nipple then the other, working both into hard nubs, I then attach those clamps, watching her gasp as she becomes accustomed to the sensation, seeing her squirm as the pinch arouses her even more.

"Ink!"

I draw back a little, studying her face. "You doing okay?"

"Fuck yeah," she breathes out, her body writhing making those clamps bounce.

"I think my little girl likes having her nipples pinched, doesn't she?" I breathe against her skin, noticing how smooth it is. I've never taken my time to think much about the whores, they were there for one thing, mutual satisfaction which involved a cock in a cunt or other available receptacle. Beth's more than that, much more. I twirl a strand of her blue hair around my fingers, it's silky and fine.

"I do," she replies to my question. "Ink, I feel so good."

"Gonna make you feel better."

I get to work immediately. Staring into her face, cataloguing every expression, I bring her to her peak on my fingers, then slide down her body, and hear her come again, this time on my tongue. Then, after clothing myself with the promised condom, I slide my cock home, pausing for just one moment to enjoy the sensation, just as good as I remembered.

"Legs, wrap them around me," I order, hissing when she obeys, the movement allowing me in deeper.

She's a runner, I remember as her limbs grip me tightly. She moves with me as I start hammering in, pushing back against me, taking all of me.

"You good?" I rasp out.

"So good," she responds, her hands curling around the chains as if bracing herself. "So fucking good Ink, I'm coming."

"That's right, babe. Squeeze my..." I lose all thought as her muscles grip me. This isn't the frantic coupling of last week when we both seemed to want to prove something. This is sweeter, more than just fucking, though I'd hesitate to put a name to it.

When we're both spent, I kiss her deeply. I fucking love how responsive she is under my tongue, against my fingers, and on my cock. The feeling of her long legs wrapped around my waist had taken me to heights I never knew existed.

Then I untie her hands, and we do it again. And again.

Several hours later, I let her sleep, exhausted in my arms.

It never crosses my mind to do different. When morning comes, she's still there—as if she belongs.

What do you say to a bitch who's spent the night in your bed?

Who the fuck knows? Not me, that's for sure. "Mornin', babe." Well, it seems a good start when at last she opens her eyes.

She stretches, much like a cat, even arching her back. I swear, she purrs. "What's the time?"

"Nine-ish."

"In the morning?" Her eyes widen.

"Yeah. How about that?"

"I thought you didn't sleep with bitches." She grins widely.

"I don't," I reply, placing my lips against her forehead, unable to resist saying with a chuckle. "Think you must have worn me out, babe. Didn't have the energy to kick you out of bed."

She pokes her finger into a gap between my ribs, making me oomph. "You didn't, huh?"

I brush a lock of blue hair out of her face. For a second, I stare intensely into her eyes. "Or, maybe, I just like you right where you are."

She snuggles against me. "I like being where I am too, Ink."

Nuzzling against my skin, she breathes in deeply. "Mmm, you smell nice."

Nice? I smell of sex and sweat, hers and mine both. Perhaps she's right. I'm not objecting to her odour either. Crazy.

"How many did we use this time?"

I laugh and leaning over check the wrappers on the floor. "Didn't beat our record. Only five."

She rolls over on her back, opening her legs in invitation. "Think we ought to rectify that?"

She doesn't need to ask me twice.

"What have you got on today?" I ask her after we've dirtied the last condom and cleaned ourselves up in the shower.

"First, I'll get a run in if it's not too icy out there. Then just chores. Sundays I usually help mom around the house, do laundry, stuff like that. What about you?"

I grin. "Well I suppose I'll need to put clean sheets on the bed." She blushes delightfully. I grow serious looking at what kind of day I might have ahead, thinking of the implications of what happened last night, not with her, but our wasted trip out. Cad will have gone back over the footage, and will have analysed it all by now. If he's found anything, the bets are we'll be checking it out. But I can't tell her that as it's club business. "I reckon Demon will need to talk through some shit. Wouldn't be surprised if he calls a meeting later. Hey, what's that look for?" She's biting her lip. "Come on, babe. Spit it out."

"I, er, no. It sounds bad."

"What?" I prompt, starting to worry now, rapidly running back over the conversation to see if there was something wrong with what I'd said.

Now her lips press together, and she looks away. Placing my hand under her chin, I turn her face back. "Tell me, babe."

"I just wondered, I was..." Then it comes out in a rush. "I was wondering if you'd like to come around to mine, later. Mom does a great roast on the weekend, and she always cooks too much." Her face goes red.

Meet her mom? "I'm not boyfriend material," I tell her, wondering why the expected horror at the suggestion doesn't materialise.

Her face falls. "I know. I'm sorry…"

"Look, Beth, I don't know where this is going to go. Done a few things already with you that I haven't done before." I lean in and whisper the next right into her ear, "Used six condoms at a time for a start." I pull back. "You're the first civilian I've gone back to for seconds, let alone let spend the night. As long as you're okay with just seeing where this goes, and not pushing for a commitment I don't feel ready to make, if I'm free, I'll come meet your mom and get fed."

"I don't know where this is going, either. And I promise, Mom won't be planning a wedding, not yet."

I shake my head but laugh. Her mom won't be planning a wedding at all. Closest I'll ever get is claiming a woman, that's all I'd need to do, and Beth and I are nowhere near the place where I'd start thinking about that.

Claim Beth? It's the nearest I've come to even thinking about making a woman mine. But that's only one step removed from when hell freezes over to maybe when I consider getting a foreign-built bike.

I see her out to her car with a promise to call as soon as I know whether I'll be able to make it later, then thoughtfully watch her drive off, wondering what the fuck I'm getting into. What is it about her that's making me act out of character? *I let her stay the night.*

I even liked waking with her in my arms.

As I'm belatedly considering whether I should have made her a coffee or got her something to eat, and thinking I'm only one step above a Neanderthal, a voice brings me out of my thoughts.

"Did I just see that?" Lizard asks, putting his hands over his eyes, and then removing them. "I think I might be having fuckin' hallucinations. I may have laid one on last night, but I didn't think it was as much as that."

"What the fuck are you talking about?" I round on him.

He shakes his head as if to clear it. "Yeah, I must be fuckin' seeing things. You waving a bitch off in the morning? She was with you all night? Nah, my imagination must be playing up."

I punch him in the stomach hard as I walk past him.

He's not the only one. Christ. Were they all watching out the window? Haven't they got better things to do on a Sunday morning?

I threaten Mace with loss of a body part if he doesn't shut his mouth. Pal gets promised a painful death.

"What the fuck business is it of yours?" I yell at Pyro waspishly when he joins in.

Mel's man shrugs. "Only give back to you what you like to dish out."

I suppose he's right. If it was any of my brothers, I'd be the one making jokes at their expense. But hey, I don't like the tables being turned. I throw up my hands and walk off into the kitchen to get something to eat. Of course, I bump into Jayden who gives me a frosty look.

"What? No apology?" I challenge her.

"I think you should say sorry to me," she huffs.

Pal's come in behind me. He taps me on the shoulder and when I turn around, he leans in. "Her ass is a little sore this morning," he explains.

I raise my fist, he bumps his against it.

His woman snorts, but when I turn back to her, she hasn't been quick enough to hide her grin.

"Demon wants us!" comes a shout from the clubroom.

As I predicted, an emergency church is called.

His birthday passed and over, Demon's all seriousness now and wastes no time getting down to business. "Cad, you've gone back over the footage from yesterday?"

"I have. There was only what I saw at the time. A couple of

men talking, cash changing hands, behind Tits Up, where we installed those cameras. You know, the ones we've disguised."

"That all?" Lizard asks.

Cad shoots him a look. "It's enough, isn't it? We're looking for people dealing, that could have been what this was."

"But by the time we arrived, they'd disappeared," I observe.

"Left evidence," says Mace, grimly. "While you were getting your dicks wet this morning, I went back and checked in daylight."

Shit and fucks are exclaimed as Mace throws some baggies down on the table.

"They were shooting up around there?"

"There, or close by," the enforcer confirms.

Last thing we want is people leaving used needles around our premises. We don't deal in drugs and don't want that reputation.

"Worse than that," Mace nods at the bags on the table, "one of those came from Devils' Pins which I thought I should also check out."

Rusty draws in air through his teeth as our bowling alley is mentioned at the same time as Demon's hand slams down on the table. "Thought we'd seen the last of this type of shit when Taser set the club up. Tits Up is one thing and we can keep an eye on it, but discarded needles where kids play? That's just fucked up."

"You think we're being targeted again?" the VP asks. Beef might not have been around at the time, but it didn't take long for him to bring himself up to speed with all matters affecting the club. The reference to Taser does indeed show where the prez's head might be at.

"Could be," says Thunder, "or it could just be we've got good locations which other people don't use. The Wretched Soulz and Mafia are active in their own areas and know to stay out of ours."

He's right. Someone new dealing would easily stick out

where the dealers are well known, so they'd avoid taken territory.

"We need to make sure we have a visible presence around our premises to chase anyone off and let them know their trade isn't welcome."

"That was my thought, Mace. Hate to put more on us but can't see anything else for it. We keep drugs out of these areas, it makes less work for the law."

Beef nods. One of the first things he did when he was voted in was to start a dialogue with the cops. A new police chief had arrived in Pueblo just before Beef. After checking his reputation out, Beef had gotten a meeting with him and had come to an understanding where our decisive position on drugs was made known. Might be an easy way of earning money, but there's too much chance of a brother getting addicted or going inside. Devils have been clear of that shit for years now. Not only don't we touch it, we don't tolerate it in the part of town we control. Got some respect for that, can't afford to lose that respect now.

"I want to know who's fuckin' with us," Demon says, meeting Hellfire's eyes across the length of the table. "We find someone, we fuckin' bring them back and question them."

"From what you said it's not someone local," Thunder observes.

"The Soulz suspect it's someone from out of town. Some small-time op seizing a chance right here in Pueblo," Prez confirms.

"You need bodies to stake out Devils' Pins and Tits Up tonight?" I ask, hoping I can still make dinner with Beth. I've actually been looking forward to that, and bringing her back here afterwards, of course.

"I'm in," says Judge.

"Me too," Wills offers.

"I want to see what's going on under our noses," mutters Rusty. "I'm up for it."

"Right, Judge, Wills and Rusty are on the bowling alley," Demon decides. "Now who's for Tits Up?"

"I'll go," offers the sergeant-at-arms.

Pyro waves his hand.

"I want to check the position of the cameras, so I'll go myself," says Cad.

I start lifting my arm, but Demon shakes his head. "Three at each location is plenty for now. And this probably isn't a one-night thing. If there's any action tonight, we'll have to think about assigning regular teams to take on the patrols."

"With luck we'll run them off tonight," Ro states, his face set as if he's already sensing blood. "They could move on and find somewhere less obvious and no Devils around."

Growls, stomps and fist bumps on the table show our agreement with his words.

"Isn't that still a worry, Prez? Even if they're not at our premises?"

Demon sighs loudly. "Yeah, Liz, you're right. But don't forget, the Wretched Soulz and Mafia are also looking out. While I'd like to string up the fuckers myself, I don't mind who catches them just as long as the result is we end their fuckin' trade. We'll concentrate on our territory; RIP and the Mafia can watch theirs. With luck, we'll run them back to the hole they crawled out of."

Relieved I'm free this evening, when church lets out I make sure to have a word with Beef about making sure my name's added to the rotation if Pyro and the others aren't successful tonight. I check the time, then text Beth to let her know if the invitation is still open, I'm on my way.

Her reply comes fast.

Beth: See you soon

I grin, then have a moment wondering what the fuck I'm doing. Have I met anyone's parents or parent before, or at least since I picked up my prom date? Not that I can remember.

The weather's kind for riding, so I take my bike, still uncertain why I'm acting so out of character. My Sunday would normally end with maybe a card game or a turn at pool before taking a whore to my room, or letting her suck me off in the clubroom. Until last weekend, I thought I had everything worth having in life.

Beth unsettles me, and I'm not sure how I feel about that. Why should I give up all the good things to go for a polite dinner with a woman in her fucking mother's house?

I can't explain why I'm eagerly anticipating doing normal boring citizen stuff. Must only be the thought that if I want to get into her cunt later, I'll have to play it her way first. Yeah, that's all it can be.

I pull up on her road and taking out my phone, check the address to make sure I'm heading to the right house, then ride up and park on the driveway behind Beth's car. There's another beside it, which is why I've chosen to block in hers. She won't be leaving before I do.

When the thunderous sound of my engine dies, I'm not greeted by the expected silence. No, instead I hear the sound of shouting from inside. Very angry shouting.

CHAPTER TEN

Beth

"You are not dragging me and Beth into whatever you're up to."

The argument has been going on for some time. I step in between my mom and her wayward son, my brother. "Connor..." I growl in warning.

Angrily he pushes me to one side. "Mom, see sense. I'm not dragging you into anything. You're my fuckin' mother. All I'm asking is if I can use my old room when I'm working in Pueblo."

"Working? Is that what you call it?"

"Yeah, I work."

"Connor," I tug at his arm, moving him away from Mom. "You could stay at a hotel..."

"Why the fuckin' hell should I?" He rounds on me now. "Mom's got a perfectly good room sitting empty." He brushes back some hair that's flopped down over his face. "There's even some of my old shit left in it. I'm asking for a night or so a week. I'll even pay a bit of rent."

I look from one to the other. To be honest, I'm not certain why Mom's so against Connor staying here. I thought she might be pleased to help out. When he first mentioned it, she did seem okay with the idea, it was only after our father's name came up, she changed her mind.

"I don't trust your father," she shouts at Connor. "And by association, I don't trust you. I'm not giving you a key so you can come and go at all hours and bring God knows who into my home."

"I won't bring anyone else here." Connor tries once more, but he's inherited my mom's Irish temper, and there's no stopping either of them now. "Jeez. Isn't there a fucking way of making you see sense, woman?" Connor yells. "Beth's okay with it."

"Beth doesn't own the house," I mumble.

"Why's this so important to you, Connor? What's your dad got you doing now?"

He throws up his hands. "Shouldn't have mentioned his name. You always were irrational about him. He's got nothing to do with this. Look, it's just me. Your son. I need a place to stay. You good with that now?" For some reason, he's starting to look desperate.

When Mom turns her back, he reaches out his hand, roughly turning her around to face him. "Don't you walk away from me, woman!"

I hate confrontations—particularly between those I love. I don't know what to do to stop them, and for the first time in my life, worry this is going to turn physical. Connor's as tall as I am, but compared to us, my mom is tiny, albeit she's the average woman's size. I've never seen Connor so angry and can't understand why. On her part, any mention of my father, and my mom sees red. I'm not sure either of them is capable of calming down and being reasonable at this point.

Now Connor's put his hands on my mom, I worry she'll slap his face, and don't quite trust him not to retaliate. The boy I grew up with wouldn't have, but who knows what he'll do now living as he does under the influence of my dad?

As I'm trying to summon up words to make peace between them, my brain registers a loud rumbling roar. *Ink.* Oh, not now.

I don't want him walking in on this. What a great introduction to my family that would make.

I ease myself out of the room and walk swiftly to the door. I open it, then, when he walks up, step out. "Er…" I was going to make an excuse why he can't come inside, but he physically moves me out of the way as, from behind me, I hear the loud slap that I feared.

Then it's Ink's voice that reaches me, and I run quickly after him to see one of my brother's arms twisted behind his back, and the other, still raised in the air, held in the other of Ink's meaty paws.

"I don't give a fuck who you are, but you do not hit a defenceless woman."

"She hit me first," my brother whines, trying ineffectually to free himself from Ink's grasp. "And who the fuck do you think you are, coming into my house and attacking me?"

"I'm not fuckin' attackin' you, asshole," Ink observes. "You okay?" This thrown toward my mom.

Mom's eyes are wide open, flicking between her son and the man who's got him restrained. "I'm fine. But this is *my* house, and my son's not welcome here. I would appreciate you taking the trash to the door."

"Trash? Fucking trash now am I, *Mother*?"

"You are in this mood." Mom thinks for a moment, then offers, "You can stay, but you come in at a reasonable time. I am not giving you a key…"

Connor growls and throws her olive branch back in her face. "I'm not a fuckin' kid, *Mother*. I'm allowed to stay out late. This is past ridiculous, I give up." He starts to walk out, then turns back. "There's some shit I left upstairs I might as well now take. It's clearly not my fucking room any longer."

Shit? Last time I looked there was a closet full of clothes more suited to a teenager, schoolbooks he'd have no use for, and old computer games.

"Take what you want," Mom says, tiredly.

"You heard your mother. Get what you need and get out." Ink lets Connor go, then stands with his arms folded across his chest.

A strange look comes over Connor's face. "I'll just go get a box, I've got one in the car."

"I've got…" But Mom's offer goes unheard as Connor has already stepped out.

Ink raises an eyebrow at my mother. "You okay with him getting his stuff? Trust him not to rob you of the family silver?"

Mom gives a small smile. "After raising two giants, there's not much of that left. But yes, if there was anything to steal I trust him that far, and there's not much in his room, anyway. Just some old computer games, and an out-of-date Xbox, not much more than that."

"Everything's old," I mumble, wondering what Connor wants with his defunct things.

"He might be able to sell it," Ink suggests.

A stomping of feet tells us Connor's reappeared. He comes back in a few moments later, this time carrying a full box. As I expected, he's got the console and games, but it doesn't appear he's bothered to pack his clothes or anything else.

With a rueful look down at the pitiful contents, he approaches my mom. His voice sounds a lot calmer. "Patsy, I'm sorry. Look, I know how you feel about Phil, but, I, well, I can't say more, but I don't want to leave with bad blood between us."

"Then don't leave. Don't go back to him. Stay here with us."

A flicker of something crosses my brother's face, so quickly I could have imagined it, then his features become hard again. "Can't do that, Patsy. I work for him, remember?"

"Your room will always be here," Mom says, but qualifies, "if you put space between you and that man. But not if he's still in the picture. I'm not risking that."

"Fuck it, woman," Connor starts, getting angry again.

"I don't think you're welcome here." Ink steps forward, not letting him finish.

"Beth's man is right," Mom says.

"Beth's *man*?" Connor almost squeals as he looks at me in surprise.

I'm taken aback by Mom's description myself and think I'll have to have an explanation for her incorrect assumption ready later. Ink's probably wondering what the hell I've told her about us.

But Ink surprises me. "Fuckin' right I'm her man. Beth and your mom are under the protection of the Satan's Devils and you better not fuckin' forget that."

As he says that he turns and comes over to me, and my brother must get his first proper look at Ink's colours on the back of his cut. His eyes open wide. "Fuck it, Beth. Thought you'd have more fucking sense than hooking up with a Satan's Devil." He turns back to my mom. "They're criminals, Mom. You best put a stop to this right now."

Mom takes a step closer to him and leans back her head so she can stare into his face. "More than one thing wrong with that statement, *Son*. First off, pot, kettle, and black comes to my mind. Second, Beth's a grown woman and can do what she wants. She says the Devils are okay? Then it's her word I'll be taking."

Ink's clearly had enough. "Come on, asshole. Think it's time we get to see the dust from your tyres." He pushes Connor hard.

My brother takes the hint. He swings to face the door, then he turns back. "Mom, Beth… Look, I don't want to leave like this. Like I said, I'll be doing some work here from time to time, I'll pop in when I'm passing. Maybe next weekend?"

"That okay with you, Patsy?" Ink checks. He doesn't seem to have taken to my brother at all.

Mom closes her eyes then reopens them. "He's my son," she tells Ink. "I don't mind seeing him, I'm just not letting him bring trouble to my door."

Ink nods. When Connor leaves, he follows him out.

Quickly I move forward and put my arms around my mom.

"I'm sorry," she starts. "What a way to welcome your man."

"I suspect Ink's seen worse," I reply, drily.

I hear the sound of a car starting, then wheels squeal as it peels out of the driveway.

Ink comes back through the door that's still open, brushing his hands together as though removing dirt from them. He eyes me holding Mom. She barely reaches my chest so it looks like our positions are reversed, with me taking the parent's role. "You want me to leave you two alone?"

"No," Mom says, determinedly. "I'm sorry you were a witness to a family fight. I'm sorry you had to walk in on that. But please, stay. That's if you still want to."

Ink considers for a moment, then his lips curve up in a smile. "A bit of friction isn't going to chase me off."

"Jeez, I'm forgetting my manners." Mom moves her head side to side. "I'm Patsy, Beth's mom. And you must be Ink."

"I kinda guessed that, though I imagined someone a lot taller." Ink grins. "And yeah, I'm Beth's *man*." He winks at me, letting me know he has no objection to the label.

"Thank you." Mom waves her hand toward the front of the house. "My son—"

"You don't have to explain anything. Got a lot of brothers who come from fucked up homes. We can't choose our blood family." He pauses. "Makes a fuckin' difference when you can choose the one you want."

"Like you've chosen your club," I interpret.

"Too fuckin' right I have." Breaking off, he looks first toward me, then toward Mom. "Might need to know a few more details, but you'll have the club behind you if he or his father cause you any problems. Here's the thing, Beth is Mel's friend, and Mel's a claimed woman. I'm… with… Beth for now. Club will help if it's necessary."

"Already knew you were going to be a good'un, Ink. My Beth doesn't read people wrong, and you've proved it this afternoon. I'll go rescue the roast, then I'll satisfy your curiosity while we're eating."

I send an apologetic look Ink's way. "I'll help, Mom."

Ink looks around, seeing the bare dining room table asks, "Tell me where you keep the silverware and I'll set the table if you want?"

Luckily Mom had turned down the oven during the argument, so dinner is soon saved and back on track. Shortly, she's putting everything on serving plates and Ink's carrying them to the table. After we sit down, we take a moment sorting our plates out, then a minute longer to appreciate the food Mom has lovingly prepared.

"You see much of your son, Patsy?" Ink asks at last.

"No." Her brow creases with the pain I know doesn't lessen. "Six years ago, he discovered his father. Didn't care he'd neglected him for most of his life, hit it off apparently. Left home as soon as he turned eighteen and lives with him now in Denver. He's only been back a few times, full of his father's praise."

"Which you aren't buying," Ink observes.

"Which I'm not buying," Mom agrees. "Know it makes me sound like a bitch, but I kicked his dad's ass to the kerb when I found out just what he was into."

"Which was?"

"This and that and anything else that brought the dollars in without him doing an honest day's work. Money laundering was what I caught him doing, but there's probably worse."

"You kept him away from his children?"

"Huh," she scoffs. "He didn't have much to do with them when he was here. I'd have let them stay in contact, he's blood after all, but he didn't make any effort."

Ink's eyes meet mine and soften. I shake my head slightly, any abandonment I'd ever felt was long gone now. Lucky escape was how I saw it instead. I wouldn't want to be involved in criminal activity, not in the way I'm convinced Connor is. Sure, that's why I'm dating a biker, I grin to myself, then I roll my eyes, and pull myself up. We're not dating. I don't know what would describe it, but it's not that.

"What's your ex's name?" Ink asks Mom, deceptively casually.

"Phil Foster," she supplies.

Ink's eyes close briefly, then his head moves side to side. "Can't say I've heard of him."

"He relocated to Denver years back," I explain. "And Connor didn't sound like he was a fan of the Satan's Devils."

"He certainly knew our reputation," Ink notes. "Though perhaps more from the old days. Phil ever live in Pueblo?"

"Until he moved out, yes. He left, what, eighteen years ago now? Connor would have been four."

"You get your height from him?"

Ink has addressed his question to me, but it's Mom who laughs and replies, "No, Phil's not much taller than me. It must have come down from my side, a recessive gene or something. Beth's maternal cousins are all over six feet tall. I used to wonder whether Beth would ever stop growing, and Connor turned out the same." She pauses, and a glint comes into her eyes. The glint that makes me swallow rapidly. "You're not on the short side yourself, Ink."

"No, ma'am, I am not."

Mom's not finished. "I always wondered whether Beth would find a man big enough for her." There's a twinkle in her eyes that shows she's well aware of how her comment could be misinterpreted.

I take it the safest way it could be meant, and say airily, "Oh, his club's full of tall, single men, Mom. I've started with Ink, but I'll be working through them all in time."

Ink makes a noise that sounds like he's choking, then turns to me with steel in his eyes, to find me winking. Mom's bent over the table wiping tears of laughter from her cheeks.

Leaning closer so only I can hear him, he whispers, "You've earned yourself another punishment with that quip, little girl. One for each of my single fuckin' brothers."

Whispering back, I ask, "Er, how many are there?"

His eyes close as though he's thinking, then he gives me his reply, "Eight." He raises his eyebrows.

I grin and give an uncaring shrug. Sounds like I've been there before. And though it had surprised me, it hadn't been punishment at all.

Ink's still staring at me intently. The next thing he says *sotto voce* is a complete surprise. "I hope you've chosen wisely, little girl, as mine is the only biker cock you're going to be riding. You won't be fuckin' any of my brothers. You understand?"

I gulp, not completely comprehending. Not that I like any of them more than him, but is he saying once we're over, I'm out of the club, or, is he suggesting, we won't come to an end? I don't ask for clarification, uncertain he'll provide an answer I want to hear.

"Who wants dessert?" Mom asks cheerily, completely oblivious to our quietly spoken and entirely, seated as we are around the dining table, inappropriate conversation.

"I could manage dessert." But Ink's eyes are focused on me, and somehow, I doubt it's my mom's apple pie he's contemplating.

CHAPTER ELEVEN

Ink

Beth's mom is a hoot, coming out with inappropriate shit which makes me laugh. I'm enjoying myself being here with the two women, something I'd never have predicted. Rather than wishing I was back at the clubhouse playing pool, I'm perfectly content right where I've found myself.

I settle into their home, fast feeling nothing like a visitor. Patsy suggests we watch a movie, and with my feet up on the coffee table—which apparently isn't a sin in this house—and a beer in my hand I'm quite agreeable. Though my face falls when they put something called *Love Actually* on, but it turns out to be hilarious and I'm doubled up half the time.

The character who visits the United States reminds me of when our chapter went to help Tucson out of some trouble they were in, and I met Wraith, the VP's wife, Sophie. Part of me had wondered whether he'd married her just to hear her accent every day and those quaint UK English terms. I chuckle as there's one in particular I remember.

"What?"

I enlighten Beth on what's amused me. "The VP's ol' lady in the Tucson chapter is from England. She comes out with some shit. Calls Wraith a wanker when he's done something foolish and when something's good it's apparently the dog's bollocks."

After laughing in disbelief, Patsy asks, interested, "You've got other chapters then, Ink?"

Half watching the film which they've clearly seen before, I run through our other chapters. That starts a discussion of the history of the Satan's Devils. Then we get onto hobbies. I don't have time for many other than the things I do with the club, so I describe how I love just taking off on my bike. Patsy proudly tells me what I already know, that Beth runs half-marathons. Gets placed regularly too.

A grin slides onto my face, and my eyes sneak down to her legs, relishing how they feel around me.

But I'm interested enough to ask for more information.

Beth replies, "A half-marathon is thirteen miles give or take. I can do that between two and two-and-a-half hours. Want to join me sometime?"

I work out, but I prefer muscle building. I'm not even certain I could walk thirteen miles without my feet blistering. "Tell you what," I wink, "I'll ride along behind you."

A gentle snore from the armchair shows even in my stimulating company, Patsy has fallen asleep. Beth and I exchange smiles, and I take it as my cue to leave. Especially when I see Beth try to hide a yawn.

While I'd love to spend a few hours with my cock buried deep inside her, I have too much respect for Patsy to subject her to hearing me fuck her daughter in her house. As for my earlier idea to take Beth back to the club, time's gotten away from me, and I know she has work tomorrow. For the first time that I can remember since I was in my mid-teens, I prepare to take my leave of a woman without my dick getting any satisfaction.

Beth sees me to the door, and stands there, hesitantly. When neither of us move, she says a goodbye and turns to go back inside.

It's then I strike. I curl my hand out and grasp her shoulder, swinging her back around to face me, then pull her tight against my chest and bring my mouth to meet hers. It seems lazy, I don't need to bend, just reach forward and she's there. For some reason, I find that her body parts mirroring mine as they rest against them, immensely satisfying. We stand, kissing, the only movement being lips against lips and tongues against tongues, our pelvises pressed together, but both keeping still, as if each of us knows a little thrust here or a swerve of the hips there would drive both of us crazy.

Her taste is like summer, her perfume as intoxicating as any drug I've ever imbibed. Her touch, firm, demanding, her little moans showing her frustrated desire clearly matches my own. She's beautiful, with brilliant blue eyes which sparkle in the light of the porch lamp overhead.

When at last we part, I lower my forehead so it rests against hers and run my hand through the loose strands of her hair. "Is it always blue?"

She laughs, the sound like a stream's burble, happy and bright. "Nope. I go through the full range. Had this done to match my bridesmaid's dress. May go purple or pink next time. Or even multi-coloured like a rainbow."

"They can do that?" My eyes open wide.

"With a lot of time and money," she informs me. I tilt my head to one side and half close my eyes trying to imagine it. Sounds like it could be a good investment.

The possible reason why she alters her appearance comes to me. "Do you colour your hair to give people something to focus on?"

"Other than my height." Her eyes narrow. "Yes. It's easier to deal with a 'oh your hair is blue' than a 'just look at the size of you.'"

Because one she can alter, and one she's stuck with.

"You are absolutely fuckin' perfect." I swallow hard and reach out my palm to place it against her face. "There's no one else like you, Beth. Or no one I've ever met. I like what's inside of you here," I drop my hand so it rests over her heart, "and I love the package it's in. I wouldn't change anything about you. Nothing at fuckin' all."

She literally shrugs off what to me was a compliment. I suppose up to now I haven't done anything to make her believe she's special to me, but she is. I want to explain, but where do I start? I've no experience to draw on.

"I fuck, Beth, I told you that. I don't go to a girl's house, meet her mom, watch a god-awful film that actually turned out to be quite good. I don't leave without getting my dick wet. Never done anything like this before, let alone fuckin' enjoyed it."

I can see she doesn't know what to make of what I've told her. Truth is, I don't know myself. There's a notion growing inside me that I'd like to replace the seat on my bike, get one with a pillion pad and sissy bar. Have her riding up behind me? Heading out just the two of us and the open road? Put up with the shit I'll get from my brothers?

Well, fuck me, but I think she's worth everything they'd throw at me. I think of what we've got in stock at the shop, sure I can find something and make it work. Payback's a bitch, as I expect I'll find out. Pyro and Mace will find me fitting a double seat too big a chance to pass up. For her though, I'll do it.

"Want to go for a ride with me next weekend, babe?"

She looks confused, and I realise maybe Mel has told her of the significance of a woman riding two up on a bike. "What? Where?"

"A ride. You and me. If the weather allows that is. And wherever we want."

She looks down, and I feel like I've been punched in the gut. "You don't want to go on my bike? I'm a safe rider, Beth."

"It's not that. Don't laugh, but I've always wanted to ride one myself."

What? I frown, then feel my lips start to curve as I wonder why the fuck not? She's tall enough to be able to handle anything. "Well what's stopping you? How about I teach you?"

You'd think I'd offered to buy her the fucking world. She starts jumping on the spot. "Really? When? Wouldn't I need to buy one first? Where do I start—"

"Whoa, hold up. One of the prospects has got a Sportster, that's a good learner bike that you'd be able to handle alright. I'll get him to let you ride it to see how you get on. And next weekend, if you want."

"Ink I… I really like you." She leaps forward and into my arms. Caught off guard, I stagger back laughing as I catch her.

"We'll talk, later in the week, okay? Firm up on arrangements once we know how the weather is holding up?"

After that we say our goodbyes, then I'm straddling my bike with a huge grin on my face. Never did I think I'd gain the affections of a woman by offering to teach her to ride a motorcycle. I'm still chuckling as I pull on my balaclava, my safety glasses, and bandana, and finally, my riding gloves. Then, with a wave at the woman who's still waiting at the open door, ride off in the direction of the compound.

I blow on my hands to warm them after getting off my bike, grimacing at the grit I've driven over, but knowing it's better than ice. Beaver's at the bar, I go straight over.

"Bourbon no ice. Oh, and get my bike washed tomorrow. And on Saturday I want to borrow your Sportster."

"Sure." The first request is fulfilled within seconds. Then he replies positively to the second as any good prospect should. "I'll do it, and for the last request, can I ask why?"

I shrug. "It's a Sportster, isn't it? Got someone who wants to learn to ride and thought yours would be a good one to try on."

If I'd thought about it, I'd have had my phone out and ready to take a picture of the expression on his face. I have to try hard not to laugh as his mouth opens and shuts a couple of times.

Lizard has overheard, and comes over, saying into my ear, "Let's see how much he wants that patch."

Beaver, though, hasn't heard the worst of it yet.

He looks from me to Liz, though he hadn't heard what was

said. "Who's learning? A new hangaround?" His expression shows how little he thinks of a novice touching his ride.

Keeping my face as straight as possible, I respond, "Nah, Beth."

Beaver goes absolutely still. His face slowly goes red. "That tall bitch?"

I bristle at the term he's used for her, though fuck knows why. Can't blame him when I call all women that myself, though Beth's become more elevated in my mind. *My woman* has a better ring to it. *What the fuck am I thinking?* Not coming anywhere near close to claiming her. Unable to offer an alternative description for her, I just nod.

Lizard snorts beside me, making me look at him. He's staring at Beaver who's clearly not keen.

Then the prospect lets out a defeated sigh. "She's got the physique to handle it. As long as she doesn't drop it or put a scratch on it, I suppose it will be alright." He thinks for a moment. "I was actually thinking of selling it, so if she likes it, she might be interested."

Shit. This could work out. While I've been coming around to the idea of Beth riding behind me, beside me has just as good a ring to it.

"What you thinking of getting, Beaver?"

While Liz and Beaver discuss models that the prospect might be considering, I turn away leaning my back against the bar. Sheila spies me and sashays over. When she's up close, her fingernails gently rake down my face.

"Want to have some fun?"

I remove her hand. "Not tonight, darlin'."

Lizard must have finished his discussion with the prospect in time to witness me sending Sheila away. "Think I'll have me some of that if you don't want it. You feeling okay? Or have you just been serviced in town?" His eyebrows lift up and down suggestively.

"Yes, and nope. In that order."

His mouth drops open.

We live on the wild side which means making use of the sex on tap. Not often that a brother's not feeling it. I'm not surprised when I feel the back of his hand on my brow.

When I slap it away, he tells me, "You feel a bit heated there, Brother. Why don't you have a chat with Rusty? May have an infection if your cock doesn't work."

He's faster than he looks, and my fist, aimed for his stomach hits only air. Though he certainly doesn't miss my raised middle finger as I walk off to the stairs. I hear his bellowed laughter ringing out behind me.

For the next couple of days, I find myself in a quandary. I want to see Beth, but I don't. Just for a fuck, of course, as I could do with one and I promised I wouldn't go near a whore. Seeing her would ease my itch, suspecting as I do it wouldn't be diffi-cult to persuade her back into my bed. But meeting up again so soon might suggest I couldn't stay away from her.

Problem is, I'm finding it hard keeping my distance. As that's unlike me, I do the extremely unmanly thing and take a few moments out of my day to analyse my strange thoughts.

The night of Ro's wedding I'd used my normal ploy, explaining to a civilian bitch that I've nothing to offer her except for my cock, and that she was only getting once. Beth had told me that was all she had wanted. I wouldn't have touched her had I not believed she'd meant it.

At the time I think we had both been completely honest, but can our wants change? Could I really yield to this craving inside me, and admit it's her I want to see again, and for more than just to get my dick wet. Has the unthinkable happened and I've started to feel something other than just sexual appreciation for her? Or am I, as Lizard suggested, coming down with the flu.

If I am skirting around the word relationship that would normally give me hives, would she be on the same page? I can't see her as the type of woman who just wants me as a temporary fuck friend, but can I be sure? I bang my hand against my head.

Christ, that would be some retribution if my feelings for her are stronger than ones she'd reciprocate. What a joke if I find a bitch I'd consider claiming, and she were to throw it back in my face?

Surprised at the direction of my thinking, glancing downward, I check my cock is still there, and that my balls are still attached to my body. Wouldn't surprise me with the thoughts going through my head that they've fallen off and I've grown a vagina.

I make a concerted effort to stop thinking about her and pick up the paint gun to continue my work instead.

Tuesday I nearly fold but, after a fight with myself, find some resolve and don't get on my bike and ride to see her. I can't, however, prevent myself picking up my phone and tapping out a text.

Ink: What you doing Friday?

Beth: Sounds like I'm seeing you.

She got that from a four-word text? Amused, I have a vision of her giggling at her presumptuousness.

Ink: Fucking right you are.

Beth: Can't wait. Oh, and go commando.

I roll back on my bed, laughing like a loon.

Ink: Babe, I'm not that easy.

Beth: Yes, you are.

I decide I can't argue and leave it at that. Never laughed so hard at just a few line texts. Is that why brothers have hooked up with old ladies? Because not only do they make them feel good in bed, but they also brighten their lives out of it.

Thinking of her predictably makes my cock perk up. I take myself in hand, realising it's not just the pledge I'd made that's keeping me away from the whores. It's like Beth is the juiciest steak and I've no desire for cheap burgers anymore. Closing my eyes I summon up a vision of the only woman it seems that I want and soon I'm shooting my load, only just refraining from shouting her name out loud.

Wednesday passes the same as any other day. I service a

couple of cars, jealously eyeing the bikes Pyro's working on, then scrub the oil off of my hands, shower, throw on a fresh tee shirt then walk into church.

"Your dick working now?" Rusty calls out. "Heard you might have a problem."

"My dick's fuckin' fine," I snarl back, sending a death stare toward Liz, but it only has the effect of causing him to double over with laughter.

"Could have worded that better," he splutters when he comes up for air.

"Yeah, heard you have difficulty getting it up." Mace grimaces in sympathy. "Might be your age, Leatherneck—"

"I'm thirty for fuck's sake, *Ground Pounder*." I kick out my chair more violently than I intended, then have to reach down and pick it back up before I can sit. I decide fast, Liz is soon going to be taking his last breath.

"So, what else could it be?" Bomber enquires, but he addresses his question to the rest of the table.

Christ! Have my brothers nothing better to do but comment on the status of my dick? Which, as I told them, is working fine.

If I admit I haven't been using it as I'd made a promise to a particular woman, they'd never let me live it down. Briefly, I consider the idea of fucking Breezy later just to get the heat off me. I'd have no problem rising to the occasion, but I'd have Beth's face at the forefront of my mind. Nah, I can wait a couple more days. Not fucking a whore just to prove a point to my brothers. My promise to Beth tops that.

Comments are still flying around me. I tune them out, instead thinking of the end of the week and the possibilities. Friday we'll fuck and Saturday, I'll find out if she was serious about wanting to ride a bike. I'm smiling as I think of it, already knowing I'll be proud as fuck if she ends up wanting her own.

I'm even dreaming of her riding out beside me, when belatedly Demon, Beef and Wills walk in. The table settles down as they sit, and Demon picks up the gavel. The loud manner in which he bangs it brings my mind back to the meeting fast.

"We got a problem," Prez starts, getting to the serious shit immediately. Any remaining conversations come to an abrupt halt as all eyes focus on the man sitting at the head of the table.

Mace gets out a packet of cigarettes and taking one out, lights up. Liz taps the table and gets the packet moving in his direction.

As smoke rises, Demon begins to explain, "The group who went to Tits Up on Sunday didn't see anything going on, but for two nights in a row now, we've had signs someone's been dealing behind the strip club. Wills has chased them off, but he's supposed to be managing the place and can't have eyes on them all the time."

"Picked up nothing on the cameras." Pal's eyes crease. "I thought they'd gone."

"Nah," Wills explains, "they set up at the end of one of the alleys, in a blind spot. I've taken to doing a walk around to check."

"Did you confront them?" Thunder asks.

Wills shakes his head. "First night they saw me, they fucked off. Second night, all I found was a user staggering home having scored."

"Time?" Bomber asks.

"Two a.m. by the time I managed to get out. Kinda got my hands full with the girls."

It shows how serious the situation is that no one quips a comment at his choice of words.

"We need people there all night as back up," Demon says. "Can't expect Wills or Sparky to run the place and be fuckin' night watchmen as well."

"We can put in more cameras," Cad suggests. "Got a couple spare and can do it tonight."

"Damage may already be done. Wills has also found discarded needles in the fuckin' bathroom."

Hellfire's fist meets the table. "So, they come to Tits Up to score, then bring that shit into our club?"

Wills nods. "That's what it looks like. Can't tell if it's our regulars or visitors."

"Latter is more likely. Have you spoken to the bouncer?"

"Sure have. Jake says there's been a few new faces, but that's not unusual. We get tourists coming in for a look around, and guys who may come once in awhile rather than often."

"We need to put a camera in the bathroom?" Pal asks.

Beef raises his eyebrow at Cad. "Don't feel comfortable with that. What's the legal position, Cad?"

I know Cad went into where he could place cameras when Pal and he started the security business, so I'm not surprised he has the answer at hand. "It would be frowned on as an invasion of privacy were we to simply install them, unless we suspected criminal activity going on, and drugs come under that category —more specifically drug dealing."

"I don't mind what the assholes get up to," Bomber puts in, "but it's the needles that worry me. One of the cleaners or another customer could get stabbed by accident if they're left lying around."

"That's my issue. I wouldn't want to think about the legal ramifications," Wills says. "Another option is to have a Sharps bin, but that might only encourage them, and turn other people off the club."

"Hate fuckin' hard drugs," growls Hellfire. "Had a problem in this club at one time."

Rusty shakes his head. "That we did." He snaps his fingers. "Brawn, wasn't it? Nearly brought the fuckin' club down when he had more loyalty to white powder than to us."

I'd heard the story as had everyone around the table. It's been brought up as a cautionary tale should anyone ever be tempted by the easy money drug dealing brings. Too tempting for some not to sample the product, but sampling wasn't enough for Brawn. He needed more and more and was caught stealing from the club trying to fund his habit. He's out in the desert now, six feet of sand and rocks on top of him.

Demon gives a sharp nod to his father. "We've got a reputation that we want to keep. No hard drugs on or near our club or our businesses. Weed, for sure, but nothing more."

"Part of the reason why Tits Up is such a success is because people know they won't get hassled," Rusty observes.

"Keeping it that way is what we're here to discuss, Brothers." Demon takes back the floor.

"Okay. We step up the brothers that support Will and Sparky. Stake out the alley and—"

"I'm not fuckin' staking out the heads." My eyes have gone wide at the suggestion I thought Thunder was going to make.

"Could be an education in dicks, Brother. Specially as you've got a problem with yours."

It's only the wooden tabletop between us that stops me reaching over to throttle Lizard.

Demon's eyes come to me, a half-smirk half-question in them. Then he addresses Cad, "Can you get the cameras set up after church?"

"Yeah. Club opens at eight, we'll only need half an hour, tops." Cad's eyes meet Paladin's who nods back.

"Okay, we'll make sure we're finished in time."

"So, we catch the users. What about the dealers?"

"We stake out the alley as Thunder suggested. Who's up for a late night?"

I raise my hand. Well, why not? If I'm prepared to give my life for the club, I can give it a few hours. Maybe tonight we'll find out exactly who's been stepping on our toes.

Or maybe, as I find out later, it's another bust and all I'm doing is standing around freezing my fucking ass off.

"How you doing, Leatherneck?"

"Probably about the same as you, Ground Pounder." Mace is lighting up which he wouldn't be if there was someone around, the burning orange tip would be a dead giveaway. Anyone who's served would know not to be so careless. "No one fucking showed."

"Inside?" I jerk my head to the building behind me. Inside, men will be cosy and warm watching women divesting themselves of their clothes. Their dicks won't be shrivelling because of the cold.

He chuckles. "Pal's probably got a new rep for having a weak bladder, he's been to the gents that many times. But he's seen nothing suspicious."

"I've seen nothing at fuckin' all. Not even buyers looking to score."

"Which suggests they know the exact times when the dealer is around. Which isn't tonight, Brother." He stubs out his cigarette on his boot and pockets the end. Then he rubs his hands together. "Any idea when we're going to be stood down? Would prefer it to be before my junk freezes and drops off."

I shrug in reply, not having the answer. But like him, I'm hoping it's soon.

CHAPTER TWELVE

Beth

"Do you know where I put my…"

Mom's standing twirling my car keys around her fingers, she's grinning widely.

"Thanks." I reach over and take them, giving her a peck on the cheek. "What would I do without you?"

She's shaking her head. "You know Beth? I don't know."

"That's what moms are for."

She laughs exasperatedly, then asks, "I presume you won't be back tonight?"

Pointedly tilting my head toward the window, I roll my eyes. "Now, do you really want me driving home in that?"

"If you stayed home, you'd be even safer," she observes, but her lips are curved, and I know she's just giving me shit for the hell of it.

Since the unexpected text on Tuesday, I've had plenty more. Ink's been keeping in touch which had surprised me. Not long messages, and not too many of them, but that I'd had any had given me a warm feeling inside.

Today's had been about changing our arrangements. It's Friday night and he was supposed to come and collect me on his bike—the one which he'd told me he's now modified with a double seat—but the storm that had been predicted for days has at last arrived with a vengeance, meaning there was no way it was safe for him to bring his motorcycle. Instead, I'd suggested I drive to the club, where I suspect, and hope, I'll be staying overnight. That well-equipped room of Ink's, hmm, I've been looking forward to revisiting that.

I'm also looking forward to catching up with Vi, Steph and Jay again. Though Mel, when I'd told her I was coming to the club, had warned me about their weekend parties.

"Sure, Mel, I know about the club girls, remember?"

"I'm not just talking about them, Beth," she'd told me in a serious tone that warned me I should take note. "You went to Demon's party where outsiders weren't allowed. Normally it's far worse. Girls from town come along trying to snag a biker. And there'll be different men there as well, hangarounds thinking of becoming a prospect, or those who just like the atmosphere of the club."

I'd shrugged. Ink will be there, and if he's anywhere near as possessive as last time, I pity the man who tries to talk to me, let alone do anything else. *I can do this.*

But it was easier when I just thought it was the bikers who I've already met and the women who are friendly. I push the introvert inside me back down, while wishing that Ink had been able to come to collect me so I didn't have to walk into a room full of strangers on my own. He had offered, but it seemed a waste of time to drag him out and make him drive a hated cage.

Unconsciously straightening my shoulders, I smile one last time at my mom, then start to walk toward the front door, when suddenly I remember and swing back, snapping my fingers. "Mom, I nearly forgot." I'd been so wrapped up thinking about Ink, everything else had gone out of my mind. "Has Connor been in touch about coming around again?"

Mom sighs deeply then shakes her head. "Not yet. But he never does. He just turns up."

"He said he might pop in this weekend. I'll try to be here in case he does. I'll be back tomorrow by lunchtime." I don't like the thought of her being alone with him. I can't forget how last week things had gotten pretty heated. I'd been afraid for my mom.

I acknowledge her grateful nod, then I'm tugging my coat around me and bracing myself to step outside. Immediately, I feel snowflakes settle on my face and find I'm battling a wind that seems intent on preventing me reaching my vehicle.

Once sheltered inside my car, I turn on the engine and wait for it to start warming up, noticing the snow hasn't been falling long, and the hot air blowing on the windshield means my wipers can cope with what's settled as it hasn't yet turned to ice. *Thank goodness.* I don't want to have to get out again and scrape.

I drive out onto the road carefully, but it's been gritted and what snow is landing is currently melting fast. When the temperature falls further, it will probably freeze, the volume of snow predicted might well settle despite the salt. Hopefully, the roads will have been cleared by the time I drive home tomorrow.

I don't mind wintry conditions, I've lived in Colorado all my life. As long as you're careful and try and avoid lunatics driving too fast or as if they were on a summer-dry road, most times you'll be safe.

It's fairly quiet, no idiots are out tonight, so I arrive at the compound unscathed. Beaver slides open the gate, stomping his feet and blowing on his hands.

"Hi, Beth. Park around the back."

I know where to go from last week when I came to the party with Mel.

Today there are more cars. I recognise Mel's, she and Pyro will have brought that, and there's a few more that I've not seen before. I realise I hadn't seen any bikes parked out front, but they're probably garaged or something for the night.

Once I've pulled up the handbrake and switched the engine off, I gather my things together, mentally ticking them off. My overnight bag and my purse I pull to me, then take a moment to check my phone and wallet are safely secured in the zip compartment. Realising I'm delaying getting out of the car, at last I open the door and step out. I rationalise my hesitation was because I didn't want to subject myself to the elements as snow is coming down more heavily, but truthfully, it's because I'm feeling nervous. Mel's warning echoes in my head and I'm uncertain what I'll be walking into. *Find Ink first.*

Taking a deep breath, I turn to face the clubhouse. At least it should be fairly easy for me to spot Ink inside. I wonder how Mel manages, perhaps with the exception of Theo, everyone is taller than her.

But I needn't have worried. Immediately after I take my first step forward, I spy Ink, leaning casually back against the exterior wall, paying no attention to the weather conditions, simply wearing a long-sleeved tee, cut and jeans.

I quicken my pace, suddenly wondering how long he'd been there, not wanting him to become frozen to the spot due to my dallying.

"Aren't you cold?" I again pull my jacket tight around me and shiver.

"Cold? Nah. Not with the promise of you to raise my temperature." He smirks.

"Sure of yourself, aren't you?" I feel my lips curve.

"Sure of you," he responds.

Then he puts his arm around me. "You're shivering, let's get you inside where I can *warm* you up."

When he opens the back door and stands aside to let me precede him in, Jeannie immediately calls out, "Shut that damn door!"

"For fuck's sake, Jeannie. Got to open it to let someone in. Whatcha expect her to do, fly down the chimney?"

"Ain't got no chimneys," observes Pyro through a mouthful of crumbs. I guess Mel's been cooking again.

"What about a window?" suggests Lizard.

"Still lets the fuckin' cold in," observes Judge, rolling his eyes.

"Yeah, but it's a smaller area, wouldn't be so bad." Liz doesn't let the inane conversation drop.

Jeannie waves a dish towel. "Will you lot get out of my kitchen? You drive me insane." But the grinning glance she sends my way shows she's joking.

"Beth!" Mel comes in, and bats at Pyro's hand, and fast directs her attention to her husband instead of me. "You've already had a tub of cookies at home. Will you leave some for the others?"

Unrepentant he rubs his stomach. "I'm eating for two."

"It's Mel who's fuckin' pregnant," Ink interrupts with a disbelieving shake of his head.

"Yeah, but I've got sympathy pangs."

"Are they a thing?" asks Judge, giving him a serious look.

Mel rolls her eyes. "With Pyro it would seem so. The amount he's putting away, his stomach will probably grow as large as mine is going to get." She lays her hand on his abdomen and looks up at him with an impudent smile. "He'll have such a pot belly he won't be able to ride."

"Have to leave the club. No bike, no patch." Thunder walks in, having overheard. "Best leave those cookies alone, Brother." The real reason why he's suggested Pyro refrain becomes clear when he reaches over, picks up the tub, and starts to carry it out. As he passes Pyro, he jerks his chin at him. "Just saving you from yourself. You can thank me later."

"What's it like out there?" Jeannie addresses her question to Mel.

"Like a Friday night."

That seems to be all the information the older woman needs as her face tightens with distaste. I'm, however, none the wiser.

"Is Vi, Steph or Jay around?" I'd been looking forward to catching up.

"Nah," Liz supplies. "As the weather is bad, Vi's gone home with the prez, the VP's taken Steph back to their house, and Jay and Pal are having their own private party upstairs."

"Which sounds like a very good idea," Ink whispers into my ear.

Although having Ink so close to me is immediately turning me on, I don't want to act like some whore he's summoned and jump straight into bed with him. I arch my brow. "Can't a girl have a drink first?"

For a reply, he takes hold of my hand, leads me out of the kitchen and into the clubroom itself. It is busy. Heavy metal music is playing loudly, a thumping beat that goes straight through me. Wills and Sparky have their heads close to two pretty girls I haven't seen here before, probably the only way they can hear anything they might be saying. Two of the club girls are dancing, if you can call it that. They're gyrating and contorting as though advertising their services. One's wearing such a skimpy dress she's in danger of... Too late, her boob's hanging out now, but she doesn't seem to care.

Fast looking away, I spy another group of giggling girls by the bar, certainly not dressed for the weather. But then, the amount of bodies around means it is warm in here. Though there's no way I'm removing my sweater.

Ink suddenly stills beside me. He catches the sleeve of Mace and uses it to pull him close. "Who're they?" His head jerks toward two men standing close to the girls.

"Hangarounds. Not been here before. Cad's checking them out."

"Serious?"

"Could be."

If I wasn't almost Ink and Mace's height, I wouldn't have been able to hear their conversation, but I am, and I do. Shamelessly I listen, wanting to learn all I can about his club.

"Want me to have a word with them?"

"Wouldn't hurt, Ink. If you don't mind." The enforcer spares an apologetic glance at me as if I might have other plans. I do, but I've got all night.

"We were going to have a drink anyway, weren't we, Ink?"

"Come on, then." Ink leads the way through the throng to get to the bar, my having to sidestep quickly to avoid having a drink spilled over me by yet another strange man.

Ink growls at him as he passes. "Howard."

The man looks sheepish, mutters a quick sorry to me, and disappears into the crowd.

"Wannabe biker," Ink quickly explains. "Man likes to talk bikes all day long and loves coming to our parties. Hasn't even got a ride. But he's harmless enough."

I spy another couple of guys who I don't recognise. I'm surprised they let strangers into the club.

"Why aren't you worried about them?" I speak directly into his ear, pointing them out. "They're not members either."

"For a start, we keep everything locked down on party nights. Meeting room, offices, even the bedrooms. So, they can see we have a bar, so what?" I appreciate him taking the time to explain. "As for these two, I know them. They come fairly regularly. Hang around the auto-shop as well. Now unlike Howard, they are hardened bikers, ride in all weathers. Well, except for tonight. Even they're not as stupid as that. It's pretty brutal out there."

He's telling me. I just drove in it. My mind's trying to establish the hierarchy of the visitors. "Do they go with the club girls?"

He shakes his head. "No, the sweet butts are just for us. Well," he goes a delightful shade of red, "my brothers for now, anyway. But I wouldn't be surprised if they manage to go off with one of the visiting girls. I expect you've noticed there's a few around." I have. And currently one is eyeing up the man by my side. She quickly turns away at my glare and the possessive arm I sneak around his waist.

Ink narrows his eyes, then turns around. He looks back at me and snorts, with a brow raised. "Come on, let's get that drink." The blond he'd all but ignored, stands and watches us stride off, her hands on her hips. I get a warm feeling inside that he hadn't more than glanced at the pretty girl.

We get to the bar. Ink orders two beers having asked what I wanted.

As Karl opens the bottles, Ink leans in. "Any problems?" He jerks his head toward the men standing a few feet down that he'd discussed with Mace.

Karl shakes his head. "Nah, but full of questions about prospecting and the club."

Ink gestures give me more.

"They asked some serious questions, more about what the experience of being a prospect is actually like. Turns out they've both served, and when I'd described it, they likened it to being a new recruit."

"You reckon they want to come on board?"

The prospect shrugs. "Can't be certain. I did tell them it was fuckin' hard work."

Ink looks worried, and I can understand why. As the prospect goes off to fulfil another drink order, I speak into his ear. "Must be worrying, taking new people in after what happened with Skull."

I've surprised him. He looks at me sharply, then sighs. "I suppose Mel told you all about what happened."

"I was the one who found Skull in Vegas," I remind him. "Of course, she told me how that had turned out." I think for a moment. "I always worry whether I should have told her or kept quiet."

"Why would you have kept that shit to yourself?" he asks, his eyes wide. "Of course, she, *we* wanted to know."

"She lost the baby." My voice has gone quiet.

"And you think that's down to you?"

For an answer, I shrug.

"Jeez. Beth, that's not on you. That's on Skull. Motherfucker played her, played all of us. Mel wouldn't have wanted to carry on mourning him." Ink looks around, surveying the room which is packed.

I follow what's caught his eye then look away fast. I've now seen far more of Lizard's ass than I ever wanted and don't recognise the girl who's lying on the pool table with her legs up around him. Mind you, it's not exactly her face which I had the best sight of.

"Don't you need to talk to the hangarounds?" I ask. Realising if this is a typical party, I probably would be more comfortable just with Ink in his room.

"Yeah. Do you mind? Hey, Karl. Make sure Beth's okay for a second?"

The prospect nods. Showing he takes his new duty seriously, after a quick glance to check no members are waiting to be served—visitors can apparently wait—he leans on the bar. "Heard you're going to have a go riding Beaver's Sportster."

I nod, but glumly. "Had it planned for tomorrow, but with this..." I point in the direction of one of the large windows where large flakes of snow can be seen falling in the light spilling out from the clubroom.

"Yeah, winters can be crap. There's always next week. Ink tell you Beaver's thinking of selling his ride?"

I raise an eyebrow.

Karl nods a confirmation, then suggests, "You get on with it, could make him an offer."

Have my own motorcycle? That sounds great. I grin. "Think I'll have to learn how to ride it first."

"Sorry about that, babe. Thanks, Karl."

Karl, who'd straightened as Ink approached, raises his chin then moves away.

"All done?" I ask. He hadn't taken long.

"For now. Cad will need to dig into their backgrounds, but on the surface, they're saying the right shit." His eyes narrow.

"What?"

"Never thought I'd be talking to a… woman about club business."

I smile at the way he stopped himself from calling me a bitch. Progress? Maybe. Then I frown. "I'm sorry if I spoke out of turn."

"Nah, babe." His eyes stare into mine. "Won't be able to share much with you, but if there's stuff I can, don't think I'd mind talking it over. Them?" He jerks his head behind him to the men he was just speaking to. "Maybe a woman could sniff out if they carry a bad smell."

"Mel didn't." Then I rethink. "Actually, yes, she did. She tried hard to stay out of Skull's clutches at first. She should have gone with her first instinct."

"She should've." He raises his hand to my face. "Now, enough about Mel, those assholes behind me and anyone else. Have you had enough socialising and want to come upstairs?"

Oh, God. Over Ink's shoulder I catch sight of Thunder pawing at a girl… he's got her breasts out. He's licking her nipple in full view. Her head's thrown back, clearly into it…

When I turn back to Ink, my face burns.

After spinning around to see what I'd noticed, Ink turns back with a smirk. "I take it you've seen enough." The sight of his brother seems to have affected him in a very different way as his voice has dropped an octave and his pupils have dilated.

Turning my head in the other direction, I quickly swing it back having caught the sight of one of the young girls on her knees in front of the much older Rusty, her head bobbing up and down in his lap.

Again, Ink follows my line of sight. "You could get down on your knees for me, doll."

"What?" I squeak. *He can't be serious, can he?*

Oh shit. Now to my side I can see one of the club girls sitting with her legs either side of Sparky's thighs. Describing what she's doing as a lap dance would be far too tame. The way he's thrusting his hips…

"Yeah, doll." Ink's voice challenges me.

The air has become heavy as musk mingles with the smell of cigarette smoke. Wild horses wouldn't have dragged the confession out of me, but the full-on orgy that appears to have started is indeed turning me on. Though not to the extent I'm prepared to give my man a blow job in public.

Swallowing rapidly, I glance back at the expectant man by my side. "I will, but not here."

"Chicken," he leans in to tell me. Then he removes the drink I'm still holding from my hand and places it on the bar. "If I'm not getting my cock sucked here, it's time to move this party upstairs."

I swallow again, then nod, and make no protest as he wraps his arm around me and takes me to the stairway which leads upward to his room. After he turns the key in the lock, I follow him in.

Closing the door he leans his back against it and immediately instructs while pressing on my shoulder, "Down."

Heaven help me, but I do. Spurred on by what I'd seen downstairs, the competitive side of me wants to give him a blow job of the type he's never experienced before. I undo his belt and carefully pull down the zipper taking care not to trap his uncovered cock in the teeth. Then I lick the head, making him suck in air.

But he's not leaving me in charge. I might be the one with my mouth near his cock, but he takes control. Fisting his hand in my hair, he again issues an instruction, "Open."

I do. He takes advantage, thrusting inside, so far and so fast it makes me gag, but he's relentless, and pulls out a little, only to thrust in again. I choke.

"Fuck, babe, so good."

This is how he wants it?

He must have been turned on by his brothers getting their needs met downstairs. My hands rise to caress his heavy ball sac, but then fall to my sides as I realise this isn't me giving him pleasure, it's him taking what he wants. As he continues pumping his hips, my eyes are watering, I'm gasping for breath, trying to breathe but his hold on me is so tight I can't pull away. I slap his legs with my hands, but to no effect.

"Fuck, woman. Your mouth is heaven."

I wish I could say that about his dick.

I feel him start to swell and wait for him to pull out, but he's giving me no option. He's moving faster and I can't do anything to stop it. Suddenly my mouth is filled with his cum.

I swallow and gag, then swallow again until at last his cock shrinks and finally he pulls out, his grip on my hair relaxing simultaneously.

"Jeez, little girl. Jeez." He seems to have lost the ability to form sentences. "Fuckin' amazin'."

He's used me. Just like a whore to satisfy his needs.

CHAPTER THIRTEEN

Ink

Beth's not a whore.

Yet I've just treated her exactly like one. I'd allowed her no choice in how she'd given me head, taken what I'd wanted, issued no warning and came down her throat without asking permission.

It had felt so damn good I'd gotten carried away and used her.

For a second, I can do nothing but lean my head back against the door and give myself a moment to regain my breath and to avoid looking down to see the horror and disgust in her face. *She'll leave me. Maybe go with one of my brothers. I'll deserve it.*

The one thing I never feel after sex is guilt.

I blame the X-rated atmosphere downstairs together with my desire for Beth which had grown over the days we've been apart. Those factors, and my unusual-for-me abstinence had ramped up my desire until I just had to have her, and the fastest way was to get her lips around my cock.

She's not a whore. I should woo her with flowers and sweet words. Not... It seems like an age but in reality is less than a minute before I summon the nerve to glance down, dreading the expression I'm certain to see, wondering if an apology is going to cut it.

Her watering eyes are wide, staring up at me with horror. Her swollen lips are gently parted, and her cheeks are red. She looks like she's been properly face fucked as she wipes her mouth clean with the back of her hand.

I'm unable to do anything as slowly she gets to her feet. "Stand aside, Ink."

"Beth—"

"I'm not one of your club girls, Ink. I deserve better than that."

"Beth—"

"I don't mind giving you a blow job, but it's mine to gift, not for you to take."

I'd try saying her name again, but I don't know what to tag on the end. She's right. One hundred percent. Breezy, Tulia, fuck, any of the girls here would have taken what I've just done without complaint, but I've no excuse for the way I've used Beth. She's not a toy for me to play with, she's a woman I should respect.

"Move, Ink." She steps closer, her eye on the wood of the door I'm still standing against.

I have no words. No excuses. After sending her a plea with my eyes which has no effect, I take a step to the side.

She wastes no time, turning the handle and stepping out.

She's at the top of the stairs by the time I catch up with her. My fingers curl around her arm, a touch she could easily evade, but it does stop her forward progress. "Beth, don't leave like this, please. Come back, let's talk."

"Talk?" she huffs, not even turning.

"I'm sorry." The belated apology at last escapes. "I don't know what came over me. I… you… You're too fuckin' irresistible. I got carried away."

"You scared me, Ink."

That shocks me. "I'd never hurt you, Beth."

"You just did." She sounds like she's about to burst into tears. The shudder I see running through her body suggests she's only just holding it together.

"Please, Beth. Come back. Don't leave like this." I'll beg if I have to. "Please."

"Why Ink? I'm sure any of the girls downstairs could give you what you want—"

"They can't," I interrupt her. "They're not you, and they're not who I want."

At last she turns. Her eyes stare into mine. "I can't be used, Ink. Not by you."

I take the liberty of brushing her hair back from her face. "I know, babe. Look, I'm learning here. I'm going to make some fuckin' mistakes. I'm a man, I fuck up. I got carried away. You think one of those girls down there could satisfy me? You think their mouth is anything like yours? You think I come so hard with anyone else? Fuck knows I want to, but I don't. But if you don't like it, I'll never do that again."

"How can I trust you?"

My arm lowers, my other one joins it; I take the risk of pulling her into my arms, she's pliant and comes to me, and thank fuck her trembling has stopped. "I don't know how to convince you. But we find something you don't like? We don't repeat it, or not without making some adjustments. You don't want to swallow my cum, duly noted."

"It's not that I don't, it's that you gave me no choice. I want a partner, not someone who takes."

My hand eases up and down her back. "Partners eh? Partners reciprocate, don't they?" Taking a liberty, I run my lips over hers, kiss her cheek, then say into her ear, "Come back to my room, and I'll give you my mouth."

Fuck. I've never stood in a hallway trying to persuade a woman into my bed. They don't give out the right signals, don't want to have sex, I don't force them, just move on to someone who does. She's right, there's a room full of sluts below who'd come running at just one crook of my finger. But I don't want any of them. I meant what I said, it's her, and only her, I want.

"I didn't totally hate it," she says at last. "I wanted to be on my knees, wanted to please you, but it felt like I could have been anyone kneeling there. I felt I was being used, that you didn't care who's mouth your cock was in."

I turn her to face me. "Oh, Beth, that's so far from true. It's you I wanted, you I was with. Only you. Look, I'm an idiot, what can I say?"

I feel her eyes burning into mine. "What are we doing, Ink? You don't want a relationship, and I don't want a man without one."

"Fuck, knows, babe. With you, I'm breaking every one of the rules I've ever imposed. But, pretty Beth, there's just something about you that means you're worth all the shit you're putting me through."

She's quiet for a moment, still staring at me. Then she rests her cheek on my shoulder. "I think you said something about giving me your mouth?"

"Fuck yeah," I say fast, before she changes her mind. "Come on, babe." I take a deep breath, then gently reaching down and wrap my hand around one of hers. Then I lead her back into my room, thanking fuck I was able to persuade her.

Inside, I push her back against the door. Placing my palms against her cheek, I lower my lips to hers. When she opens and lets me in I can taste my cum in her mouth. It's fucking exhilarating, but a reminder that I pushed her too far, too fast.

As I continue to kiss her, her breathing speeds up. She becomes an active participant, one of her hands holding my head to her. I deepen the kiss, she responds, her tongue following mine when it retreats. Her hips start moving against my own, and my cock hardens again. Who am I kidding? I'm hard all the time I'm with her; any time I have my hands on her my dick responds.

I nearly lost her. Fuck. I'm not even sure why the thought makes my heart beat fast in something like terror, how close I came to seeing her walk out of my life. The relief I feel that I have another chance with her has taken me by surprise. It's too early, I don't know what's at our destination if we ever reach it at all, but I'm determined I'm going to stick in there and hang on for this ride. *She's worth it.*

Her hands are now clutching at me, little moans coming out of her mouth, she's grinding against me and I wonder if she knows she's doing it. My cock throbs as our kiss grows more frantic.

Still with my tongue toying with hers, I push her backwards and roughly tumble her down onto the bed. At last parting our mouths, I gasp, "I need you."

"I need you, Ink."

That's all the permission I require before I make short work of removing her boots, jeans and panties, leaving her top on as I'm too impatient. Then her legs are over my shoulders and my mouth finds her cunt so fast it makes her gasp.

"Ink!"

I'm relentless, remorseless, when I find her wet and oh so ready.

"There, no… Up a bit… There."

Her instructions make me chuckle, knowing my voice is vibrating against that sensitive bundle of nerves. "Now who's trying to take what they want?"

She stills, then giggles softly. "But Ink—"

I growl and raise my head, while slapping her ass cheek. "You'll get what I want to give you. When you're in my bed this is mine, understand?" Then I go back to what I was doing.

I already know it turns her on when I take charge, or at least when it's her pleasure I'm chasing. I certainly don't need her guidance, I know my way around a woman's body, and it hasn't taken me long to learn hers. It's only a minute before her thighs start to tighten around me, her muscles rippling and clenching and then she's screaming.

Her taste has got me so hard, it's only this side of painful.

I stare down at her. "Fuck, Beth. I don't know what you do to me."

"Is this going to be another six condom night?" she asks, impudently, a challenge in her eyes.

"Christ, you're going to be the death of me. Is that all you're here for?" I give an exaggerated sigh.

"Why else do you think I'm here?" She chuckles, brazenly.

Good question. "Because you can't resist me?" Fuck knows, I can't resist her.

"Well you have got a magic cock."

That pulsating organ is what she homes in on now, reaching down, circling my length with her hand, and I hiss, even her touch feels better than anyone else's ever has.

Stretching over to the bedside table for a condom, I push her hand away and quickly sheave myself. "I can't wait," I tell her, my voice sounding harsh with my need to be inside her.

I turn her, manoeuvre her onto her knees and thrust inside. Her cunt clutches at me as though trying to pull me in further. There's a handprint on one cheek that's reddening nicely, so I place a matching one on the other side making her jerk.

"Ink!" she cries out, thrusting her hips back against me.

I love how much she likes my hand on her ass, how it arouses her.

Now I regret not fully undressing her, so I reach around and improvise, pushing her top up and squeezing my hands on those tits. I always thought I preferred them larger, but that they fit nicely into my palms is actually a turn on.

Thank fuck her bra is again another which fastens in the front. When I flick it open her breasts topple out, leaving me free to pinch her nipples.

Christ, I love it when she jumps and I'm deep inside her. "Ink," she cries out, but not in protest. "Will you move for fuck's sake," she wails while I'm concentrating on her tits.

I slap her ass again. "Who's in charge?"

For an answer, she pushes back against me, rolling her hips which makes my cock jerk. I might think I'm driving this, but she's giving as good as she gets. Christ, I fucking love her reactions to me. She takes everything I give her and still comes back for more. Testing me, pushing me. Keeping it spontaneous.

I squeeze her tits tightly and thrust once, hard, inside her. "Who's in charge?" once more I ask.

Again, she pushes back against me, making me smile.

Leaning over her, I place my lips next to her ear. "I think you'll find I'm the one in control."

Sliding my hand under my pillow, I remove what I'd left there. Those nipple clamps in the same shade of blue to match her hair.

I take her by surprise when I clip one on. She jumps. "Ow!"

"Breathe." I'm grinning when I make the helpful suggestion and clip on the other one. "You've worn them before."

"Ouch! Oh my God!"

She's arched her back as if to get away from the feeling. I smooth my hand up and down her back, repeating my instruction that she should draw in air. She does, and a delightful shudder goes through her, playing hell with my cock.

"How are you feeling?" I check in.

"Like I want you to fucking move."

Laughing out loud this time, I do oblige her. Starting with a fresh thrust in, pulling out, then pressing in. Each time I slide out, her tight cunt feels like a vacuum trying to draw me back. Suddenly this position is not good enough. I want to see her red nipples adorned with the clamps. She objects when I pull out, but I've soon turned her over and am back inside, my arms hooked under her legs, and her ass resting against my thighs. With each renewed thrust, her breasts jiggle, making those clamps bounce.

Our eyes meet as I start hammering inside her. Our gaze fixed, hers only breaking when she suddenly tenses and screams. The rippling of her muscles makes it hard for me not to give in and follow her over. But I pride myself on giving the woman I'm with a good time, and she's got another orgasm or two in her.

I slow my pace, waiting until she's ready to start building again, then fasten. This time, just as she's at the point when she begins to tense, I reach forward and remove those clamps.

She gives out a piercing scream and her body convulses from the joint assault of both pleasure and pain at the same time.

The sight of those cherry red swollen nipples and the feel of them under my hands as I try to soothe them makes me lose it myself, and I come hard. So fucking hard I see stars.

Has it ever felt this good before? If it has, I don't remember.

Slipping out, I roll over onto my back, pulling her to me, loving the feel of this woman in my arms. We fit, like I have with no other.

Big men often say they like a small woman they can feel protective over, that's certainly true of Pyro and Mel. For some reason that's never appealed to me. Someone by my side literally sharing my view of the world, I find far more alluring. Someone I don't fear will break when I manhandle her. Someone who can take what I want to dish out, well, within reason of course. I risk a glance at her face, her eyes are half-closed, but she's smiling. Seems she's got no objections to the way she's just been fucked.

I'm driven to check. "Beth. I'm dominant. I can't help it. Was it too much?"

She turns, and her eyes rest on mine, and her lips curve. "Not enough. Can we try that again?"

I laugh and do my best to oblige.

CHAPTER FOURTEEN

Ink

We make love again, this time more gently, and then predictably a third condom wrapper hits the bin. She's fucking close to perfection, and it hits me I don't want to see her leave in the morning.

Without stopping to analyse the reason, I ask her, "Want to hang around here tomorrow?"

Her brow creases. "Not much point now my riding lesson is cancelled. Maybe it's for the best if I'm at home in case Connor comes around."

I've never asked a woman to hang out with me before and it irks me she seems to be slapping me down. It isn't just my cock she's after, is it? I frown. Would be turning the tables for her to just want some dick. Nah, can't be that, surely?

"What's up?"

I decide not to go there, talking about feelings isn't my thing, asking instead, "Has your brother been in touch?"

"No, but that doesn't mean he won't just turn up." I might not like discussing my thoughts, but it seems she's fine sharing hers. "I'm worried, Ink. I don't know him anymore. Sure, him doing business in Pueblo and needing a base isn't too much of a stretch, but Mom's right to be suspicious about what he might intend to use the house for. Even him coming or going at all hours would be disruptive. He's a virtual stranger nowadays, and it feels like he's exploiting his relationship to us."

"What kind of shit is he into?"

Her head moves to one side then to the other. "I'm not sure, which is why I'm worried. Not doing an honest day's work, that's for certain. Anything where there's easy money to be had, I suspect. You've seen him, Ink. He's big, threatening looking. Wasn't shy of using his fists. So I wouldn't be surprised to find Phil running a protection racket, and Connor being the muscle to collect."

"But you don't know."

"I don't know."

My brow creases. *Couldn't be, could it?* A new business venture in Pueblo? As casually as I can, I ask her, "Connor ever have anything to do with drugs?"

She startles and turns to me. "No, and he wouldn't."

"Why so certain, Beth? You said, you don't know him now."

"I know the boy that he was," she insists.

I'd meant to ask Cad to check out both him and her dad, now I've got another reason to know. One thing I don't like is coincidences. What was her dad's name? Philip… Phil Foster. That was it. I make a mental note to ask our tech expert soon. See if I can find out what Phil and Connor are into, and what trouble it might bring to Beth and her mom's door.

I can understand why she'd want to be at home. In my view, whatever Connor's involved in, he's a waste of space and they're right not to give him the run of their home. He is also intimidating. I feel relieved she's not leaving without good reason.

"Tomorrow morning, when I leave here, first I'll go to the gym. It's too icy to run at the moment, so I'll train there instead."

"We've got some shit here. I train with weights. What do you need?" I get a vision of her all sweaty, wearing skimpy shorts and working out alongside me.

"Elliptical trainer. Treadmill."

Those we haven't got. When I train, like everyone else, I just use a corner put aside in the basement. Maybe I'll get the club to invest in getting our own gym facilities. Beef might be keen, Tucson had a fully kitted out one. I'd often considered utilising one of the large derelict outbuildings that used to be part of the mill. Now it's lodged there, I can't get the image of Beth and I training together out of my head.

Set up a gym so I can train with her? That's starting to sound long-term. The idea doesn't make me squirm. Beth, me, and a future?

In the meantime. "Which gym do you go to?"

She mentions one of the popular ones where I wouldn't be seen dead. Not serious in my view, but good enough for citizens who want to keep fit. It's not got a bad reputation, so at least she'll be safe.

"How long will you be there?"

"A couple of hours." She huffs a quick laugh. "I'll have plenty of time. If he's coming, Connor wouldn't arrive until much later. My brother's always been allergic to mornings."

"You want me to come around to help deal with him?" I may have an ulterior motive. That would give us more time together.

But she shoots me down. "I can't impose on you to do that. As long as I'm with Mom, he should behave."

"You call me," I tell her. "I'm just a couple of key presses away." Then a thought occurs to me, *Keep your friends close, your enemies closer.* "Ever considered giving him a place to stay could mean you find out what he's doing?"

"Mom and I have talked about it, of course. But she's worried he might bring people back who we wouldn't want to stay. Or, he might want a place to store stolen goods. Maybe Phil's a fence, I don't know."

"You and your mom don't think much of your brother, do you?"

She sits up fast. "I love my brother," she says forcefully looking down at me. "It's Phil I don't trust. Connor's a good man deep down inside, and if we've got a chance to bring that side of him back out, Mom and I will do everything we can to achieve that."

"But you won't let him stay in your house."

"No. Not unless he breaks it off with Phil. That's the bargain. We'll let him back into our lives when he's not in Phil's clutches anymore."

Will they be able to extract Connor from his life of crime? Pulling her back down, I let her head rest on my chest, while thinking I'm not sure. Easy money is hard to give up and exchange for a nine-to-five.

"If he gives you any trouble, you use my number. I mean it Beth. Hell, tell me if he turns up. I'll come around anyway. I don't like the idea of him losing his temper again." I didn't take to Connor, didn't take to him one bit.

"You mean it, don't you?"

"I couldn't mean it more." I nuzzle the top of her head as she yawns, then give her as much as I feel I can. "I care for you, babe. Don't want you hurt."

"You've worn me out Ink."

"Go to sleep, babe."

As she turns her back toward me, I pull her against my chest. Gradually her body goes limp, but I lie awake in a quandary, uncertain of what to do. Every time I see her, I just want her more. I already know it's going to be hard to let her go in the morning, and not just because that asshole of a brother may turn up, but because I'm starting to think of giving her a place in my world.

What would it be like to have a woman of my own? Could I commit to just one pussy for the rest of my life? How did my brothers know when it was right to put their patch on a woman? Hmm, my patch. Seeing my name tattooed on her? Fucking amazing.

What the hell am I thinking? I'm Ink, I'm a confirmed bachelor. Surely, I couldn't see myself with a woman and kids in tow? That isn't me. Is it?

I think of Mel, and how she looked before she lost her kid, that baby bump beginning to show. What would Beth look like? Would I find the same look of amazement and joy on my face that I'd witnessed on Pyro's when Mel had announced she was pregnant again?

Does Beth even want kids?

As I lie here, each breath I breathe in carrying her scent, I realise why I've never wanted to spend the night with a woman before, it's because they weren't right, they weren't Beth. I know right now I'd be happy to have her in my bed every night.

Tomorrow, we'll have a talk. I need to find out where her head's at, and whether she's thinking along the same lines.

With thoughts I never expected in my head but also a feeling of contentment, my own eyes close and I follow her into sleep.

"Hey." Feeling movement as she gets off of the bed, I stretch out my hand and pick up my phone, then glare. "It's six am, babe."

"Gym, I told you."

Can't deny she had. But at the ass crack of dawn?

"You want to do something later?" I try to sound nonchalant, but inside I'm crossing my fingers, hoping she'll say yes. Now's not the right time, but later I'll broach with her, some of the thoughts I had last night. See if we can move this on, admit it's not just sex.

"Tonight?"

I shrug. "Why not? Unless you've got to be home in case Connor turns up."

She considers for a moment. "I can't spend all my time sitting around waiting. If he doesn't turn up, I could come back later on. If that's what you're asking."

"You up for another party?" I wink at her.

She raises a brow. "Like I saw much of last night's, you didn't give me much of a chance before you dragged me back to your cave."

"We could have stayed." My eyebrows waggle suggestively.

"I don't see myself taking part in a live porn show, Ink."

"Never say never, doll." I don't mind a bit of exhibitionism myself. Hmm. The idea of thrusting into Beth while my brothers watched, all knowing she was mine and while they could look, they couldn't touch, makes my cock hard. I palm it.

She ignores what I'm doing. "Right. I'm off. Er, thanks for last night, Ink."

"Come here, doll." I pull her to me and, ignoring the fact I haven't yet brushed my teeth, meld my lips to hers and make sure she says goodbye properly. I place her hand on my cock, but she's having no mercy.

"Save it for later," she whispers with a wink.

And then, she's gone.

I'm totally fucked. As soon as the door closes behind her, I realise I miss her.

I take care of my throbbing cock myself then wipe my chest clean with last night's discarded tee, after which I go back to sleep. At a decent time, I awake and shower, regretting I'm washing away her unique perfume. Then at last I'm ready to face the day.

I see him as soon as I descend the metal stairs to the club-room. "Cad!"

His pale as death face stares up at me, reminding me why we call him Cadaver. "What can I do for you?"

"Phil Foster. He lives in Denver. Dabbles in illegal shit. Can you try and dig up some info on him? See if you can find out exactly what he's into?"

Cad bows his head for a moment and rubs red eyes which look sore from staring too long at a screen. "I can try if you don't mind it going into the queue. Got some other shit I need to do first. It would be good to have a few more details."

I can appreciate that. I nod. "I can probably get you more to work on. All I've got now is he was married to Beth's mom, Patsy, until about eighteen years ago. His son, Connor, now lives with him. Before he moved to Denver, he lived here in Pueblo."

"Okay. When I've got a moment, I'll see what I can dig up. Presumably you don't know if he's a Philip, and whether that has one or two Ls?"

I shrug which gives him the answer. But Cad's found people on less, so I've no doubt about his abilities. If he's there to be found, Cad will discover him.

"I've got to get through last night's footage from all the cameras before I can start taking a look."

Demon would have my hide if I took Cad away from his club work for no reason. "No hurry." I don't miss Cad's thankful look as I leave him.

The rest of the day passes like any other Saturday when I'm not needed at the shop. I eat, watch some TV, then looking out at the weather regret it's not a day to go for a ride on my bike. It's a fucking shame I had to postpone teaching Beth to ride. I'm actually looking forward to seeing whether she can handle a bike.

Maybe it's because I'm anticipating seeing Beth later that time seems to pass slowly. It's only mid-afternoon when I see Wills and Sparky with their heads together. As I walk past heading for the kitchen to top up my caffeine levels, Sparky catches my eye.

"Wills had trouble at Tits Up last night. More of the same. Cad's been staring at the screen all day, but the new cameras haven't picked shit up. Think we need to widen where we're looking."

"Didn't we have a team there?"

"Yeah, but only Judge and Bomber out front and out back. Obviously not in the right place, 'cause shit was brought into the club."

Mentally I go over the location of the strip club. There are alleys either side, and a dimly lit parking lot discreetly placed at the back. Another alley runs behind that. But I thought we had security shit set up so we could see all over. It would appear not.

"What's behind it?" I ask to refresh my memory.

"The Jade Lion. The Chinese place. Cad's asked for permission to set cameras up there, but they weren't particularly cooperative."

Hmm. Wonder what they get up to at night? Wouldn't bother me what, if it wasn't affecting us keeping our own businesses secure. "When does the Jade Lion shut?"

"Midnight."

"Could be whoever it is has figured that out, and that's where the dealing's taking place."

"That's what I was thinking." Sparky, our road captain who loves diagrams and maps, produces one now. He's marked a number of crosses on it. He kicks out a chair and I sit my ass down, leaning in for a closer look. Tapping on the paper in front of him, he informs Wills and myself, "These are the locations we've not got eyes on right now. Close enough to be associated with the strip club, but not near enough to be in camera range."

"Or," Wills sits back with a frown, "they could be dealing inside."

"Nah. Cad's said cameras show nothing in the gents or the ladies come to that."

I raise my eyebrow. "And just who's checking that feed?"

"Pal and Cad."

Pal's got a woman, but it doesn't mean he doesn't have hormones. I chuckle, but Sparky says, "Cameras don't cover the stalls."

"Yeah, but it still gets interesting at times." Wills winks. "Bitches adjusting their underwear. Or so Cad says." He adds the latter fast, but I've got a sneaking suspicion he's had himself a look.

Sparky's letting me in on all this for a reason. "We've got to get those blind spots checked."

"Yeah, most of us are going out later rather than just two or three. That way we can make sure everywhere is fuckin' covered this time. You in?"

Seems like my plans for another fuck-session with Beth have just been put on hold as well as that conversation I was planning on having. Suppressing my personal regrets, I say without hesitation, "I'm in." I'm sure she'll understand. She'll have to, if she wants to be an old lady.

Beth? An old lady? If she's going to be anyone's, it would have to be mine. Is that really the direction my thoughts are heading? I suppose that's the logical conclusion of what I've been thinking.

Beth. *My* old lady. Well I'll be damned if that doesn't sit easy in my mind.

Perhaps I did get that bump on the head that Mace had suggested. Am I really thinking I'd be happy being tied down? No doubting how much my dick likes that woman in my bed, but take it to the next level?

But fuck it. I can't get her out of my mind.

Should I ask Beef or Pyro? Is this how it started with them? Is this how they knew they'd found their one? Hell. Thing is, I know the answer without asking.

When you've tried fucking a woman out of your head and that didn't work... When you wanted to wake up with her, not just today, but every day of your life... When she brings out every protective instinct you possess... When you fucked up and knew you'd never again make that mistake if you could only have another chance with her... If you were told you could only have one cunt to sink your cock into for the rest of your life and you would be quite happy as long as it was hers.... When you enjoy spending time with her talking, and her texts brighten your day... That's when you know she's going to be your old lady.

Me with an old lady?

What the devil's gotten into me?

Thank fuck I'm out on a job tonight. Clearly we need time apart. I try to convince myself I don't mind not seeing her.

I'm lying.

Beth's like a devil who's gotten under my skin, tempting me to sin. For the first time since I was patched in, I resent having to do my duty for my club. When we're called in for a meeting to discuss tonight's plans, I'm so annoyed I kick my chair over.

"What the fuck's up with you, Leatherneck?"

"Fuck all," I snarl at my brother and friend. "Leave it."

CHAPTER FIFTEEN

Beth

"**I**s it serious between you and Ink then, if you're going back tonight?"

When I left the gym, I didn't bother to change thinking I'd sort myself out when I got home, so I'm still in my running gear and in desperate need of a shower. The fact Mom has hardly let me in through the door before starting her inquisition shows her eagerness to hear my response.

"It's not serious, Mom," I reassure her. "Despite Mel finding her happy-ever-after with Ro, bikers are men you use for fun."

I'm lying.

Last night had been different, and while I was on the treadmill, I'd let my mind drift, trying to sort out how. I still couldn't put my finger on it.

It had started off badly, but Ink had listened and had got my point when I'd come so close to walking out. I'd let him off with a pass this time, and something tells me he won't behave like that again. He is trying, but whatever's between us is new to him.

We'd had the same type of sex as we'd done before, Ink being his usual dominant self and me unable to resist him, but at times it had felt more like we'd been making love. There was never any question right from the start that I would spend the night, and for a long while after we'd used the last condom, he had just held me, and we'd talked. He'd even offered to spend the day here with me and Mom in case Connor put in an appearance.

Coupled with the texts we'd been exchanging all week, that doesn't sound like the behaviour of a man who just wanted me for sex.

Would he run a mile if I told him I'd like us to date? To have a relationship, not just in bed, but out of it.

But what if he's not in the same place? I'm already in deeper than I'd ever intended, and it won't be easy to casually wave goodbye when Ink gets bored with our arrangement. Unless... it's no longer a cold arrangement for him either.

Love?

Not sure I'm there yet, but the involvement of my heart is certainly not far over the horizon.

"I'll be seeing him again, but don't read much into it," I warn her.

Mom opens her mouth to say more. Not wanting to hear parental words of wisdom for now, I pull my exercise tank top away from my armpit, sniff and wrinkle my nose, then seeing she's got the message, run upstairs to jump into the shower.

As I stand under the hot water, my hands smooth over my breasts. They might not be huge, but Ink seems to like them. He seems to find me as perfect for him, as he is for me.

Maybe I've just chosen wrongly before, but my experience with men who are shorter hasn't been good. They've felt the need to prove themselves, the worst one I'd left when he'd used his fists on me to make a point that despite my height he'd been physically stronger. Then there were a couple more who saw me as someone to support them, that my broad shoulders could take the weight of their worries. If I wanted a pet to take care of, I'd have gotten a dog or a cat.

Ink offers himself for me to lean on, and he's definitely a take-charge man in bed which I've found I enjoy immensely.

Even if my ass is still a little sore, I grin, as I reach around and massage my buttocks. He wouldn't want me to sort his problems, instead, he'd take on mine as well as his.

He makes me feel cherished and cared for. That's why I need to shield my heart. Ink made it clear this is only a temporary arrangement, and nothing he's said has hinted otherwise. If I read too much into his actions when he's made no other promises, I'll end up getting hurt. Which would be my fault for overstepping the boundaries.

I rinse my hair, thinking how hard it is for me to put myself out there. I've had enough hurt and disappointment to be wary, and my natural inclination is to hide in my shell. The only men I meet are friends of friends or people I meet through work. I could never use an app like Tinder. My shyness at odds with my looks, it isn't what most people expect.

Mel knows me though, that's why she was surprised I went after Ink. Sure, I'd been bolstered by alcohol, but when I'd seen him that day it was as if I'd been possessed by a devil telling me I couldn't let this one escape, not without at least making an attempt to get him to notice me. Just for sex? Well, that would be worth something on its own. Something more?

Ink had immediately knocked that idea on its head, but I found I was happy to stay for scraps, even if the full meal was beyond my reach. But now, it would seem, I'm developing a hunger for more. But I worry the cost of that dinner is way out of pocket.

As I dry myself off after the shower, I muse what would have happened if Ink had turned me down. Could I have actually gone with another biker?

No, I hadn't been that desperate. I'd taken a calculated risk coming on to Mace. If it hadn't had gotten Ink riled, I'd have backed out soon as I could. Luckily, my gamble had worked.

Though, I grin, as my mind circles back to the behaviour of the town girls last night, I doubt any of the bikers would have been a disappointment in the sack. Something about these rough tough men keeps the girls coming around. Coming, obviously, I give a childish giggle to myself at the double entendre as I sort out some fresh clothes.

"Bethany? Want some lunch?" a voice floats up the stairs.

"Sure, Mom," I call back.

I go down, help her make some sandwiches. Give her a side-eye look when she tries to bring Ink into the conversation again, which gets her changing the subject.

"I've come up with some new designs I'd like you to look at."

"Yeah?"

"I'd like a picture of you wearing those pants and shirt I did last week. Would you mind modelling again?"

The business mom is just starting up is designing clothes for taller teenagers and women, ones which actually fit. She's had a lot of interest on her Instagram page.

"No, of course not." As long as I can turn my head, or the picture just shows me from the neck down. I hate having my face on photos.

The afternoon passes like any other Saturday, and to my relief Connor doesn't make an appearance. I do start getting fidgety, anticipating seeing Ink again later. Surely the fact he wants to see me again so soon means something?

When my phone rings I stand and leave my mother alone.

"Missing me already?"

"Huh," he laughs. "Not yet. But babe, gotta tell you, I'm really sorry, but I need to reschedule. I can't make tonight, something's come up."

"Reschedule, You can't, huh? And what's come up, has she got a name?"

"There's no bitch involved, babe. Trust me." His chuckle shows he knows I was joking. "Just need to do something for the club."

Mel's learned to accept Pyro disappearing at odd hours with no explanation, I suspect I'm going to have to learn to do the same if my relationship continues with Ink. "Is this club business?"

"You got it, doll." He's quiet for a second before adding, "But how about I make it up to you tomorrow? Storm's moved off now, it's already warmer. Forecast is dry with sun for tomorrow. How about that first ride?"

"That sounds really good, Ink. I'd love that."

"Okay. I'll call you in the morning. Might have to wrestle Beaver's keys off him first. Oh, and if you're worried about leaving your mom alone, bring her with you. I'm sure she and Jeannie would hit it off, and she already knows Mel."

I'd giggled when he'd mentioned Beaver and the key to his bike, but my eyes had gone wide when he'd talked about Mom. What fuck buddy thinks of his partner's mother?

"I'll talk to her," I tell him.

"I'll be in touch tomorrow. Take care, babe."

"You too, Ink."

"Me? Come to a motorcycle club?" Mom's eyes twinkle when I tell her, and she nudges me in the ribs. "There were a couple of older bikers I noticed at Mel's wedding."

"Mom!" I stare aghast at her. "Hellfire and Bomber are taken."

"What about the redheaded man? He was quite striking."

"Rusty?" I roll my eyes. "Mother! I am reconsidering this if you're going to make a play for your own biker. If Rusty hasn't taken a woman in all his life, what makes you think he'd start now?"

She nudges me again. "He obviously hasn't found the right woman as yet."

I'm speechless.

She laughs loudly. "Just messing with you, Beth. Anyway, I'm fine staying here. Connor probably won't even turn up."

While I'm having doubt about the wisdom of Mom coming to the compound, I'm also against her staying here on her own.

"Come on, let's watch a movie if you're not going out with your man."

We do. Mom, as usual, goes to bed fairly early. When she does, I turn off the lights and go to read in my room.

I miss Ink.

Sitting cross-legged on my bed, I stare down at the phone lying on the comforter, wondering whether I could text him. But I don't know what he's up to tonight, maybe it's not right to disturb him.

My finger is actually hovering over Ink's name when the phone rings making me jump.

"Yo," I answer evenly, trying to hide how overjoyed I am that Ink's called.

"Beth?"

It's not Ink. "Yup. What d'ya want, Connor?" Nothing good, I muse, not at this time of night. "You coming to see us again?"

"I can't." His voice sounds croaky.

"You ill?" I ask, suddenly feeling sympathetic. He is my brother even though I may not agree with the choices he's made in his life.

"I'm hurt, Beth."

Oh my God. No. I sit up straight. "Hurt? How? Have you been in an accident?"

There's a pause, then, "Beth, I need help."

I grip the phone tighter. "What do you need?" He's my baby brother. I might not think much of the man he's grown into, but I was his protector while we'd been growing up. If he was bullied, I'd step in to help. My immediate reaction to offer assistance is automatic.

"Be certain, Beth, I've no one else to ask. It's a matter of life or death."

What? He must be being overdramatic. "Whose life, whose death?" I ask fast. "What the hell's going on, Con?"

"They've hurt me and threatened worse if I don't do as they say." His voice certainly sounds rough.

"Oh my God," I exclaim. "What? Who's they? Why? Have you told the police? Do you want me to call them? Where are you, Connor?"

"No cops, Beth," he croaks urgently. "Promise, no cops. They'll kill me if I get the law involved."

Kill him? "Con, you're sounding like someone out of a movie. What the hell is going on?" I wouldn't have believed him for a moment, except for one thing—his connection with our father who is very bad news.

"Promise, Beth. Promise you'll keep this between you and me. You can't tell Mom, or that man of yours. Promise me. You tell anyone else, I'm dead, I swear. Sis, I need you to promise. If you want to see me again, you've got to give me your word."

Nothing he's saying is making me feel any easier. I might not have had much to do with him lately, but there's a sincerity in his voice, an underlying fear that warns me the situation is serious. A cold lump has settled in my gut. "What help do you need, and what can I do? You say you're hurt? How badly? Where are you? Should I come to you? Should I ask Phil to help?" I never call my dad by a more familiar title.

"No, no and no," Connor says fast. "I don't want him involved. I got into this, I'll get out of it. Look, I've got broken ribs, cuts, bruises, but I'm alive. I need your help to stay that way."

I've gasped as he's run through his injuries. He's my brother. What can I say? "Christ, Con. Surely it's best..." But there are probably reasons he can't involve the cops. The reason why Mom hadn't wanted him to have a key to the house was she thought he was involved in something illegal. From what he's saying he probably is, but more importantly he's hurt. What do I know about how things work on the side of the line which I'd never cross over? Nothing. All I can do is hope that my younger brother knows. "Anything, Con. Tell me what you want me to do. I'll do it."

"Anything?" His voice sounds sharper. "Do you really mean

that Beth? Will you help?" If he was going to add more, it's swallowed up by a fit of coughing interspersed with stifled moans of pain.

"It sounds like you need a doctor." My heart's beating so fast, my hand goes up as if to hold it inside my chest.

"When I can, I think I do, yes. But I can't now, I'm being held."

"Held?" I squeak. "Who by and where?"

"The first doesn't matter, the second, I don't know. I was unconscious when they brought me here. They let me have my phone, so I can arrange what I need to do to get me released."

"Which is what, Con? What do you need from me? Shall I try to find you? Maybe I can locate you using the phone." Maybe Ink's friend Cad can do it. Or, "Have you an iPhone? I could use Find a Friend. I can come get you—"

"Beth, no. And I don't have a fuckin' fancy phone. No, the only way to get me out is to help me. That's if you care about seeing me again."

He's an asshole, but he shares my blood. Of course I don't want him hurt or worse, dead. "Anything, I've already told you. I'll do anything to help." My hand holding the phone is shaking.

"And you won't tell anyone?"

It goes against the grain, but I can't make his situation worse. "You promise, if I do whatever you ask me to, you'll be safe?"

"Released straightaway. Beth, I hate to ask you, I should do this myself, but I can't."

"Just tell me, Con. The sooner I do it, the sooner you'll be safe." And then I'll have to find a way to get him out of the life he's living, get him away from the clutches of our father. He's behind this, I'm certain. "What is it you need? Is it money?" I don't have a lot, but it's his if he needs it to save his life.

"Beth? You listening, Bethie?"

"I'm listening."

"I don't need money. That won't help. I do need you to make

a delivery for me. If you go into my old room, I left some pack-ages at the back of the closet, under a pile of old clothes."

Left some... "What the hell, Con? You said you were picking up your stuff..."

"No time to argue, Beth. I needed somewhere to store some-thing. Now I need some of it taken somewhere else."

"Is whatever it is stolen?" If so, perhaps the person who it was taken from wants it back.

"What? No. But someone wants it in trade for my life. I need you to make the exchange."

"Connor. Are you lying to me? Are you just trying to get me to do your dirty work for you?"

"Bethie." His childhood nickname for me drops again from his lips. "Bethie, I promise. This is the truth. I won't get out of this unless you help. Please Beth, I'm begging you. They'll kill me."

His tone has the ring of truth to it. Can I afford to doubt him? My eyes are leaking as I realise, I have no choice. "Okay, I'll go to your room. What do you want me to take?"

"Thank fuck. Thank you, Beth. Take two packages. Take them to this address." He rattles off a location. "Hand them over. Once that's done, I'll be released. Beth, I'm relying on you. I need you to do this."

"Who do I give them to? What if... What if they take me too?"

"Beth, this will be simple. You don't need to know who he is, he'll be the only one waiting for you. And no, you won't be hurt or taken. I promise you that. It's not a difficult task. I wouldn't put my sister in danger."

He sounds certain I'll be safe. But even if there's a chance I won't, what choice have I got? *Find out the details and ask Ink's advice.* Yes. That's what I'll do. Now I've a hastily thought up plan, feeling easier I ask, "When?"

"Now. The rendezvous time is 1 am."

I glance at the clock. Shit! "You've not given me much time."

I'll be pushed to make it by then, let alone waste precious minutes discussing what I've been asked to do with anyone else.

"And what time you've got you're wasting. Are you going to do this, Beth? Or do we say a final goodbye?" He sounds desperate, and his new bout of coughing reminds me he's hurt, or at least says he is.

I pull the phone away from my ear and stare at it for a second, wondering whether he's being over dramatic. Worried about what low-life I'll be handing whatever it is over to. But what if it's all the truth? What if I say no and never see my brother in this life again?

There's only one answer I can give. "I'll do it."

"Beth. You're going to save my life. If there was any other way, I wouldn't ask you, but there's not. I love you, Sis."

Then he's gone.

Love you, Sis.

When was the last time Connor expressed such emotion for me? It must be years. *What if that was his final message? What if, even if I try to help him, he ends up dead?*

I stand, putting back on my warm sweater, wondering whether whoever it is will stop hurting him now he's enlisted my help. Or will they kill him anyway?

No. I can't think that.

I slip my phone into my pocket, then immediately pull it back out. Despite what Connor said this is too big. I need help. I'll go to the police... I don't place a call. What the hell do I know about this sort of situation? Connor might be right, and I'll only be making things worse, or my little brother might be rescued but immediately arrested. I'm convinced he's caught up in something illegal.

Prison might be better than being dead.

But people are killed in prison, aren't they? And if he's not quite irredeemable yet, he probably would be after being locked up with criminals. Connor would never forgive me.

Ink. Ink's club might be able to help him. But what am I to

Ink? Have I got the type of relationship where I could presume on his help? He offered to help if Connor came around, but could I really involve him in this?

Why should he lift a finger to help him, or draw his club into a fight which isn't theirs? What if the club agreed to help find Connor and rescue him? What if Pyro stepped up and he was hurt or killed? While everyone says it wasn't down to me that Mel lost her baby, if I hadn't told her Skull was alive, would that have prevented events turning out as they had? Even if she had found out later, just a few more months and she'd have been holding a living, healthy baby.

I owe it to her not to involve them in my brother's shady business. I'll do nothing to hurt her again.

I can't find my car key. I start emptying my purse, my hands shaking as I look for it again, my mind racing.

No cops, I can't risk it. I can't risk involving Ink's club. I can't tell Mom, she'd not want me putting myself in danger. I'm sure she'd choose me over her errant son. I pull back my shoulders. What choice have I got?

What if Connor's lying to get me to do something?

It hadn't occurred to me while I'd been speaking to him, but now he's no longer on the line, doubts are entering my head.

Would Connor put me in that position? He coughed, yes. He sounded hoarse and husky. Could be he's just got a cold and is going to pass an unpleasant task off onto his sister. He'd pressed enough of my buttons to do whatever he wants.

Damn this niggling voice inside that says, *I can't trust him.*

One thing I know, I can't be responsible for the death of my brother. I'll do what he wants, then somehow I'll find him, get him to a hospital if he needs one. If he doesn't, he just might by the time I've finished with him.

Got my key. I listen carefully, there's no movement from Mom's room, but it is past midnight, she'll be asleep. As I tiptoe to my brother's old room, my mind is still whirring as again and again I run over my brother's words. I'd taken everything at face value. It wouldn't be the first time he's fed me a line which I've swallowed.

Say you broke it, Beth. Mom will go easy on you. She hadn't. I'd been grounded for a weekend that had turned into a week when I tried to shift the blame onto my brother and he hadn't backed me up. *Just say I'm already in bed, I'll be back soon.* He hadn't been, he'd stayed at a friend's all night and I was in the wrong because being older, I should have known better.

He's also no stranger to embellishing the truth when it got him the result he'd wanted. An *I've been sick, Mom* accompanied by *my stomach hurts so bad* had gotten him off school coincidentally, when he hadn't done the assigned homework.

Christ, I hate this. Hate being sucked down into the world of secrets. This is completely outside of everything I've ever known.

Take two packages and deliver them at one am in the morning. What could go wrong?

CHAPTER SIXTEEN

Ink

"Change of plan,"

I've barely stomped in and had my chance to take my seat before Demon starts speaking. Not entirely unexpectedly, Prez has gathered all those who are going to stake up Tits Up tonight, together.

Sounded quite simple to me. Allocate each of us to watching certain areas, and we were done. I'm still seething that I won't be able to see Beth tonight, and for once not because I'll miss wetting my dick. The more I've been thinking about her, the more I want to get her view of where she could see us going. No point in me making plans in my head if she's only going to be turning me down. I'm also angry at myself. This isn't me. I'd give my life for my brothers, and today all that's being asked is to give them some time. Not the first occasion my own plans have had to be put on the back burner for the club, but it's the first time I've been rankled because of a bitch. I make a concerted effort to calm myself down.

I see Mace looking at me warily. I throw a chin lift back and a shrug. He narrows his eyes, then turns his attention to the VP who's just cleared his throat to speak.

"I was picked up by the cops earlier today."

Murmurs of surprise go around.

"What d'you do, Beef? Push that Fat Bob too hard?"

Beef glares at Lizard, who makes as if he's sinking down on his chair, then continues, "Someone's ratted out the club, or rather put in a report that there's dealing around our business-es." He waits for our exclamations to die down, then lifts his chin. "I suppose it was only a matter of time. Needles in bathrooms, shady people around. Anyway, I was interrogated. I had to decide fast what to tell them and decided 'no comment' was unlikely to help. I settled back, drank my water, and reminded them of the meeting I'd had with their chief a few months back. Told them again how they already knew we do our part to keep drugs away from our part of town."

"They happy with that?" Thunder enquires.

Beef shakes his head. "Nah. Suspicious fuckers said things might have changed. I pointed to that report they had in front of them and asked how the hell they thought that fitted with what we were trying to do, that is, trying to make an honest living. As we have done for years." He pauses for a moment. "They still weren't convinced, so I shared our thinking of who was behind it, or rather, what little we surmised. That someone is coming in from out of area and using our businesses either as everyone local knows to stay clear, or because they saw a vacuum and filled it."

"We've no rep for dealing or using," Hellfire says, sounding annoyed.

"I told them we'd be fuckin' stupid to shit on our own doorstep," the VP responds. "Seems that got through their heads. I reminded them no member has been picked up with more than marijuana for a number of years now."

"Ever since we became Satan's Devils," Hellfire states.

Beef raises his chin in acknowledgement. "I may also have given the impression we were fuckin' angry about the situation, and they told us firmly not to address it ourselves."

"General warning?"

"Nah. They're planning something." The VP grins widely. "When they'd finished questioning me, they went out in the corridor, but hadn't closed the door properly. Maybe Steph's rubbing off on me, but I've got excellent hearing. I heard a few words, didn't have to hear it all. Tonight, Tits Up and SWAT. That was enough for me to put together there's a bust planned for today. Look," Beef leans forward, "the last thing I want is for us to be caught up with a trigger-happy SWAT team."

"So our stakeout is off?" Sparky catches my eye and grins. Guess he might also have plans for later.

Demon looks at Beef. "I'm not happy. I want to know who's fuckin' with us. Cops have Tits Up in their sights, and may well have gotten info we haven't dug up yet."

Mace completes Demon's thoughts. "They may only end up with a dealer. A bit player who's too scared to talk to them. Someone will be behind this, I'm fuckin' certain, and it's more than just one or two fuckers outside our club."

"They catch someone, he might make a plea bargain," Hellfire challenges.

Beef gives a slow nod. "That depends on who he can give up. Snitches don't last long inside."

"But you are saying we should stay clear tonight?" I ask, my brow creasing. It doesn't settle easy with me to sit back and let others do what I see is my job. Protecting my club. Like my brothers, I hate drugs and the problems they cause, but it's understandable the cops want to be involved and catch the dealers. Getting whatever's being sold off the streets would look well on their record. Conversely, there's a very good personal reason why I'd be happy to not be out with my brothers tonight.

"We leave it to them?" Rusty is obviously reading the VP's words the same way as I am.

Sparky's eyes roll. "They couldn't find their assholes with a flashlight and a map," he states. "Leave it to them and whoever it is might get away."

"They'll know we won't let others handle it for us," a voice interjects. "If they expect us to sit on our hands, they don't know who they're dealing with."

Beef grins and nods at Pal. "I didn't let on I'd overheard, obviously. But I told them we were doing what we can to stop this shit going on. In legal ways, of course, protecting our premises and businesses. That we're beefing up security at the strip club. They sort of huffed and exchanged glances at that. They weren't going to admit to getting a SWAT team ready, but hopefully they'll have their eyes out for Devils and we won't be caught in their crosshairs."

"Or we'll be rounded up if they catch no one else." Like any one-percenter, I know the risks of getting too close to the cops. I start to be certain we'll be stood down tonight and that evening with Beth could be back on the cards.

The VP gives another grin. It's not a very warming one. "Oh, we'll be there. Just not where they expect us. My fear is this is organised crime, and we're not faced with someone who's stupid. I'm certain the dealer will have an escape route ready. My proposal is we go along and block any way out. Hopefully we can nab him ourselves and bring him back here. Our methods of persuasion," he takes a moment to jerk his head toward Mace, "are probably more effective than those of the cops."

Mace's answering expression is even more chilling than Beef's smirk. I happen to think that's a much better suggestion, even if it means I've again lost my chance to be deep in Beth's cunt tonight.

"So no one's being stood down," Beef surmises, and then looks around, but as could have been predicted, there's nothing but nods and murmurs of agreement.

"I want the fucker here," says Mace, cracking his knuckles. "I want to give him payback for fuckin' with the club."

"Twenty years would do that if he lasts that long inside," Demon observes, then pinches the bridge of his nose. "Look, I hear you, but I just want him and his crew off the streets. If that means letting the law deal with him, well, that's one less body we've got to bury."

"When you put it like that," Thunder grins, "it almost sounds better. Hate digging fuckin' graves." He murmurs the last almost to himself.

"You're suggesting if we get him, we pass him over to the cops?" The road captain's face is creased in confusion.

"No, Sparky. But what I don't want is us to be caught spiriting him away. It can't look like we're protecting him." Demon frowns. "That's my only objection. If it comes to that and we're seen moving him, I'd prefer to hand him over. I don't want anyone risking this club just to get up close and personal with our revenge."

"I don't like it." Pal grimaces. "We'll get a reputation for helping the cops."

Beef hits the table with his fist. "Don't fuckin' care. As you well know, Pal, Tucson has helped the authorities out a time or two. We don't want a gun battle behind Tits Up. So what we're doing is staying out of sight to intervene if necessary. They'll be going in loaded and armed. Just stay out of the line of fire and make damn sure nothing comes back on us."

"What about the bowling alley and the tattoo parlour?"

Demon glances at his VP. "Beef and I talked this through. The cops' focus is Tits Up, which makes us suspect they've had a tip off. Somehow, I think the SWAT team expects the strip club to be where the head honcho will turn up tonight. They must have something to convince them it's worth their time."

The VP takes over again. "Tits Up is where they've got their eyes tonight, so we'll have ours there too. We'll keep a presence at the other locations, but the aim is to be visible and make it too hot for anyone to make a buy. Their customers won't want to face a Devil, so hopefully they'll move on."

"So at Tits Up," I just want to make it clear, "we block the escape routes. If SWAT loses him, we pick him up."

"Or them. We may be wrong assuming it's just one man. He

may have protection with him," Beef confirms, "but that's the essence of it. Pick him or them up, or herd him or them into the loving arms of the cops."

There are a rumble of chuckles at his description. Yup. I expect the cops will get very up close and personal with whoever they catch.

We thrash around the details for a while until Prez and the VP are confident we all know our roles. Then the gavel comes down and we're dismissed.

"What do you think about going in when we know the cops will be there?" Sparky asks me as I go to get myself a beer after the meeting.

"Couldn't care less one way or another. We know the area like the back of our hands, the SWAT teams are probably working from Google maps." I chuckle. "I know of at least one escape route that's not shown. It's not wide enough to be called an alley, but there's a gap between buildings a thin man could squeeze down."

"Hmm." He frowns. "Must admit I'm worried about stray bullets heading our way."

A hand claps down on my shoulder. "That's why I'm making sure everyone wears their Kevlar vests." It's Thunder, who's clearly in his sergeant-at-arms role. "Handguns only, nothing else. For self-protection. And we shoot anyone dealing, not cops."

My eyes widen. Hell, if bullets start flying and a cop goes down, if it was from one of our guns... Christ, I don't even like to think of the implications.

Thunder nods as though he's reading my mind. "I expect the SWAT team to be closer to the action, using a pincer movement to catch the dealer red-handed. We don't care about catching him in the act. It's possible someone will spot the cops and double back. We'll be there to nab them."

If the cops do make an arrest, hopefully Cad will be able to discover who they've caught and we can try and track who's behind it back from there. With any luck though, we'll get him, or them, ourselves and do our own questioning.

According to Wills and Sparky backed up by the camera footage, any dealing that takes place is when the club's been open a few hours. We aim to get there by eleven, so we can take up our positions well before we expect any action to start.

It's not often nowadays that we do more than most citizens do, get up, go and do an honest day's work, come home, drink, fuck and party, then go to bed. A few hours later get up and do it all over again. So to be sitting checking guns and ammunition, going over plans, and making sure everyone knows what role they're to play gets the adrenaline rising. I find myself slipping back into the mindset I wore as a Marine.

Like all my brothers, I'm sick to death of someone fucking with us, and with any luck, tonight, it stops. Either we'll get the bastard or the cops will. One way or another they'll be off the streets. We can go back to running businesses clear of the drug trade and the mess that goes with that. At least we've got a heads-up about the police operation, and Beef was able to warn them we'd be around. Doesn't sound like much can go wrong.

"Hey, Leatherneck. You found your temper yet?" Mace plonks himself down beside me. He takes some ammunition out of his cut, checks it, then puts it back.

I don't apologise for snapping at him earlier. "Looking forward to seeing some action tonight?"

"Yes and no. Yes, as I want to take down this motherfucker. No, because I'm worried about the cops. They're a bit too close in my estimation."

I know what he means. "Take care, Mace," I warn.

He now takes out his phone and checks the time, then replaces it. He's fidgety. I know how he's feeling. "So, this bitch, Beth. Twice she's stayed over."

I look at the ceiling, then back down. I could give him shit or admit the truth. "Reckon you might have to get used to seeing her leave in the morning."

"Like that?" His eyes open wide.

"Like that," I confirm.

"Cad run a check?"

I raise and lower my shoulders. "Don't think there's anything to find. But I asked him to look into her father. Something's not right there."

"But she's not involved?"

"Nope." My eyes narrow as I challenge him.

"Ink…"

"Mace," I say as I start to stand, and lean with my hands on the table. "It's early days and I don't know where my head is as yet. Don't fuck it up for me, okay?"

He stares intently, then nods and huffs. "Your funeral, Brother. Just be sure what you're getting into."

Why is it that Mace's caution has made me more determined? They don't know her like I do. I grin, as I follow my brothers out to the bikes. No, they certainly will never *know* her like I do, as I'm the only biker who'll be fucking her.

"Night's warmer."

"Above freezing, that's for sure," I reply to Sparky. The weather's looking up, Beth will be able to have that first ride tomorrow.

And after that? Well, she can ride my cock. Then I may broach the subject of us giving a relationship a try.

Demon circles his hand over his head, engines start and exhausts roar, then we're rolling. Me with a smile on my face and, as I'm thinking of Beth, a semi-hard dick in my pants.

A large number of motorbikes arriving at the strip club isn't unusual. Sometimes we have a new dancer who brothers want to check out, or, when we had a permanent manager, visiting artistes to pull in the crowds. Something perhaps Wills and Sparky will get back to arranging once they get themselves better organised.

We don't need to be discreet or hide our arrival, it's only after that there's a difference in our normal procedure. Rather than all the brothers disappearing inside, I and some of the others peel off to take up our assigned positions.

There are cops, I can see them, but only because I was looking for them. I act nonchalant as I pass them, going to my allocated spot, a back-stop position should the dealer escape and come in my direction.

We're early, of course. There's currently no action. Sparky, who's my backup tonight, leans against the wall while I take the stance and mentally prepare like all those times I stood on guard, staying motionless but hypervigilant for hours. Once trained, you never forget.

We don't speak, we just observe.

A man shuffles past us, kicking an empty crumpled can out of the way. He's a user, not a dealer, and from the twitching I see as he passes me, he's in desperate need of a score. His arrival confirms we're in the right place. Sparky nudges me to check I've noticed but doesn't say a word.

I wait to see what the police are going to do, but there's no commotion. Unless they're making a silent arrest and their victim no audible protest, they're at least being clever. If the dealer turned up to find no customers, he'd know something is wrong.

Another figure appears, this one it's hard to tell whether he's a dealer or customer, but he takes up a spot, unbeknownst to him, near the hidden cops. They leave him alone too. I know they need to catch the right person and hopefully with drugs in his hands.

Now another. A tall, slender man in a hoodie. A customer for sure. The way he's walking shows he's nervous. His head is down as though he doesn't want to be recognised and he's carrying a bag.

Sparky nudges me. "Dealer?"

I return in the same almost inaudible voice Sparky had used, "If it is, he's new. Christ, I can see him shaking from here." The bag is dangling at arm's length as though the man's carrying a live snake.

Damn it. If this is the dealer, it's a small player and not the top man himself, he's far too nervous to be that. Maybe the real culprit got word of a possible bust but didn't want to lose sales, so sent a new minion instead. That's what it looks like to me.

There's something about the gait of the slim man that's familiar. As he passes under a light, I get a flash of blue from under his hoodie.

Immediately, I know who it is.

Immediately, I know I have to stop her.

Everything about her screams that I'm right to think what she's carrying could mean she'll be looking at a long stretch in jail, and from what I know of her, she'd never survive. *How the fuck is she involved in this?*

In a flash, I estimate distance and calculate there's a chance I can stop her before she gets too close to the cops. I rise like a dark avenging angel…

"What the fuck, Ink?" Sparky grabs at my arm. "Leave him to the cops…"

But I shake him off with a violent blow that throws him back into the wall. Then silently, I move up behind her.

"Get out of here, Beth," I snarl quietly, while covering her mouth with my hand. As she relaxes and realises who I am, I release her.

"Ink?" she whispers, turning. "I can't, I—"

"I think you've got something of mine." The other man we'd noticed earlier moves out of the shadows twenty yards away. He's still some distance from the cops.

Without thinking, I take the bag from her. "Get out of here, Beth," I repeat in the most commanding whisper I can summon, the tone that she obeys in bed.

Now relieved of her burden, she turns and flees.

"Bring it here." The click and the reflected light bouncing off the weapon shows I've got a gun aimed at me.

Yeah, if she was carrying the small holdall like a snake, so do I. If she was delivering his stock for the night, then I'll do it for her. Then he can go make his sales and the cops can pick him up. All this goes through my head in an instant. The bag feels heavy, unless I'm totally wrong about the contents, it's a fuckload of shit I'm about to turn over. No wonder he's keen to get his hands on what Beth had brought. *How the fuck is she involved in this?*

But there's no time for second thoughts. *Hand this over and disappear.* I step toward him and hold the bag out.

The area is floodlit.

We're surrounded by cops.

It happens so fast. The dealer was so focused on me making Beth's delivery, and I was so intent on giving her space to get away, I'd forgotten the imminent danger for one moment. One, dreadful, life-changing moment. Now, I'm lying face down on the ground, a knee in my back, and my hands rapidly hand-cuffed behind me.

Then I'm pulled to my feet, searched, and have my weapons taken away.

The dealer, if my suspicions are right as to who the man is, well, he too is subjected to the same treatment.

As I'm led to a police car and pushed roughly inside, all I can wonder is how the fuck this evening has ended like this, and whether this is the last night of freedom I'll ever have. Fuck. Fuck. Fuck and fuck. My head spins with the rapidity with which I went from a free man to a prisoner.

I'm a Devil. They'll throw the book at me.

CHAPTER SEVENTEEN

Beth

When I entered Connor's old room and flicked on the light, I went to the closet. There's a musty smell from old shoes. I move the clothing aside and then find packages piled up against the back wall.

Where had they come from? How did they get here?

The heel of my hand hits my forehead. *Connor hadn't been bringing an empty box in to collect his stuff.* No. He'd obviously brought these in and left with the garbage that I thought his old Xbox and games were.

I might never have come across anything like this before, but there's only one thing he's got stored. Here. In my home. In our mother's house. Drugs. *Oh, shit no.*

I sit back on my heels, not even wanting to touch the Saran-wrapped blocks. I'm no expert and don't know what type, it could be anything. But it's highly illegal, and to me seems one hell of a lot. There are ten packages in all, and Connor had asked me to deliver two of them. *I want nothing to do with this.*

And what's he planning on doing with the rest? Storing them here indefinitely? Using me as a... *what do they call it?* Drug mule?

I feel sick as realisation goes through me and puzzle pieces start to fall into place. If this is what Connor is involved with, that he's really in danger becomes more believable. Has he stolen the drugs from someone? Is he now supposed to be giving them back? Or are they his, and he's using me?

What's does he plan to do with the rest?

Taking his words at face value, he'll be dead if I don't do what he's asked. His story is now far more credible.

He's also been clever. Leaving it so late, I've no option if I'm going to try to save him, but to follow his instructions to the letter. I don't have the time to call for help or stop to wonder whether there was a better way to extricate him from whatever trouble he's in. If I'm going to make the meet, I can't involve the cops, tell Mom or go to Ink for help. There's no time.

But still there's a niggling doubt at the back of my mind, there's a chance he might just be using me to do his dirty business. *Can I take that risk?*

No, I can't. He's my brother, I couldn't live with myself if he died because I hadn't done what he's asked. *But if he's stringing me along, he'll wish he was dead later.*

I've got to get moving.

I'm not stupid. It's cold, and I've got gloves in the pocket of my jacket I'm already wearing. Taking them out I slip my hands into them, then pick up two blocks and, already feeling like a criminal, take them back to my room and place them in an old rucksack I remember being hidden behind my winter boots in my own closet. The packages drop to the bottom and feel heavier than their weight.

I don't want to do this. I don't want to be part of the drug world. I don't want to feed someone's habit when they should be getting help instead. How many children are going hungry because their parents are shooting themselves up?

I could sacrifice my brother and take this all to the cops.

But Connor could die.

I've barely enough time to get to the place I'm supposed to go. No time to think about how to handle this better. Connor's played me well if it is a game, an appeal to my caring nature, an appeal to his big sister who still wants to redeem him which wouldn't, couldn't, go unheeded.

I stifle a sob. Why Connor, why? How did you come to this? Is this what Phil has gotten you involved in?

I hear a sound and freeze, but it's only the house settling and not, thank goodness, my mom stirring. She must never know what Connor is up to, it would kill her. As for finding out I was going to be driving around Pueblo to deliver drugs? I don't think I'd survive her fury.

I can do this.

His instructions were simple. Get to my destination and hand the bag over. I won't even bother taking the drugs out, I'll gladly forego the rucksack if I can get out of there faster. Then I'll return, report that it's done and hopefully save Connor.

I get in my car and start the engine and reverse off the drive-way. *Tomorrow I'll speak to Ink.* He or his club will probably know better than I how to dispose of the remainder of the drugs that have been left in our house. One thing's for certain, the other packages won't be staying there one more day. I'll set fire to them myself if I have to. *Once I know Connor is safe.* I can salve my conscience by believing the bulk of the drugs will never hit the streets.

I drive carefully, obeying all the rules of the road, scared witless I'll get pulled up in a traffic stop. If they find this amount of drugs on me, I'll surely end up going to prison. While I don't want my brother to hurt, I don't want to end up doing serious time for him either. To be locked up in jail? Not something I think I'd be able to survive. There's also the very good chance that if I'm caught, Connor will be killed as I'd have failed to make the delivery.

I keep to the speed limit, not one mile above or below it. I eye every traffic light ready to come to a halt. At intersections, I check very carefully. A cruiser passes by on the other side of the road, and I sneak glances in my rearview, holding my breath until it disappears out of sight.

The short journey across town seems to take ages, and I'm violently shaking by the time I pull up. I pass a building with an unimaginative name and glaring neon sign, then doing what I'm told, navigate around it until I'm parking in one of the back streets to the rear.

It was Tits Up I'd passed, the strip club owned by Ink's club. *Help could be near.* There were motorcycles parked up in a line out front.

But Mel's assured me the club doesn't run drugs. They may want to stop me handing them over, preferring them off the streets instead. What help would that be to Connor? He might end up dead if I don't play my part. I thump the steering wheel in frustration. I don't want to deliver drugs, but if I want to save Connor, I don't see I have any choice. The clock on my dash shows time has all but run out.

I shrug off my jacket and pull up the hood of my hoodie, shoving my dyed blue hair inside, trying to make sure no strands are showing. My distinctive feature a drawback tonight.

I can't stop trembling as I turn and lift the bag gingerly off the back seat as though it's going to bite me.

Only a few hundred yards and I'll be passing it over. Then, my one and only foray into a life of crime will be finished. *Fuck you, Connor.* I decide to make sure he's alright, then cut him out of my life. If he's going to live a life where he puts himself in danger, then that's on him and shouldn't fall back on me or Mom.

Mom has still got the remaining eight packages in her house.

I'll call Ink and ask him for help as soon as I get back.

Connor might die if someone knows there are more, and they don't turn up.

I don't care. Tonight I'll do what he wants. Tomorrow I'll get help. I shouldn't have come here right now, but it's too late to have doubts.

Almost paralysed with hopelessness and fear, I glance at my

phone. *Time to go.* A couple of minutes to get to the rendezvous, and then I'll be in the clear. And Connor will be safe. *Fuck Connor. Fuck my fucking brother to hell and back.*

Getting out of the car I glance around, checking the landmarks Connor had told me to watch out for. I'm parked by the Jade Lion just like he said and easily spy the alley I'm supposed to go up. It's narrow and runs up beside the massage parlour, closed now, of course.

My fingers curl around the strap of the bag and then locking my car carefully—heaven forbid someone steals it and leaves me stranded—I take the first step into the night.

It's dark. The light from the streetlamps behind me quickly fades and it takes me a moment to adjust to the light only from the moon. I shiver, the temperature has dropped, and after slipping on a patch of ice which stubbornly had refused to melt, start picking my way more carefully.

A shadow appears in front of me, still tens of yards away. It doesn't draw closer, as though waiting for me to go to him. I'm certain it's the man I'm supposed to hand this to. Who else would be waiting in an alley in the dead of the night?

But before I can reach him, I feel a presence behind me and a hand clasps over my mouth. Instant terror floods through me and I freeze, my body preparing to kick out when I recognise the voice that speaks right into my ear.

"Get out of here, Beth."

"Ink?" It can't be. Why is he here? He can't be part of this. His club doesn't do drugs. But there's no time to explain, the man who holds my brother's life in his hands is waiting. "I can't, I—"

"I think you've got something of mine." The man moves further out of the shadows twenty yards or so away.

I was right. This is the man I'm supposed to meet.

A tug and I lose my uncertain grip on the rucksack. Ink's got it in his hands instead.

"Get out of here, Beth," he commands, strangely in that voice he normally uses during sex. My brain, already attuned to him, interprets it as instruction. Wanting nothing more than to escape, I start to back away as Ink moves toward the man. Then, not understanding Ink's involvement, or how he'd turned up, I take my opportunity and flee.

I'm aware of a commotion behind me and am thinking maybe I should stop when powerful arms come around me and I'm yanked up against a hard chest. I open my mouth to scream, but for the second time tonight, it's covered by a palm.

"Shut the fuck up, Beth."

In my mind's depths I recognise this voice too, but not being Ink's, panic takes over. All I know is, I'm trapped. I kick out with my leg hearing an oomph as I hit his knee. I bite down on his hand.

"For fuck's sake, Beth. It's me, Sparky." As he talks, he's dragging me back. "I've got to get you out of here. Ink would go apeshit if you were caught up in this."

Sparky? But what's he doing here? Then I register his desire is the same as mine—to get as far away from here as possible. But I've failed, haven't I? Or did Ink hand over the drugs.

I stop fighting. *Connor, I'm sorry. I tried.*

He doesn't let go of me completely, but now has just one hand with a firm hold of my arm, and he's tugging me along. Then we're running. I easily keep up with him, my long strides matching his.

"Where's your car?"

I stop. "I've got to go back…" I've got to make sure the drugs were handed over. An image of Connor with a gun to his head, a bullet flying… "Sparky…"

"Where's your fuckin' car, Beth? There's no time." He grabs hold of my biceps and shakes me.

What can I do? Ink's here, so's Sparky. There could be more bikers. My head's spinning. What's happened to the drugs? And what will be the outcome for Connor?

I'm so far out of my depth, I'm drowning.

"Your fuckin' car?"

"There." I point to the end of the alley. "It's just there."

When it comes into sight, I press the key which is in the pocket of my hoodie and it unlocks with a loud beep.

Sparky curses then opens the passenger door. "Get in, I'll drive."

What? "No."

"Don't argue, Beth. This place is crawling with cops. I've got to come with you. Give me your keys."

"Aren't we waiting for Ink?" Maybe he's gone the other way to his bike.

Sparky looks at me, the streetlight shows he's incredulous. "Didn't you fuckin' see?"

"See?" I frown. All my thoughts had been on the fact I'd failed my brother as Sparky had dragged me away. I'd left Ink and the man behind me, more intent on getting free.

"Keys," Sparky repeats tersely.

Cops, Sparky had said. What the hell does he mean? I'm not a criminal, but I've probably just knowingly committed a crime. I don't want to be arrested, what help would I be to Connor then? He wants my car key. Wordlessly I hand it over. He doesn't have to adjust the seat, just slides in and starts the engine up, then we're moving and we're off.

I'm hyperventilating as though I've just run the best part of a marathon. It's not long before I realise it's probably lucky that I do have a chauffeur. Tears prick in my eyes as I bow my head, struggling to breathe. One minute I was holding a bag full of drugs, scared witless in case the man I was to give them to proved violent, the next, Ink had them instead. My brain tries to make sense of it all.

Ink.

"What happened to Ink?" I ask, suddenly convinced something has.

"He was fuckin' arrested," Sparky snarls.

Oh. My. God. I draw in a sharp breath. "What? Why?"

"You fuckin' tell me," he snarls. "In fact, you can tell the prez."

Sparky sounds so angry. Looking sideways, I notice his jaw is set. I also notice he's not taking me in the direction of my home.

"Where are we going?"

But it seems he's done talking to me, and anyway, my question quickly becomes pointless as the compound comes into sight.

I don't want to be here. "I have to get home," I wail, needing to try and call the number Connor rang from to check he's okay; to find out whether somehow this clusterfuck of a night turned out right. If I take his words at face value, now I'd failed, he might be dead.

Sparky spares one glance for me. "I suspect Ink will prefer to be heading home too."

Ink. Oh my God, Connor. What have you done? What have I done? My mouth opens to ask what exactly has happened to Ink, but everything happens so quickly.

The gates slide open after Sparky leans on the horn. He throws the car into park then dives out. My door is flung open. His fingers curl around my arm once more and I'm pulled roughly out.

I try to remove his hand, it's impossible as his grip is too strong. He doesn't seem to care I stumble as he drags me along and in through the door of the clubhouse.

"What the fuck's gone wrong?" Demon is standing right inside. "Mace called but I couldn't make any sense of what he was fuckin' telling me. Why the fuck have the police taken Ink in?" I swear sparks are flashing from his eyes. Then they land on me and flare. "What the fuck is she doing here?"

"*She*," Sparky starts in a tone full of disdain bordering on hate, "was delivering fuckin' drugs to the dealer. She's obviously deep in this shit. Ink saw, took the bag off her. Cops got him in possession of them."

What?

Suddenly it all falls into place. "No!" I scream, but my body goes weak as my head spins, it's only the biker's tight hold on me that's holding me up. In my panic and confusion, I hadn't joined all the dots or realised the implications. *Ink arrested for possession of the drugs?* The drugs I took there. Ink's got nothing to do with this. Me, yes, by association with my brother and my desire to save him. But Ink? He's not to blame at all.

"Fuckin' yes." Sparky rounds on me.

Demon pinches the bridge of his nose while looking over his forefinger and thumb to Sparky. "Are you fuckin' sure?" he asks, in a voice as cold as any I've ever heard before.

Sparky has one moment of hesitation. "What was in the bag, Beth?" It's easy to see he's praying to some deity that he's got it wrong.

"Drugs," I miserably confirm.

The word seems to hang in the air. Then their prez issues an instruction, "Basement. Now."

Again, Sparky drags me. A door is opened which leads to a set of stairs, then I'm being taken unceremoniously down them.

"Wait, please. I have to make a phone call. Wait, please." My eyes open in horror as a light is flicked on when we get to the bottom, my gaze immediately landing on a variety of tools laid out on a workbench. "Please, I can explain…" My voice trails off as I wonder what I can say in my defence as the results of the actions I'd taken tonight begin to sink in. Ink, my lover, and one of their brothers has been arrested, and it's all my fault. It should have been me instead. *Surely the cops will let him go?* He's innocent. They must.

Demon kicks out a chair. "Sit her down."

"No," I cry out, turning around to face him. "I can explain. I've got to go to the police. Ink's done nothing wrong."

"No, Ink's done nothing wrong except it sounds like he's been stupid. But you fuckin' have. You are going nowhere until I get answers. Sit. Her. Down," Demon shouts at Sparky, enraged.

I try to stop them forcing me onto the chair, somehow

sensing I'll not be leaving anytime soon after they get me seated. Again, I try to get loose. Someone comes over to help, and I recognise Mace. Together they manhandle me, keeping just shy of painful as they kick my legs from under me and push me down.

Within seconds, my arms are pulled around the back of the chair and secured. This time, I don't feel the slightest bit aroused at being tied up. Instead I struggle, protest and kick out.

They overpower me, of course. Sparky takes one leg, Mace the other. Despite having strong leg muscles from all my running, soon my ankles are restrained to the chair. Demon was right. I'm going nowhere.

A thunder of footsteps and Beef appears in the doorway. "What the fuck's going on, Prez? What's this about the cops getting Ink?"

"That's what we're just about to find out," Demon calls over his shoulder, then focuses his stare on me. "This bitch got him arrested. She's about to start fuckin' talking."

I'd admired the height of the bikers, I'm revising that opinion as I start to feel small, me with my height advantage taken away sat as I am on the chair, and them towering over me.

It's human to be scared, but my fear isn't for me, but for someone else. Two someones in fact. But I'm a bad sister, as there's one who concerns me most. "Ink?" I cry out. "What's happening to Ink?"

"Fuck if I know, but whatever it is, it will be something he doesn't fuckin' deserve." Demon couldn't have said anything I'd agree with more.

"Let me go!" I demand, knowing there's only one thing for me to do. "I'll go to the cops, hand myself in. Tell them it was me and not Ink..."

But Demon shakes his head, and snarls, "Not until we know what the fuck's going on, and whether that would make things better or worse. Right now, I don't give a fuck if you rot behind bars, but I need to know what's best for Ink."

"Just talk, Beth." Beef steps into my line of sight, his words are unthreatening, his tone and expression are not. "Don't like hurting bitches, none of us do. But a brother of ours has been arrested, and from where I'm standing, that's all down to you. You've got no choice but to tell us fuckin' everything."

CHAPTER EIGHTEEN

Beth

They seem to think they're going to need to use force to get me to speak to them. But why should I hold anything back?

My eyes water with tears I can't wipe away. Ink's in trouble, there's no denying it's my fault. Mine, as I was persuaded by Connor to be some sort of drug mule for him. I've been a fool from start to finish.

Had Connor been lying about everything? Had anything he'd said been the truth? Was he really injured, being tortured and under threat of death? Or did he play on my sympathy? Did he involve me as he thought it would be too dangerous to deliver the drugs himself? Had he set me up, knowing there were going to be cops there tonight? Preferring to see his innocent sister arrested, rather than risk doing time himself? *Could he hate me that much? If so, why?* What have I ever done to hurt him?

Or had he been totally honest? In which case, now that it's all gone south, my failure could mean whoever's holding him will kill him anyway. I should have refused to help. Connor would get what he deserved for living the life that he does, and Ink would be free to live his. *I made the wrong choice.* But, the devil on my shoulder whispers, *How could I have stood back and done nothing?*

Another thunder of footsteps comes down the stairs.

"Brought her purse in. Bitch received a call today close to midnight. Cad's analysing her phone now."

"Who?" Demon snaps my way. "Who were you fuckin' talking to?"

"Connor—" I respond, but don't have a chance to add more.

"A fuckin' man," Mace snarls, interrupting me. "Always a man at the bottom of it. And here I was thinking you were cosying up to Ink. Knew he was a fuckin' fool to fall for a bitch." He directs his words to me, and his look of disgust has me reeling and spitting out the explanation fast.

"Connor's my brother, not a boyfriend."

My explanation doesn't help in the slightest, as the enforcer just scoffs. "You in this together? You got a nice supply chain going on between you?"

"No," I cry out. "It's not like that!"

Beef looms over me, but his eyes flick to meet those of his prez. "Seems we've got to the bottom of who's bringing drugs into Pueblo. A family fuckin' business at that. Is that why you've been cosying up to our brother?"

My eyes can't open any wider. "No," I cry out.

"Then what the fuck is it?" the VP snarls.

I'm scared. My mouth doesn't seem to work, my brain can't find the words. These men are terrifying.

Mace steps closer. "I'm the fuckin' enforcer, darlin'. Prez gives me the signal, and it will be gloves off. You get what I'm putting out here? Start fuckin' talking."

The threat is obvious. I don't need his pointed glance toward the implements laid out on the workbench. As if a dam's opened, it all starts tumbling out. "My brother lives in Denver with Phil, our father..." my voice trails off. That's not the right place to begin. I try again. "My brother left packages in mom's house, in his old bedroom. I wasn't aware he left them, not until tonight."

Beef snorts loudly.

"I didn't have a clue. Not until tonight." Poor Mom is still in the dark. *She'll be devastated and scared when she finds out.*

Demon pinches his nose, then shakes his head, he pushes Mace to one side. "Right. I'll ask you questions. And I'll warn you, I know when someone's lying to me. One word that's not truth and I'll take the leash off Mace." The glance he exchanges with the enforcer isn't comforting.

I nod, having nothing to gain by lying.

"You and your brother got an operation going?"

Emphatically, I shake my head. "No. I'd never go near drugs."

"Think you did tonight," Demon reminds me. "You said no for yourself. Your brother?"

"I don't know. He moved out several years back. Lives with Phil—as I said that's our father—in Denver, but I've not seen him for years. He, er… Mom chucked Phil out when she realised he was a criminal. But I don't know if he's got anything to do with drugs. I wouldn't have said Connor did either, but I don't really know who he is nowadays."

"You have much to do with your brother?"

Another shake of my head. "I don't. Occasionally he'll visit, but not often. It's been almost a year since we last saw him. But he's come a couple of times lately. He asked to stay in his old room, Mom didn't want him to have the key to her house… Look, I'm sorry, I'm trying." I plead with my eyes, asking for time as I try to get my thoughts straight. "When she refused, he asked to pick up some of his stuff he'd left in his bedroom. When he carried a box in to collect them, we'd assumed it was empty, but I think that's when he left the packages of drugs. Then he'd come down with it full of old junk, so we weren't suspicious."

"He started visiting you, why?"

"He said he had a new business venture in Pueblo."

"He must be the one behind the fuckin' drug dealing," Beef says in an aside to his prez. "And I don't buy she knew nothing about what he was leaving."

There's nothing wrong with my hearing—with my common sense, perhaps, but not my ears. "I swear I didn't know about them. And I'd point the finger at Phil. Connor would have been working with him."

"So you're keeping to the story that he brought in the drugs without you knowing?"

At the same time as Mace asks his disbelieving question, Beef throws out, "Was it Heroin or meth?"

"Yes," I direct at the enforcer, and then, "How the hell do I know?" to the VP.

Beef is clearly not convinced.

"I didn't know until tonight," I insist.

Mace cocks his eyebrow at Demon, who nods back. He approaches me menacingly. "You got close to Ink. Fuck, at the wedding it could have been any of us, as long as you got a biker ensnared by your presumably magical pussy, you didn't care who. Shame it wasn't me you fucked, I'd have never been so fuckin' stupid. So what was your plan? To cosy up to Ink to find where we weren't looking? Were you finding where it was safe to deal?" At the stunned look on my face, he changes tack. "'Cause I don't believe you, *darlin'*." He snarls the last word. "You want me to believe you had no ulterior motive? Tell me this. You were fuckin' him, why didn't you speak to him, as soon as you knew there were drugs?"

Demon, clearly getting on Mace's wavelength asks. "Or, did you tell him? Did he know you were going to be there? Did he know what you were going to do and was trying to stop you?"

"No!" I all but scream. "I didn't know he was going to be there. I didn't have time to try and speak to him. Yes, that had been the first thing on my mind. But I didn't have a chance to call. No, he didn't know I was there. He must just have recognised me. Please," I beg them. "Please let me tell you what happened when Connor called."

When Demon gives me a sharp nod, I try not to think of how this morning had started, with me saying goodbye to Ink with every expectation of seeing him later. Instead, I focus on what happened after Ink had bailed, and I'd gone to my own bed alone.

"I was reading in my room; the book was good, I wanted to keep on with it. It was getting late, almost midnight. My phone rang, I'd hoped it was Ink, but instead, it was my brother. That in itself is unusual, I didn't know he still had my number, must be years since he used it." My eyes crease as I recall the desperation in his voice. "He said he was being held by someone and they were hurting him, and that he needed me to do something for him to make them stop. If I didn't, there was a risk they could kill him. He told me they'd broken his ribs, beat him, he sounded in pain, as if it even hurt to talk."

"Who had him?" Beef asks the question, but his expression shows he's finding my words hard to believe.

"He didn't say. I asked, but he wouldn't tell me. I got the impression they were listening to the call."

Mace snorts.

Demon purses his lips, but his only words are, "Go on."

"He gave me instructions. I was to open a box, take the packages, and deliver them to a man who'd be waiting for me in the vicinity of Tits Up." I pause to take a breath. "He'd left me no time to do anything otherwise. Of course I wanted to tell Ink, but Connor said I wouldn't see him, my brother, alive again if I didn't do what he asked. I couldn't risk that he was telling the truth." I glance up, but no one looks the slightest bit convinced. "I said I'd do anything to save him, and I would. He's my baby brother after all." I swallow down he'd been known to take advantage of that relationship, sensing it wouldn't do me any good. "I said, *anything,* and I meant it. I didn't know what the task was. I thought he might need money, heaven knows how I was going to get it that time of night, but I'd have emptied my bank account if that's what it would take."

Demon's raised chin and a quick look toward Beef gives me a slight hope they can understand such a desire to save a brother. Then he signals to me to resume.

"As I said, he'd left it until the last minute, and I had to rush to make the meet. It was only then that I found what he'd left and knew the packages were obviously drugs." I pause, then stress, "I thought about calling the cops, then realised that would get my brother locked up, that's if he was allowed to live. I thought about calling Ink, but…" I sob, I can't help it. Fresh tears run down my face, and I feel snot drip from my nose. "I couldn't risk dragging him into it, or your club. This was *my* mess to sort. Those were my thoughts in the few precious seconds I had if I was to get there on time. I took two packages, and well, you know the rest." I raise my watery eyes and look Demon straight in his, trying to convey how earnest I am. "It should have been me who was arrested, not Ink. I feel so fucking bad about that." My words end on violent sobs which shake my body.

"I bet you fuckin' do," Mace snarls from behind me.

"She didn't have much of a chance." Sparky surprisingly comes to my defence. "If we hadn't been there, it would be her sitting in jail now. Ink made a split-second decision, and well, it's him there instead."

"Jail is no more than she fuckin' deserves," barks Mace. "Ink, Christ…" his voice trails off, and he turns away and wipes at his face.

"I didn't ask him to help me," I cry out in desperation. I still can't believe he got involved. Just look what happened. It would have been me arrested if he'd not intercepted. If he'd had any idea, he wouldn't have done it, would he? In an attempt to get the scary looking enforcer to believe me, I continue, "Ink appeared out of nowhere. Took the bag from my hands. He told me to go." And I had. "I should have stood my ground, should have stayed with him, insisted he'd given me the bag back. That was what I did wrong." But I hadn't. Instead I'd obeyed that tone he'd used. I have no excuse for that. I weep again, this time, more quietly.

"Ink knew." Beef slaps one meaty fist into his palm. "Ink fuckin' knew the cops were there."

Ink knew?

"So why?" I wail. "Why did he step in? Why did he tell me to run? Why didn't he leave me, as Mace said, to get what I deserved?"

It's Sparky again who's voice is calmer than the rest. "Because he knew, Beth. Because he knew it was you. Because if he guessed right what you were carrying, you'd have been taken by the cops. Because… he's Ink."

More feet on the stairs and Cad enters. He pauses at the bottom, and Demon gives him a nod.

"Got a location for this Connor fucker?"

They're trying to find Connor?

Cad shakes his head. "Nah. Tried ringing the number, but it goes straight to voicemail. Tried several times now. From Beth's phone and another."

My head blasts with sudden pain. I don't know who to worry about more, Ink, locked up in jail because of my stupidity, or Connor, because despite all that I'd done, he might have been killed anyway.

"They've killed him," I cry out weakly, knowing he would have answered the call from my phone if he could. He'd have been waiting for me to confirm I'd done what he said. "Connor must be dead."

As an anguished sound escapes me, Demon looks at me again. "You think your brother was telling the truth? He was being hurt? That he really was, is, in danger?" His tone suggests he has no patience for what I'm feeling. "Assuming you've told us the truth and had nothing to do with this before your brother called, could he have been using you to make the delivery as he got wind there might be trouble at the drop tonight? Could he have been using you?"

Tonight. It seems I've lived a whole lifetime, but it's still only the early hours of the morning.

"It's more likely that Beth was part of it all along." I tune back in to hear Mace, who's clearly not convinced of my innocence.

"Ask Ink," I cry out, then realise that's impossible. As incredulous eyes look toward me, I try to explain, "Ink was there when Connor was arguing about staying and then taking his gear. Ink saw him bring in a box and leave with it filled. He knows neither I nor Mom had a clue Connor had brought something into the house."

Demon enters the conversation again. "You said you took two of the packages. There were more?"

"Eight," I tell him. "There are eight packages of drugs left." I raise my eyes to him. "I don't care what happens to them, I want them out of our house. Please, can you help?"

The prez draws himself up and looks incredulous. "You have the fuckin' nerve to sit there and ask for our help?"

"I care about my mother, she might be all I have left. She doesn't know... what if someone else does? What if someone turns up for the rest?" My voice rises higher. "They're worth money, aren't they? You could take them, sell them—I don't care..."

I'm forced to stop as there's a roar from the bikers surrounding me.

"Shut up!" snarls Demon, to get them to stop.

But Beef is eyeing me carefully. "Drug dealers don't offer up their stash, Prez. If she's got eight bricks of whatever that fuckin' shit is, she's offering it freely. I'd bet she's no clue of the value."

"She could just be following her brother's instructions." Mace isn't giving me an inch.

"You reckon he'd instruct her to simply hand over that shit? One brick, Mace, maybe, to get us onside. But fuckin' eight? She could be telling the truth." Beef turns to his prez. "She could be trying to save her skin, yes. But I warn you, Demon, don't make the same mistake you made with Skull, before he was patched in and was the prospect Runt. Don't go looking for answers when there may be none to be had. Focus on the information she does have instead." His eyes flash something to Demon. I don't know why they mentioned Skull, there must be some things Mel hadn't shared, but his words seem to do some good.

Whatever, Demon seems to take what his VP has said at face value. "I asked you a question, Beth. Could your brother have been using you?"

I press my lips together, and more tears leak as I start speaking my thoughts aloud, "If you'd asked me a week, a day ago, I'd say he was on the wrong path, influenced too much by Phil, but that there was still a familial affection there. That he wouldn't have wanted any harm to come to me," I give a little shake of my head to show I haven't finished, "as I wouldn't want physical harm to come to him. All I can tell you is that he sounded hurt, it sounded like it was painful for him to breathe, so I believed he had broken ribs. But when you come right down to it, I don't know my brother anymore. He could have been setting me up. There, that's the truth of it."

If anything, Demon's eyes seem to darken until they become a solid black. "Either way we need to find him."

He makes a slight turn, raising an eyebrow at Cad. Cad nods and gives him the answer he's clearly seeking. "Haven't been able to trace where the calls were made from, it was probably some type of cheap burner, but I can carry on digging using the signal from hers. Will involve triangulation, but I'll get there."

"I want men ready to roll as soon as you find out where we're heading."

"Want us to get to Denver so we'll be waiting?" Mace asks.

Demon again raises a querying brow in Cad's direction.

"I'm doing what I can. It may well be tomorrow," he grimaces, clearly remembering the time and corrects, "later today, or even Monday before I know anything. And, you're only assuming he's in Denver as that's his hometown. He could be here in Pueblo for all we know."

That they're searching for my brother should give me some satisfaction, but it doesn't. He could already be dead, or, he could be having the time of his life, completely unharmed and laughing as he'd avoided the fate I'd so narrowly escaped and Ink's suffering instead. Neither option is attractive. Alive or dead, Connor will be gone from my life. *Ink. What must he be feeling? Does he now hate me for landing him in this mess? He probably regrets ever going with me. Oh God, Ink. Why did you step in? Why didn't you just let me accept my fate?* I realise I'd tuned out for a moment as Demon's still talking.

"You find him? I want him back here. He's got access to large quantities of drugs, and whether or not he's the ringleader, is probably up to his neck in the new trade coming into Pueblo."

I glance at those tools again being under no illusion what would happen if my brother's alive and they get their hands on him. But if Connor's whole story was concocted, I don't feel much sympathy about the Devils hurting him. With Ink locked up, they'll show little mercy.

"How many do you think should go?" asks Beef.

"I'll go," offers Thunder. His voice surprises me. I hadn't noticed him descend the stairs, though the expression on his face shows he's been here for most of the conversation.

"Me too," agrees Mace.

"Four more," Demon proposes. "Just in case we need to extricate a hostage." But a glance in my direction shows he thinks it's unlikely. *He thinks I've been had.* Maybe I have. Or, perhaps, he still doesn't believe one word of my story.

"One more thing…" Cad holds up his hand and interrupts. "Don't know what this has to do with it, but Ink already asked me to look into this Phil Foster."

"He asked about Phil?" It must have been after last Sunday. I'm confused, why would Ink want to know about him?

Demon ignores me. "And have you?" He gestures at the tech man to give him more.

"Yeah, he's one shady motherfucker," Cad obliges. "Cops want him but can't pin enough on him." He glances my way as if to see how I'm taking it.

It's not news to me. I'd known all my life my father was a criminal.

"Drugs?"

"That's what I was looking for but haven't found a connection as yet. I'll get back to digging." Then Cad turns to leave, presumably to resume what he was doing. I call out to him. "Cad, find Connor. Please?"

Sparky waves Cad off, and then he comes over to me. For the first time since the alley he sounds a little sympathetic. "If your brother is being held against his will, we'll find him and get him out. If he's not there, we'll find out what's happened to him." He crouches down in front of me. "While he's still got the rest of the drugs, he's got a bargaining chip."

I hadn't thought of that. The implications slam into me. "Are you saying we've got to leave them where they are? Oh my God. Mom's alone," I cry out. "What if someone comes for the rest?"

Demon stares at me, then voices his thoughts. "If they're left there, someone may not take them gently. If they're not, they might take it out on the person who was storing them, unknowingly or not. Fuck." He turns to Mace. "Know you're suspicious of Beth, Mace, so am I. But her mother?"

With a glance my way as if the last thing he wants to do is something to assist me, the enforcer gives a resigned lift of his chin. "If you don't need me here, Prez, and we're not setting off anywhere, I'll go check it out. I'll take Rusty with me, and we'll bring whatever's there back."

He means take the drugs. "But wouldn't it be worse if they turn up for them and find them gone?" I'm so worried for my mom. She's done nothing wrong. "What if they hurt my mom, trying to find out what happened to them?"

"Bring Beth's mom back with you." Demon shakes his head. "Fuck, this is getting complicated."

Now one of the older bikers, Bomber, appears. "Ink's not been charged yet, but that will be coming. Got Sykes out of bed and he's at the station."

"Bet the lawyer liked that," Mace scoffs.

"For what we pay him, he better be there with a smile on his fuckin' face," Demon retorts.

Ink. Them talking about cops and a lawyer makes it real. I start to cry in earnest, saying through my sobs what I tried to tell them from the start, "Let me go. I'll go to the police. I'll tell them what happened, I'll say Ink had nothing to do with it—"

"No, you won't," Demon says.

"But this is all my fault," I protest, and hiccup. "I don't know why Ink took the bag off me, but he was arrested when it should have been me."

"Exactly." Now, Prez is crouching in front of me. He brings out a knife and slices first through the ties holding one leg, and then the other. He nods at Beef who goes behind me and frees my hands. At last able to, I wipe at my eyes. Demon continues, "Ink knew whoever was caught with those drugs could be arrested—he knew the area was swarming with SWAT. He made a call that that wasn't going to be you. Until I know what was in his head when he did it, you're doing nothing to put yourself in the sights of the cops."

Demon rises, I get to my feet as well, rubbing my wrists to get the circulation going. We stand looking eye to eye.

"Fuck knows why Ink did what he did," Demon eventually tells me. "For some reason he thought it was better to be him than you. Maybe he thought there was a chance he could get away with it..."

"Could he?" Hope stops me breathing.

"No fuckin' chance." Demon's eyes flare. "He was caught handing drugs to a fuckin' dealer."

I slump, my hand reaching out and finding the back of the

chair I'd so recently been held captive on, needing its support to remain standing. The stark words sounding dreadful now they've been voiced.

Taking pity on me, Demon suggests, "Maybe Ink cares a lot for you Beth. Face it, doing prison time is not something anyone would do lightly. The question whether you're worth it or not hasn't yet been addressed."

My head moves side to side. *Is there anything in what Demon is saying? Does Ink really care for me? Is that the explanation for what he did?* I try to work it through, speaking my thoughts out loud, "Ink took the rap for me. He *knew* he was likely to be arrested." Never in my life would I have dreamed anyone would do so much. It makes it ten, a hundred times worse. I would never have asked him to do something as reckless when any trouble should have landed on my head. "He shouldn't have, Demon. I could have explained to the cops…"

"Could you?" Demon doesn't look or sound convinced. "Beth, what would you be doing if you were questioned right now? Would you be dropping your brother in it? What difference would that make? You knowingly took drugs to deliver to a dealer. That's as bad as selling them yourself. You were caught supplying them. You think they'd buy your story of being coerced?"

Would I drop my brother in it? If he was telling the truth, involving the police would mean he'd be killed. Connor's life or Ink's freedom? What a choice. But Demon's is a moot point. I'm not being questioned by the police. I have damned all idea where my brother is, whether he's alive or dead, or whether he'd been lying or truthful. All I know is the man who I'd started to have strong feelings for is in a jail cell right now. I'm vaguely aware tears continue to fall down my face as I acknowledge how helpless I'm feeling.

"We're going to have to sort out how to deal with this." Beef steps up beside Demon, delivering a scowl in my direction. "Christ, what a fuckin' mess."

Is he talking about me? Startled, I realise I'm a blubbering disaster at the moment. I scramble in my pocket to find a tissue and blow my nose loudly.

My brother could be injured, dying, or already dead. My lover could rot in jail. My mom's life could be in danger if my brother told whoever's got him the location of the rest of the drugs.

This is too big for me to handle. There's only one thing to do, even though Demon had told me not to. I straighten my back. "I'm going to the cops. I'll tell them everything. At the very least I'll get Ink out of jail. I'll go now."

"No, you won't," Demon announces equally firmly. "You're staying here. Where we can keep an eye on you."

"Demon, it's the right thing to do. I need to take responsibility for any decision I've made. The cops may let me off, I didn't think I had a choice…"

"You think that would clear you? Christ, woman, I've already told you. You were an accomplice at the very least. In their view, as soon as you found the drugs you should have turned them in. I doubt they'll accept any excuse."

"So, I get arrested. I'll do the time." It might kill me. I've never been enamoured by the thought of being locked up. I shudder as I recall what I've heard about going inside, but I can't let an innocent man suffer for actions I'd taken. *Why Ink? Why?* What had made him decide to do what he'd done when he must have known what was likely to happen when he took that bag from me? "It's the only way, Demon. I'll give myself up. Admit it was me and that Ink knew nothing—"

"No, you won't," Demon says, his tone broking no argument. "Ink made the choice. He knew what would happen."

"But maybe he didn't," I protest, trying to justify Ink's actions. "He can't have known the cops were so close."

"Ink knew exactly where the SWAT team was positioned tonight, and what they were looking out for. Odds on that he'd be arrested. If," he holds up his hand as I go to speak, "if Ink thinks enough of you that he'd do the time instead, then I'm not letting his fuckin' sacrifice go to waste. You go to the cops? They've got you both. You'll probably achieve nothing, and I doubt that they'll let him walk."

"But it wasn't his fault. It was mine."

Demon shrugs. "He handed the drugs over. That's what they saw."

I turn away, my hand covering my mouth feeling as though I'm going to be sick.

"What the fuck's going on?" A new voice, one I know well. It's Pyro. "What's this about Ink being arrested and that it's Beth's fault?"

I zone out as I hear Beef explain. Since Connor had called the first time today, I've been running on adrenaline, caught up in a world I know nothing about. Suddenly thrust into a universe where people use torture to get what they want, narrowly escaping it being used on myself. I'd got my lover arrested, and all for what?

"Mel's upstairs, love. Come on, let me take you up to her." Pyro's voice sounds close to my ear. "Come on," he repeats, patiently, when I don't move.

"Mel shouldn't have come," I say, absently. "She's pregnant."

"Yeah, but not fuckin' ill. I couldn't keep her away once she heard something was up with you and Ink."

"Ro," Demon attracts his attention, "I know your wife and Beth are close, but in other circumstances, Beth would be a fuckin' enemy of the club. She's no friend of ours, but it appears she might mean something to Ink."

"We're offering her our protection?" Pyro gives me an assessing look.

Demon's statement hadn't surprised me, I'd be a fool not to sense the animosity in the air. Shifting a little uneasily, I don't blame them and can appreciate the conundrum they're now in. They might offer protection to me and my mom, but it's not out of the hand of friendship.

"Yes," Demon tells him, having come to a decision. "For now, Beth and Patsy are under our protection. At least until we know what's happening with Ink, and what part this Connor played in the drugs flooding into Pueblo." He turns to me. "If I get word you turning yourself in could help Ink out of his predicament, I'll take you to the cops myself. And," his voice deepens, "if you've been telling me a pack of lies, you'll be taking your last breath."

I gulp. Knowing he means it. But my only danger is him catching me out in a lie, and all that's come out of my mouth is the truth.

Pyro nods as if a message has been telegraphed and understood, but warns, "I need something to tell Mel if we're keeping Beth away from her."

"Nah. She can talk to Mel." Demon turns to me. "But for fuck's sake do not give her any details of what happened tonight. Can I fuckin' trust you on that?"

It's Mel's man who persuades me. "Keeping ol' ladies out of club business is keeping them safe. You get dragged into this mess? Your friends might be questioned. If she doesn't know anything, she can't implicate herself or the club. Got it?"

I nod. I've got it. "She's pregnant, Pyro. I won't hurt her again. I promise I'll keep my mouth shut. I'll do nothing and say nothing that could upset Mel."

"Yeah." Pyro gives a twisted smile. "Just say it's club business, and she'll give you sympathy without questions."

I suppose that makes sense, but I highly doubt Mel will be able to stop herself from interrogating me. But as I don't know what's going on myself, there's little I can give away. If I'm honest, I'd prefer not to admit I have a brother I never talk about, who's tried to get me involved in criminal activity carried out by the man who, however much I dislike it, is my dad. Not quite the kind of family you bring up in idle conversation.

CHAPTER NINETEEN

Ink

As a Marine, I was used to making split-second decisions. I'd been a sniper and it's ingrained in me how to quickly assess what is a threat and what is not. Any hesitation might mean the death of my comrades. I see a situation and sum it up fast.

Her stature and figure were immediately familiar, and then that telltale blue hair left me without the slightest doubt it was Beth. I didn't even stop to think why she was there. One split second was all it took to realise that I couldn't let her get taken in by the cops. I didn't stop to rationalise anything, just acted entirely on instinct to save the woman I must have serious feelings for. Else, why would I put my freedom on the line?

I was brought to the station and searched. My cut, wallet, phone and belt had been taken from me—my gun and knife had already disappeared when they'd handcuffed me at the scene. I'd been photographed and fingerprinted even though my prints are already on file, as previously, I'd been rounded up before with other members of the MC for something we hadn't done.

Beth's appearance, my arrest and processing, it had all happened so fast, moving me along like a stone crashed against the rocks by the tide. Now the action has stopped, I have the first chance in hours to consider what's happened. As my situation catches up with me, I realise what a fucking bind I'm in.

Pushed inside with the door clanging behind me, I get my first taste of where I'll be spending the remainder of this god-awful night. It's a Saturday, the station is crammed and busy. Clearly no cells are available, I've ended up in the drunk tank of all fucking places.

Most of the inmates around me are currently sleeping off their excess, those that aren't, I intimidate with a glare and a flex of my muscles. Then, confident I'll be left alone, I sink down onto my haunches and, ignoring the snores, belching and farting as best I can, take a moment to process and think.

Beth. Fuckin' Beth. What the fuck was she doing there? If she were here standing in front of me, it wouldn't be my palm on her ass she'd be feeling, but my hands wrapped around her neck as I shook whatever it was that had gotten into her out.

Fucking hell. I'd all but decided to claim her, and she was carrying drugs to a drop-off point. Is she the one fucking with my club?

Too frustrated to rest, I abruptly stand. One of the drunks staggers to his feet.

"You fuckin' kicked me," he slurs.

"I'll fuckin' kill you if you don't sit back down." I'm longing to hit out at anyone, and he'll do if he doesn't shut up.

My rage gets through his alcoholic haze, and wisely for him, if disappointing to me, he sits once again.

What the fuck was Beth doing there?

Beth supplying drugs?

No. That's not the woman I've come to know, that's not her, is it? I rake my hands through my hair, trying to understand, thinking back to what I saw. She'd emerged from the alley nervous and on edge, not as though this was something she did all the time. When I took the drugs from her, she'd tried to protest, had been hesitant when I told her to run. That's not the reactions of a supplier of drugs. Why was making the drop so important?

Why the fuck was she there?

Why did I set myself up?

My fist hits my palm.

A loud window-rattling snore reminds me where I am. I've given up my freedom, for her. For a bitch who most likely doesn't deserve it. A fucking bitch who I thought of making my old lady. Well, being locked up has at least saved me from making that mistake. Women, never good news.

I glance around, almost hoping one of these fuckers gives me a hard time. I won't start a fight, but it sure would be me as the last man standing.

I'm in jail. I've done nothing wrong. *Cops will never believe me.*

I may not get out. Unless I can come up with a story that's convincing. *How the fuck do I do that?*

My—I snort at the idea I refer to her as mine—woman may have let me down, but my club will never desert me. I can depend on them and know they will already be arranging a lawyer. Sykes, if I'm not mistaken. Maybe between us we can work out something that the cops will accept.

Fucking Beth. And fucking me. My desire to protect her had me doing just that, when more thought may have stopped me acting impulsively.

Why had Beth appeared, at that time of night and at that place and carrying what I know now, and at the time assumed, were drugs? Is she not the innocent civilian I'd thought her to be? Nothing about her behaviour seemed to suggest otherwise. But I could be wrong. Take Skull, for example, he'd lived a double life which none of us had ever expected. Was Beth an undercover cop? No, unlikely. She works for the government, yes, but does something with Mel in the land registry department. From what she'd said, and Mel would have caught her out in a lie, she'd worked there since she'd left school.

Was she not as innocent as she'd appeared? Was she in

cahoots with her father and was he responsible for the drugs flooding into Pueblo? Unlikely. The way Beth and her mom had talked about Phil, nothing would have convinced either to get involved with him. Unless both women were good enough actors to be nominated for an Oscar, there's no way they had me fooled.

Had Beth known I was going to be there behind Tits Up tonight? Devils run the strip club, it was obvious some of us would be around. But unless there was provocation, and in this case, the drug dealing which I hadn't told her about, we were unlikely to frequent the alleyways behind the club. So, no, my presence had to have taken her by surprise.

How did she know the dealer was going to be there? Is she earning extra money by being a courier, or even dealing? After all, working for the government is not the highest paying of jobs. While I hate drugs with a passion, having seen a childhood friend get hooked and finally overdose and die, she might think they're fairly innocent. Fuck it, no. Who could look at that shit in a rosy light?

My head drops into my hands as my brain goes around in circles. *Connor.* That waste-of-space brother of hers. It makes more sense he's involved. Both him and his father he thinks so much of and works for. Could he have put pressure on Beth? Persuaded her to drop drugs off with the dealer? Was Connor there himself tonight? Was it an associate of Connor's who I'd passed the stash over too? If so, why the fuck is he involving his sister in that shit? Or, are they in it together? And why the hell hadn't I insisted Cad drop everything else and investigate him and his father?

Fuck my life, which now as I know it could be over. The cops are going to throw the book at me. After all, I was found with drugs in my hand. Enough witnesses in uniform to properly finger me for whatever they want. They won't go easy on a Satan's Devil. *Fucking hell.* I'm done for. *Will I ever see the outside of a prison cell again?* Age wise there's every possibility, not that I know offhand how long a sentence for possession with intent to sell would carry, but say even if it was thirty years, I'd be sixty. *Christ, Hellfire's age or thereabouts.* Trouble is, while I've not been inside, I've known people who have, and some who've never gotten out. Being a Devil would plant an immediate target on my back, everyone wanting to be the big man and take a member of an outlaw MC out. It's quite possible I, too, wouldn't be alive at the end of my sentence.

I didn't serve my country to go to prison for a crime I didn't commit. But it now seems, because of Beth, I might.

I should have stood by and let Beth take responsibility for her actions, but I hadn't. Now I've got to live with that. I only hope she knows how she's fucked up my life.

Would I rewind the clock if that were possible?

Of course I fucking would.

A drunk rolls over, falls off the concrete slab covered with only a thin plastic mattress that serves as a bed. He's so out of it he doesn't even wake up. I move over to take advantage of the suddenly vacant space. An automatic action which doesn't interrupt my train of thought.

I imagine Beth sitting in a similar cell, along with whores and drunken women. I see her cringing, her arms wrapped around her long legs as she tries to make herself invisible. I can almost hear her quiet whimpering of fear as she faces the unknown. Then she'd go to jail and become someone's bitch and be bullied and ridiculed. She wouldn't fight back, she wouldn't know how. It wouldn't take long for that sparkle in her eyes to dim, and for her joy of life to seep out of her.

She'd deserve it.

I conjure up Beth's face, but surprisingly it's not the image of her lying beneath me as I thrust into her that's the strongest memory I have. I'm not recalling the way her tight cunt squeezes my cock. No, I'm remembering just talking and listening to her, the way she smiles, the feel of that long silky hair, and thoughts of that evening I spent with her and her mom.

I'm in here because my instinct was to protect her, like an old man does his old lady. Rhythmically, I start banging my hand against my head. She's not my old lady, not yet. But it seems a part buried deep inside me believes that she is, and it was my duty to care for her.

I'd known in an instance Beth wouldn't be able to cope, locked up. Me? Well, I'm better equipped. I can look after myself. Mentally, would I last? I'd have to.

If Beth is the woman I believe her to be, *if* she got caught up in something it was impossible to stop, then no, I wouldn't want to turn back the clock. My only regret is that she didn't feel she could come to me.

It's just sex, I'd told her. How was she to know it had turned into more?

But if—again I bang my hand against my head—if she's involved in running drugs. If I'm taking the rap for something she did willingly, then... I grin evilly to myself... the club is going to make her life a fucking misery, or what's left of it. Her life, for the best years of mine.

She must have an excuse.

A man, clearly locked up for being drunk and disorderly, awakes and noisily uses the open toilet on the other side of the room. The sound wakes a couple of others, one rushes to push him away and vomits, but misses the bowl. My surroundings are dirty, disgusting, probably vying with some places I'd been on my tours for the worst I've ever seen.

The thin plastic mattress I'm sitting on feels sticky with substances I don't want to imagine when I accidentally touch it with my hand. The jeans I'm wearing, I've already decided, will go straight into the trash.

That's if I have the choice. I may be exchanging them for an orange jumpsuit any day now. All for the sake of one woman. A woman who should be here instead of me.

Tonight should have gone smoothly. Tomorrow, I should have been teaching Beth how to ride a bike, then, taking her to my room and fucking her. If it had gone to plan, I'd have suggested us starting a relationship, and one day soon, asked her to be my old lady. What would she have said?

Ignoring the unpleasant sights, sounds, and odours around me, I let my mind run amok.

"Yes, Ink. I'll be your ol' lady."

"Ink, I'm pregnant."

"Ink, we're having a son."

As I summon up the words that I once thought would make me run a mile despite my environment, there's an unidentifiable feeling churning inside. Something that has a kernel of excitement, of expectation and… longing. Now when my future is distinctly likely to involve me doing serious time and I'll have lost any chance of ever hearing those words from Beth, I admit they wouldn't make me jump on my bike and ride as far away as I could. No, I'd want to stay and hear her repeat them. If, that is, she's the woman I thought.

Could there be a good reason why she was there tonight? Could I forgive her?

I imagine myself doing just that. Imagine holding her in my arms.

How would her voice sound when she tells me she loves me for the very first time? Would her hoarse whisper echo the emotion and reverence in mine?

Love?

What a fuck of a time to admit that's where my feelings were going. Maybe had already arrived. What other emotion would have driven me to step in last night except for an affection so deep I'd do anything for her.

Her blue hair made me look at her twice. Her personality a third time. Her shapely, athletic body kept my eye. Her love for her mom, support for her brother even though he's an ass, everything about her showed me Beth's one in a million. I'd have been a fool to turn my back on the woman I'd thought she was.

A dream snatched out of my reach.

It was my perfect woman herself who tore it into pieces.

I huff a mirthless laugh. Always knew bitches were bad news. Best I forget all about her.

Despite my misgivings about the mattress, exhausted after the long night, I lie down and turn on my side, my eyes closing as I tune out the disgusting sounds around me and my traitorous mind conjures up thoughts of riding with the wind in my hair and Beth's arms tight around my waist. Or, better still, her on her own Sportster riding along beside my Fat Bob, glancing at each other, sharing the enjoyment of being free and out with just nature and our bikes.

Jeez. For fuck's sake get out of my head woman.

Who's going to teach her to ride now?

There may be a chance I'll get out.

Yeah, and I just saw a flying pig through the bars of the too high up and too small window of the cell.

I turn on my other side, but it still doesn't put a brake on my thoughts. Wishful thinking or not, maybe Beth's innocent. Maybe it was her brother who got her into something way over her head. Would it be too much of a leap to assume her brother had something to do with the drugs in Pueblo and somehow persuaded her to get involved? If he'd heard word the cops were out in force tonight, *last night,* I correct seeing daylight brightening the room, he could have set her up. I think back to when I'd so briefly met him. Was he a man to throw his sister under a bus to save himself? Yeah, I could believe that he was. I'm going to fucking kill him if he did, or, as it's unlikely I'll get the chance to do it myself, get the club to dispatch him to meet Satan by proxy.

If Beth is the woman I believed her to be, I've got a problem. If she's as sweet natured as I thought, there's a good chance she'll sacrifice herself to give me a chance to walk free. That certainly wouldn't work. Cops cheer when a biker goes down, and they've got me, caught red-handed. She wouldn't free me, she'd only convict herself.

I've got to convince her to let me go down. *How the fuck do I do that?*

I could do my time as long as I knew she was happy and free. *Cops can't stagger across a hint of anything that connects me with her.* But how?

I've got to cut all ties with her.

No visits. No enquiries. No putting herself in the sights of the cops. It's the only way I can protect her.

Fuck, but I must have it bad. Even knowing she's the reason I'm here, and I'm unclear as to her motives, there's still this urge inside to keep her safe. If I can't enjoy my life, knowing she can, will make up for a lot. Even if she deserved the punishment, I can better serve it. If she has made a mistake, this is her chance to learn from it. Do my time knowing she's happy and protected? There may not be much sense to it, but it makes me feel easier.

My club will know what to do.

Suddenly I turn on my back, my arm flung over my face. *Am I being a fucking idiot? The club's not going to throw themselves behind Beth.* Not when she's the reason I, their brother, is inside.

She's new to the club, and I haven't led anyone to believe she's anything to me but a casual fuck. I sit bolt upright. *What would I feel if Mace or Liz were in jail when it should be their fuck buddy instead?* Christ. *Will they blame her?* Running it through in my head, I realise of course they fucking will. Instead of protecting or helping her, they might already have banned her from the club. Or worse, sort their own retribution on my behalf. Especially if they think she had anything to do with the drugs.

A drunk farts loudly, a few seconds later the foul stench reaches my nostrils. But even that doesn't distract me. *How can I get the club on Beth's side?*

Ask them, tell them what I want. Hell, I'd probably sound as deranged as I think I am. Especially when I come up with the answer, the one thing I can do to extend my protection to her when I'm not there to do it myself. *I claim her.*

I almost laugh aloud at the ludicrousness of it. Me, claim a woman? Commit to her for life? If I was a free man, that could be where Beth and I would be heading, but I'd have taken my time and made sure it was right. Fuck knows if she feels the same way, we hadn't exactly discussed it. In fact, we discussed anything but that, and persuaded each other we were happy with a few fucks. If I claim her it would be in name only. I couldn't expect her to wait three decades until I get out.

But, if the club know she's mine, they'll have to support her. To give me peace of mind, knowing she's safe and being cared for while I'm locked up, it's the only answer.

Then what would she do? Act like an old lady? Would they allow conjugal visits in prison? Or would I have to marry her for that? Perhaps I wouldn't mind putting a ring on her finger if it gave me her cunt to look forward to while I was doing serious time.

My mouth twists slightly upwards, then turns down when I realise the problem. I can't have the cops looking into Beth, not if I'm right about Connor. Who knows how deeply he's dragged her into his world? Nope, don't want the cops to go sniffing around her. They can't have any idea she was there last night.

She'll be feeling guilty. So it won't be much of a stretch for her to believe I want nothing to do with her. If I was in my right mind, that should be where I'm headed. I've got to make her believe I hate her.

I shake my head slowly. She'll never know I'll have done the stupidest thing in my life. I'll claim her to get her the protection I can't provide. Her believing I've cut her loose is the only way to keep her out of this mess. If she gets arrested and goes inside too, my sacrifice would have been for nothing.

Fuck being sensible. The thought of never seeing her again hurts worse than any other sentence I could be handed, but I can't see any other way around it.

Hate. Love. One coin, two sides. She'll never know which landed up.

"McNeish. You're wanted."

It was only a matter of time.

Standing, I walk to the door feeling the indignity of my pants slipping down as I'm missing my belt. My motorcycle boots have buckles so at least I don't need to shuffle in the way I've seen men who are missing their laces have. Hoisting up my jeans as best I can, I straighten my shoulders and follow the guard down the short corridor and step into the room that he opens. I let out a breath as a sigh of relief when I see who's waiting and step forward with an outstretched hand.

"Sykes. It's good to see you."

He shakes my hand automatically. "Fuckin' Sunday. Why's it always a Sunday? If you could have heard my wife—"

"What you get for us paying you an extortionate amount to be our lawyer."

"There is that." He nods, seriously, then points to a chair one side of the desk. "How about you sit down, and I do my job and get us both out of here as soon as I possibly can?"

Sounds good to me. Impossible, though it may be. He'll soon be going home to his wife and me? Well, I'll be going back to my cell, and from there to a penitentiary.

"So, Damon—"

"Ink."

He knows us well so doesn't argue. "Ink. What happened?" He stifles a yawn suggesting he has indeed been pulled from his bed.

"This room got ears?"

"Shouldn't have. Lawyer-client privilege. But I do need to know everything that happened, then I can best prepare your case."

"What am I looking at?"

Sykes shrugs. "The charge will be possession with intent to sell. You had two kilos on you. Depends whether they try to link you with large-scale heroin distribution, if that's the case it could be anything up to thirty-two years. At the other end of the scale, the minimum is two."

"It was heroin?" As I ask for confirmation, I huff a mirthless laugh. I hadn't even known what was in the bag.

At my strange question, Sykes sits back and folds his arms. "Mexican brown," he confirms. His eyes sharpen. "That you didn't know what you were carrying suggests there's a story there. Now give me something to work with."

For the next half hour or so, I explain why I had been there in the back alleys behind Tits Up, and how I'd come to so briefly be in possession of two kilos of a controlled substance.

"Unbelievable," he says at last. "You're prepared to do serious time for a woman you've known only a couple of weeks? Who could be up to her neck in this business?"

"She's not," I say firmly. I don't know why I've come around to that opinion, but while I can't think of the explanation, I've become convinced there must be a good reason why she was there last night. "I don't know what went down or why, but I do know she doesn't have anything to do with drugs."

He rolls his eyes as if I'm the biggest idiot he's ever seen, and working for the likes of us, he's seen quite a lot. "You had the bag for less than a minute?"

"Sparky will back me up."

"You didn't know it was even drugs." It's a statement, so I stay quiet.

"Right, what's her full name?"

I don't give him his answer but explain instead. "I don't want her dragged into this, Sykes. I don't want the police to get her in their sights. I can deal if I go down, she can't."

"She could prove your innocence—"

"Only by trapping herself. As you said, they've got me on possession. I'm a Devil, they're not going to cut me loose. We'll both end up fucked." Or not, I think with disappointment.

"You don't make my life easy."

"That's why we pay you so much," I mutter under my breath.

"This brother of hers. You think he might be involved? Have you got the club checking him out?"

"I haven't spoken to anyone in the club." I haven't had a chance.

"Of course, you haven't," he confirms. "It's early. Forgive me. I'll speak to Demon and give him the heads-up. Trouble is, Ink, we don't know how much the cops saw. Did they see you take the rucksack from someone? If so, they'll be trying to find out who it was."

"The fucker who was expecting the delivery held a gun on me," I tell him. "They might have seen that. I had no option but to pass the bag over."

"Useful." His hands move in the way the prez's son, Theo, does when he wants something. A 'gimme more' gesture.

"I found the bag and was taking it to the cops? The dealer saw me?" I think more. "A fucker was coming along, saw me and Sparky, dropped the bag and ran? That's why I picked it up?"

"That's something I can work with. Of course, it all hinges on how much they witnessed. Any cameras that might have picked something up?"

Fuck. Again my thoughts go to her and not me. Where had Beth parked? Was there CCTV on the street? "Tell Demon to get Cad reviewing footage. I'm serious Sykes. I want Beth kept out of it." If she'd driven there as I suspect, her car might have been clocked all over Pueblo, but only if they're looking for it. They couldn't follow up every vehicle driving last night, so Cad just has to try and doctor sightings of her in the vicinity. Even while I won't be directly able to speak to him, I know my computer expert brother will do what needs to be done.

Suddenly Sykes leans forward. "Throw her to the wolves, Ink. You barely know her, and I earn my money for the club. My instructions are to get you out of here."

I shake my head. "No. I'm claiming her. She's mine." She just doesn't know it, and unless I get out, never will. "Her being brought into it doesn't exonerate me, just makes her an accomplice, and she'll go down as well."

Sykes breathes in loudly through his nose. "I can't guarantee you're not wrong in that. Okay, I'll stay away from her. But she may come forward herself, if what you obviously feel for her goes both ways."

That's my worry, the nail he's hit right on the head. "She'd do it for anyone, Sykes. She's not the type to see an innocent man locked up. But in this case, she has to be persuaded she has to, for her sake and mine. If we're going with the flimsy story of the man who dropped the bag and ran away, she'd only make things worse if she starts telling the truth." It's hard to tell him what I've decided, but it's for the best. "I've got two messages for Demon." I pause while my eyes find those of my lawyer's and wait for the jerk of his head that shows he's noting what I'm saying carefully. "First, impress on him she's mine, I've claimed her. Second, get him to tell her to keep the fuck away. Hell, let her believe I hate her if that's what it's going to take. She's got to understand I don't want to and won't see her." Fuck, it hurts, but to protect her, Beth must believe whatever this was is over between us.

His brow creases as he jots down some notes. "You clearly think a lot of her, Ink. If she's of the same mind, might be hard keeping her away."

"Then Demon will have to find the right words to say. He's got to convince her." He's inventive and resourceful. It's why we voted him in as the prez.

A warning knock, and then the door opens.

"Detectives Barker and Hastings are ready to speak with Mr McNeish."

Sykes raises his brow, I give a returning raise of my chin. Guess I'm ready as I'll ever be.

Following my lawyer, I shuffle, now with my hands and legs

in chains, and am taken into an interview room. This one kitted out with a recording device, and high on the wall, a camera.

"I'm Detective Barker, this is Detective Hastings. For the recording, please state your names."

"Joseph Sykes. Attorney at law." Sykes nods at me.

"Damon McNeish. Otherwise known as Ink."

"Thank you. Now, Mr McNeish, our reports show you were found in possession of two kilos of heroin on Third Street behind Tits Up, the strip club owned by the Satan's Devils MC. Your club."

"No," I refute.

"No? Please explain." A raised eyebrow and a small challenging smile suggest Barker thinks I can't.

"I was there with other members of my club. Dealing behind Tits Up had been going on for some time, users were shooting up in the bathrooms, leaving used needles around." I frown. "That isn't good for business. The Satan's Devils MC do not deal in drugs, and every member hates dealing and using with a passion."

"Is that so?" The detective smirks.

"It's so unless you have evidence to the contrary," interjects Sykes.

"It appears to us that you are very much involved, Mr McNeish. Our evidence shows that you were caught handing over a vast amount of heroin to one Fender Childs."

"At gunpoint," Sykes puts in.

Barker continues as if that point is of no interest to him. "What is your relationship to Fender Childs, Mr McNeish?"

"I don't know the man."

The detective seems to sneer at my honest reply. "Mr Childs has a record for dealing. Only small fry up to now, but it looks like he may have upped his game. Do you deny you were passing him his stock?"

And admit I was supplying drugs for sale? No way. "I do deny it." My tone is forceful, my voice strong.

Now Hastings steps in. "If you weren't handing them over, and it was as your lawyer purports, at gunpoint, perhaps you were intending to sell them yourself?"

I shake my head fast. I'm becoming frustrated. "No. Are you interested in hearing what actually happened?"

Barker leans back and folds his arms, half turning to Hastings, he raises an eyebrow seeming to telegraph *this will be good.* When Hastings smirks back, he offers magnanimously, "Go ahead."

"As I said, dealing had been going on behind the club, and at our other premises. Satan's Devils are known for keeping that shit away, so we presume someone saw sites other dealers were staying away from. Somewhere with a demand and no one supplying." I draw in a deep breath, knowing I need to choose my words carefully. "We don't need the wrong sort of reputation. We were there last night to try to keep that business away, not encourage it. We even knew there was going to be a heavy police presence and a SWAT team coming in."

Barker's eyes widen. "How?" he snaps.

I shrug. "You brought our VP in for questioning. He overheard a conversation." I'm not dropping Beef into anything. He'd done nothing wrong, it was them who were careless.

"You should have known to stay clear in that case."

"I did. Or tried to, at least."

He waves to indicate I should carry on, but his yawn suggests he's bored.

"I was waiting with Sparky. A man appeared from behind us. He was tall, not far off my height. Slim build. He was carrying a rucksack and something about him looked suspicious." *He, him. Keep emphasising he was male to throw them off the scent.* "I knew he wasn't the dealer."

"How?" Hastings interrupts.

My shoulders rise and fall. "Supposition. This man was nervous, scared. Could have been a user himself. He didn't have the confidence to be dealing. Also, he was totally unaware of his surroundings, whereas a dealer will always be on his toes, keeping one eye open for danger. Anyway, as he came past me all I could think was that bag might be holding drugs, and that he was a delivery boy. So, I went to confront him."

"He was heading toward the cops," Barker interrupts.

"I didn't know exactly where you'd set up. I thought there was a chance you could miss him. Tits Up is important to us, we have sworn to protect its reputation. Perhaps I wasn't thinking straight, all that was in my head was stopping drugs coming onto our premises."

"Carry on," Barker prompts, but his disinterested tone of voice suggests I'm not convincing him.

"I confronted him. There wasn't time to tell Sparky, and I needed to be quiet." I grimace as though annoyed. "I thought Sparky would be right behind me, instead he stayed where he was. Turns out he isn't a mind reader."

"So, you say you challenged this man?"

"I did. I grabbed the rucksack, and he ran off. I didn't think I could catch him, so decided to bring the bag and its contents to your lot. I was walking with it when the dealer… what did you call him? Fender? Like the guitar?" I wait for their nods. "Well, this Fender stepped out from the shadows and held a gun on me. I had no option but to pass him the rucksack, and the rest you know."

"You are correct that Mr McNeish had drugs in his possession, but only for a matter of seconds. He also was unaware exactly what was in the rucksack. Mr McNeish was performing a civic duty at the time." I could kiss Sykes for his excellent summation, but refrain.

"That's your story?" Barker scoffs.

"That's the truth," replies Sykes, giving his own look of challenge. "Mr McNeish has never met this…" he looks down at the notes he'd been taking, "Fender Childs in his life. He has no connection with Mr Childs."

"Then he was going to be dealing himself."

Sykes eyes widen. "Few things wrong with that. First, the Satan's Devils have no reputation for dealing drugs, in fact, the opposite. The police know they keep them away from that area of Pueblo."

"That could have changed," Hastings suggests. "Or Mr McNeish is the person responsible for dealing either with or without the blessing of his club."

Sykes shakes his head and continues, "Second, Mr McNeish and his club were aware that the police were staking out Tits Up and the surrounding area that night. Under those circumstances, if the dealer was aware of the presence of the cops, he would be a million miles away from the action. Not walking toward it as my client had done."

"So, Mr McNeish isn't the brightest tool in the box. Maybe he had customers he couldn't disappoint and thought he could get away with it."

Sykes eyebrows rise almost to his hairline. "My client is a Marine. I presume he's passed his aptitude tests."

"Mr McNeish is an ex-Marine. People change."

I seethe. *Once a Marine, always a Marine.* But I keep dumb. I'm worried about opening my mouth and anything I say being twisted.

"Do you need money, Mr McNeish?" Barker asks. "Are you dealing on the side?"

"I have a good job. I'm a mechanic and I work at our auto-shop. I live at the club, so my expenditure is small. I have more than enough for the things I want in life."

It's Hastings turn to scoff. "Anyone can get greedy." He taps the table with his fingers, then after a few seconds, proposes, "If we buy your story that another man was there, how about you just being opportunistic? Seeing what you thought were drugs and taking them, not to give up, but to sell yourself, or share with the club to provide funds?"

I do not want the club being dragged into this.

But Sykes gets in first. "Mr McNeish has just told you exactly what he was doing. He was heading *toward* the cops. He was going to turn what he'd found in. It's a shame the man slipped past him, but you have gotten the drugs off the street and have arrested this Fender Childs who presumably was going to sell them. I do not think you have a case against Mr McNeish and ask you to release him."

"We are continuing our investigations. While we do, Mr McNeish will stay on remand."

As I expected, I won't be going home to my club. Not today. Maybe never. Barker and Hastings weren't at all convinced by my story, and if I'm honest, I wasn't myself.

CHAPTER TWENTY

Beth

"What's going on?" I ask for the hundredth time, as Demon walks past.

"Beth," my mom says, "when they know something, they'll tell you." Her voice sounds tired and she looks pale. It had come as a shock to her to have been woken at dawn and then to find out she had boxes containing an unbelievable amount of drugs in her son's old bedroom, which Connor had stored without her knowledge and definitely not her approval. When she'd appeared in the clubhouse, she'd been shaking and demanding to know what was going on.

I think partly to shut her up, Demon had agreed I could bring her up to speed. She wouldn't have stopped without a full explanation of why I, and now she, were here. One question led to another, and I found I'd been unable to hold anything back as Mom used her best mother's investigative techniques to get to the bottom of what, who and why. With the result, she's now also having to deal with the information that her son is missing, and possibly injured or dead. In my view, she's holding up remarkably.

Demon's eyes flicker with concern as he views my mom

before his expression turns stern when he addresses me, "I've got no news, Beth, other than what I've already told you. Cad hasn't been successful getting any answer from the phone, and he's still working on finding your brother's location, or at least, where he made the calls from."

Yes. I knew that. Cad's been doing all he can to find Connor. That I can understand his difficult task, doesn't mean I like it. "It was more than twelve hours ago I last spoke to him," I cry out, reminding Demon. "Connor might be dead." I ignore the gasp from my mom, but it's not the first time I've voiced that fear. She already knows that either willing or not, her son set up her daughter, and that it was only Ink sacrificing himself that means it's not me locked up in a jail cell right now. I get to my feet and take hold of Demon's sleeve as if to stop him moving away. "Demon, there must be something we can do. Let me try to contact Phil…"

"Beth," he says sharply, "Phil Foster is a man we've got in our sights, but I want more information before I confront him. We've got to step carefully for now. I will do nothing that could jeopardise Ink getting his freedom—unless you know more about him than you've already told me?" When I shake my head —neither Mom nor I have anything other than the belief Phil's into shady dealings with no specifics at all—Demon continues, "I need to know whether Phil Foster is involved, and if so, in what way, before we approach him."

"Beth, come and sit down." Mom clearly realises Demon is fast approaching the point where he's going to stop being tolerant of my constant questions.

I release my hold on his sleeve, and Demon steps away. I sit again beside Mom on the couch. Jeannie appears, and two fresh cups of coffee are placed in front of us.

"You okay?" she asks, looking from one of us to the other.

Mindful Demon asked me to keep what I know to myself, I meet her eyes, and just confirm the little she already knows. "As much as anyone can be when the man they've been seeing has been arrested."

Her expression softens. "Seen it too often before, sweetie. Just sit tight and let the club sort it out."

That would be easier were it not all my fault, and if I wasn't the reason Ink had been taken by the police. Something everyone other than the women are very aware of.

Jeannie might have been sympathetic, and Mel, of course, is supportive though doesn't know the half of what's gone on. On the other hand, Ink's brothers who know it all give off a vibe they really don't want me here. So much so, rather than a friend of the club, I feel like an intruder. I shiver at just some of the looks sent my way and wish I were anywhere else but here. Question is, where's better? Cad's my best hope of finding Connor, and Demon is waiting on information about Ink. I'll just have to grow a thick skin around men who are blaming me that Ink isn't here.

Without Ink here, I'm nothing to the club, other than a friend of Mel's. No greater connection than being the fuck buddy of a brother who, down to no fault of his own, is now in jail.

I wanted to be something to Ink. Hell, I was going to talk to him about starting a real relationship, wasn't I? That he'd done what he did, stopped me from being arrested, surely suggests he's got feelings for me too? Fuck Connor for messing up two lives. Though I'm trying to hang onto the hope that Ink might walk free and we can have the discussion I've been planning. Though it's more likely, he'll want nothing to do with me. No one else has bought my explanation for what I did.

Everyone here, including Mom, thinks I've been stupid. I can't criticise them for that. There are a hundred other routes I could have taken, none of which would have ended with their innocent brother behind bars. In the cold light of this Sunday morning, my reasoning last night is questionable at best, and it's not just me being punished for it. That the man who could have been the love of my life is lost to me now, tears my heart in two.

But what shreds it into pieces is when I wonder what he's going through. *What's he thinking?* I feel so damn miserable, and so damn guilty.

When Jeannie walks off and is out of hearing, Mom turns to face me. Her lips thin. "Take me through it again, Bethany. Starting with why you didn't tell me Connor was in trouble."

My lips, copying her expression, press together and I shake my head. "I don't even know if that was a lie, Mom. Maybe he knew the cops were staking it out and didn't want to be caught himself."

Mom frowns. "I don't have any time for your father, you know that. But I thought Connor would come to his senses one day, not that he was beyond redemption. If he set you up, Beth, then there's no hope for him. I can't believe my son would do that."

Neither can I. "Perhaps he's an addict himself, Mom? Perhaps he'd do anything to score."

"Score?" An incredulous laugh escapes. "He doesn't need to score. Not with ten spare kilos of H he can leave in his old room."

She's got a point.

"You okay?" The older biker with ginger hair comes over and sits down. Like Demon, his concern is for my mom. "Still feeling shaky?"

Mom shakes her head. "I'm not *okay,* but I'm starting to deal. I'm just so pleased you've taken that stuff away." She shudders. Rusty leans forward and puts his hand on her arm, then moving his fingers down feels her pulse. She lets him. He'd introduced himself as a medic. He doesn't appear to have much time for me but does for my totally innocent mom.

Anxiously I watch his face, but he doesn't seem worried.

It's been a shock for us both. For a week we've stored an incredible amount of drugs in our home. What if the police had come searching? Or rival criminals? Or disreputable friends of my brother who'd left it there? He must have known he was putting both of us in danger. There are so many unanswered questions. Who do the drugs belong to? If Connor, where the hell did he get the money to buy them? And if, more likely, it's someone else, who, and what lengths will they go to, to recover them?

My thoughts prompt me to ask, "What did the club do with it?"

Rusty's eyes narrow at my question. He rests back in his chair. "Don't you worry about that."

"Has it been destroyed?"

He doesn't deign to answer. Instead he gives Mom such an intense look, she shifts a little uncomfortably. "You've had a shock, darlin'. You start to feel rough? You just say." With that he stands and moves off.

"I wonder what they've done with the drugs?" It seems I can't get that off my mind.

Mom considers for a moment. "They might not destroy them immediately. Might need them as leverage, I don't know. Offer them up to the cops, perhaps? Plant them on someone?"

I stare at her, my eyes wide.

"What?" she shrugs. "I watch crime shows. You know, where bad guys are set up."

Just like that she's reminded me of Ink. "Like I set Ink up," I say, glumly.

"I still don't know why you did something so crazy, Bethany. You should have informed the police as soon as you found that Connor might be in danger, and definitely when you found what he had stored. Then Ink wouldn't be in the position he is."

"What would you have done, Mom?" I challenge angrily. "Connor could have been, might still have been, telling the truth. His life could have depended on me doing what he said. I didn't have any time, I was too scared for him to think of myself. Of course I knew what was in it as soon as I'd opened that damn box. The last thing I thought of was calling 911. It didn't even cross my mind. I couldn't take the risk that Connor would have been killed."

"Or that's what he told you."

"That's what I believed at the time, or if those drugs are his, he could have been arrested."

"Then the right man would be sitting in jail."

I gasp. Her blunt statement is the truth. Trust Mom to give it to me straight. "I've been so, so stupid." She's right. If Connor's dealing heroin, he'd deserve a long sentence, much more than the man who is locked up.

Her hand comes out and rests on mine. "You're a good sister," she says, her tone gentling. "What would I have done?" She thinks about it for a few seconds, her brow creasing. "If I had been put on the spot, needing to make a fast decision while being told it was a matter of life or death, I'd like to think different, but have to say, I'd probably have done the same thing as you under the circumstances." She pauses, then looks straight into my eyes. "Ink must think one hell of a lot about you, Beth, to do what he did."

I could tell her Ink's a good man, that he'd have done it for anyone, but I'm pretty certain that's not true. He did it for me, even though I didn't ask him to. "I think he must," I reply at last.

"And what about you? What are your feelings for him?"

"I think I could love him, Mom." I might even be there already. What more could a girl ask for but someone who's as good as Ink in the bedroom, fun out of it, and prepared to do anything to keep her safe?

"You're not someone who'd be happy with a brief fling, Beth. You might have tried to kid yourself you could have walked away if he asked you to, but I reckon your heart would be broken. I was scared, I admit, when you started this relationship, not about him being who he is, but that I thought you would get hurt."

"The thought of not being able to be with him again, Mom. The thought of only seeing him in a visiting room…"

"It might not come to that," she rebukes firmly. "We'll find Connor, build a case, and get Ink out."

If only that was going to be so easy to do. Now the cops have gotten ahold of a Devil, they're not going to casually let him go. But Mom's right, for now, I've got to stay as positive as I can.

"You doing okay, Beth?" Mel comes over, indicates I should scoot over, and sits beside me.

It's down to her that I'm not a quivering wreck. When I'd been brought up from the basement, she'd been there and just allowed me to cry without asking questions. All I could tell her was Ink had been arrested, but I couldn't tell her why. Surprisingly, she'd seemed to understand that I couldn't give her more. Just her being there was a comfort to me. When Mom had arrived, she'd made herself scarce so we could talk.

"I'll be better when we know what's going on," I tell my friend. "This isn't me, Mel. I don't sit on my hands when I could be doing something to help."

"But what could you do? Ink obviously got himself into this mess. He's got to get himself out of it." She frowns. "The club will be doing all that needs to be done."

But she hasn't a clue of the part I played, nor that if I could go to the cops, Ink would surely be released. Unless Demon is right, and they'd still implicate him as well.

At that moment the door to the clubhouse opens and a cold draft sweeps in, along with a man wearing a suit. Immediately I freeze, and it's not from the temperature drop. *Is he a detective?*

But when Rusty goes across and warmly shakes his hand, then leads him in the direction of Demon's office, I realise he looks more like a friend of the club, or, possibly, a lawyer.

If that's what he is, maybe he's got news.

Mel's talking about anything and everything just trying to distract me, but I can only concentrate on the thoughts in my head and everyone about Ink.

I hate this. Hate sitting around unable to do anything. I'm

upset, frustrated, and furious at Connor and at myself, as well as angry at the bikers who don't seem to be doing anything.

Suddenly I stand. Mel stops her conversation with my mom as the latter narrows her eyes suspiciously. "What are you doing, Beth?"

"I'm going to ring Phil." I don't care what Demon says. I need to do something.

"No, you're not." Mom gets to her feet fast, her hand landing on my arm, and leading me out of earshot of my friend. "You are not getting yourself in any deeper with this. You heard Demon. You could be making things worse and not better." She wipes a hand across her brow. "You were a little girl when he left, you don't know what he's capable of, Beth, I do. He'd never do anything to implicate himself. If he's behind this, he wouldn't be beyond letting you, or especially a man he doesn't know, take the fall for him."

I open my mouth to say it's down to me to try to sort the fix Ink is now in, when Beef comes out of Demon's office and walks over to me.

"Can you come and speak to the lawyer, Beth?"

Try and stop me. I walk so fast the VP struggles to keep up. Opening Demon's door, I barge straight in.

Demon eyes me tiredly and shakes his head. "Do come in," he starts, pointedly, then proceeds to the introductions. "Beth, this is Sykes, the club lawyer. Sykes, this is the woman Ink was involved with, Beth."

"I gathered that," the lawyer says drily as he stands, shakes my hand, and glances up into my face.

"How's Ink?" I ask fast. In my mind I imagine him hurt and bleeding. Yeah, well, Mom's not the only one who watches crime shows on TV and knows about the police brutality.

"Ink's fine. I'm working on getting him out."

Words I want to hear but find hard to believe. For some reason, meeting Ink's lawyer has made this all too real. I can't let this go on, if it's in my power to stop it. "I want to go to the police," I tell him. "Would it do any good?"

Sykes stares up intently, then motions me to a seat. When we're sitting, and he can look me straight in the eye, he gives me an answer, "From what I hear from Ink, it could make matters worse. I don't see how you could help him without you both ending up locked up. At the very least, they'd have Ink for aiding and abetting." He sighs. "Look at it this way. You brought the heroin with the intention of delivering it to the dealer, Ink ended up doing just that. If I were prosecuting, I'd present the case as that having been the way you arranged it between you."

I digest that for a moment, reluctantly coming to the conclusion that I have to agree he's right.

"It's all my fault." When the lawyer raises his chin and lowers it, I know he's not going to argue my point. "I was the idiot who believed my brother. I was the one who took the drugs to the drop. I was the one—"

Sykes holds up his hand. "Demon's filled me in. Let me play devil's advocate here. Your mother had a serious quantity of heroin stored in her house for a week. Who says she didn't know it was there? Your brother sounds like he could very well be a criminal. Who's to say you're not as well? Your father is thought to run a gang out of Denver. You're associated with him too, just by your relationship."

"None of that is true…"

"May not matter to the cops. Once they start digging who knows what they'll put together?"

"Should Beth hear Ink's story?" Demon asks.

Sykes nods. "Yes, for the reason that if she came forward now, it would make Ink out a liar. Ink's saying," he turns to me and looks me up and down, "that a man, tall and slim appeared. Ran off when Ink confronted him and dropped the bag. Ink picked it up and was taking it to the cops, when the dealer took it off him at gunpoint."

"Plausible." Demon nods.

"Flimsy, but it's up to the cops to prove otherwise."

"I'll make sure Sparky knows what Ink's putting forward."

"Is Ink allowed visitors? Can I at least call him?" I want to tell him how sorry I am, that however long it takes, I'll be waiting for him. If he ends up in prison, whatever sentence he'll be serving, I'll do that time too.

Demon exchanges glances with Sykes, and it's the MC prez who tells me, "Ink doesn't want to see you, Beth. He doesn't want to talk to you."

"But…"

"Beth. Whatever relationship you had with Ink, well, consider it over."

"He blames me?" Of everything I'd been thinking, even when I was paralysed by my guilt, I hadn't imagined he'd cut all ties with me. Why put himself in this position if he didn't care for me at all? I bite my lip. Seems like he's regretting his actions, and that in saving me, he's looking at years inside. Unless his story holds up. I'd suspected I wouldn't be his favourite person but hoped he'd at least have heard me out. Now it seems I won't have a chance to give my side of the story. "Demon—"

"Beth, no. It's over between you. Best you forget you ever knew Ink."

My anguished eyes meet his firm ones, and oh God, while I'd thought I'd prepared myself, I hadn't. A tear rolls down my cheek, and I wipe it away

The lawyer clears his throat, then stands. "Well, I'll leave you now. You'll keep me updated, Demon, with anything you find out?"

"I will and thank you."

"You'll get my bill."

With that Sykes opens the door and leaves. I swallow hard to keep back the tears that threaten to follow the first one that had fallen. Believing the meeting must be over, I start to get to my feet.

"Sit, Beth."

I obey, my brow furrowed.

Demon drums his fingers on the table. "Look, Beth, I'll be honest. Brothers aren't happy with you right now. They believe you're responsible for putting Ink into the position he's in. You know yourself this situation is fucked up, how much of it was your own making or your brother's we don't know yet. Our focus is Ink, and well, if there's blowback on you, maybe you deserve it in their eyes."

I stay dumb. I could protest my innocence again, but it wouldn't do me any good. While I think Demon believes me, I could understand why Ink's club brothers don't. And even if they did think I'd been telling the truth, because I tried to save my brother on my own, I brought trouble on a member of the club.

"Can't put this plainer, Beth. Ink's cut you loose, for more than one reason." I just stare at him dumbly while he lists them off. "First, he's angry as he's entitled to be. He doesn't know yet why you had two kilos of H on you last night, but he's not in a place where he's willing to give you the benefit of the doubt."

"But when he knows…"

Demon moves his head side to side. "It's over, Beth. As I said, for more than one reason. The other being, he's managed to find a way to keep you out of it. Think of your mom if not yourself. Ink and the club have attracted the interest of the cops. They'll investigate anyone connected to him and to us. Ink gave up his freedom so you could walk free. You owe it to him to keep out of trouble, and that means keeping well clear. You have to deny there was ever anything going on between you and Ink."

"A lot of people know I had a relationship with him…"

"Not a relationship, Beth. Ink fucks. Nothing more to it."

I lower my head, letting it rest in my cupped palms. Ink obviously hates me, even if he were to get out, there's no me and him and won't ever be. All because I fucked up. Now the club is washing their hands of me and I can't deny I deserve it.

"What about Connor? Are you still going to try to find him?"

Demon's eyes harden. "Yes, Beth. We won't stop tracking him down."

"If you find him, will you tell us?"

I don't like the expression on his face, it's so cold it makes me shiver. Well, there's no point them telling me he's alive if they're only going to kill him shortly after.

All Demon gives me is, "I'll tell you what I can."

"It's no good me begging for his life, is it?"

Demon stays quiet.

"Mom and I will go home." I frown, thinking we'll just have to put our heads together and decide what to do. The drugs have been removed, of course, but what if someone comes calling for them? I try to shelve that worry, there's no point mentioning my worries to Demon. His focus is trying to get Ink out of jail, not looking out for the woman who put him there.

Demon raps his knuckles on the desk, getting my attention. "You can't stay here, Beth. One thing's for certain, police love to raid us, and Ink has given them just the excuse they need to get a warrant for searching the compound. I don't want them to find you here, it would be impossible to deny a connection if they did."

"You didn't bring the drugs here?" I say fast, worried that I've brought more trouble to the club.

His raised eyebrow speaks volumes. Of course, they didn't.

"You need to go home, go to work. Keep up appearances. But we won't be leaving you unprotected, Beth. I'll arrange someone to be at the house with you, just in case, until we know whoever owns the drugs won't be coming looking for them."

For a moment I'm stunned, replaying his words to make sure I understood them correctly. That was the last thing I'd expected. "You don't need to do that, Demon."

"Not doing it for you, Beth. I've got a man inside and I want to look out for his sanity. He might not want you, but what he did was for you. Makes his actions a bit of a waste if you end up dead after all."

"Will you tell me what happens with Ink? I know he doesn't want to see me, and I'll stay away. But it's my sanity at risk here, too. Please, Demon, whatever happens, let me know how he's doing."

Demon's eyes flare as they focus on me. "I'll tell you what I can, Beth."

CHAPTER TWENTY-ONE

Mace

I'm the enforcer for the Colorado chapter of the Satan's Devils, a role I'd stepped into a couple of years back, and one I feel I was made for. Of course, I'd rather not have had the vacancy arise in the way that it had, when Ingot, the previous enforcer, had been killed. One of my first jobs had been to deal with the man who we belatedly discovered had murdered him. As it turned out, he'd been killed by one of our own. Taser had died screaming. I'd made sure of that.

I'd been voted into the position as I'm not afraid of doing what has to be done. It was partly Taser who'd spurred me on to be the best fucking enforcer the MC ever had. Having cast doubts on my abilities, I'd set out to prove him wrong.

The natural leanings inside me which make me good in my role are also probably the reason I'm not coping well right now without a target to vent my frustration on, or someone to question in ways that would ease this beast inside.

I'm seething with rage, way beyond angry. My brother's been locked up and in no way does he deserve it. My hands curl into fists, and I hit them against each other, wishing I could use them on someone's head. There's a particular someone I have in mind.

That bitch Ink hooked up with, whose fault it is my brother is where he is, deserves my anger. Fuck, I wish Demon had let me loose on her. Firstly, because my methods would have left us in no doubt whether what was coming out of her mouth was the truth, and secondly, it would have made me feel better.

For more than one reason, I wish it had been me she'd targeted at Pyro's wedding instead of Ink. Selfishly, I wouldn't have minded those long legs which go on for miles wrapped around me, and second, I'm not so much of an idiot about women as Ink has turned out to be. If I'd been the one seeing her walking into a trap, I would have stood by and happily watched her put her head in the noose. No bitch is worth doing time for, particularly when she'd been the one committing the crime. He should have left her to get what she deserved.

This story about her brother and her not knowing she was storing drugs? Who the fuck can believe that? Not this man, that's for certain.

Disbelief is the primary emotion for most of us this morning. A morning when I didn't wake from my bed—no, I've not even lain in it since the night before last—a morning which has seen me having to fist my hands to stop torturing a woman I'm sure knows more than she was telling, and then to top it off, a morning which saw me collecting said bitch's mom from her house and delivering her back to the compound.

Thank fuck Rusty had been with me. I'd gone in, all guns blazing, well, hypothetically that is, but the old man had kept calm. It was his arm that had supported Patsy when she had what seemed a very genuine reaction to finding she was still storing eight kilos of heroin in one of her bedrooms.

I'd left her with Rusty when we'd returned, making sure Beaver had instructions to take the drugs immediately up to the cabin that isn't registered in our name. Now I'm back at the club-house, an energy to burn off, and no target I can touch.

"This is the fuckin' pits, Brother." Thunder comes up by my side. "I'd kick that bitch down to the cops myself if I had a choice."

"Demon seems to think it wouldn't get Ink off." I feel crease lines appear on my brow. "Could be he's right. Cops might work it to say they're in it together. You know what it's like when they get one of us behind bars."

"Hard as fuck to get out," Thunder reluctantly agrees. "Still her fuckin' fault. Even if she was telling the truth, she should have left her waste-of-space brother to wallow in his own muck."

I answer with a chin lift. That's my view as well.

I have a beer, and then another. I turn down a third, then looking around, nudge the sergeant-at-arms. "Hey, looks like our visitors are leaving."

"'Bout fuckin' time." He, too, turns and views Patsy and Beth's backs as they head out the door. Beth's head is down, her chin almost to her chest. "Wonder what Prez said to them?"

Get lost and stay lost, I hope. Seeing her face just reminds me Ink's not here.

"Mace? Get your ass in church. Thunder?" As Demon's eyes go around the room, he only has to name a few people before everyone stops what they're doing and heads his way.

Cad's the last into our meeting room, and when he enters, I notice every seat bar one is filled. Not surprising, everyone's staying close, eager to offer whatever they can to help, even if it's no more than giving each other support. My rage rises again as I stare down the table at the empty space where Ink should be sitting.

"Don't need to tell you why we're here," Demon starts. I notice, like most of us, he looks drawn, running on adrenaline and too little sleep. His eyes, like mine, survey the occupants of the seats around the table before he continues, "Only one topic on the agenda today. But before we get to discussing his situation, I've something to kick off with. I know how you're going to react to this, so no point delaying the inevitable. Ink's gotten word to me via Sykes." He pauses, clears his throat, making me suspect it's something I don't want to hear.

Is Ink going to plead guilty? Surely not.

When Demon finally opens his mouth to enlighten us, what comes out is quite possibly worse.

"Okay, let me get this out in the open. Ink wants to claim Beth."

Loud exclamations and snorts of derision go around the table with a loud 'Fuck no' from me. The commotion is such, Demon has to bang the gavel and call two or three times for silence. When we've calmed sufficiently, he points toward Hellfire who's indicating there's something he wants to get off his chest.

"Ink and Beth weren't heading that way," Hell observes. "Least not from what I saw. What the fuck's changed?"

I look down at my hands, wanting to keep my mouth shut, yet in fairness to my brother know I have to speak up. "There was more to them than just fuckin'. Ink told me I'd better get used to seeing her in the mornings," I admit. "Before... Well, he didn't mention anything about claiming as such. And why the fuck now? After what she's done to him?"

Demon shrugs. "Obvious, isn't it? Do I need to remind anyone claimin' an ol' lady puts them under our protection? By claimin' Beth as his old lady, he's making her part of the club. Bringing her into it as we abide by our rules and regulations. One of which is, I need to stress, if a brother goes inside, we look after his ol' lady."

"You suggestin' prison rights?" Liz perks up. "Don't mind taking over."

If Thunder hadn't reached over and clouted him hard around the head, I would have done it myself and used more force. As it is, Liz reels and puts a hand to his skull, ruefully rubbing it. But his cocky grin has been replaced by a look of regret.

"Too fuckin' soon, Bro," Judge tells him.

I turn my attention back to the prez. "No. Just... No. That shit ain't happening, Prez. She's already got one of us locked up. We're now in possession of eight kilos of H which we shouldn't have. We don't know who the rightful owners are, but knowing we have it, Beth now holds information that could bring down this fuckin' club. I'd prefer her six feet under where she can't talk. No way in hell is she getting my vote."

I get murmurs of agreement from quite a few directions, coupled with growls of 'I'm not fuckin' voting her in.'

"Sparky," Demon says, tiredly, as I notice the road captain trying to get Prez's attention.

Unusual for the normally mild-mannered man, when he's given permission to speak, Sparky's hand slams down on the table causing all eyes to go to him.

"Can I fuckin' remind you that our brother is currently sitting in a jail cell looking at thirty years or more behind bars? I say the very least we should be doing is making his mind easier. And if to do that means taking his woman under our wing, maybe we shouldn't dismiss it."

"But Sparks, we don't know how the bitch is tied up in this. Bring her inside the club, who knows what she could infect us with."

"You trust Ink?" Now Sparky's got the floor, he's not giving it up. "Think he doesn't know when something's right or not? He's sacrificed his freedom because of her, which shows how much she means to him, and how important to him it is that she's taken care of by the club."

"Sparky's got a good point," Demon says sharply after banging the gavel to get us to quiet down once again. "Never expected Ink would claim anyone, but his actions last night showed this woman clearly means one fuckin' lot to him." He pauses. "I agree, if she's up to her neck in drugs coming into Pueblo, we can't vote her in. Yet I, for one, am inclined to believe what she's saying is the truth. But we're not bringing her into the club. As far as she knows, Ink's cut all ties with her. He doesn't want any contact with her."

"Let me get this right. He's claimin' a woman and not telling her shit?"

Demon grimaces, but just raises his chin in reply.

Guess it makes it easier that I'll not have to watch her living it up while her man, which Ink now is, is inside. "You say you believe her, Prez? Why?" I don't.

"She was too fuckin' gullible if she believed her brother," Bomber sneers.

"Not gullible, Bomber," Beef refutes, "too innocent. We look for a hidden motive behind everything 'cause we're suspicious bastards and we have to be. Wouldn't survive otherwise. But Ink's girl has lived a sheltered life."

"With that father?" Thunder sounds incredulous.

"She doesn't have anything to do with her father. Hasn't seen him since he walked out when she was what, nine?" Pyro rolls his eyes.

"Got a suggestion." Hellfire's voice booms from the end of the table. "We give her the protection that Ink wants, but we don't vote her in until we've caught up with Connor and hear what he has to say. If he's still breathing that is."

"And if he's dead?" Bomber asks.

Hell shrugs. "Sort of confirms she's telling the truth."

Demon gives his father a quick nod. "I'm inclined to agree with Hellfire. We respect Ink but hedge our bets. All in favour?"

I think we can all live with that. I, for one, expect to find Connor Foster very much alive, kicking back and enjoying his freedom while my brother is suffering in hell. I give my agreement with a caveat. "If Beth's played Ink, is playing us, I want her taken out." And I'll be the one to fucking do it.

Demon raises an eyebrow, but it seems in the case which I believe most likely, I'm not the only one who'd want her dispatched to meet Satan. Would balance the scales if Ink loses the best years of his life.

Buzzard hastily records our decision. Prez gives him time to do it. When his pen stops scratching, it's Thunder who asks, "What else did Sykes get from Ink?"

Demon enlightens us. "The story Ink's told the cops might be full of holes, but with any luck it should hold enough water to stay afloat. Look, I know we all hate that he's inside, but he is, and we've got to rely on Sykes that he can spin it the right way. In the meantime, with Sykes working the legal angle, we'll keep digging to see if there's anything we can find that might help."

Demon jerks his chin at Cad. "The man who was arrested, the man who pulled a gun on Ink and was obviously expecting the delivery of H was called Fender Childs. I want you to dig up all you can on him."

"On it." The tech guy makes a note on the tablet he'd brought in. "Black? White?"

Demon shakes his head but makes a note on the pad. "No idea. I'll ask Sykes. Did you see anything, Sparky?"

"Not Black. White, or maybe Hispanic. It was dark, remember, and I was too intent on getting Beth away to take much notice."

Cad's tablet pings. He fist bumps the air and sits forward, not waiting for permission to interrupt. "I've come up with a location for Connor Foster. Or at least, where his phone call originated from."

Now that's a step forward. I can't wait to start asking Beth's brother questions in any one of my preferred ways. Men tend to talk while their fingernails are being pulled out.

"Where is it, Cad?"

"Prez, it's a warehouse on the very outskirts of Denver."

Beef looks concerned. "Warehouse? We're talking large quantities of drugs. Could be a base for their operations. Could be a fuckload of manpower there. Don't like the thought of us going in blind."

Yeah. Beef's observation makes sense. You don't have your hands on that amount of shit without being able to protect it. Then there are the workers packaging it up. We've no idea of how it's brought in, or how many might be needed to process it—

"We'll use the new drone."

As his voice breaks into my thoughts, my eyes snap to Pal who, I notice, looks smug.

"Yeah," Pal continues, exchanging a smirk with Cad. "Cad and I were trying it out last week. We don't need to get too close to send it in. It means we can see what's going on, or at least, how many vehicles there are and whether people are going in and out. If there's a convenient window, we might even be able to see inside."

Well that's a great fucking idea. Hands bang the table in appreciation.

"Good plan, Brother," Demon says.

"I've also got a home address for the dad, Phil Foster," Cad states. "Beth seems clear Connor lives with the man. Might be worth checking out to see if Connor's gone home."

"This Phil, anything to connect him to drugs?"

"Not that I've found, but then he'd hardly have it on his resume. Extortion, money laundering… those are the charges the cops have brought but have never been able to make stick."

Sounds like this Foster's some crafty fucker to me.

"Could be that Connor's branching out on his own," Beef puts in.

Demon's fist bumps the top of the desk. "That's why we need to find him." He closes his eyes for a second, then reopens them. "I say we go to the warehouse first, that's where Connor was last night and might still be there. Mace, Thunder. You head out with… Liz, yeah. You okay to go Ro? Right. Pyro, Judge and Wills, and of course Pal to operate the drone. You take the warehouse. I want to get inside and tear that place apart. If you need more manpower, we'll be right behind you and rolling. Beef, Hellfire…" he pauses.

"You want us to check out Phil Foster's place?" Hell asks.

Demon thinks for a moment. "We don't know how or whether he's involved, or if he is, how deeply. It could be him who's behind it. Going straight to his lair tips our hand. See what we find at the warehouse first. That will determine any future conversation with Phil."

"Makes sense, Prez," says his VP. "Hell and I can be ready to roll once we know what kind of words we'll need to exchange with Foster Sr."

In case they'll be telling him, his son is dead, I presume he means. Doubt it. If anyone asked me, I'd say my money was on Phil Foster being up to his fucking neck in this shit, along with his son and Beth. Fuckin' family affair. Patsy? Maybe not her, it's hard to feint that degree of shock when she found she'd been storing heroin in her home, but who the fuck knows? Green talks. Loudly.

"You want us to leave now?" I offer, getting ready to stand. I'm eager to be doing something, anything.

Prez glares at me. "Rushing off half-cocked could get us killed. We need to have a plan. If Connor's dead, there's no rush, and if he's alive, he'll have no idea we're coming for him. There're other things at play here, and I want to be as prepared as we can."

I'm just itching to get my hands on Connor. He and his father can confirm if Beth was in on it the whole time, or whether they set her up. If they did, they'll be the ones largely responsible for Ink going down. Only half listening to the meeting, I remember last night and her offer to go to the cops herself. Had that been genuine? I couldn't be sure at the time, my anger perhaps clouding my judgement. Ink had made the decision though, he preferred to be taken than her. What does he know that I don't?

If she really is as innocent and unworldly as Ink must think, she could have been the victim of expert criminals and the very people who were supposed to have her best interests at heart. Christ, she'd be gutted if that turns out to be the truth. I realise the edge of my anger toward her has been taken off at that thought.

CHAPTER TWENTY-TWO

Mace

My embryonic sympathy prompts me to ask, "What are you going to do about Beth and her mom, Prez?"

Demon purses his lips. "I sent them home." I know that. I saw them leave.

"Drugs are gone, Prez," Beef reminds him. "What if someone goes calling expecting them to be right where they were left?"

Demon frowns at Beef. "You think I haven't fuckin' considered that? Two defenceless women against fuck knows who? Ink's claimed her which brings her under our protection. But he also wants to deny his relationship with her to the citizen world and keep her out of the clutches of the cops. And," he pauses and looks at each of us, "as far as Beth knows, Ink's finished with her for good. There is no relationship, and if anyone points the cops her way, she'll confirm all they did was fuck a couple of times."

Ouch. That must have been a slap in the face for her. No wonder she looked down when she left. Perhaps I'm getting some of the payback I was hoping for.

"All that falls apart if they stay here on the compound," Prez finishes up.

"Would they be safer in a safe house?" Pal asks.

Pyro is frowning. "Beth's kept no secret of seeing a biker from her friends. Anyone who was at the wedding saw them go off together, and that includes her work colleagues. It's possible when the cops start digging, they'll want to know how closely she was involved with him, and what she knows about where Ink was last night and why. It will be mighty suspicious if she's not at home."

"Or what if the cops manage to trace the drugs back to Connor? What if somehow it becomes known they were hidden in that house…"

"Oh, so, he left a return address in the packaging…" says the sergeant-at-arms sarcastically.

Beef is fast on his feet and around the other side of the table, his fist, quite rightly, gets Thunder in the gut. Then he returns to his seat calmly and continues his train of thought. "There are always signs, fingerprints perhaps. We're talking about someone who left a million dollars' worth of smack in boxes casually stored with his mom," he reminds us. "So yeah, Thunder, he may have left a calling card."

"Beth picked up the packages," I remind them. "If her fingerprints are in the system, they will know she has to be involved."

"Why would her fingerprints be in AFIS?" Pal asks. "Doubt that girl's ever been arrested in her life."

"She works for the government," Pyro observes. "Same as Mel. Think it's standard practice to take them when they're first employed."

"Do they automatically pass them on?"

Cad's nodding his head. "Yup. Since 2015, the FBI stores fingerprints taken by employers and anyone else, together with personal info in their criminal database. If she's been working there longer than that, then she's probably okay. But it's a risk they already have them."

"Hey," Pyro stares at Cad, "I had my fingerprints taken when I applied for a motor vehicle dealer license. Does that mean mine are now in the system?"

"Since 2015?" Cad queries.

"Yup."

Cad's nod back gives Pyro all the confirmation he needs. "Fuck." But he follows it up with a chin lift of his own. "Good to know, brother."

"Alright, alright. Anyone worried speak to Cad later. Mace, you've got something?"

My lips press together. Ink wants us to protect her. The only way we can do that is if we know all the cards the cops hold. If Beth's fingerprints turn up on the packages of H, we need to know they can't be traced back to her. If they can, we could be facing another whole level of problems. "Yeah, Prez, I think we need to ask her whether her fingerprints have been taken recently." Christ, I hope they're not. Ink's sacrifice could be for nothing if the cops pick her up after all.

Demon's fingers drum the top of the desk again. "I agree. We might end up having to hide her from the cops." He rakes his hands back through his hair. "Jeez. Ink's given up his freedom and put her under our protection. If we don't keep her out of jail, we're failing him. We'll be a brother down, and his woman will suffer as well."

It seems incredible that Ink has claimed a woman. For a second, I wonder whether Demon's heard wrong. But why he did it is obvious, it was to force our hand, so we'll look after her. Serious step to be taking though. No one claims a woman lightly, and never just temporarily even if that's what I think is in Ink's head. Whatever his thought process, we've got to proceed as if it's permanent. Or at least until there's proof that she's lying, then all bets are off.

"That was a serious amount of shit hidden in Patsy's house. Where did the dough come from?" I wonder aloud. "Someone will have paid out for that. I can't believe it was Beth's brother."

"Phil Foster seems the obvious candidate."

Cad dips and raises his head, then backs up the prez. "His

lifestyle might suggest he could put his hands on that amount of cash."

"He was an accountant." Buzzard's obviously up to speed. "I certainly wouldn't discount him."

Buzz has got a point. Mind you, he's a money man, which is why he's our treasurer.

"The drugs could have been stolen."

"In which case," I reply to Prez, "we won't be the only ones looking for Connor." This is the reason Demon held me back from being a hothead and rushing off. Looking at a problem from all angles may use up time, but it helps to be prepared. I exchange a look with Thunder. We'll need eyes at our six. Best man to have with us would be Ink, he was a Marine. But if he was here and not locked up, I wouldn't be facing a ride out to Denver. "We need more men," I suggest.

Hellfire's quick. "Beef and I will ride with you. Then we're in town to go see the old man should Connor not be at the warehouse."

Demon raises his chin. Seems he agrees. Then he turns to me. "Mace, can you check with Beth about her fingerprints? Want to decide what we do with her and her mom. I want to be prepared when the cops come calling as they invariably will."

Prez is right. They're probably getting a warrant as we speak. If Beth's name's going to come up, we'll need to have thought how to manage it.

Half an hour ago, talking to Beth in a reasonable tone would have been the last thing I wanted to do. While she's not exonerated in my eyes, I have come around to the view that by claiming her, Ink's shown she means something to him. If keeping her safe brings him some peace, when there's little else I can do to help, I'll do it. I nod, and without delay, get out of my seat to go do the task I've been given.

Outside the meeting room, I stand for a second with my forehead resting against the wall. I'm tired, there's a throbbing ache behind my eyes, but the day is far from over. Lighting a cigarette, I breathe in smoke, then exhale as I collect my phone from the box we leave such devices in while in church, then tap on the number Cad had already texted me.

I know I've got to handle this carefully. It's not a stupid woman I'm dealing with, even though she may be ignorant of the darker side of life.

"Hi, Beth. It's Mace. Need to ask you something. Were you fingerprinted when you got your job?"

"Yes. Years ago, when I first started there."

"Before 2015?"

"Yes. Why?"

The magic date. Seems like she could be in the clear. I ask another question to make sure. "Have you ever been arrested and fingerprinted?"

"No," she replies quickly, "I have not. Why the questions, Mace?"

"Thank—" I start to say, but she's speaking again. Now she sounds timid and scared as the implications sink in.

"I haven't been arrested but have had my fingerprints taken. A couple of years back we were burgled. They took both Mom's and mine for the purpose of elimination." She gives a squeak. "But surely they won't have kept them?"

Well, fuck. From what Cad says, nowadays once they have them, they go onto AFIS.

Now she's continuing, she sounds thoughtful as though she's thinking back, "I wore gloves, Mace. My fingerprints aren't on the packages. I made sure of that." Her voice lightens as she remembers.

"The bag. Where did that come from?" I want to cover all bases.

"Oh, shit. The rucksack was mine. I've had it for years."

I think fast. "What was it made of?"

"Canvas. With a plastic handle and strap."

Jeez. They can lift fingerprints from that. She might as well have placed a flashing neon sign over her head.

"Will they be able to tell it's mine?"

Yes. "Look, Beth. Try not to worry. If they examine the bag, all they can tell is that you touched it, but not the drugs, okay? Let me take this back to Demon."

"Try not to worry?" Beth huffs, her incredulity coming down the line.

"I, or someone, will call you back."

Returning to the meeting, I don't waste time, knowing Beth and probably by now her mom, will be worrying themselves silly now they realise there's something that links Beth to the crime.

After I deliver the bad news, the prez and VP seem to have a conversation without words. Incongruously, it strikes me how well they've adjusted to working as a team, almost as smoothly as Hellfire and Demon used to. Thunder, while a great sergeant-at-arms never wore the VP hat so comfortably, whereas Beef seems a natural.

At last Demon speaks, his forefinger touching his nose. "We could hide Beth and her mom which would scream their guilt, or they could stay home, and Beth could continue to go about her daily routine. She already knows she's got to deny she had a relationship with Ink."

"How good an actor is she?" Hellfire asks. "If she can act normally, she could get away with it. There's nothing for the cops to find if they search the house. And nothing to link her or Patsy to any wrongdoing."

"Except for the rucksack that would take them there in the first place," I point out.

"They threw it out? Good enough story, nothing to disprove? Or lost it?" Sparky suggests.

Beef nods. "Yeah. Weak, but might throw them off the scent. I can't see how they can charge a civilian with no record, no obvious need of money, nor signs of a habit with being in possession of heroin."

"She could say she gave the rucksack to Connor. Drop her brother in it?" Cad suggests.

I purse my lips and shake my head. "If she's telling the truth, she got into this as she thought her brother was in trouble. Doubt she'd want to offer him up, unless she has proof he set her up."

"We'll deal with Connor," Demon says tersely. "Don't like any man, family or not, setting up females. Doesn't matter if he had an excuse."

"Which leaves us with the problem of what happens when Connor finds the rest of his drugs are missing," I observe. "Or whoever else is looking. Just how are we going to provide protection for Beth and her mom when the cops may turn up any moment, and we're trying to deny there's any relationship between them and the club?"

Demon again does that characteristic thing where he's thinking, then suddenly raises his chin. "I told them we'd send them protection, but I don't like using any of us. Cops find a Devil in the house, it links her straight back."

"You've already got something cooking, haven't you, Prez." Beef leans back on his chair and waits.

"Yeah. The new hangarounds."

"Dirt and Nails?" The VP waits for Demon's nod. "Hmm. Early days, Prez. But Cad's looked into them, seem pretty legit. Very intent on joining, even after Karl told them what they could expect. He laid it on pretty thick as well. I like your thinking. The benefit is, so far there's nothing to link them to the club."

Thunder gives the Prez an 'are you mad?' look. "We haven't been able to test them."

But Hellfire's looking interested. "Dirt's actually a plumber. A blocked sink gives him an excuse to be at that house if the cops turn up. All they need to do is be on-site to alert us to anything suspicious, and we'll muster up support. And Beef's right. Currently, they've nothing at all to do with us."

Prez thinks for a moment. "I can't see anything else for it. Ink's asked us to protect them, but we can't give visible support.

I want the records correct though. Get Patsy to place a call to Dirt's business number asking for a plumber. Nails can go as his assistant. I want one of them there around the clock. Cops take their time to come? The excuse is that they've just arrived back with a part or something. Let them know, Beef, if they screw this up, there's no chance of them wearing the Prospect rocker."

"Heaven help us if one of them is another Skull." Thunder shakes his head.

Cad waggles his hand. "Learned lessons from Skull. Dug deeper. That I couldn't turn anything up doesn't mean there was nothing to find, but I'm satisfied I've done what I can."

"Pyro can go visit with Mel. That wouldn't look suspicious. Mel and Beth are best friends."

"I'm going to Denver," Ro points out. "Not having Mel go there on her own, not when there could be someone searching for their stash."

No, he wouldn't. Mel's pregnant and he's rightfully treating her like she could break. He wouldn't risk this baby.

"You're right, Ro. Point taken." Demon stands. "Let's get all our pieces in place. Those of you going to the warehouse, get ready to roll. You've got a two-hour ride ahead."

But before any of us can get a chance to put our plans into action, there's a commotion outside the door. Glances are quickly exchanged. You wouldn't need to be a genius to gather from the yelling and shouting that as we expected, the cops have turned up.

Demon takes a moment to let his best prez expression slide into place and then steps purposefully out. The rest of us follow.

"Down on the floor. Keep your hands where we can see them."

Even old ladies and prospects aren't exempt it would seem. Not my first raid, but it's hardly top of my list of fun things to do. I catch sight of Beef glaring fiercely as Pyro helps Steph down, Max, dropping beside her gives a lick to her face as though to reassure her he's close.

There are cops with guns aimed at us, and two officers going around, handcuffing hands behind backs, and removing weapons. I catch Thunder's eye and give a little shake of my head.

"I presume you've a search warrant?" Demon asks, refusing to drop to the floor. "If so, I want to see it. If not, you can set my men free and leave."

A cop, obviously the leader of the team, steps forward as another wrenches Demon's hands behind his back. "Oh, we've got a warrant alright. Saves us all time if you just tell us where you store the drugs."

"Nothing here, or on any of our premises," Demon says, confidently. "Maybe some grass, but that's legal in the state."

"We know the law," the SWAT leader growls. "And that piece of paper shows we've got the rights to tear this place apart."

"And you'll pay for every bit of damage," Demon says seriously, clearly meaning it. "You've got no grounds to suspect the club of anything."

"Judge disagrees. Damon McNeish who's in custody is a member of this club." With that, the SWAT team leader turns away.

Grounds to search Ink's room, but the whole club? Well, I bet they just love having an excuse.

Belly flat to the floor, I raise my head and watch as another man enters, accompanied by an excited looking cocker spaniel, his tail wagging furiously. At least someone enjoys their job.

Max rises to his feet, his hackles rising. I even hear a low growl come from his throat.

"Keep that dog under control," a cop barks out, "or I'll fucking shoot him."

"He's a seeing eye dog," someone shouts back. I think it's Pyro.

"Down, Max," Steph orders, and Max obeys, while still keeping his eyes firmly fixed on the intruder. He's still grumbling, and his body's vibrating. Guess he's picking up a vibe from us and has taken a dislike to the canine cop.

"Let your sniffer dog search," Demon orders. "He won't find anything here. Devils don't have anything to do with drugs."

"No? Then why is one of your members sitting in jail on a drug charge?"

"Because he was trying to help you do your fuckin' job," Demon snaps back, but his answer is ignored.

It's a waiting game now. First the dog sniffs each of us, the hair on the back of Max's neck rising again when he gets too close.

He's just got to Thunder who's at the end of the line when Bitch appears. Now Max might be able to be instructed to control himself around a four-legged interloper, but Bitch is under no such constraint. She flies across the room toward the strange dog and there's a loud yelp.

Followed by a shot and an agonised screaming meow. Fuck no! My reaction startles me. Fucking cat did not deserve that.

I watch in horror as she gets to her feet, and staggers from the room, a trail of blood left in her wake. She's not dead. Not yet.

I think that action stunned us all more than the raid itself.

"You bastards!" Beef roars.

"Bitch! What's happened?" Steph, an animal lover to the core cries out, clearly distressed.

Someone reassures her that the cat is still alive, for now. *Dying*, I think to myself, surprised at the amount of anguish I feel for the feline who hates men.

"Just get the fuck on with it and get gone. We need to take our pet to the vet," Demon roars.

"That cat attacked a valuable trained animal," a cop says unrepentantly.

"Your fuckin' dog's fine," Demon snarls back. "He just got a scratch on his nose."

From the shocked and disgusted growls all around, I know everyone's feeling the same way. We all pretend to hate the cat who only tolerates women and kids. She'd just turned up one day, such a misfit, we let her stay. We might not want to get close to her claws, but to think of her injured and dying, well, that's just fucked up. Especially knowing the SWAT team will leave here finding nothing, unless they plant something, of course. That's always a concern.

"I'll go find her," offers Mel. "If they let me search."

"Look, my wife's pregnant. Let her up," Pyro pleads. "Let her go find the fuckin' cat."

The pleading doesn't work, of course, and our general mood worsens.

Two fucking hours. Two hours they take to complete the search. I don't even care about the mess they're making, and I doubt I'm the only one to worry about finding Bitch dead at the end of it.

The dog, fully recovered from the surprise smack around his nose, still has his tail wagging happily as his handler tosses a ball in the air for him as a reward. I care fuck all about that dog, it's the cat I'm surprisingly worried about. Had anyone asked me earlier on today, I'd have said I couldn't give a fuck if she was living or dead. Turns out, I haven't yet run out of fucks.

It's obvious they haven't found anything just by observing how they're acting. But we told them from the start, Devils don't touch drugs. Surely that must help Ink's case? They've left such a mess everywhere, I hate to think what Ink's room looks like, that they'll have turned it inside out. Well, that's what brothers are for. We'll make sure it's sorted before he comes home.

One by one our handcuffs are removed but we're told to stay down until they make their exit. In case we suddenly jump up and rush them, I suppose. Then, at last, they're gone. Our weapons, all having been checked they're legally owned, left in a box by the door.

"Bitch!" Mel screams. Pyro holds her back, presumably not wanting her to get upset any more than she already is by finding a cat's dead body.

"I'll go," says Vi, then glares at Demon. "She'll hate men even more now."

But I'm the one in the lead with Judge right behind me and Demon and Vi hot on my heels.

I'm expecting to find a cold dead fur-covered body. The trail leads into a closet. I thrust the door open wide and find someone's pushing a flashlight at me. I turn to see Judge, his features fixed, his brow furrowed. I nod, then flick the switch and the beam provides enough illumination for me to see Bitch paused, tongue half out, a paw held up which she'd clearly been in the process of calmly washing. I get a cat's narrowed-eyed glare as if wondering why she's being interrupted.

Vi pushes me out of the way and steps up close, picking her up in her arms. Well, fuck me. The top half of one of her ears has been shot clean off, but otherwise she looks unharmed. It's even stopped bleeding.

Incredulously, I shake my head. "That cop must have been a lousy shot. Reckon she's just lost another of her nine lives."

As Vi strokes her, examining whether she has any other injuries, she glances at me. "Doubt it was her first. And I think we need to take her to the vet to get her checked out, she might need a shot."

While that sounds a good idea, as Bitch hisses loudly when Vi moves her a little too close to me, I reckon she'll need to make sure it's a female vet.

CHAPTER TWENTY-THREE

Beth

"I should go to the police." I pause my pacing and turn to look at my mom who's violently moving her head from side to side.

"And get arrested for something that wasn't your fault?" Mom spits back. "Anything you could say might just incriminate Ink further. And your brother as well."

"What else can I do? My fingerprints are on the rucksack…"

"They should have destroyed them after the burglary. They might not have them at all."

I roll my eyes. "I don't think that's how it works, Mom. Isn't it better to get in first with my side of the story? Or one I concoct that is."

"What would that be?" she interrupts. "That you found a package of drugs and just wondered around Pueblo trying to find the owner? You know what cops are like. They'll try to trip you up, even if you're telling the truth. Trying to keep to a complicated story will be too difficult. The truth would be hard enough for them to swallow."

She's right. I know it. But it goes against the grain to think that Ink is sitting in jail for something he didn't do. If they're going to be coming after me anyway, there must be something I can do to swing it to free him.

"Mom, I've told you. I had no choice—"

"I doubt that's the way they'd see it. We've been through this, Bethany. As soon as you feared Connor was in trouble, you should have contacted them. Not tried to sort it out for yourself. You should have at least told me what was going on."

"I couldn't Mom. It would have upset you."

Her expression speaks volumes, telegraphing *as if I'm not now.* Then her shoulders rise, then fall and a quick sad grin covers her face. "I understand why you thought what you did was right. Bethany. I love both my children. I know Connor and I don't see eye-to-eye at the moment, but I'm hoping in time he'll become the man I know he can be if he just removes himself from the influence of his father." Suddenly she stills. "That rucksack. When was the last time you used it, Beth?"

I shrug. "I don't know. Years?" I hate throwing stuff out, always thinking it might come in handy one day. In fact, I'd forgotten all about it until I needed something to carry the packages in. Mom's tapping her fingers to her mouth. "What are you thinking?"

"What if it got 'stolen' during the robbery?"

"A fraying, old bag?" I scoff.

"Thieves could have needed something to carry stuff away in."

I pace again, thoughts flying through my head. Suddenly, I stop. "That could work. They couldn't disprove it. Sure, we hadn't reported it then, but who'd care about a rucksack worth nothing?" I begin to feel lighter thinking perhaps I could get away with this after all. Simple enough to remember if I just stick to the plain facts. Better than the story I was concocting about throwing it out with the trash. One worry eased, my mind settles on another—my brother and whether he's dead or alive. I wave toward the phone I've barely put down since we'd returned to the house. "I keep trying to call him, Mom. I'm worried about him."

She's quiet for a moment. "I'm worried too about whether he's okay, and also, well, what do we do if he does make contact? What if he wants the other packages delivered somewhere? Are we going to pretend they're still here?"

We're talking about Connor as if he's alive, and again, believing that puts me in a quandary. If he's unharmed, it means he cares nothing about me. *It could be me in jail and Connor would have been responsible.*

If he's alive, he'll want the rest of the heroin. He knows me and Mom, knows now we know what he left in our unknowing care we'll want shot of them. He'll be so angry to find them gone.

I can't imagine there's any excuse to explain Connor's behaviour. I may not have been arrested, but Ink has. And that's all down to my brother. I swallow rapidly when I think of the man I lost, the man who, quite rightly, now hates me.

"There must be something I can do for Ink." I feel so helpless and useless. Giving myself up would be easier than doing nothing at all. The possible loss of my freedom means little to me, the pain in my heart hurts far worse. *I'd found the man perfect for me.* Right now, he's sitting in a cell, cursing my name and that we ever met.

"I'm sure there is, will be. But right now, I don't know what." Mom's holding her head as if it hurts.

"I'll be upstairs if anything happens," I tell her. I just need some time on my own. Something I haven't had since Ink was arrested, and I was taken back to the MC.

I don't blame Ink's brothers for being suspicious of me and my involvement in the events of last night. When you think about it, my story is pretty lame. If I'd had more time to think, I might have done things differently. But I'd had none. Connor had made sure of that. On purpose? Or at gunpoint? Whatever, the result wouldn't have changed.

My hands cover my face, and I blink rapidly to push back the tears. I'm done with crying, it doesn't help. But the anguish I feel is all but paralysing.

I'd hoped to persuade Ink we could have a future. What would it have been like to make my life with him, like Mel has with Pyro? To have his baby like Mel's pregnant with Ro's?

I'd been unlucky in all my relationships, had all but given up searching for my one. Now that I realise Ink may well have been it, our chance has come and gone.

I sit on the bed rocking back and forth. Demon telling me Ink wanted nothing to do with me was perfectly understandable, but next saying he'd help protect me and Mom seemed at odds with that. Not that anyone's come around as yet, maybe he's already forgotten, or reconsidered, and our plight's been washed off his hands?

Once again, I wonder why Ink had taken the bag out of my hands when he must have known what would happen. If I could wind back time, I wouldn't have let him. Or, I'd have stayed by his side so I'd been able to explain. Despite my fight, my eyes again start leaking.

Vaguely, I become aware of a door being slammed, and loud voices from downstairs. The noises gradually filter through the sadness in my brain. Numbly wondering whether it's Connor and he's come in all guns blazing at Mom, I grab a tissue and wipe my eyes, and descend the stairs. The way I'm feeling right now, Connor's lucky I don't have a gun to hand.

But it's not my brother. It's worse.

Mom's there, examining a piece of paper, and she's surrounded by three cops.

She turns when she hears me approaching. "Bethany, the cops have got a warrant to search this house. Do you know anything about it?"

There's a message in her eyes, I let mine widen. "Search this house? I've absolutely no idea."

The two uniformed cops glance at each other and roll their eyes.

"You're upset." A plain-clothes detective approaches.

Again, wiping my reddened eyes, I ignore his observation. "What's all this about? What are you looking for?"

"That warrant," he takes it back from my mother and shows it to me, "gives us the right to search anywhere and everything. Is there anyone else in the house?" His eyes sharpen as though expecting me to lie.

"No. It's just Mom and me. What is this all about?" I repeat my previous question, having gotten no answer before.

"Ms Bethany Foster?" another cop enters the front door and asks.

I nod, fear settling in my stomach. "I've been asked to take you in for questioning."

"What on earth for?" I stare at him, my mouth dropping open, as beside me, my mom gasps.

He shakes his head. "We think you may have information which will help an ongoing investigation. Will you please come along with me now?"

"But you're going to search the house. Shouldn't I stay here?" I don't like leaving Mom on her own.

"Mrs Foster will be here."

"Ms Stephens," Mom corrects from behind me, even now hating the reference she was ever married to my dad.

"The car is waiting, Ms Foster."

"Where are you taking her?" Mom steps beside me, her forehead etched with lines of concern.

The police officer states the name of the precinct.

"I don't understand," I tell him. "I've done nothing wrong." On the outside I'm trying to convey confusion, while inside, I'm wondering what and how much they know. It has to be enough for them to have obtained a search warrant. "Am I under arrest?"

"Not yet," he tells me ominously. "For now, Detective Barker just wants a word."

An innocent person wouldn't refuse, would they? Right now, I'm not sure what is the right reaction to have, because I am guilty.

"You go," Mom says from beside me. "If you're not back soon, I'll get someone to help." She presumably means a lawyer to represent me.

"If you will, Ms Foster?" The police officer steps to one side, indicating I should precede him.

I might not be under arrest, but that doesn't make me feel any easier as I'm helped into the back of a police cruiser aided by a hand on the top of my head. The grill between me and the officers makes it feel like I'm in a cage, and the fact there are no door handles on the inside makes me feel claustrophobic. Luckily this won't be too long a journey, my hands are already beginning to sweat. I feel like a prisoner, and it's wearing me down.

I'm trying hard to maintain what composure I have left as I exit the cruiser and step out, wondering whether I'll say something to incriminate myself and this will be the last time I breathe in fresh air as a free woman. *What is the sentence for being in possession of drugs?* A long time, I suspect. The amount I was carrying would earn me more than just a slap on the wrist.

With the thought that I could be going inside for many years, I take one last deep lungful of clean air, suppress the instinct to turn and run a marathon's distance away, and step inside the precinct.

If I thought being in the police car was intimidating, walking into the station is even worse. First, accompanied by the two officers, my purse is searched, then I'm taken through an electronically controlled gate, hearing the thick steel door slam shut behind me. I'm now in a different world. As prisoners wearing handcuffs are escorted along the corridor, I glance around wondering whether I'll see Ink. There are also men in uniform all heavily armed. People are talking all around me, mentioning numbers which I presume relate to various crimes. I'm a tall woman, but I feel myself shrinking, becoming some insignificant being dumped into an alien world.

At last I'm shown into an interview room, grateful of the peace that suddenly descends. Though the iron bolts which could hold shackles on the floor tell their own story.

The cop who'd escorted me stands with his back to the door. We wait.

Another impulse, this time to bite my fingernails has to be resisted. Even if I was totally innocent, I'd be inclined to admit to something I wasn't guilty for just to get out of this environment, were it not that such admission would lead to me being somewhere worse. *Did Ink sit in this very chair protesting his innocence?*

Somehow the thought he very well might have done gives me a kernel of comfort.

Eventually the door opens and a man in his fifties walks in. He's got a weary look on his face as though he's seen it all before, and he probably has. He's followed by a younger man in his thirties, who has sharp, intelligent eyes.

The second man introduces himself first, "I'm Detective Barker, and my colleague is Detective Hastings." He indicates a device he's just switched on. "We'll be recording our conversation."

I have never been questioned by the police before. "What is this about?" It's the third time today I've asked. Perhaps this time I'll get an answer. "Don't you need to tell me my rights or something?"

Ignoring the question, they ask me to confirm my name for the tape. I do.

Now seated, the detectives lean forward, and at last enlighten me. "We wish to question you in relation to illegal substances which were recovered during a drug bust yesterday."

"What?" My eyes actually widen in horror, but I hope it conveys mystification to the officers. "Why on earth would I know anything about that?" I shake my head. "Are you asking if

I saw something? I went to the gym in the morning." I crease my eyes now, as if deep in thought. "I didn't see anything—"

"We will indeed be asking what you saw," the detective interrupts impatiently. "At the moment we're inclined to interview you as a potential witness. However, if you suspect you may be about to say something to incriminate yourself, I will read you your rights."

I freeze. "I don't understand. You're talking about drugs. Wait, is that why you're searching our house?" I meet his eyes directly. "I have never taken, or had any inclination to take, any drug whatsoever." I frown and decide to be honest. "I did try marijuana in college, but that's legal. I don't understand why I'm here. Are you arresting me?"

"At this moment we don't intend to charge you with a crime." His words would have been comforting were it not for the expression on his face which seems to add *not yet.*

"Look," I'm tired, confused, and not about to drop myself, or Ink, in it, "how will I know whether I'm incriminating myself? I don't have any idea what you're talking about." I consider for a moment, wondering if the next question could be interpreted as pointing to my guilt, but ask it anyway. "I have never been questioned before. I know you've not charged me, but have I the right to get legal representation?"

The detectives exchange snide glances with each other. "You do have the right to have a lawyer present. Have you an attorney on speed dial?"

"No, but I have his daughter who's my best friend. Her father lives in Denver, but he must know someone local who could help." It's only been two weeks since I was at Mel's wedding. I'd spoken to her parents there and found her dad an approachable sort.

They seem reluctant, but they give me some time to make a call. Mel immediately agrees to contact her father. He's fast. It's only a couple of hours before a lawyer, a Mr Ottoman, is shown into the room. He's a big, black man who regards the detectives with sharp eyes, while gentling his expression when it lands on me. He must be about Mel's father's age and immediately gives me twin feelings of confidence and comfort.

After he's seated beside me, he nods to the detectives and immediately takes control. "You're interviewing Ms Foster as a witness, I believe, and that she has not been charged with any crime?"

"Not as yet," Barker confirms, unpromisingly.

Ottoman turns to me. "Go ahead and answer their questions. If you feel unsure about anything, let me know and we'll discuss it. Likewise, if I'm not happy with a question or whether you should answer, I'll indicate."

I feel a little more relaxed now he's here.

"If we can begin?" Barker asks but starts without waiting for an answer. "Ms Foster, can you tell me how well you know Damon McNeish."

I frown and shake my head. "I know no one of that name." I'm being completely honest.

Impatiently, Barker elaborates, "You may know him as Ink."

"I don't know him at all."

"Ms Foster," Barker says sharply, "your lawyer should have advised you to tell the truth."

"I didn't say I hadn't met him, but we didn't have much time for conversation. As you must realise, he didn't even tell me his real name."

"So, when did you meet him?"

"At Mel's wedding. Melissa Evans as she is now. She married her man, Pyro, Brendan, two weeks ago."

"And what relationship have you got with Mr McNeish?"

I shrug. "You know what weddings are like. A lot of drink flowing, people looking to hook up. Look, it may have escaped your notice, but I'm tall. Ink's taller and that was refreshing. He intrigued me, and with the alcohol in my blood, I was attracted to him. We… er… made love. That was it."

"You only saw him that one night?"

"I went to the Satan's Devils' clubhouse the following week-end. I'd been one of Mel's bridesmaids, the other were women whose partners were Satan's Devils. I'd gotten to know them quite well. Mel invited me back as they were having a surprise birthday party for Violet's man Demon—he's the prez. As I knew everyone going, it sounded like fun. Ink was there. We hadn't planned on meeting again, but well, we again hooked up." I'm having no difficulty so far. Everything I've said is the truth. Except I hold back that the sex was amazing and the best I've ever had. But there's no way I'm divulging that.

The older detective, quiet until now, speaks up. "You're saying you only had a physical relationship with Mr McNeish?"

"I wouldn't go so far as to call it a relationship, but that's not a crime, is it? I'd be stupid to imagine anything other than that. Most bikers enjoy the single life."

"So, you're leading us to believe you're a woman who just goes with a man for sex?"

"That, as Ms Foster has observed, is no crime," Ottoman puts in calmly, no judgement at all in his tone or expression. "Perhaps you can explain what you want to know about Mr McNeish, other than trying to establish a relationship where it appears there was none."

"Did Mr McNeish use any illegal substance in your presence?"

"No," I say fast. "If he had, there would not have been a second time. I wouldn't trust a man with a habit. I saw no drugs being used in the club, I wouldn't have felt comfortable if I had. Of course, the odd joint, but nothing more." And a live porn show, but that's no crime.

Is this all they're going to be asking? I start to feel less tense.

Barker opens a folder in front of him and passes a picture across. Ottoman takes it before I can glance at it, but after a second, slides it in front of me.

"Ms Foster, do you recognise this rucksack?"

It's mine and has clearly been photographed as evidence.

"I had one just like that," I point to the picture and admit.

"Had?"

"Yes." I frown, trying to summon up all my acting skills. "It's been ages since I've seen it."

Barker sighs. "Ms Foster. Define ages please."

"Years?" I shrug. "I really can't remember. It was old, not fashionable, not even good enough to carry my gym stuff." I frown. "Why have you got a photo of it? Or one very much like it?"

"Why so much interest in an old bag, Detectives?" Ottoman asks.

He's ignored. "Your fingerprints were on this particular rucksack, Ms Foster. And we found none from anyone else." The stare from his eyes is unblinking. I set my features and try not to shrink under his gaze. "I'd like to know just how this rucksack ended up in our evidence room."

Tapping my fingertips together, I steeple my hands under my chin. "I haven't seen it since the burglary," I tell them.

Barker rolls his eyes. "You were burgled?"

"Our house was, a couple of years back."

"Did you list the rucksack on the inventory of things stolen?"

I move my head side to side. "What with putting the house back straight and cataloguing everything for the insurance, I didn't notice it gone. Forgot all about it until now. And even if I had noticed, it wasn't worth making a fuss over."

Ottoman holds up his hand. "I have no idea why you're asking about this rucksack, but your interest carries the implication it's been used, or appears to have been used, in committing a crime, or was at a crime scene. Ms Foster has told you she hasn't seen the rucksack for a very long time. She's also given a plausible explanation of how it could have come to be in the hands of someone who did commit a crime."

As the detectives go to speak, Ottoman continues, "I gather the only reason Ms Foster has been brought in for questioning is her fingerprints came up as a match for those on the rucksack."

The detectives exchange glances. "We are also interested in the relationship between Mr McNeish and your client. Mr McNeish is being questioned in connection with a serious crime and was carrying the rucksack in question. Ms Foster has admitted to knowing Mr McNeish and of having a relationship with him. That's a lot of coincidences in my book. I suggest Ms Foster did not have it stolen in any home invasion, but instead gave it to Mr McNeish to use in connection with a crime."

"Hold up," Ottoman interrupts. "Coincidence yes, but tentative at best. First, a relationship of any substance between my client and Mr McNeish has not been established. Second, however Mr McNeish used the rucksack which appears at one time to have belonged to Ms Foster, there's no logical leap to suggest she had any knowledge of what it was used for."

The detectives stare at me, I try not to fidget.

Barker sighs. "I'll ask a straight question. Did you or did you not give Mr McNeish the rucksack, Ms Foster?"

"No." The word is accompanied by an adamant shake of my head. It's true. Strictly he took it from me, I didn't give it to him.

"Could Mr McNeish have taken the rucksack from your house? Has he been to your home?" Barker won't give up. He seems like the proverbial dog with a bone.

Don't drop him in it.

"I honestly don't think so. Ink only came to the house once."

"To collect the rucksack? Were you involved with what Mr McNeish was carrying last night? Did you know where he was?"

"Look, I've told you, I have no idea what happened to the darn rucksack. I have no idea how Ink came into possession of it. I don't know where Ink was or what he was doing last night, let alone what he was carrying. If I'd thought about it, I'd have presumed he was at the club."

"Who else has access to your house?" This from Hastings.

"My friends often visit. My brother. They've been there far more often than Ink."

"I think Ms Foster has helped you answer your questions as

best that she can. That she had a rucksack which you say is the one found or used at a crime scene doesn't seem a crime by itself. Unless you have other evidence that links my client to any breaking of the law, I suggest we draw this interview to a close."

I hold my breath, waiting for the detectives' response.

Barker nods thoughtfully. "Where were you last night, Ms Foster?"

"Last night, I stayed in. I read a book and went to bed early."

"Witnesses?"

"My mother." Or that's where she'd thought I'd been. Quite truthfully, she'll be able to cover for me, I'm sure. Or at least, perhaps I better start praying that she does.

CHAPTER TWENTY-FOUR

Mace

Cad had managed to pull up the driver's permit photo of Connor Foster and has sent it to our phones. At least we'll be able to recognise the motherfucker. There is definitely a familial resemblance to Beth. Facial features, that is—his hair is blond, not bright blue.

As predicted, the storm moved off, temperatures have risen overnight, and the forecast looks promising enough that we can take our bikes. It's late afternoon by the time we arrive in Denver, and we draw up in an almost empty country park on the outskirts. The crash truck pulls up behind us, and out jumps Pal carefully carrying his and Cad's most recent acquisition, the drone.

"What's the range of that thing?" Beef asks him, his eyes critically examining what looks like little more than a toy.

"It's limited by battery power and the time it can stay in the air," Pal informs him. "What's more important is that the warehouse is a quarter of a mile away from here, so for our purpose, it can easily get there and back, and I can have some time to fly it around to check the lay of the land and what's going on."

"What do you need to control it?" I ask, noticing Pal's not carrying a control device.

Pal grins and pulls out his phone. "I just use this."

A fucking app. Who'd have believed it? Well I suppose there's one for everything now.

"I'll get it set up. I'm using here as the home point it will automatically return to, should I lose contact for some reason. I've already programmed in the coordinates of the warehouse. I'll get it in the air while we've still got some light."

Pal looks excited, it's the first time he's using his new toy in a real situation. For me, it's anti-climactic when, without fanfare, the drone lifts smoothly into the air, rises above the trees, then disappears behind them.

Pal's attention now switches to his phone. Looking over I'm impressed by the quality of the image as the drone flies over the park and out across the landscape. It's not long before it reaches its destination and the warehouse appears below. I have to admit I'm impressed and already thinking how useful this shit is.

"That's the place." Looking over Pal's shoulder, Beef points to the screen. It's easy to recognise from the Google images Cad had pulled up and shown us back in Pueblo, but now we can home in on the detail. It's small, hardly worthy to be called a warehouse but must have been useful for someone at some time. What it's being used for now is of more interest. At first glance it would appear not much, it's almost derelict. But that could be a cover of course.

"No cars or trucks." Pal sounds disappointed.

"None?" Beef takes the phone for a moment and examines it. "Could they have parked inside?"

Pal takes it back from the VP, then taps and slides his finger across the screen. After a couple of minutes, he informs us, "No loading bay they could have driven into. I've circled the whole of the outside."

"Doesn't mean no one's there," observes Hell. "Could be they've left people behind, dropping them off then picking them up to hide what they're up to."

"Or, it's not a base at all. Just somewhere he used to make the calls from in case they were able to be tracked. Look at that." Thunder points to the device Pal's holding. "It looks abandoned to me."

Fuck. I smash one fist into my other palm. "Wild goose chase. There's nothing there." Frustrated I pull out my cigarettes. Liz is the only other person to take one though I offer them around. "What's the plan?" I ask the VP. "Go to the dad's place instead?"

"I still think we need to check it out." Beef frowns. "I've known meth labs set up in places like this. Just because it looks abandoned doesn't mean it is and could be a disguise. Maybe if we go in we won't find anything, but what we do know is that Connor was there yesterday. There may be something we can find."

"If Beth's brother was hurt, there could be blood," Hellfire suggests. "If he's dead, there might be some sign, or even a body."

"And if there's no evidence of a scuffle, he was lying through his teeth." I state what I fully expect to find. Nothing at all.

"Hang on. Look." Pal waves us back over to him. I finish off my cigarette, stub it out on the heel of my motorcycle boot, and pocket the end. It's an ingrained habit not to leave evidence behind.

I glance over his shoulder. "Well, fuck me. Can you zoom in?"

Pal does, and a face of a man who shares the same bad habit as I comes into view. He's just lit a cigarette himself.

"Not Connor." I've just compared his face to the photo on my phone.

"Hey, what's that. Under the lean-to there?" Pyro's looking more carefully now.

"Bikes," says Judge. "I can see two rear wheels."

"Connor ride?" Hell asks but gets no answer. None of us know.

"You sure you're not missing a car or truck, Pal?"

"Certain. I've double checked everywhere."

As he zooms back in at the man having a smoke, I chuckle, getting a few looks of surprise. I point to Pal's phone. "He's got no fuckin' idea we're watching him."

"Move it away," Liz says suddenly. "I don't want to see his fuckin' cock."

Sure enough, the man's turned, and is taking a leisurely piss against the wall.

"Offends your sensitive eyes, does it, Liz?" I chuckle again.

"See enough fuckin' cocks in my line of work," he complains. Well, he was the one who suggested extending the tattoo business to include offering a piercing service.

"Circle the drone around so we can get an idea of how best to approach, then bring it back," Beef suddenly decides. After Pal's done exactly that, the VP stares off into the distance for a moment, then states, "Going by the transport they've got, we've got two, possibly four of them if they doubled up on their rides. There's nine of us."

"How do you want to play this, Beef?"

He looks around. Dusk is falling fast, and the last citizen car has pulled out of the parking lot and gone. "We'll leave the bikes here. Everyone will squeeze into the crash truck, then we'll take the road that runs along the rear. Didn't notice much traffic using it, but I saw at least one car. Pal, you drive. Drop us off, then come back here. If they're listening out, that shouldn't be too suspicious."

Pal nods.

"We'll go through the back fence. Everyone see that gap?"

I nod, and so do my brothers. Seems we're all as sharp-eyed as the VP.

"Put those fuckin' vests on," says Thunder. "Don't want anyone going back with a hole in their chest."

"We don't know what we're heading into," Beef agrees. "They're into drugs. If they're sampling their own product, they could be unpredictable."

"Or have a fuckin' good reason to protect their investment," Hell observes.

"What about damage?" I ask as I slip into my Kevlar armour. "Do we mind if they get holes in them?"

"We need to have a conversation, so disarm and capture if possible," Beef instructs. "We definitely want Connor alive if he's there to be found. Ink's freedom may depend on what he says." He focuses his gaze on me and Liz. "You up for going first and doing some reconnaissance?" Both of us nod. "Right. Once you report back what we're dealing with, we'll firm up on a plan."

It all goes like clockwork. Pal drops us off then zooms off with the crash truck back to where the bikes are parked. Though the car park was empty, none of us like leaving the bikes unattended for long. Pal had joked it was like being a prospect again, but he needn't feel bad about being away from the action, he's played his part well today. That drone had been a fucking good idea, the information it fed back meaning we're not going in completely blind.

Liz and I slide through the gap, while the others stay outside. Under the cover of the now darkness, we carefully pick our way across the uneven ground. It was concrete once, now that's cracked and overgrown with weeds. If we hadn't seen the man and two bikes with our own eyes, we would have dismissed this place as totally deserted.

Lights go on in two of the windows. Lizard and I glance at each other and nod. We now have a destination to head to.

Once I estimate I'm within range should anyone look out, I drop to the ground and begin the military leopard crawl. Dressed as we are in black, it's unlikely anyone would spot us as Liz copies my action, and on our bellies, we approach. I take one window where a dim light glows from inside. Liz takes the other.

There are two men that I can see. They've got a bottle of amber liquid in front of them, and cards in their hands. Two metal cups alongside. As I watch, one takes a long swig. I study them hard, but neither looks like Connor. The drinking man is Hispanic which immediately rules him out, the other is white, but his hair is dark.

I glance toward Liz who makes a few hand signals that show he's seen no one inside, in response I hold up two fingers. Again, he makes signs, this time letting me know he's going to circle the building going around to the right, I reply I'll take the left side.

I peer in windows, then edge along cautiously with my back to the wall as I move to the next. By the time I meet up with Liz I've seen no other sign of life. It appears he hasn't either.

Jerking my head toward the fence where Beef and the brothers are waiting, I drop and start crawling again, just able to hear Liz doing the same right behind me.

When we're at the point where it's safe to stand up, I notice Liz holding his hand.

"What's up?"

"Fuckin' piece of glass. Put my palm down hard right on it. Pierced straight through my glove."

Shit. "Deep?"

He holds out his hand and looks the other way. The shard is still in there. Shielding the beam from my Maglite by turning my back to the warehouse behind us, I examine his injury. "That needs to come out."

"Pull it," Liz instructs, still with his head turned.

"Fuckin' pussy," I tell him. But I waste no time. As soon as it's out, I take his glove off to get a better look, but blood is now flooding out.

"Is it bad?" he asks, sounding like he's talking through gritted teeth.

"Nah, just a scratch. Give me your bandana and I'll wrap it up."

He does. I do.

"Can I look?"

I remember and chuckle softly as I reassure him, "My temporary bandage is doing its job, Brother. Nothing to see now." Well, only a slight reddening where the blood's seeping through.

Doctoring done, Liz and I make our way back to Beef and the others.

"What happened to you?" Thunder asks, noticing how Liz is cradling his injured hand.

"Liz got a piece of glass in his palm," I explain. "Went in deep."

"Fuck," says the sergeant-at-arms with feeling. "You need to stay back, Brother?"

Beef steps forward, his flashlight landing on Lizard's hand. Then he turns to Thunder. "What the fuck you talking about? Man's got a scratch, that's all."

Like I'd done moments before, Thunder chuckles. "Liz might pass out if he sees his own blood." Yeah, Lizard tends to faint if he gets cut. If someone bleeds out in front of him? He doesn't blink an eye.

Beef looks at Lizard, he's shaking his head in disbelief. "You're a fuckin' tattoo artist. You see blood all the time."

"Yeah, but it's not mine," Liz protests, shifting awkwardly on his feet. "And I'll be fine, Thunder, thank you for fuckin' asking. Now we doing this, or what?"

Beef's still staring at him incredulously, then after a moment, asks, "Well, what did you find?"

"Two men. Drinking and playing cards casual as you like. No sign of Connor."

Beef exhales loudly. "Still need to talk to who's there. They might know where he is."

I nod sharply. If they do, they won't be keeping that information to themselves. Not when I apply my trade.

"There's a door at the back, flimsy looking." Liz notes what he'd found.

"Can we pick the lock?"

"What fuckin' lock? It's hanging off its hinges. One kick and I reckon the whole place would come down."

"Good enough. Where are the men in relation to that point of entry?"

Liz bends down and draws a diagram in the sand. "Don't know about internal walls, of course," he taps at a point where he's drawn an X, "but that's where we should be heading for once we're inside."

He's seen more than I did. Useful shit too.

"Okay," says Beef, his head turned toward the building we'll be entering, "me, Ro, Liz, and Judge will take the front entrance. Mace, you, Thunder, Wills and Hell will come in the rear. We'll go in at," he checks his phone, "nineteen hundred zero five."

This time it's eight of us crossing the open ground carefully. The hairs on the back of my neck stand on end, half expecting to be spotted any moment. By the time I get into position by the rear door, which, as Lizard had said, looks like a strong gust of wind would blow it in, my forehead is covered in sweat, even though the evening air is chilly.

My heart is beating fast with anticipation, along with a kernel of excitement and hope. Right now, my brother's sitting in a cell which is down to the man I've come to Denver to find. I'm determined I won't be going home without him. He might not be in this tumbling down old warehouse, but the men who are will give me their secrets. I'm the enforcer, and everyone does, in the end. I've got a one hundred percent success rate at making people talk. Lizard might be immune to other people's blood, in my role I've become impervious to their pain. Administering my torture with surgical precision when it's the safety of my club, or one of my brothers, at stake.

Thunder's got his eyes trained on his phone. "*Thirty seconds,*" *he mouths. Then* "*Ten, nine... one.*" I turn to face the door and push on it. It swings open with a slight creak. With a mental image of the hastily drawn diagram in the sand, I move forward alongside my brothers.

This place is indeed falling down. There's a big open area for storage, and presumably what were once offices off to the side.

Drywall has come away and fallen so the wooden partitions are almost see-through. The room where I'd seen the men is probably in the best condition. Maybe they're there because they can keep it heated.

Beef's approaching from the other direction. When he signals with the gun that's in his hand, Judge, Wills, and Ro fan out to check the hidden areas of the interior. The rest of us wait outside what looks to be another weak door.

Beef kicks it hard with his steel toe-capped motorcycle boot. It puts up no fight.

The two occupants are taken completely by surprise. From the way they stagger as they stand, I reckon most of that bottle of what I can now identify by the smell is whiskey, has gone down their throats tonight. They reach for guns, but their hands drop as they belatedly notice ours are already pointing at their heads.

Quickly, Thunder and I step forward and relieve them of their weapons, searching to make sure they've no second piece or knives concealed on them. Then, I zip tie the hands of mine behind him, and none too gently.

From the protest by the other, I take it Thunder has done the same.

"Who are you? What the fuck are you doing here?"

"Hellfire, can you find Ro? Tell him he can search with lights now and to tear this fucking place apart."

Hellfire snaps to it. If the situation wasn't how it is, I'd be amused at how my ex-prez takes orders from the new VP. Another reason why it was good to appoint someone from a different chapter. I think the years when it was ingrained we had to obey *him* would make it hard for any of us to dare tell Hell what to do.

A quick glance behind me shows lights have now come on in the warehouse.

"Right. Where's Connor Foster?"

"Look, man, don't know what you're talking about. You must be in the wrong place." The one who asked who we were looks shiftily at his companion, his expression making me not trust him one bit. "We're just two dropouts finding a dry place to stay for the night."

"Not buying it." Beef picks up the whiskey bottle. "This is malt. Dropouts would buy a cheap blend."

"Dropouts wouldn't have that kind of dough either." Thunder points to a pile beside the cards. I can see at least one fifty-dollar bill.

Beef growls. "Connor Foster. Where is he?"

CHAPTER TWENTY-FIVE

Mace

"We don't know any Connor Foster, man. Why would we? We're just squatting here for a few nights." The Hispanic looks scared. It's the worried look in his eyes which keep going to the area that Pyro and the others are searching that makes me think there's something here to be found.

"Look, just let us go. We'll collect our things and be out of here. Didn't know this place was owned by... who are you anyway?"

Out of our territory we're not wearing our cuts so we could be anyone.

Beef gives me a tired look. I'm not the only one who's been awake for thirty-six hours. "Mace."

My name, spoken in a tone of voice which only means one thing. I look from one to the other, quickly assessing which man can least handle pain. The Hispanic looks scared, but the white man? He's all bluster, I'm sure.

"Sit him down," I snap to Thunder. "Hold him tight."

Taking my pliers out of the utility belt I'd thought to bring with me, I kneel on the floor and roughly pull off the man's right boot. When he tries to kick out, Beef's there with two sets of handcuffs. The VP soon has the captive's legs fastened to the wooden legs of the chair. I nod my thanks at him when he stands.

When I remove the man's sock, I could puke, and wish I'd started with his hands. But trying to breathe through my mouth and not my nose, I take a strong hold of his ankle. As I'd hoped, his personal hygiene isn't good, and he's neglected to trim his toenails for some time and gives me something to get hold of. Yes, I might have done this a time or two before.

"What the fuck you doing?"

"Where's Connor Foster? Who are you working for?" Beef's barking questions at him. "Start talking and we'll stop this now."

"I don't know anything," the man protests.

Glancing at his face, I see his eyes widening as the pliers approach his smallest toe. "You can hurt me all you like. I can't tell you what I don't know."

I've heard similar words before, from Skull. Then, they were true. I hesitate only a moment. As things had turned out, if I could go back, I'd do it all over again, and this time, I'd kill him. Save one hell of a lot of pain that was to come. My remorse at what I'd done has gone. There is no such thing as an innocent man.

I attach the pliers firmly, then with a practised upward pull and a twist of my wrist, the yellowed nail comes away from the nail bed. Blood floods the area immediately.

The man lets out an unholy scream, and tries, unsuccessfully, to pull his restrained leg up toward his body. It will burn, sting, and then throb. Even stubbing your toe hard seems to cause a disproportionate amount of pain.

"Where's Connor?"

"I don't fucking know who Connor is," the man wails.

"Who owns this warehouse? Who's your boss?"

Silence. Right. Toe number two it is.

The man is crying with pain. It's only when I have worked my way along to his big toe that he screams out, "Alder. It's Alder. We're working for Alder."

"Beef? Mace? You need to see this." Ro appears in the doorway. The expression on his face is grim.

"Thunder. Hell. Stay here," Beef orders.

I follow Ro. He leads us across the main floor and into a maze of passages and storerooms beyond. There in the last is a pile of bloody rags on the floor. Next to that, lying prone, is my brother.

"Liz?" I start forward, filled with concern.

"Never mind him," Ro says, tersely. "He saw blood dripping from his hand. He'll be fine. It's *him*."

The light in here is dim, so I switch my flashlight on. Shit. The bundle on the floor has a head. A very, bloody, unrecognisable head.

"Is he dead?" I'm making the presumption he's a man. It's hard to tell from here.

"Not quite," says Ro.

The body groans as if to confirm it.

"Is it Connor?"

"Man," Ro's face twists, "I can't tell."

Christ, it is impossible to identify him, I realise, stepping closer. Even hair colour is difficult to determine as it's all a combination of bright and dark red, some fresh blood, some dried.

"Pal, get here fast. Need to take someone to the hospital." Beef is already on the phone.

"No… no…"

"Hey. You're Connor, right?" Making the assumption, I sink down to my haunches, wary of even touching him. There doesn't seem any part of him that's not hurt. We need to fix him to the point he's capable of talking. Beef's made the correct call, if he's going to live, which at the moment seems doubtful, only an expert could help.

"Ye…" I take it he's trying to say yes.

"Looks like he was telling the truth," Beef says dourly. "If we want questions answered, we need him alive."

"No hosp… No…"

I realise he's passed out. Or possibly, dead.

"What are we going to do with him?" I ask. "He didn't want a hospital."

Beef looks at Pyro. "We got a doc on speed dial?"

"Yeah. Rusty's our medic, but this is beyond what he can handle. I know a man who's dug a bullet or two out for us before now. Decent doc, but expensive."

"If he's got info that could free Ink, don't care about the cost, Brother."

"We're taking him back to the clubhouse?" Staring down at the unmoving bundle at my feet, I doubt if he'll still be alive when we get there. I wouldn't be surprised if he hadn't already taken his last breath. "I still say we drop him at a hospital."

Beef turns stern eyes on me. "Then what? State he's in, the cops will get called, and we lose our chance to talk to him. Taking him back, fixing him up—if possible—means we get the info that he's got for ourselves. You get to do your job, Mace."

Fix him up so I can hurt him. From the state of him, there's not much more I can do that someone else hasn't already done. Seems I'll have to get inventive. The reference to my skills reminds me we've got another problem. Well, two of them.

"What about the men tied up back in that room?"

"Pyro, Wills, go and get the main entrance open so Pal can drive straight in. Mace, you come with me." He pauses and looks around to where Judge is kneeling beside Lizard. "He okay?"

"I'm okay," Liz answers for himself with a hand to his head. I take it he must have knocked it when he went down.

"I've bound his hand again," Judge says, shaking his head. "I'm worried about him being able to ride."

"Of course I can fuckin' ride," Liz objects.

"You're not riding. In fact, you're staying sitting down until Pal arrives. Not risking you keeling over again. We'll load up your bike. Look at it this way, Pal's driving. Need someone to keep an eye on him." Beef points to the bloody heap on the ground.

It's not a moment for mirth, but the thought of how sheepish Liz must be feeling makes me suppress a grin. It's far from the first time Liz has been struck down because he's injured himself, but Beef has made a good observation. Pal will need to concentrate on the road and can't doctor his passenger at the same time. The thought he might be pulled over with a dead or dying body in the rear seat, well, it wouldn't just be Ink who's looking at life on the inside.

"Look for something you can use as a stretcher," Beef instructs Judge.

"I don't need—"

"Not for you, asshole." Beef sounds exasperated. "For Connor."

Already on board with his allotted task, Judge looks around, his eyes narrowed. I'm sure they'll find a plank or something. Getting the unconscious man onto it shouldn't be hard. Getting Lizard out to the truck without him looking at his hand, more difficult. I only hope the second bandana Judge has wrapped around his wound will do the job.

I follow Beef back into the room with the table and cards. One man is crying in pain, the other is looking distressed.

As soon as we walk in, both look up, both scared for their lives. As they should be.

Again, Beef takes the lead. "We found Connor. He's dead."

Well, will you look at that? If I thought the men seemed scared before, they're petrified now.

"No," cries out the Hispanic. "He's not. He can't be. Only gave him a few taps to soften him up."

A few taps? They'd used him as a punching bag then gave him a good kicking as well, if I'm any judge. And I'd be surprised if some of his blood hadn't come from stab wounds.

"He bled out." Beef shrugs as if a man's death is of no importance to him.

The look that goes between them is interesting to say the least. So are the Hispanic's words. "We're in trouble now," he tells his friend whose injured foot doesn't seem to be bothering him as much as the words he's just heard.

"We're dead," his friend replies.

So, they weren't supposed to let Connor die? Just torture him so he'd call Beth and then keep him here alive. Trouble is, they got carried away. Enough so, it's not too hard for them to believe Connor isn't dead.

"This Alder want him alive?" Beef asks.

The look on their faces suggests that he does. But without encouragement, they're not going to elucidate.

It's at that point when my ex-prez jerks his head toward me and raises his eyebrow at the VP. Beef nods, then says tiredly, "Do your stuff, Mace."

I do. Conscious we haven't got much time if we want a chance to keep Connor in the land of the living, I go as fast as I can, figuring out weak points, their greatest fears, and concentrating on those areas which cause maximum pain while leaving them still able to talk.

Their pleas for mercy quickly change until, with their pants around their ankles and their dicks exposed, they're giving us more information than I've asked for. I think at this point they'd give me their bank account numbers and PINs were I to ask.

We learn little about Alder, they don't know much. They're foot soldiers, left here to make sure Connor didn't escape. Alder wanted him alive, but for what, they don't know. But they'd been the ones getting their hands dirty when Connor was forced to ring Beth.

They'd had 'fun' with Connor after Alder had left. We have a description to go with the name, man in his fifties, grey hair almost white, neatly trimmed beard and a slight paunch suggesting he overindulges. Whether Alder's the first or last name, they don't know. Or, apart from the obvious drugs, what business he's in, or who, if he has them, are his partners. I'm satisfied they've told me all they know and haven't held anything back.

"Finish them off?" Hell suggests, when Judge puts his head around the door saying we're loaded and ready to go.

"Nah." Beef's eyes land on the pair, and he shakes his head. "Connor's dead. Reckon Alder will kill them himself once he knows, may as well leave it to him to dispose of what's left." He then addresses our captives directly, "We're taking Connor's body. Reckon his sister will appreciate having something to bury."

Yeah, we'll leave them alive to get that message across, and hopefully the heat will be taken off looking for a man who no longer exists in this world.

As we leave the room, I overhear two men speaking in pain filled voices behind us.

"I told you not to fucking kick him in the head," says the Hispanic who we now know is called Al.

Diego—fuck me, when I'd heard I'd laughed thinking it would be more apt were the names the other way around— replies, "It was probably your kick to his fucking balls."

I wince on Connor's behalf.

When they realised we were leaving, their cries to at least pull up their pants went unheeded. Why cover a target that Alder could aim for? Mind you, as we've turned off their heater, there probably won't be much exposed when he turns up to check on his prisoner.

We pile back into the truck to go the short journey to get our bikes. Back at the parking lot, Lizard's ride is soon in the back. We're practised at loading up a bike and tying it down, and then Pal drives off. We let him go alone, a smoke for me giving him enough time to get clear. An unescorted truck obeying the rules of the road, less likely to be stopped than one surrounded by bikes in the middle of the night.

Pyro hadn't wasted time making his call. Two hours later when we draw up at the compound several minutes after Pal, there's already a man in the back of the truck. It's Dr Ironside who I've met a time or two before. Not for treatment, thank fuck. But there was a time Buzz caught a bullet which had lodged somewhere beyond Rusty's abilities to pull out.

Pal is standing by the side of the truck. "Want us to get him out, doc?"

"Not until I've seen what I'm dealing with," Ironside snaps. "Christ, this man's more dead than alive. You do this?"

"No," Pal replies, sharply.

No, but if doc can patch him up, it might only be to hurt him again. Depends on what Connor says. But I do admit there are signs that I'd been wrong. Beth had been right to believe her brother was being tortured and could have been killed. May still be the result, if the doc can't fix him up.

"Go get some rest, Mace." Demon's hand lands on my shoulder. "You too, Hell, Beef. I've got this."

I don't take much persuading. Christ, it's dawn on Monday morning. Been times I thought the weekend would never end. Almost forty-eight hours after I last left it, I'm finally crawling between my sheets and lying my head on the pillow. My eyes immediately close.

CHAPTER TWENTY-SIX

Beth

The cops had let me go, but I'd be a fool to think that was the last of it.

When I got home, Mom was pacing the room, her eyes widening with relief as she changed direction and ran over to hug me as soon as I entered the door. By the time I've completed my second interrogation that afternoon, I'm brain dead.

I'd had some questions of my own. After the cops had finished searching the house, they'd questioned Mom about where I'd been the night before, clearly taking the opportunity of asking before we'd had a chance to collude and get our stories straight.

As I'd hoped, she'd told them precisely what I'd said, and what she had known at the time. That I'd been tired, took a book and went off to bed and hadn't gone out. My alibi, such as it is, stands.

I may only have been gone for a few hours, but much had happened in that time. After the police had left, Mom had received another visitor who'd ignored the front door and strangely come in over the back fence. It had been one of the prospects from Ink's club. Under his watchful eye, she'd placed a call to a number he'd given her, telling the person who'd answered that she had a blocked sink. The prospect had disappeared as quietly as he'd arrived.

Shortly after, Dirt, an apparently qualified plumber, and his assistant Nails, had drawn up in his van to fix said fictional block. A couple of hours later, Nails had driven the van off, but Dirt had stayed. It turns out one or the other will be keeping us company in the house while the club tries to find out who the drugs belonged to, and whether they'd be back.

As hangarounds, Dirt explained, neither currently have a known connection with the club.

To complete the cover story, the kitchen floor is now covered with bits of pipe from the sink, as if waiting for a workman to return. It means Dirt could look busy should the police reappear.

Dirt seems pleasant enough, but I wasn't keen on having a stranger in the house. I remember him from the party as one of the men Ink had spoken to briefly. My concern then returns to me now. *How do they know who they can trust?* I know only too well how even the Devils can be deceived.

"Be careful Mom," I whisper quietly, out of his hearing. "You remember Skull?" She'd met him when he'd come to one of our barbeques with Mel. When she nods, I continue, "You also know he turned out to be an undercover cop."

"For heaven's sake, Bethany. Now you don't know who to trust?" Her eyes go to the ceiling and come back down. "Seems you should have been more cautious yesterday. I, for one, am just glad there's someone here, and that Demon's thoughtful enough to spare him to help us. Don't forget, someone out there thinks we've still got a king's ransom in heroin in this house. Your brother for certain, and maybe someone else."

I'm tired, worried about Ink, and feeling irritable. I'm not going to give up easily. "What's one man going to do, Mom? Dirt's okay, but even I could take on Nails." Not quite fair, but as he's around five foot ten, I tower above him.

Mom's sighs. "They're not going to be taking them on. They'll get in touch with Demon if anyone turns up."

"And the club will, what? Send reinforcements? How's that hiding our involvement with the Devils if a dozen motorcycles turn up outside?"

Mom places her hands on her hips. "So what do you suggest, Bethany? I send them away? Would you prefer we were here on our own?"

"I don't know," I cry out. And then to my horror, tears start leaking out of my eyes. I had no sleep last night, had to keep my wits about me during my visit to the police station. Have learned the man I was starting to love, now, quite rightly, hates me. As for my brother, he could be dead or dying, or free when it should be him who's locked up. And I should be allowed to tell the truth, but nobody wants me to. No wonder I'm not thinking straight.

Mom's arms are fast around me. "Oh, Bethany, honey, come here. The last twenty-four hours have been hell on you. Come on, cry it out."

She pulls me to the sofa where it's easier for her to hold me, and I lean my head against her chest and just sob. From the moment Connor called me to when the police took my statement, it seems I've been existing on adrenaline, reacting rather than doing anything with any rhyme or reason. I'm running on empty now. I cry in the arms of my mother until I've no tears left to fall.

When I finish, my throat feels dry and raw, my eyes are swollen, and my face is red and blotchy. She tries to get me to eat something, but neither of us have any appetite at all. The stress and the long hours during which I've been awake have me yawning widely, so when she suggests an early night, I don't argue.

But in bed I can't get my brain to switch off. Instead I keep wondering how Ink is now, trying to accept even if by some miracle he walks free, I'll have lost my chance with him. Then, when I try to stop thinking of what he and I have lost, my thoughts turn to my brother, see-sawing between hoping he's alright, to wishing he's hurting if everything he'd said to me had been a lie.

He'd set me up. My fingerprints showed I had my hand on the bag if not the drugs themselves. Though Ink's brothers want me to stay in the clear to make what Ink did worthwhile, all that might fall apart. I thought I'd been careful wearing gloves, I hadn't. I'd not given a thought to the bag. Huffing, I realise I'm not cut out for a life of crime.

Eventually, I drop into an uneasy sleep and doze; my dreams are haunted by Ink appearing and taking that bag from me over and over again. I try to run as though through molasses to stop him and take it back, but he gets further and further away, and I can't catch up to him.

Three times I've woken twisted up in the bed clothes and covered in sweat. This time, it's something else that awakes me. A quiet knocking on my door, and a man's voice saying, "Beth."

"Hold on." I reach for my robe and pull it on, at the same time glancing at the clock by the side of my bed. *It's Monday morning, five am?* The time makes me worry. *What's happened?*

I waste no time rushing to the door and opening it. "What's up?" I can tell by the look on Dirt's face that it's not going to be anything I want to hear.

"A car's pulled up outside. Two men look like they're checking out the house. I need you to ring the police now, Beth."

Call the police for help? After they questioned me?

"Now, Beth."

If that's what Dirt's advising, it's advice I should probably follow. Immediately I run back into the room, pick up my phone and dial 911.

"I think someone's trying to break in," I tell the dispatcher who answers my call fast. I give the address and hear the reassurance that the cops are on their way.

I hear noises from downstairs, and then, a crash. "What do I do?" I speak into the phone, while quietly opening my bedroom door.

"What's going on?" Mom appears, wrapping her dressing gown around her.

"Shush," I hiss loudly, then explain into the phone. "Sorry, I wasn't speaking to you. But there are men here, coming into the house."

"You've got visitors," Dirt says fast and softly to my mom. I notice for the first time there's a gun in his hand. "Beth's on the phone to the cops—it was Demon's suggestion—it's just a matter of staying safe until they arrive." He pauses, and his brow creases. "Normally you'd lock yourselves away until the cops get here. So, go into your room, or your bathroom if that's got a bolt on it. I'll stay hidden and won't intervene unless things get nasty."

The same advice comes down the line and straight into my ear. "Keep yourself and your mom out of the way. The squad car is almost with you now," the calming voice says. Well, she's trying to be calming, but it's not working.

I'm vaguely aware of Dirt slipping back into the shadows as the hall light is switched on downstairs, illuminating both me and mom standing at the top. There's a man with a gun, and he's pointing it our way.

"Get down here."

We've dallied too long. No chance to hide away now.

"I've got to go," I tell the dispatcher fast. "There's a man with a gun."

"Stay on the line," warns the voice on the phone.

But he's seen me. "End that fucking call and get down here."

I've no choice but to do what he instructs. Dirt must have slipped away unseen, as when I grab hold of Mom's hand—whether to give comfort or receive it, I'm not entirely sure—and slowly descend the stairs, the man makes no comment about anyone else being in the house.

"Where is it?" the man almost screams when we reach the bottom step. "Where's the fuckin' smack? Connor said it was here."

"What are you doing in my house?" Mom sounds scared, and I don't blame her. I'm shaking too. "I have no idea what you think I've got. Please leave."

"I've called the cops," I warn him. "They're on their way."

His eyes widen. "You stupid bitch. So you better talk fast. Where is the stash? Where did Connor put it?"

"Stash?"

"He's talking about drugs, Mom. But why the hell he's asking us, I don't know." I open my palms and gesture that I have no idea what he's talking about, noticing my hands are trembling.

"There are no drugs here," Mom states shakily and truthfully. "Please get out of my house."

The man steps closer, he looks from me to my mom, then for some reason, homes in on me. He takes another pace which puts him in front, his head only just above the level of my shoulders. As he looks up into my face, I recognise this particular sneer. He doesn't like feeling at a disadvantage. I've seen his reaction often, like many short men, he doesn't like women being taller than him.

"Give me what I want, or I'll kill this one." He raises a gun and points it at me.

"No," Mom screams. "No. And I can't give you what I don't have. This is all a mistake!"

I look at the barrel of the gun, wondering if this is the last thing I'm going to see, wondering whether the police will get here in time. As I stare death in the face, the thoughts which hurt most are that I'll never have a chance to see Ink and explain, will never be able to tell him how much he means to me, that I under- stand why he hates me or how I'd give everything to be in jail and him walking free. Those are the regrets I'll take to my grave.

Time seems to stand still.

"You've got one more minute, then this one here takes her last breath."

"I can't tell you as I don't know," Mom cries out. She starts to move toward me.

"Stay back!" I swear he's frothing at the mouth as momentarily the gun points at her before swinging back to me.

"Leave us alone, please." Finding my voice, I begin to beg. The thought of Mom being killed worse than if it was me.

Suddenly another man runs through the smashed front door. "Cops are on their way." He looks panicked. "Just heard this address on the radio. Have you got the shit we came for? We've got to go, *now*."

The cheeks of the man standing close blaze bright red. His jaw tightens. Maybe my senses are all on high alert as adrenaline floods through me, but I read his intention almost before he decides what he's going to do. No drugs. He's failed. And that threat he'd made? Well, he's going to follow it through. But before his finger has a chance to even twitch on the trigger, my arm shoots out and chops down on his with all my strength behind it.

Not expecting a woman to fight back, he's not got a tight grasp on it and his gun flies out of his hands.

Mom might be aging, but she's not old. She is, however, fast, with all her faculties intact. She's quick to make a dive for it with a rather impressive improvised roll and has it in her hand and pointed in his direction.

"Get out of my house!" she roars like a lioness protecting her cub. "And don't come back. We don't have what you're after. I have no idea what you're talking about."

"Arch," the man standing by the door calls out, his voice shrill with fright, "we don't have time. I'm going with or without you."

To my utmost relief, Arch, proving he's not deaf and hearing the gradually loudening sirens, doesn't argue with his companion and they disappear the same way they came in. Moments later I hear a squeal of brakes. Only seconds after that, another vehicle draws up, and now it's state troopers in uniform entering the house.

Neither Mom nor I mention they were looking for drugs as I don't want to give the cops more ammunition to use against me. Instead, we say they'd broken in, and we're in the dark as to the reason.

They bag the gun, complimenting me for disarming the intruder, but don't take the death threat seriously. Then they go through the motions which don't take long, the broken door is the only sign the men had been here. Even though I was almost killed, they write it down as a failed home invasion where nothing was actually stolen.

After being given unnecessary advice about calling someone out to fix the door, Mom, driven by fear of the men returning, snaps, "They held us at gunpoint. What if they come back? Aren't you going to do anything?"

One of the cops shifts awkwardly. "Look, ma'am, it's very unlikely they'll come back. Just keep your phones with you and call us immediately if you hear or see anything suspicious. They've probably moved on to another house. I doubt you've got much to worry about." He glances around the room which is pleasant enough but doesn't scream money. "We can get a patrol car to cruise past when they're in the area." *That's supposed to be comforting?* "There's been a spate of home invasions recently, looks like you've just been unfortunate. Ma'am," he addresses her directly again, "you said they wore gloves, so there're no fingerprints unless we find any on the gun. You can come to the station and look through our mug shots, see if you recognise them, but unless you can point them out, there's nothing for us to go on."

If it really had been a home invasion I'd have been annoyed, but as it is, I'm just glad to see the back of them when they leave.

As soon as the troopers pull away, Dirt appears.

"Those were some slick moves," he says approvingly, but his face is tight. "Thank fuck you disarmed him and got the gun."

"I thought you were supposed to protect us," says Mom. I notice she's looking extremely pale.

"I couldn't take a shot as Beth was blocking him." He almost glares as he adds, "Why do you have to be so damn tall?"

Glancing back at the stairway, I see what he means. I was directly in his line of sight, and the man completely hidden by me.

"You can't go and identify them," he warns. "If you do, there's no doubt the cops will know they have something to do with drugs, and that will just bring more trouble to Beth's door."

He's right. Christ, what a mess.

"What's happening to us?" Mom suddenly cries out, her hand finding the back of a chair and she eases herself down. "I've a son leaving a fortune in drugs in my house, a daughter who's having to lie to the cops and now strangers holding us at gunpoint demanding to know where their drugs are, and I can't admit they've been taken by an outlaw MC."

Suddenly she's crying, and I'm rushing over, pulling her into my arms.

"What the hell is going on, Bethany?" The bravery Mom had shown when faced with a gun-toting criminal has fled now. I'm surprised to feel my own cheeks are wet, as the situation catches up with me too.

Vaguely from behind me, I hear Dirt talking into his phone.

CHAPTER TWENTY-SEVEN

Ink

"The cops have spoken to Beth? What the fuck for?" I hiss at Sykes. I've tried my best to keep her out of it. Why would they speak to her? I'll tan her backside if she's fucked up and dropped herself in it. The only thing keeping me sane is the thought that they haven't got both of us locked up.

Sykes frowns. "I don't know. But you did have a relationship. I suspect they're talking to all your contacts."

I suppose that makes sense.

"Oh, and Demon rang this morning. I didn't let him say much." Sykes reads my irritation. "If I as your lawyer know too much, and especially if I pass that on to you, then it's possible something will slip out while you're being questioned. But what he did say was, Beth's got a story that holds up and he's satisfied with it."

I sit up straighter. "She's innocent?"

He shoots me a look. Yeah, okay, so she was carrying a fuck-load of H and was the reason I got locked up. But if Demon says she's in the clear, he means it. *There could be a good reason for what she did.* Though fuck knows I'm unable to see it. Could she have been coerced or forced in some way? Jeez, now I'm worried about her. If she was, it must have been that asshole brother of hers.

"Is that all Demon said?"

"You know he wouldn't give me much. He had nothing to help with your case. Unless you're going to give her up?"

No fucking way. Especially now Demon's given me hope. If she's gotten herself into trouble, I'm not going to worsen it.

"Cops let her go, though?"

Sykes nods.

At least that suggests she didn't give herself away. Maybe she got my message that I wasn't interested any longer and is happy to leave me here to rot. I lower my head into my hands. Christ, this place is making me go nuts. That's what I want her to do, isn't it? Truth is, the thought hurts, and it's not likely to be the behaviour of the Beth I remember.

Now I've been locked up for thirty-six hours, my anger has started to fade and another sentiment is taking its place, a sense of loss. Lost chances. Knocking my palm against my head, I'm not sure how the confirmation that Beth acted with good reason helps me or not. Christ, I wish I was out of here and could talk to her.

The idea police are presumably trying to connect her to me is extremely concerning. Fuck. What I did becomes worthless if they arrest her. Should I change my story to some bullshit, shifting all the blame from her? Fuck it! I need answers.

"Has she got a lawyer?" If not, she'll need one.

"Mel's father arranged it. Good move. It shows her independence. If the club had sent her to me, the cops would try to make something of that."

"Do we know what she told her lawyer?"

He shakes his head. "Eventually, witness statements will be shared with me, but not now. Ottoman, her lawyer, plays it straight down the line. As do I. It would be unethical to step on each other's toes or share confidential information."

Unethical be damned. But if Sykes got a reputation as being

crooked, he wouldn't make a good lawyer. I try to suck it up. "So what happens now?"

"You'll appear in court for your first advisement hearing tomorrow, Tuesday."

I frown. Looks like I'll be spending yet another day locked up without hope of bail. "That's more than forty-eight hours."

He shrugs. "Seventy-two isn't unknown. It could be a good sign if the prosecutor is having difficulty building a case."

I just raise an eyebrow. Sounds fairly solid to me. I was caught with a bag carrying two kilos of heroin.

The detectives want to speak to me again, it's why Sykes has come in. It's the old familiar routine. I'm shackled with my hands in front of me linked to a chain on the floor just in case I get the sudden urge to reach over the desk and strangle one, or both, of the pair. Looking at it that way, it's probably lucky I'm handcuffed. At least it stops me acting on the impulse.

Barker takes the lead once again. "How well do you know Bethany Foster?"

Shit. Dive straight in why don't you? I think fast how to approach this. *I don't know what she's told them.* Fuck straight lawyers. I decide fast and wink. "Very well."

I swear my answer makes both of them sit straighter. "Would you care to elaborate on that? How long have you known her, and would you say you and she were an item?"

I wish that I could say what we were. I've claimed her, for fucks sake, just to make sure my club protects her. But somehow the idea of having an old lady has got stuck in my head, and it doesn't feel as dreadful as I used to think it would. Having Beth to come home to? Her to fuck for the rest of my life? Her to hold, to sleep with? I could get pretty comfortable with that.

Only one problem, I doubt she'd wait thirty years for my release. Even if some magic is worked and I get out sooner, I have no idea whether Beth would want me, or whether I've been too successful pushing her away. *How long does it take for a woman to lose interest?*

Restricting myself to what I fear is the truth isn't hard. I shrug. "She targeted me at a wedding. There was a mutual attraction. We fucked. I liked it, so we fucked some more when her friend brought her to one of our parties."

Hastings can't keep the look of disgust off his face. "Ms Foster feel the same way? That the only thing offered was a physical relationship?"

"It's what she wanted," I say, daring them to contradict, mentally crossing my fingers that our statements won't contradict. "What can I tell you? Ms Foster wanted to take a walk on the wild side, I was only too happy to oblige. If you saw her, you'd know that body offered on a plate would be hard to turn down." I don't let on I know they've interviewed her.

"You've been to her house?"

"I have," I confirm. No point in denying it.

"Did you collect the drugs from her there? Or did she hand them to you when she met you somewhere else?"

What the fuck? How have they linked her with the drugs? It's my turn to look genuinely confused. I turn to Sykes, but he, too, isn't showing any sign he knows what's going on. "I don't understand the question," I reply at last. "Why the fuck would Beth have anything to do with drugs?"

"The bag you were caught with had her fingerprints on it."

It did? Damn. I hadn't time to ask her anything at all. I hadn't thought that she might not have been wearing gloves. Fuck, didn't everyone on such a cold night?

"I know nothing about that," I tell them at last. "I can't imagine Beth would have anything to do with drugs, but as I said, I barely know her." I'm hoping my words won't get her into trouble.

I'm stared at by two pairs of eyes for a moment. I stare unerringly back.

Barker breaks the silence. "Where did you get the rucksack? Did it already contain drugs?"

Sykes glares at them. "My client has explained exactly how

he got possession of the rucksack. He picked it up when it was dropped, only moments before he was arrested."

Barker ignores him. "Did you go through Ms Foster's house, perhaps? Take the rucksack while you were there? Decide she wasn't putting out enough and get her back by trying to frame her?"

Christ. His version is more fanciful than mine.

"Whoa," Sykes steps in. "Mr McNeish told you what happened quite clearly. Mr McNeish had nothing to do with the bag prior to him taking it off of the man he saw down the alley, the man who I suggest you should be looking for instead of keeping my client locked up. My client handled the bag for little more than a minute. How would he know where it came from?"

The detectives confer for a moment.

"Is there anything else you'd like to tell us about Ms Foster? Think carefully, Mr McNeish. If she gave you drugs to pass on to Childs, maybe you were just the messenger and indeed had no knowledge of what was in the bag. A bit of cooperation here might go a long way."

I've already made the decision I'll sacrifice all that I am to keep Beth out of this. I can't go back on that now. I wish there was something I could do, some way to talk to her, to tell her not to give a hint that she knew what was going on. I wish I knew the story why she was there in the first fucking place. But I don't. All I know is that message from Demon that she has a story which checks out. I can only surmise that her brother is somehow involved and rely on my club to find out. "I've nothing more I can tell you," I respond at last.

Seeing they won't be getting an admission out of me, I'm returned to the cell.

The drunks have mostly sobered up and gone. There's a man snoring off alcohol in the corner, but Monday night isn't a busy one. The place still stinks though, and I already know what to expect when the drunk awakes and his hangover hits. Obviously depends on how much he imbibed, but I expect to be woken by vomiting or retching sounds again, or at least, a loud long piss hopefully in the correct receptacle.

I never thought I'd long to be sent to a proper jail where I'd have a cell, hopefully with a bunk to myself even if I had to share the room. Anything would be better than this. It's a punishment all in itself.

My chin lowers to my chest and I allow myself to doze, keeping my senses on alert in case the drunk isn't as incapacitated as he seems.

It's another long night. When dawn breaks, I'm almost pleased that I've got something different today, my time in court. I tamp down any optimism of thinking I might make bail, it would only cause disappointment if I don't. I resign myself to not being away long before I'm returned to a cell.

I expect the advisement hearing to be a formality. In Colorado, there's a brief appearance before a judge, and then the arraignment will follow sometime later. Most people are allowed to walk free between the two court dates, but I already know from what I've seen with my brothers, wearing a one-percenter patch means those niceties aren't often afforded. The prejudgement you're a criminal is already made.

Obediently, I hold out my hands for the handcuffs to be attached before being led out of my cell. Sykes is waiting for me in the courthouse.

I've been to these hearings before, but only to give support to my brothers, never as a suspect myself. I'm shocked at how nervous I am, and how there's an underlying feeling of guilt even though I've done nothing wrong. It seems all set up to intimidate.

We wait our turn, then I'm called in front of the judge. I notice Demon in the courtroom, but nobody else from the club, and no Beth which both pleases and disappoints. He gives me a chin lift of support, then my attention returns to the most important man in the room. The man who controls my future.

The judge takes off his glasses, stares at me for a second, then turns back to the paperwork in front of him.

After I've confirmed who I am, the judge asks, "Are you aware of the purpose of the advisement hearing, Mr McNeish?"

"I am, Your Honour." I've seen it before, and Sykes has already taken me through the process.

"Hmm." I seem to have taken the wind out of his sails, but then he continues his normal spiel apparently just in case. "I will advise you of the crime you have been arrested for, and the charges the district attorney intends to prosecute. We will then discuss bond and whether it's applicable in your case."

A legal man coughs, making the judge glance at him. When they exchange nods, I presume it's to acknowledge the judge has already been advised against setting bail. I didn't expect they would, so their unspoken conversation comes as no surprise.

The judge looks down at the documents again. "Mr McNeish, you are accused of being in possession of two kilos of heroin that you were supplying with intent to sell. These are the charges which will be brought up at your arraignment. Do you understand?"

At this preliminary hearing there's no need for me to admit or deny my guilt, but I can't help getting my dig in. "I understand how the police are twisting it."

"A simple yes or no will suffice, Mr McNeish."

As Sykes shoots a warning glance at me, I shrug. "Yes."

"Have you got an attorney, Mr McNeish?"

I want to ask if he's blind as Sykes is sitting right there in front of him but bite my tongue. "I have."

"The DA has advised bail is not appropriate in this case—"

"Objection, Your Honour." Sykes gets to his feet, tossing a glare at the other lawyer. "Mr McNeish is a Marine veteran with an unblemished record. This is his first arrest. There is nothing in his background to suggest he'd commit the crime of which he is accused, and in fact, everything points to it being unlikely."

"Your Honour, Mr McNeish is a member of the outlaw

motorcycle gang, the Satan's Devils." the other lawyer gets in fast.

The judge raises his eyebrow toward Sykes.

"He is indeed a member of a local motorcycle riding club," Sykes refutes sternly. "The club runs several businesses in Pueblo and pays their taxes like everyone else. They contribute to the local economy and create employment for the community. That they ride motorcycles should not count against them." He holds up his hand when the other lawyer tries to speak. "There's been no trouble between the police and the Satan's Devils MC for many years now, and in fact, the reason that Mr McNeish was arrested was because he was trying to help the police in their drug raid on Saturday."

"We're not here to try the case, Mr Sykes."

"I am aware of that, Your Honour." Sykes humbly accepts the rebuke. "I will confine myself to expressing Mr McNeish's family is the Satan's Devils Motorcycle Club. He lives and works in Pueblo where he's been since leaving the Marines. Mr David Carter, the president of the MC will personally vouch for him and is prepared to put up bail."

"We object, Your Honour. Mr McNeish is a flight risk."

Again, the judge takes off his glasses and studies them. He then looks over toward me. I try to make myself look as small and unthreatening as possible, which isn't easy for a man of my size. I have no expectations other than being returned to jail.

The judge doesn't disappoint me. "Application for bail denied. Mr McNeish will be remanded in custody until his arraignment."

CHAPTER TWENTY-EIGHT

Mace

"**B**ail denied."

We're all waiting in the clubhouse. Prez had wanted to refrain from a mass presence at Ink's hearing as he didn't want the judge to feel threatened, so only he'd been in attendance. But keeping our distance apparently hadn't worked. I hated staying away, wanted to be there to show Ink he's loved, missed and supported. Will he think we've abandoned him? Fuck, I hope not. We'd never do that.

"Church," Prez announces, as he quickly spies everyone waiting around. Our businesses are today being left to the civilians to run having all hoped, rather than expected, Ink to be coming home even if only on a temporary basis. Everyone had wanted to be here to greet him.

Prez waits for us to sit down. "Where are we at?" he starts.

There's nothing more to say about Ink. He's in jail. Now we've got to concentrate on what little we can do to get him out, or, if that fails, to seek vengeance.

"Connor will live," the VP pronounces. "I'm going to be able to question him today. Up to now he's been circling in and out of it."

"I've stopped the strong shit as per Ironside's instructions,"

Rusty announces. "He's just on normal pain relievers now. Should give him a clearer head."

Connor had been unconscious since we brought him back Sunday night, partly it sounds, due to medication. It's good news he has improved and maybe we can start getting some answers. I'd hoped that would be the case. When I'd looked in on him earlier, his eyes were less swollen, and Rusty had assured me he was sleeping, rather than in a coma. Seems once all the blood had been washed off, his injuries, while painful, aren't fatal now the deepest cuts had been stitched and his blood levels topped off.

Demon's looking down at his hands which are clasped on the table in front of him. When he looks back up, he states, "I didn't expect Ink to be granted bail. Not for the charge they think they've got him on. But I tell you, Brothers, I'm not certain how he's going to get out of this. Judge didn't even attempt to put a monetary value on his freedom."

"What's Ink's state of mind?"

Demon stares at his VP for a moment before answering. It's not that he doubts the veracity of the question coming from the man who perhaps knows him least, it's because he's deciding how to answer.

"Hard to tell from his brief appearance. But Sykes says he's holding up okay. He's worried sick about Beth being interviewed by the cops. What's most important to him is that we do what we can to watch out for her. If she goes down..." Demon pauses to shake his head. "Well, everything Ink's sacrificed will be wasted."

"Did you tell Sykes about Connor? Does Ink know?"

"I called Sykes yesterday morning, but all I said was Beth's in the clear, just to give Ink some comfort. The less either he or Sykes know, the better at the moment. Any temptation to embellish his story, or drop Connor's name into it, might do more harm than good."

"The only reason he's inside is to keep her out of it," Thunder, serious for once, states. "If he knew the truth of it, he'd go crazy. Does he know about the incident at her house? Or that Connor stored drugs there?"

"Fuck no," Demon says, adamantly. "You think I want to heap that on him too? How would any of us feel if we had an old lady and couldn't lift a finger to protect her?"

I wouldn't know and am unlikely ever too. But from Beef and Pyro's reaction, even Hellfire, Buzz and Bomber's reaction, it wasn't something they'd want to even contemplate.

But I add mine to the murmurs of agreement around the table. It's best not to add to Ink's worries. If anything happened to Beth, either as a result of the law entrapping her or physically because of those fucking drugs, if he knew she'd been moments away from eating a bullet, Ink would go out of his fucking mind.

Since Sunday night I've been revising my opinion of how Ink had come to be arrested, and the part Beth had played. Beth's close brush with death had focused my mind, had made me realise how high the stakes were and to what lengths people would go to continue their drug trade. I'd started to understand the pressure that must have been brought on her to make her act out of character and deliver those drugs. I decide to give my brothers the benefit of my new thinking.

Raising my chin, I sum up, "I know none of us like the fuckup that happened on Saturday night, or like Ink's woman for her part in it. Simply put, if Beth hadn't been there, Ink wouldn't be inside." I pause for the inevitable nods, and some growls of agreement. Then, carry on, "There's now no doubt in my mind having seen the state her brother is in, that he must have come across as convincing. As it turns out, it's only by luck that he didn't bleed out. Doc said that if he'd been left unattended in that state for much longer, that may well have been the result. Beth did what any of us would have done for a brother, she did what she could to help him. Beth was right to be concerned."

"She should have come to us," Pyro objects.

I find myself doing what I never expected, advocating on her behalf. "She had no time to think what to do. Whether she'd called us or gone to the cops, she was told Connor would be dead if she didn't act there and then. Remember, she didn't know what she was being asked to deliver until she found the drugs."

"She's a bitch." Liz opens a pack of smokes. "Can't expect any sense from them."

Some laugh, some grumble. I leave it at that. I've said my bit.

Prez glances my way, then gives a slow nod. "I've spoken to Beth a few times and have had to be pretty forceful to stop her turning herself into the cops thinking it would get Ink out."

"See? No sense as I said."

"Liz," Prez growls. Then starts again, "She's doing no more than Ink. She's prepared to sacrifice herself to help another. Just as she was prepared to do to help her brother."

"Ever get the impression she's had no one to rely on? That she's used to doing shit on her own?" Eyes go to Hellfire.

Bomber scoffs. "Girl lives with her mom."

Hell shrugs. "Sure. But look at Beth. Does she look like someone to lean, or be leaned on?"

I've got a suspicion I think I know where he's going with this. "Whatever Beth is like, she comes across as big and strong, not a woman who needs someone to stand up for her. So it makes sense she didn't call for help, she's used to doing shit on her own." I think about it a bit more and find myself uttering words I wouldn't have thought would come out of my mouth a day or so ago. "You have to admire the bitch, she's probably got no one in her corner."

"Even her brother went straight to her for help," inputs Judge. "He didn't give a thought to her safety, just offered her up."

Hell picks up when other voices trail off, "Look at what she didn't know rather than what she did. She didn't know the cops were there that night, didn't know Ink was anywhere close. Even if she did, his actions took her by surprise. Pure accident the part she played in putting Ink behind bars."

Lizard is frowning, looking at his now properly stitched and bandaged hand. "I suppose you, Prez, or you, Ro, can better understand why Ink is so intent on protecting Beth. Can't myself, never found a broad who would make me give up the life that I know. In some ways, I wonder whether it's how Ink's justifying what happened, rather than what he feels for her. He's looking at being charged with something he didn't do. He can't get out of it, but if he's doing it for a reason, it becomes worthwhile. Fact is, as we all know, if he hadn't stepped in, it would be Beth looking at thirty years."

"I'd do the same for Steph," Beef offers.

"For Sindy too," echoes Buzz.

Hell and Bomber look at each other. Then laugh. Hell puts it into words. "May have to think on it for a moment. Things look a bit different after you've been married darn near forty years."

Demon's eyes go large as they look down the opposite end of the table at his father. His mouth opens, shuts, then opens again. Then Hell snarls, "Fuckin' with you. Damn it, I'd do the same as Ink, even though Mo can be a pain in my ass. What this club is about, isn't it, Brothers? Protecting those we love. Especially the weaker sex."

Liz snorts. "From what Dirt said, Beth's not weak. She disarmed that fucker who went to her house." His observation is acknowledged with comments of begrudging respect.

"Her mom was no slouch either," Rusty reminds us all.

I think to what Dirt had said. If Beth hadn't reacted so fast, she'd probably be dead. I can't blame Dirt though, he couldn't shoot through her and had been unable to see the fucker's head.

"Seems like it's time to bring this up. They were threatened at gun point. I really don't like leaving her and her mom in that house," Beef puts in. "Those motherfuckers could be back. They want answers and they want the heroin. The next time, they'll know they're not dealing with two powerless women."

"Agree with you, VP. But I can't see another option." Demon wipes a hand over his brow, drawing attention to the crease lines on it. "It's likely the cops will question her again because her fingerprints were on that bag, and not unlikely, cops will pay us another visit. Any other time, I'd pull them in, but a link between us and them would only do more harm. The fact we're not visibly watching out for her cements the view she was a casual fuck to Ink, and not his old lady."

Beef slams the table with his palm. "Then we protect them another way. Find out who the fuck we're facing, and deal with them. If we can't keep them out of danger, we stop it touching them. We need answers from Connor, and I'm in the fuckin' mood to get them. Mace?"

"I'm in." Won't even take much to make Connor hurt. All we were doing was waiting until he was fit enough to feel it.

"Okay. We've covered everything we can for now. I agree with the VP, we get these fuckers and stop them. Connor's got answers, VP and Mace will get them. Church over. But stay fucking close. Soon as we know anything, we'll reconvene."

Like Beef, having gotten Demon's blessing, I waste no time getting to my feet.

As I walk past him, Hellfire stays me with a hand to my arm. "Wring that fucker dry," he instructs unnecessarily. I raise my chin back. That's exactly what I intend to do. We might have filled him back up with blood, but I'll soon let it out again if I have to.

When I open the door, I'm pleased to see Connor sitting up and spooning broth into his mouth, well more accurately, raising his spoon to his lips, then sucking in the contents, his jaw still being swollen. But hey, the man can eat, the man can talk. And I'm in the mood to make him.

He pauses with his spoon halfway to his mouth, looks to me, then the man behind me, and replaces it without partaking of the contents, putting the bowl down on the bedside table.

"This is it, then?" he says, the words understandable if not well-formed. He glances from one to the other of us again.

"You're a dead man, Connor," Beef tells him, pulling up a chair and turning it around, folding his arms over the back.

Connor's eyes close briefly. When he opens them, he asks, "You get far with that approach? Letting me know whether I speak to you or not, you're going to kill me."

If he thinks we don't know what we're doing, he's very mistaken. Though I must admit I was taken a bit aback by Beef's opening words. My face, however, remains impassive as I wonder where the VP is going with this.

"No," Beef contradicts. "But whoever did this to you," his hand indicates Connor's bandaged body, "thinks that you expired because I told them you had. So yeah, it doesn't matter what we do with you now. But it does, however, leave you with a choice, should you choose the right one."

Connor looks confused, but I understand Beef's opening gambit now. If it works, I may not be called on to ply my trade.

"A choice suggests you might let me live." Connor's eyes are swollen yet manage to convey a glimmer of hope.

Beef shrugs. "Maybe." He waves toward the broken body on the bed. "I'd bet good money if whoever did this to you finds out you're alive, you wouldn't be that way for much longer. You tell us everything, we find it to our satisfaction, then you have the option to start over. A clean slate because Connor Foster is dead."

He frowns and stares at the VP as if trying to process the words he's heard and clearly wondering about the implications. "I'm dead?" The lines etched on his forehead deepen. "I could start afresh?"

"Being dead gives you certain freedoms. But you'll be dead for real if you don't talk. This is my promise to you, Connor. We won't make fiction fact unless your answers aren't anything but the truth." I step up closer to him, flexing my hands.

His swollen eyes close as he thinks. "If I were alive, they'd kill me for speaking to you. But if they think I'm dead, they won't know I'm telling you anything." Some of the tension in his face seeps away. "You said, I could start again somewhere new. Why would you do that for me?" He seems disbelieving, and his face tightens again. "From here it seems like you've done me a favour. Wouldn't it be easier for you to kill me once I've told you everything I know?"

I chuckle. "Probably, yes. I can oblige if you prefer. Could still be the outcome if you don't give us everything we need."

He presses back into the pillows as though trying to get further away from me. "What I don't understand, is why you're involved?" he says after a moment. "Why were you at the warehouse? Why did you bring me out? Why did you let them think I was dead?" His brow furrows. "How you knew who I was when you found me? If you were after the drugs, there weren't any there. But why would you be? You're wearing Satan's Devils' cuts, but everyone knows Satan's Devils aren't in the drug business." He sounds puzzled.

"Which was why you were dealing around our premises," I put in. "Because we don't touch heroin or anything else."

"No, man. Not me. I wasn't dealing. Never have, never will."

My eyes narrow as I look at Beef. It dawns on me, Connor probably has no idea what went down Saturday night. Oh, he knows he asked Beth to deliver the drugs, but he doesn't seem to know the outcome.

"What's your relationship to Fender Childs?" Beef asks. I'm content to leave the questioning to the VP. I'm just here to enforce any answers which aren't forthcoming.

"I haven't one."

I start to mentally prepare myself, certain he's already lying.

"But you know him?" Beef probes.

Connor shrugs. "Met him. Why?"

Suddenly Beef is off the chair and diving forward so his impressive hands land on the bed either side of Connor.

"Because that's who you fuckin' told your sister to deliver drugs to."

"Beth? What's she..." His eyes narrow. "That fuckin' boyfriend of hers. He's a Devil. He's behind this, isn't he? She went to you when I told her not to." His eyes close then open. "No wonder they went so hard on me. I thought they'd ease off once I'd done what they asked, but no..." He grimaces. "Look, I was in trouble. I had to ask her. They... well, you can see what they were doing to me. Told me they'd kill me if I didn't get the drugs delivered. I just knew a place and time, I didn't know who'd be there waiting."

"You haven't even asked if your sister is alright," Beef snarls.

Connor tries to sit up, not easy when he's caged in by Beef. "The fact they darn near killed me suggests she's alright. That she went to you and didn't go to the meet." His face falls like that of a little boy. "She didn't care what happened to me."

"She fuckin' cared," Beef roars back. "Though why she'd care about a piece of shit that got her involved in this business, I've no fuckin' idea." He pauses, glances at me for an instant and I see him shudder as he tries to get a grip on himself before turning back. "What if I told you the person delivering the drugs and Fender Childs have both been arrested?"

Even if there was a million dollars at stake, I wouldn't have been able to predict Connor's reaction. As far as he knows, Beef has just told him his sister had been arrested. Instead of horror, instead of regret, Connor... smiles.

Beef's face glows, his shoulders straighten. He leans even closer. "What type of fuckin' man are you? Getting a woman to do your dirty work for you? You might not think much of us, but we'd never, ever, put an innocent woman in the position of being hurt. Or arrested."

"She's been arrested?" Connor still doesn't look upset. "She'll be okay."

"Okay?" Beef roars. "Fuckin' okay? The person found with

drugs on them is looking at thirty-plus years for possession with intent to supply."

Connor frowns. He scurries up the bed as far as he can to get away from Beef. His groan of pain as he moves doesn't affect me at all. "Look, it's bad timing. That's all. She must have gotten bail, first offence and all that?"

"First offence counts for fuck all in these cases. No bail."

Beef's not admitting it's not his sister who's locked up. Not yet. I'll leave it to him to decide when or whether to enlighten him. Would it make Connor clam up if he knew just exactly what our vested interest in this was?

"What day is it?" he suddenly asks. I realise he's been out of it for a while.

"Tuesday," Beef replies. "You've been here since Sunday night."

"I can sort it in a few days." Connor looks hopeful. "She's just got to hang on until the weekend. It will be fine," he adds, sounding like he's trying to convince himself.

"Ever been inside, Connor?" I ask, unable to hold back anymore.

He shakes his head.

Beef stands up straight. His hands clench, and for a moment I wonder if he's going to step into my role. "Thing is, Con, whether who you've gotten locked up will be fine, or whether it's okay for them to hang on a few days, isn't for you to decide. You see, we knew there was a SWAT team standing by that night. It was our fuckin' premises that you and your friends were targeting. We wanted to make fuckin' sure the cops caught whoever was there, and if they didn't, we wanted to get our hands on them ourselves. My brother, Ink, saw Beth. Saw she was walking straight into a trap. He swapped places with her, and it's him who's fuckin' inside."

Connor's mouth forms an O as he processes this new information and its implications.

Beef gives him a moment, then says in a deceptively casual tone, "So tell me, why shouldn't we kill you?"

"Because I can help you get your man out," Connor says fast.

Beef's jaw drops. "How the fuck do you think you can do that?"

Christ, he's a cocky little bastard. Or is he thinking he can swap information for Ink's freedom? Not sure that would work. Not without dropping everyone, including Beth, in it.

I wait for Connor to answer Beef's question. He swallows a couple of times and rubs his neck. "Look, I'll tell you everything. But first, man, can I have a beer? My throat is parched."

Pushing himself up, Beef lurches away from the bed and goes to the wall and starts banging his hand against it. The sight would be comical were it not that I share his frustration. Connor thinks he holds the key to getting Ink out but squeezing blood out of a stone would probably be easier than getting the words out of him.

I go to Beef's side. "Want me to kill him?" I ask, casually.

Beef huffs a laugh and offers a heartfelt response, "Yeah." Then his head shakes. "Get him his fuckin' beer."

Taking out my phone, I shoot off a quick text, then turn to the man on the bed. "You okay to drink with the painkillers you're on?" I don't really care, I just don't want him comatose and unable to talk.

Connor gives me a sly look. "Can't hurt if I'm already dead."

It's hard to argue against that.

It's not more than a couple of minutes before there's a knock on the door. On the other side is Karl with three bottles. Opening one, I pass the others to Beef and Connor. The latter takes a long drink, then sighs and wipes the back of his hand across his mouth.

"Was a moment when I didn't think I'd taste that again," he says, looking almost adoringly at the bottle he's holding.

"Our brother might not," Beef reminds him tersely.

Connor shifts, clearly trying to get comfortable, I don't offer to help. He takes another, smaller sip, swallows, then starts, "I'd lived with Mom and Beth all my life. Mom was always on at me to do well at school, to go to college and get a good job. Beth was held up as a shining example, but what did she do? Work for the government offices in town. Sounded boring as hell to me."

"There a point to this history lesson?" Beef asks.

He nods. "Yeah. About six years ago I set out to find my dad. Wasn't hard, Mom didn't try to hide him from me. Dear Phil didn't want the bother of raising a child, but a kid nearly grown into a man? Now that he could work with. He didn't live a boring life, he had money, knew people. Well, it sucked me in. When I was eighteen, I moved in with him."

"And worked with him?"

I lean back against the wall, content to listen and let Beef do the prompting.

"For him, yeah. I'm tall, could do with muscling up a bit but he could use what I was." He tries to laugh at himself, but bursts into a fit of coughing which obviously pains his broken ribs.

It's a few seconds before he summons up the strength to speak again. Although both the VP and I are anxious to move this along, it's clear he's going to go at his own pace.

"At first, I was working in one of his clubs. Got a job as assistant manager, fuck knows why. Nepotism at its best. But I was too young to realise I was there in name only, the manager used to put me on the right track and clear up any mess I created. All I could see was at eighteen I'd stepped into a job I'd never have gotten back in Pueblo. I felt important to him, more so than I ever did with my mom."

"He was proud to have you as his son?"

"Nah. We never had that kind of relationship. Anyway, stuck that out for a couple of years, then I tried flexing my muscles and fucked up. Lost him one of his best employees. That's when I saw his other side, but hey, I deserved it."

"He hurt you?"

"No. But I lost my job in the club and my rank in his organisation. I'd have done anything to get that and his respect back. And I did. I took on anything. That's when he got me working his protection racket."

"You enjoyed that shit?"

"Hell no. But hey, he was offering a service and expected to get paid." His brow creases. "The women with kids were the worst. Hated taking whatever they had." His face twists as he remembers. "But I still gave my dad a pass. He was a successful businessman, and for a while, I wanted to be just like him. Until I found out what else he was into."

"Drugs?"

Connor nods at the VP. "Yeah. He was feeding people's habits. Worse than that, getting them hooked in the first place. One of the things he'd do was send a man into a student party, passing around free shit. Made sure they knew where to come to when they wanted more. Cheap at first, then the price increased. I came across that by accident, heard a meeting where they planned getting into one of the parties. Start them young, I heard, then you've got customers for life."

"Did you confront him?" I ask, wondering if that's why he'd gotten such a beating.

"No. I wasn't that brave. By then I'd learned what happened to people who crossed him. I kept my head down and started making my own plans to get out. Despite everything, he wasn't paying me much, certainly not enough to break out on my own. I couldn't go home to Mom with my tail between my legs, so I stuck it out. I think he wanted a son he could groom to take after him, but I wasn't made of the same stuff. But I was useful, hey, I'm big and intimidating."

"So what fuckin' happened, Connor? How did you end up like this?"

"I got arrested. Went to collect a debt, neighbour called the cops. They got me on a felony assault charge."

Beef's lips press together. "You said you hadn't been inside. What did you do, make some kind of deal?"

Connor looks at us as if to check how we're going to take what next comes out of his mouth. "Yes. They offered one and I accepted, it was the escape route I'd been looking for. Drugs were flooding Denver. They suspected my father was playing a part in it, and that he was branching out to other towns. Letting a violent man remain free was apparently nothing compared to the bigger picture."

"Like Pueblo?"

He nods.

"Where does Alder come in?" Beef asks.

"You know about Alder?" Connor's eyes widen, but he doesn't ask how. "Well Phil runs the drug trade on the ground. Alder's the man at the top of the food chain. He organises the buys. Phil takes it from there, moves it on down. He runs the dealers and makes sure they're supplied."

"Your Dad know about this?" Beef waves at Connor's broken body.

"Yeah." Again, Connor's mouth twists. "He was there when Alder ordered it."

Beef and I exchange glances. I signal I want to ask a question myself, and Beef steps back.

"Why put the drugs in your mom's house if you didn't want to touch that shit?" I'm still trying to work out how everything adds up.

Connor nods as though he'd expected one of us would get around to asking. "Thing is, I was getting desperate. My handler, Agent Caruso's patience was only lasting so long. If I had nothing useful to offer, he'd take me back in, and I'd stand trial. I kept my ear to the ground, listened when I should have made myself scarce. Overheard a convo between Phil and Alder, and learned there was a load of drugs coming in. Just so happened I saw my chance and managed to intercept the delivery. Took the drugs myself."

The hairs on the back of my neck rise with suspicion. "Why the fuck didn't you turn the drugs in? Wasn't that what you were supposed to do?" Connor would know the value of ten kilos of H. The answer is obvious. It was too much of a temptation.

Connor glances at me and clearly interprets what I'm thinking. He laughs, but mirthlessly. "Believe me, I was fucking shitting myself holding onto it. But it was bad fucking timing. Caruso's off on his honeymoon for three weeks."

"What the...?" The VP looks incredulous. "He goes off and leaves you no other contact?"

"He didn't know anything was going to go down. I'd been looking for an opportunity for a few months, too long as I'd said. So while the timing didn't work, I couldn't not take the chance."

"So how did Beth get to be involved?" I really want to move this on. Things are starting to fall into place, but there're pieces of the puzzle that don't fit. "Phil and this Alder, they found out what you did?"

A frown now covers his face, and he winces in real or remembered pain. "If Caruso could have taken the shit off my hands, he'd have gotten me straight out of Denver, put me in Wit Sec, just like you said. But as he's not around, I had to wait it out. I couldn't go to the cops with ten kilos of H, not without Caruso to back me up." He pauses again.

"Phil was dealing drugs, and Caruso wanted him sent down. At the time, I hadn't known Alder was involved, only found out his role when I overheard about that shit, and that's when Caruso was out of town. The feds had been trying to catch Phil for years, but nothing would ever stick—it's clear now why, he couldn't be linked with the major suppliers as Alder dealt with all that."

I look toward Beef. Beef raises his chin, then turns to Connor. "Alder was driving this train."

Connor nods. "Yeah. I thought I'd been careful, but I'd been hiding shit from the wrong man. Alder's got contacts I didn't know about. And the weeks when I had to hang around, trying to carry on as normal, well, that gave him the chance to find me out. I don't know how, but he got wind I was responsible for taking his H. He grabbed me on Saturday wanting it back." Another one of his sly looks. "I thought, hoped, I could come up with some story that would satisfy Alder, and still have something to give to Caruso to get out of that life. I managed to convince Alder the shipment was short, that there had only been two kilos. To buy me some time, yeah?"

It's Beef's turn to shake his head. If Alder had done any kind of investigation, he would have easily found out the whole truth. Connor would have been a dead man, whatever he thought. Alder was only keeping him alive until he had the other eight kilos in his possession. And he'd obviously figured out where Connor had hidden them. Connor wouldn't have split them up, they'd have been with the two kilos he's handed over. And Beth and Patsy had had visitors as a result.

I shake my head, Connor certainly is no mental genius.

"Phil appeared at the warehouse. He was furious about the shipment that was short, so he had dealers with nothing to sell, and beyond mad that I'd taken it. I think he'd already had a verbal lashing from Alder. He was yelling and screaming about needing stock in Pueblo that night. He saw Alder had two men there and must have known the reason. But when Alder sent him away saying he was going to deal with this—with me..." Connor breaks off and takes as deep a breath as he can with his broken ribs. I guess it must be hard to know your father didn't care how much he was hurt.

After a moment, Connor resumes, "Phil left, and that's when Alder took the gloves off his men." To his credit, he doesn't look proud of himself when he continues, "I thought if I came up with a way of getting what I'd admitted I'd taken, the two kilos, to his dealer, that he might go easy on me. I made the suggestion. At first, I offered to go myself, but Alder said he didn't trust me, and wasn't going to let me go anywhere until the drugs were with Phil's dealer. He said I had to get them there, any fucking way I could. The only thing I could think of was to involve Beth. I'd worked out the plan with him. He'd leave me capable of using my mouth if I made the calls to persuade her. His man needed stock that night." Connor's lips thin, then he adds, "I think he quite liked the twisted idea of using my sister."

The bastard's dead. Alder is going under.

"But Alder found out later there was more?"

Connor looks down, then up and provides me with the answer, "Guess I'm not so clever. There's honour among thieves. He trusted the Mexican suppliers more than his son."

"So, you admitted it, and told them where you stored them."

He grows animated. "What the fuck type of idiot do you think I am? First, I might not get on with my mom, but I wouldn't want to let loose the likes of Alder and Phil on her. And second, as soon as I told them, I'd be dead."

"Which they now think you are," I remind him.

A wan pained smile crosses his face. "I feel like I am."

"You are an idiot," I tell him with no sympathy at all. "Once Alder knew Beth could get her hands on two kilos, when they knew there was more, they knew where it had to be stored. Men have already paid your sister and mother a visit."

Fucking asshole. The moment he used Beth, he sent those motherfuckers to her door.

"They got the drugs?" This gets to Connor. "Oh, fuck, man. Are Beth and Mom okay?"

"They're fine," Beef reassures him, his face grim. "But the drugs are gone. That mean you've lost your bargaining chip with Caruso?" Beef doesn't let on they are in our possession, not his father's.

"Cops got two kilos," Connor states slowly. "Perhaps that will be enough." Then I swear a tear rolls from his eye. "I never wanted Beth to get into trouble. Thought she'd just hand it over and then walk away. How could I know she was walking into a trap? That your brother would swap places with her. Fuck, man," his eyes find Beef's, "I didn't know."

Even I have to admit he looks contrite.

"What was your plan if the drugs were still there? To offer them to Caruso?"

"Getting that much heroin off the street would look good on his record. Yeah, I'd have bargained with that."

"When's your handler back from his fuckin' sex trip?"

As Beef grins at my description of a vacation following wedding nuptials, Connor answers, "Saturday."

CHAPTER TWENTY-NINE

Mace

"So, there you have it," Beef finishes his summary of the conversation with Connor.

"He's telling the truth?"

"It's plausible and fits with the evidence," the VP reassures the prez.

Hellfire looks thoughtful. "By now Phil will have been told his son is dead, but will he take his henchmen's word for it? There's no body, only a lame story about bringing him home to bury. So, we need to do something to convince him, and my suggestion is that a burial has to take place. For that we need Beth and her mom to believe it. They've got a funeral to arrange, and a body to put under ground."

"We're going to let them believe their son and brother is dead?" Fuck. I might torture people when there's a need, but unless I've finished the job, physical wounds heal or whatever scars left can be lived with. Letting women think they're putting a family member six-feet-under? The pain will be there for life.

Hellfire sits forward, his hands clasped on the table in front of him. "We've all heard what Connor said. Though he doesn't yet know it, he's still got, or rather we have, his bargaining chip. We've got the drugs. We can pass them to Caruso, and he gets, what, ten kilos in total off the street. But it doesn't get him closer to Phil Foster, or this Alder. From what you say, Connor thinks he's a foot soldier, hasn't inherited the brains of his dad. But I reckon that's what he's been told all his life. Patsy probably thought she was right comparing him to Beth's achievements, and Connor probably read it wrong. There's a five-year age difference, of course she'd be getting ahead. Connor underestimates himself. He managed to intercept and take the drugs. Fuck knows how he did it. But he could have a lot of info in his head, info that would be of use to Caruso."

"Suppliers and routes for a start." Demon nods. "But is it enough to get our brother out of jail?"

Crease lines appear around Beef's eyes. "Caruso knows Phil's in this up to his neck, but the fed is looking in the wrong direction. Alder's the kingpin here. Ten kilos of H sounds a lot to us, but easy to replace. That shit's flooding over the border, we all know that. Caruso might play ball if Connor gives him the man at the top."

Demon's eyes snap to his VP. He looks thoughtful. "It could work," he says. "Give him the chance to stop the trade rather than just putting a dent in it."

I frown. "So, we offer that up to get Ink back? But how do you get from there to a funeral?"

"Phil and Alder are still walking free men, if they've got suspicions that Connor's alive, they'll never stop looking for him. They're still out ten kilos, remember, and by taking it, Connor's revealed just how much information he's got in his head. If they believe he's dead, Connor can start somewhere else without looking over his shoulder. And," he holds up his hand before I can ask why the fuck we should care what happens to Connor, "they won't try to use Ink's woman to locate her brother."

I hadn't thought of that. Though it will hurt them, believing Connor's dead will protect Beth and Patsy.

Demon hasn't finished. "It also buys the feds time to set up

Alder. If they think Connor's silenced forever, they won't think they've anything to worry about."

"Wit Sec," Beef says. "I know all about that. It's a fuckin' hard option. I stood by Steph, remember, when she had to give up all contact with her friends and family."

Hell shrugs. "Seems to me Connor burned his bridges a long time ago. Do you think Patsy and Beth will ever really forgive him, or trust him again? Nah. He's got to stay dead. And his mom and sister have to believe it." Hell looks at me directly. "How well could they act if they know the truth?"

I shrug. "They might be able to pull it off. They were estranged from Connor, it's not exactly a close relationship. Patsy knows what her ex-husband is and must have been half expecting it. If they don't shed many tears, won't be anyone to overly question it."

"Too big a risk, Mace. If they believe it's real, they won't have to act. Their grief will be genuine."

Fuck. Hell's right. It just goes against the grain to cause those two women such distress.

Demon looks from me to his father seated at the opposite end of the table. "I agree with Hellfire. I doubt any of us like it, but everyone outside of this room has to think Connor is dead. That includes the ol' ladies. They can shed a few tears and support Beth. You know what women are like at funerals and weddings."

There are murmurs of agreement from all around. I'm nodding my head. Christ, every female had a tissue in their hand at Mel's wedding to Ro.

"Are there any whispers about Connor being on the compound?"

Beef reassures Demon. "All anyone knows is that a Dan Forster is being given refuge for a while. Prospects have been dealing with his food, I've kept his door locked when no one's on guard. Of course they've seen Ironside coming and going, but as to who we actually have here, we've left them in the dark. The ol' ladies, they know not to ask questions."

Or if they do, they'll go unanswered, I finish in my head. Then put in, "There's no reason for Beth to think Connor is here." And even his sister would be hard put to recognise him.

The VP reminds us, "Caruso's back at the end of the week. I'm thinking we'll set things in motion. In the meantime, we'll get a funeral organised. When Connor can make contact, he can offer up the drugs and his info in return for Ink's freedom. Connor must agree to leave Pueblo and have no contact with his family again."

"And if Caruso doesn't buy it?" Lizard asks. "Soon as we admit we know where the drugs are, we put the MC in their sights. I, for one, don't want to be fuckin' followed half the time or pulled over to make sure I'm not carrying."

"I don't think that holds an appeal for any of us." Bomber looks disgusted. "Connor know we've got his stash?"

Beef gives a negative shake of his head. "I'm leaving him to stew for the moment."

Prez is thinking. His fingers are at his nose again. Used to his mannerisms, we all look toward him.

"Okay," he says at last. "Hell's made some good points. Whether or not Caruso officially puts Connor in witness protection, he's better off dead. All we need is to find ourselves a suitable body, and someone to volunteer to break the bad news to his mom and sister."

"Hopefully the body will already be dead?" Pyro asks, a half-smile on his face.

"Rusty, you still got that friend who works in the crematorium?"

Rusty grins at the prez. "If he hasn't been arrested for, let's say, his unusual attention to dead bodies, yet, yes. And sure, I'll ask if he can look out for a suitable one that won't be missed."

"So, who's up for visiting the family?"

No one meets Prez's eyes.

Ink's my fucking brother, he's often been my right hand. If I trust him to have my back, I'll not give him a reason to be unable to say the same. This won't be a pleasant job, but then mine often isn't. What's one more black mark on my soul?

"I'll do it," I find myself volunteering. "Reckon it should be someone who found him in that warehouse."

"And we've left it until today…?"

Good point. I think for a bit. "We're not exactly on best terms with Beth. Just telling her on our time, not hers."

"Well, don't leave it much longer. I'll get onto Dr Ironside, he'll make sure the paperwork stands up."

I wait only for the news there's a death certificate ready to be collected. I'm the type of person who when there's something unpleasant to be done, I get right on and do it. By the time I've detoured past the doctor's office, I'm pretty certain Beth will be home from work.

It's only a couple of hours later when, minus my cut which I left back at the clubhouse and with a beanie pulled down right down to my eyes and a scarf hiding the lower part of my face, I'm knocking at the front door of Patsy and Beth's house.

When I hear footsteps coming to answer it, I carefully school my features.

"Er, the lady of the house is… Fuck me, Mace? Didn't recognise you."

"You the doorman now, Dirt?" Glancing down I see his Glock held by his side.

"Ain't taking any chances. Told them to stay back while I check it out."

"Mace? Is there news? About Ink? Or Connor?"

"Beth," I acknowledge the woman who's appeared behind the hangaround. "Patsy around? I want to talk to you both."

"She's upstairs just finishing off some sewing."

"Patsy's fuckin' good at that shit," Dirt tells me, admiringly. "Woman's had some good news. One of the big stores has approached her wanting to use some of her designs for taller women."

I'm confused.

After going to the stairs and yelling for her mother, Beth returns. "Mom took up making my clothes when I couldn't get any to fit," she explains, her voice showing she's proud of the parent who makes her money in legit ways. Totally different from her other.

Patsy descends the stairs. "You've got news?" she's asking, before she reaches the bottom step.

"Ink?" Beth queries hopefully. "Has he been released?"

"No." I carefully examine her face as I give my one-word answer. I'd have to be blind to miss her pain. It's been increasingly harder to maintain my animosity toward her having seen the condition of her brother. I've also a grudging admiration that she hadn't wanted to involve the club or specifically Ink, so had taken the task on all by herself. I finally admit it wasn't her fault he'd been there and got caught.

As the last vestiges of my ire disappear, I soften my voice. "Can we sit down?"

"Of course." Patsy leads the way into the sitting room. "Do you want a beer or something, Mace?"

"Not at the moment. Thank you." I take a breath. "There is news, but it's not what you're wanting."

"Has Ink been hurt?" Beth covers her mouth and seems to stop breathing.

"This isn't about Ink. It's about your brother. Your son, Patsy."

Patsy's face pales at the mention of her errant child. "You've found him?"

There's no easy way to deliver this. Taking a deep breath, I get it out fast, "I'm very sorry to tell you, but he's gotten himself killed."

"Noooo!" Beth cries out.

"No," Patsy says, any remaining colour leaching from her face. "He can't be. What happened? Why are you saying this?"

I decide to tell them as much of the truth as I can, easiest way to maintain the deceit. "He didn't lie to you, Beth. Cad eventually managed to get a fix on where his calls had come from. It was a warehouse outside of Denver. We went to check it out. He'd been, he'd…"

"They beat him to death?" Beth says what I couldn't. Then her head drops into her hands, and I hear her quietly sobbing. "It was all for n-n-nothing."

Christ. It kills me to see her guilt, but I'm not sure how I can soften it. "You did what you could, Beth. What anyone would have done. You tried to save your brother."

"No. He can't be dead. He's my son. I'd know it."

I don't think Patsy's aware that she's got tears streaming down her face. I spy a box of tissues and pass them over.

"The last thing I said to him was for him to get out of my house. If…"

Beth's hand's fast holding on to Patsy's. "He wouldn't have stayed, Mom. He was too much under Phil's influence."

If only I could tell them the truth, I could admit he'd discovered too much about his and Beth's father and wanted out of that life. But in order for our plan to work, to get my brother back riding his bike, I've got to harden my heart to their distress and keep on with this charade.

"I'm sorry we didn't get there sooner." I school my features again, this time into an expression of regret.

"You did the best you could." Patsy's comfort in my direction means I'm the one now filled with guilt. "Where is he?"

"We brought his body back. He's at the crematorium." Well, by now I hope a suitable someone's body is.

"I want to see him, see for myself."

"Sorry, Patsy. It's best if you don't. He… he's not very pretty. He was beaten pretty badly. Keep your memory of him intact so you can remember him as you last saw him, not as he is now." I'm crossing my fingers hoping I can persuade her.

"What was the actual cause of death?" Beth seems intent on torturing herself. Her words might be coming out in the right order, but she's trembling, clearly having trouble holding herself together.

"Loss of blood from penetrating trauma caused by multiple stab wounds," I say quickly, as I pass over the right paperwork that they'll need to arrange the funeral. "I'm so sorry, Patsy, Beth."

Patsy reads the death certificate, then puts it down beside her. I notice her hand is violently shaking. "I disowned him when I knew he worked for his father," she says, her words punctuated by sobs. "Now I just want him back. I should have tried harder to keep him in Pueblo."

"Hey." Leaning forward, I take hold of her hands, trying to still her trembling. "I doubt there was anything you could have done to change how things turned out. He was what, eighteen when he decided he wanted a change of scenery? No talking sense to a man of that age."

"I should have tried harder," Patsy repeats.

I spare a look for Beth, she's weeping silently. It's more disturbing than if she was making a sound. She mumbles something, I struggle to hear it. I ask her to repeat what she just said.

"I should have gone to the cops. They might have found him sooner. I didn't." Beth's voice at last gets louder. "I didn't go to them when he called me, nor later because I'd have had to admit we'd been storing drugs. I didn't want to make it worse for Ink. I sacrificed my brother, and Ink's still locked up."

"You didn't sacrifice anyone," I say sharply. "You were not the one to yield the knife. You thought if you did what they asked for, that you'd keep him alive and safe. Not down to you he ended up dead." I try to make it easier. "If it makes any differ- ence, the men who did this went further than they should." Which is true. "Killing him was a mistake." Well it would have been, had they actually done so.

Hell, I'm an enforcer, not a therapist. I've made it worse not better.

"A mistake? A fucking mistake? My brother's death was a mistake?" Beth spits out. "You think that makes it any easier?"

"Who did it?" Patsy asks, suddenly. "Who killed my son?"

Do I admit her son's father was there? I decide that might be too much, so limit myself to the information I was told at the time. "A man called Alder."

"Alder?"

"You know him?" I ask sharply.

"Phil's brother-in-law." She stops her sobs long enough to speak through gritted teeth. "If he was in on it, Phil knows about it, those two were always as thick as thieves. My ex-husband killed his son." Patsy looks like she could commit murder herself.

Well fuck. I'd tried to spare her that knowledge. "Do you really think he's capable of that?"

"Oh God, I don't know." She's crying again. "There could have been a rift between him and Alder. I haven't had anything to do with him for almost two decades. Perhaps Connor got caught in a dispute between the two of them?"

I decide to stay dumb. I don't want to make matters worse, or admit I'd been talking to her son.

"Do you have anything else to tell us?" Beth looks a mess. Her face is red, her eyes swollen, but she's casting worried looks toward her mom. "Because if you haven't, I'd like you to go."

"No." I'm not surprised to be dismissed, Beth and Patsy need to grieve together, and not in front of someone they barely know. I might not want to stay, but feel I'll be remiss if I don't offer my brother's woman support. "Oh, this is the funeral home where he is. If you need help with the arrangements, just let me or Demon know."

"The Devils will help?" she says, scornfully. "Connor and I have put Ink in jail, I doubt your club wants anything to do with us. You'd probably rather dance on his grave if Ink gets the maximum sentence."

At that moment I wish I could come clean to her. To explain

what we're doing and why. But as her brother is essentially dead to her, and has to remain so to stay alive, there's nothing else to say.

"Just go, Mace."

I might not have wanted to come. Might not have had a lot of time for the two women. Didn't know what I expected, thanks for coming out of my way to give them the news? That sounds ridiculous.

But something doesn't sit right with me as I ride away from that house. I've a feeling I've somehow failed Ink.

CHAPTER THIRTY

Beth

"Dirt. Can you give us some space?"

"Sure. Look, I overheard, okay? I'm fuckin' sorry for your loss. Of course, you want to grieve without a virtual stranger hanging around."

After having him staying in the house for a couple of days now, a stranger isn't exactly what I'd call him. But he keeps himself to himself, and most of the time, we don't know he's there. But I need him out of the way. I don't want the prospect-hopeful to report back any of the discussion I'm about to have with my mom.

Dirt walks off and I wait until I've heard his footsteps clear the stairs and the door of the guest room where he's staying close.

"Why did you dismiss Mace so abruptly, Beth? He may have had more answers to give us." Mom stuffs her fist into her mouth as though to stop more sobs coming out. I'm angry, she shouldn't be made to feel this upset.

"Because Connor's not dead. Or not yet," I tell her, starting to pace.

"What?" Mom shrieks. "What are you talking about, Bethany? Why the hell did that man come and tell us all that if it's not the truth?" She picks up the paperwork Mace had handed to her and holds it up. "What's this if it's not proof that he's dead?"

"Doctors can be bought, Mom." I roll my eyes. "And we got details about how, who and where, and basically instructions to arrange a funeral."

"So, what more do you want to be told? Bethany, I know this isn't what you want to hear, but bad as it is, I'm certain it's true. Connor's gone..."

"No, he hasn't," I hiss, coming over to sit next to her on the couch. "I don't know why, or what good it will do, but I think the Devils have got him. Maybe to use as a bargaining chip to get Ink out of jail or something."

Mom stills. Her brow creases. Then she reminds me as if talking to herself, "They did take the eight kilos of drugs. Maybe it's too tempting. Would they use Connor to get more? Maybe they deserve their reputation. Just who are we dealing with, Bethany? Do you really think he could be alive?" There's a spark of interest showing through her grief. God, I pray I'm not making her hope for nothing. "The Devils aren't known for running drugs, but I suppose that much falling into their laps could be hard to resist," she continues.

"No, Mom. Do you think Mel would stay with Pyro if they got into that type of business?" I watch as she blots at her eyes, but only to mop up what leaked out previously. There're no fresh tears falling now, so that's a start. "I think it's more likely they've got a plan to use Connor to get Ink released." From what I've seen of the Devils, they'd do anything to protect or help one of their own.

"How?" she reasonably asks.

"I don't know." I hadn't thought that far. "What if they forced him to say he was the one delivering the drugs, not Ink?"

"But Ink was caught with the drugs on him. What difference would that make? And why make us believe he's dead and ask us to arrange a funeral?"

"I don't know," I repeat, almost as a wail. "But there must be something."

Mom just looks more confused.

"He's alive, Mom, I feel it. Why else would Mace suggest we wouldn't want to view the body?"

Mom stands, her hand pressing down on the arm of the sofa to provide leverage. Mace's visit had caused her to age twenty years in the same number of minutes. She crosses the room unsteadily to get to her purse and takes out her phone. When I go to ask her who she's calling, she waves me down.

She taps on the screen for a moment, scrolls up and down, and then selects a number.

"Phil?"

Oh my God. She's ringing my sperm donor.

"Yeah, it's Patsy… Yeah. A long time… Cut the crap. I've just been told my son is dead…"

"What do you mean you heard that as well?"

"His body was taken by persons unknown? So his mom and sister could bury him?"

My eyes widen throughout what I can hear of her side of the conversation. It sounds like someone's told exactly the same story to my dad.

"How did he get hurt? Alder's name was mentioned…"

"He's gone *rogue*? What the hell does that mean?"

Mom turns her eyes on me. "Could always tell when you were lying, Phil. So, tell me straight. Did you tell Connor to leave drugs in my house?" She pulls the phone away from her ear and even from the other side of the room I can hear a voice blustering. "No, they're not here now. No, I don't know where they are or who's got them…. I'm ending this call now."

"I'd appreciate it if you didn't turn up to the funeral…"

"Well of course I fucking am. I'm off to the funeral home tomorrow morning."

"No, I won't tell you which one. I'm burying a son because he became involved with you and your business."

Determinedly, her finger hits the button to end the call.

She stands, staring off into space. A minute, then another passes, before she turns to face me. "You could be right, Bethany. Or you could be wrong. Your dad's been given the same story, and I can tell he doesn't believe it. He's as angry as I've ever heard him."

My brow becomes creased. "So why all that crap about the funeral?"

"Because, it wasn't remorse and grief that I heard in his voice. Because if Connor is alive, I'm frightened for him."

My eyes widen. "You think Phil would hurt his own son?"

My question gives her pause. "Phil left and didn't look back." Her face twists. "Look, you were young when he left, I don't know how much you remember of him?"

"Not a lot," I admit. "He wasn't exactly involved in my life." As a kid I used to try to get his attention, pitiful looking back. I couldn't remember ever being successful.

"I married him when I got pregnant and he stepped up and accepted his responsibilities. It wasn't long before I realised my mistake, but stayed with him for the sake of you, and then when Connor came along, him too. But your dad had problems. He found it hard to relate to other people, empathy was something he was lacking. He could be cruel without intending it. I had a comfortable life, he wasn't overly demanding, and I could mostly turn a blind eye to his behaviour. Until he discovered there was easy money to be made and I could no longer deny he was the only one that mattered in his world, a true narcissist."

It starts to come together. "Crime was okay because he didn't care who he was hurting?"

She raises and lowers her chin. "Exactly. That's why I didn't give a damn that he forgot he had children."

"And why you were so concerned about Connor going to him."

"Phil's got an overblown view of his own intelligence and abilities. A confidence which he uses to make other people believe him. He would have seemed a good role model to an impressionable boy. He was well able to lay on the charm when he needed to." Her eyes close as if in pain. "I couldn't stop Connor when he became an adult. But I always expected—hoped—eventually Connor would see through him and realise Phil wouldn't care who he hurt if someone stood in the way between him and making a profit."

Her eyes meet mine. They signal something that chills me.

"You believe he'd hurt Connor?"

"I know Phil. Well, knew him. In that phone call just now, he wasn't upset Connor was dead, he was upset he's lost him. If he believes Connor's dead, he'll stop looking for him and he can't hurt him." She waves her hand as I go to speak. "He blustered about the heroin, I don't think Connor had told him that here was where it was hidden."

"But those men…"

"Might not have been Phil's. Maybe there were working for Alder. Alder could have tortured the truth out of him." Mom closes her eyes as though it's too painful even to think of that, but it's the truth. I'd *heard* Connor in pain. "I have difficulty believing the Devils wish us harm. Look how they've left Dirt and Nails here to protect us. Look how proud Mel is of her man. And you, are you such a poor judge of character to get mixed up with a man who'd kill someone for gain?"

"Ink took the heroin off of me, Mom. He knew the cops were there. Only a good man would do that." Or a foolish one. I'll never forget what he did, or the debt I owe him. "If Connor's alive and the Devils are keeping him that way, I don't think they'd harm him." I drop my head into my hands. "Nothing about any of this makes sense!" I almost scream.

Mom rushes over and puts her arms up. Leaning down, I hug her as best I can. We stand, like that, for a moment.

"If Connor's alive and the Devils are lying, then, maybe they're doing it to save him. If Phil's bad, Alder's worse, Bethany. If Connor's crossed them, he won't be safe."

"We need to know the truth, Mom." I know neither of us will rest easy until we do. I may be wrong to hope that my brother's still breathing, if he's gone, I need proof.

"Whatever they're telling us, I want to view who's inside the casket," Mom says with determination. "If it's Connor, I want to know."

Suddenly I have doubts that I'm right to give my mom hope. Maybe I'm wrong, and my refusal to believe it, simply that. "It could be bad, Mom. What if it is him? What if the last memory we have of him is seeing him so hurt?"

"I said me, not you, Bethany," she says firmly. "You remember Connor how he was. I'm his mother. It's my job." That's when she starts weeping again. I might have given her hope, but even after everything we've said, when the funeral home opens tomorrow, I could find out Mace had told us the truth.

Is this feeling that the enforcer is lying simply my denial that I've seen my brother for the last time?

No, no, no, and no.

I sink to the floor and wrap my arms around myself. I've tried to stay strong for my mom, but the odds are Connor is gone.

When will I stop making mistakes? If I'd called the police as soon as Connor had said he was being hurt, would he still be alive? Would I have spared him death in such a horrific way? And would Ink be laughing and drinking with his brothers?

Everything's my fault. I made the wrong choices and look where they've led.

Mom's crying on the couch, I'm weeping on the floor. After a while, we gravitate together, and hold each other. There's no more to be said. We're both determined to find out the truth in the morning, and while the hope we've been told a lie is so tempting to believe, both of us are trying to deal with the notion what we've been told may be true. Connor's no longer alive.

"Can I get you anything?" Dirt's voice sounds hesitant, unsure of his welcome.

I raise my head. "No, it's alright."

"I lost my squad." Dirt sits on the armchair opposite. "I watched them die. Only survivors were Nails and me. I know how hard grief is to deal with."

I hadn't realised they'd served together. No wonder the two share a bond.

Talking about someone else's pain is easier than dealing with mine. "What happened?"

"IED took out the jeep we were in. We were returning to camp at the time. Even had a dog with us, he was trained to sniff out bombs. If we'd been walking, he could have warned us, but in the vehicle he couldn't have known."

"What happened to the dog?" Stupid question, I know.

"He lost a leg but survived. We brought him back, well, he was part of the team. He lives with us."

"You and Nails live together?"

"Yup. Me, him and the fuckin' dog."

I wonder if they're gay, then realise it's unimportant. They're three survivors, moving on as best they know how.

"How many died?"

"Five. Including our squad leader. Two others came through the initial blast, one died shortly after in my arms before help could get to us. The other lost his leg, then died of a fuckin' infection. Nails and I only had minor injuries from the shrapnel. We turned in our papers after that. It wasn't fearful on our own behalf, it was watching our brothers die. Just couldn't take the chance of going through that again."

"That's why you want to join the MC?"

He nods. "Want men at my back again, and me to be at theirs. Nails and I have felt adrift since we've been out. Started our business, but something was missing, you know?" He leans forward, his hands clasped between his legs. "You're always waiting for the other shoe to drop. We'd been laughing that day.

On our way back after a successful mission. I'd just been handed a picture of Tinman's baby, I was staring at it when the world exploded. Tinman was killed immediately. Makes no fuckin' sense."

"That's awful," says Mom, her voice dripping sympathy.

Her tone suggests that his pain, his sharing, somehow helps us with ours. A reminder that loss happens all the time. That what we're feeling happens everywhere, every day. I'm just about to tell him, when for the second time in two days, the front door crashes in.

"Look everywhere," a voice barks.

"Phil?" Mom's on her feet as I set my eyes on a man I barely recognise.

His hair, thinning now, is more grey than black. I get the blond from my mom. His face is etched with lines, and his cheeks are reddened. He's got a gun in his hands and so have the men who've come in with him. He must have set off from Denver immediately after Mom called.

"Stay right where you are. Search him."

Dirt's standing. He sends a look of apology my way and holds out his arms to his sides. He needn't feel sorry. What can one man do against five? Nothing other than die if he tried to be a hero. Soon he's disarmed, and, for good measure, has his arms tied behind him.

"You the boyfriend?" Phil demands.

"Yes," I reply fast, my own look of contrition toward Dirt. Don't want to admit he's here as an ineffective, as it's turned out, bodyguard.

"What are your men doing?" Mom asks, her own face reddening with rage as now Dirt has been secured, four of the men have fanned out, and are opening drawers and cupboards and throwing the contents on the ground.

"Looking for my fucking stash," he rasps. He approaches and grabs hold of Mom's chin. "Where did Connor hide it?"

"The drugs are not here anymore. I told you that."

"Who took them?"

"And I told you that too," she replies steadily. "I don't know."

"Where's Connor?"

"Connor's dead," I cry out.

It gets his attention on me. He looks up into my face. "You're a fucking freak. Give you a thrill does it? Fucking a bitch like her?" The last is thrown over his shoulder to Dirt.

Dirt's face goes apoplectic. If he was my boyfriend, he couldn't be angrier.

"I'd give her a try." One of Phil's men stops what he's doing long enough to leer at me.

I'd break his freaking dick if he came near me. It's noticeable my father doesn't say a word on my behalf.

"Where's Connor?" he repeats.

"In the morgue," I say, sharply. He must see my reddened eyes; must know we've spent the evening crying at the loss of my brother. I know it's imperative he doesn't suspect we don't believe it's true for one second.

"You believe that?"

"Why should this lie?" Picking it up from where Mom had set it down, I throw the death certificate at him.

He peruses it while frowning and doesn't look as certain as he did before.

"Nothing in the garage, boss."

"Nothing upstairs, either."

One by one the four men return, presumably from searching every area of the house. Empty handed, of course.

"Where's my shit?" Phil demands once again of my mom.

"I don't know," she replies.

"Who took it?"

"I don't know. They broke in. Seemed to know exactly what they were looking for. Shifty looking men, like yours." Mom's getting annoyed.

"Describe them."

I take over. "There were two men. One was tall, dark hair, angular features. One was Hispanic." I shrug, making it all up, hoping I'm not describing a pair that he'd pick up and question for no reason. "They went straight to Connor's old room and took the stuff."

He eyes me carefully as though trying to assess whether I'm telling the truth.

"No one would fucking cross me," he declares at last. "Connor must have had a side deal going on. And you," he swings around and his narrowing eyes land on Dirt, "there's something about you I don't like."

"Phil," I snap, wanting to get his attention back to me. "You know we don't have what you want or know who has. I suspect you might get a thrill out of terrorising women, but other than that, there's no point in you being here."

"Mouthy bitch aren't you?"

"Phil, that's your daughter you're talking to," Mom snaps.

"Oh," he says, in a sly tone I don't like, "I'm well aware of that." He nods to one, then another of his men. "Bring the freak, she's coming with us." He turns to my mom who's looking on in horror. "My daughter will enjoy *my* hospitality for a time while you have a think about who took those drugs. I'm sure with the right incentive, you'll remember."

I try and signal with my eyes that Mom has to keep her mouth shut. God knows what Phil will do if we give him the information he's after and we're no longer of any use to him. But her eyes flash sympathy and her own warning. She knows what he's capable of, after all. If he could contemplate killing his son, he'd not hesitate to take out his ex-wife and daughter.

"We don't know and can't tell you," I cry out as two men approach.

"Then Patsy will have to do some investigating. If she doesn't, you won't be coming home."

Dirt, hands bound, still tries to step up, but a hard punch to his head floors him.

I struggle and cry out as one of the men grasps my arm too hard. That's Mom's undoing.

"Stop!" she screams out. "I'll tell you."

We're frozen in a bizarre tableau. I stop fighting the men who've got hold of me. Phil swings around and stares at Mom. Dirt's struggled to his knees and his face is filled with horror.

"Who?" snaps Phil when the spell is broken.

"Let her go and I'll tell you."

Instead, Phil signals toward one of the men holding me. He yanks on my hair so hard I yell out.

But still I try to stop her. "Mom. No!"

"The Satan's Devils MC. They've got what you're looking for."

She's achieved nothing.

A very unpleasant smile crosses Phil's face. "Then I'll keep Bethany until they've given them back. Connor said Beth was fucking one of them." He pauses and gives a hard look at Dirt. "You, I'm only leaving alive so you can take that message back to your club. Get me my drugs, or you won't see your girlfriend again."

My hands are yanked together behind my back and tied, then, each man has a hand on my elbow, and I'm marched out and pushed roughly into an SUV.

CHAPTER THIRTY-ONE

Mace

"How did they take it?" Beef draws me to one side when I return to the clubhouse.

"How you'd expect," I tell him. "Devastated." But I'm distracted, and the VP pulls me up on it.

"And?"

Shaking my head, I tell him what's worrying me, "They told me to leave."

He looks puzzled. "What the fuck's wrong with that? Perfectly understandable, they wanted to grieve alone."

"I'm not sure, VP. I think Beth is suspicious."

"That you weren't telling the truth?"

I shrug. "Tried to be as convincing as possible. Don't know what she could have picked up."

"Maybe you imagined it. First step to grief is denial. Probably hard to believe she won't be seeing her brother again."

I look down at the ground and then back up. "Are we doing the right thing here, Beef?"

His shoulders rise and fall now. "Fuck if I know, but Connor can't stay around here. They'll never see him again, so what difference does it make?"

"At least a mother would know her son isn't dead."

"And then she'd try to maintain contact with him. You know what Cad found out about Phil Foster. He won't give up. He's a man who likes revenge. Connor stole from him and left him well out of pocket. He's a dead man if Phil comes across him again."

He's right, but I still hadn't liked delivering the news. For some reason, I'd felt I was letting Ink down, when all I'm doing is trying everything I can to fix his situation. I'd hurt Ink's woman. Do you ever recover from the death of a loved one? I'm not sure you do. I know my great-grandmother still felt the loss of the man who died sixty years before. She was ninety when she went to join him a year or so back, and in the end, he was all she'd wanted to talk about. She'd never forgotten him, or ever got over her loss.

Would Beth?

I might not mind inflicting physical pain. But mental hurt? Seems it's there I want to draw the line. *Too late.* What's done is done.

To take my mind off the grief of the women I'd just left, I take advantage of Beef's attention, and broach my embryonic idea.

"Hey, VP. You had a gym set up in Tucson, didn't you? It get well used?"

"It fuckin' did, Brother. And does. Drummer insists on it. Monthly sparring matches in the ring too. Should have something like that here." He flexes his biceps. "I'm getting soft."

"We use a gym in town, as you well know, Beef." I raise my chin at him, having seen him there a time or two. "But Ink's been on about setting something up for ourselves."

He gives me a calculating look. "You thinking of starting the project for Ink?"

I shrug. "Ink's idea, but we'd all benefit. Thought of seeing if we could renovate one of the old buildings out the back."

"What? The ones behind the fence?"

Yeah, Beef had fenced off the more dangerous areas when he'd laid out the backyard for his old lady. "Yes. One of them is fairly sound."

"It's a good idea, Brother. Bring it up at tomorrow's church. Reckon we'd all like to chip in and do something for Ink when he gets out." The faraway look that comes into his eyes suggests he's thinking that despite our best efforts and using the drugs and Connor's knowledge of Alder to bargain with the feds, Ink could still be going away for a very long time.

"You did the yard for Steph, Bro," I remind him. "At the time you didn't know you'd see her again."

Beef snorts. "You think it worked like a charm bringing her back to me?"

I give a half-smile. "Well, it can't do any harm."

He slaps my back. "We're doing what we can for Ink, Mace. But yeah, I think brothers want to do more. A gym's a great idea in any event, but when every nail hammered in and every piece of equipment set up is for him, well, I don't see anyone turning your idea around. We'd all give our lives for each other; blood, sweat and tears would be cheerfully donated."

"And a few cuss words." I grin now.

"That too," he laughs. Then, spying Demon, walks off.

"What was that about?"

"A gym. For Ink," I explain to Lizard. He calls Judge over, and I tell him too. Next, it's Ro.

I drink beer and spend the next few hours discussing plans for the gym. The notion seems to have gone well. We're heading into spring which will mean longer, warmer days when we can get work done after we've finished our day jobs.

"Let's walk around tomorrow," Rusty suggests. "See how much needs to be done. Could always get Viper and Bullet's crew up from Tucson if the fabric of the building needs more work than we can handle. They did a fuckin' good job on the repairs to the clubhouse." He indicates the new brick matched in with the original walls, damage we'd had to repair when the Mafia came visiting a while back.

"Good call," I tell him. Looking around with a second pair of eyes would be useful and means I've got some practical suggestions to bring up at church.

"Mace. Can I do something for you?" Titsy approaches with a wide grin on her face.

Now there's an idea. I'd not have been in the mood had she asked me earlier but having spent some time talking about doing something positive for Ink, I'm certainly in a better place. As I stare down at her tits in such a low-cut top that her nipples are almost visible, my cock starts to get hard.

I begin to give her the answer which is a very definite yes. I'm opening my mouth to form the word when I'm distracted.

"See you tomorrow!" Ro shouts to no one in particular as he walks toward the door.

A usual occurrence. He normally spirits Mel home when the club girls come out to play. I turn back to what I was preparing to do. "Yeah, doll." I look over and see the pool table's not in use. Like Ink, I have no difficulty getting my rocks off in public, and the idea of my performance being watched is often a turn on. "Over there, yeah?"

My hand's on her ass as she starts to walk over, but my attention is on Pyro and Mel's progress across the room, wanting to keep it PG while his old lady's still in sight. So, I see him forced to step back and pull Mel out of the way as the door flies open, and in runs a distraught woman. "Help, I need help," yells Beth's mom, Patsy. She's followed by an anguished Dirt, one of his eyes seems to be shut and swollen.

All eyes shoot to her. She might be small, average height for a woman but tiny to us, but at the moment she's commanding the attention of the room.

"Phil's got Bethany. He wants his drugs back."

Beef moves fast and is over to her before I can get my feet moving. "Demon's office." He gives her no choice, taking her by the arm and leading her across the clubroom. His eyes catch mine and he jerks his head suggesting, or more likely demanding that I come along too. He gives the same signal to Thunder.

I pause only long enough to glare at the club girls and even spare one for Jayden who's sitting on Pal's lap. Pyro's got his arms around Mel, holding her back and talking fast into her ear.

Bella and Titsy mime zipping their lips shut.

Beef's talking on the phone as he opens Demon's door. "Prez, need you back here fast."

Then he points Patsy to a chair. Taking the one next to her, he turns it to face her, and reaching forward takes hold of both of her hands. "Tell us exactly what happened, Patsy."

She needs no encouragement. "After he," she indicates me with a tilt of her head, "came to tell me my son was dead, Bethany and I discussed it. It didn't seem right, and maybe it's just optimism, but we didn't believe it."

Christ, and there I was thinking I'd gotten away with it. I exchange a glance with Thunder, an apology in mine.

"Where does Phil come in?"

"I haven't had contact with Phil for years, but he hasn't changed his number. I called him to see if he knew about Connor's death. If he was dead, well, I wouldn't put it past him that he was behind it. And now he's got Bethany..." Angrily she wipes a tear from her eye as if she's got no time for it.

Strength runs in the family it would seem. She's distraught but will leave her inevitable breakdown until later.

But hell, she's right to be worried, and so am I. Phil stood by and watched two of his men kick and punch his son almost to death. What a fuckup of a job we've done of protecting Ink's woman. Now Beth's been kidnapped by a monster. I have no confidence she'll be returned unharmed. *What if he hurts her like Connor?* I shift in my seat, knowing I could never look my brother in the eye again. Maybe if I hadn't been so inclined to blame her, I'd have protected her myself. What did we do? Pass her and her Mom on to two hangarounds who we're not even confident enough to patch in as prospects yet.

Thunder's voice pulls me back to the here and now. "Go over the conversation you had with Phil."

For a second, Patsy bows her head. "It's my fault," she says, quietly. "I shouldn't have called. But Bethany was convinced Connor wasn't dead, and I wanted to know if Phil knew. When he said he did, I, er, I asked him whether he knew Connor had left drugs with me."

Phil might not have had that knowledge until she opened her mouth. Alder had, Connor had said his father had left the warehouse by then.

"And?" prompts Beef.

"He was mad, furious. He asked if I still had them. I told him persons unknown had taken the drugs." She pauses, and her brow creases with pain. "That was the end of it. Until, a couple of hours later he turned up in person."

"Didn't Dirt confront him?" That man is never getting patched in.

"Phil bashed in the front door, came in with four other men. Dirt didn't have a chance. If he'd tried to shoot him, he'd have ended up dead. They disarmed him and tied him up, hit him when even then he tried to help. I couldn't do anything." Her voice cracks, and she takes a pause to swallow a couple of times. "They searched the house as if they thought I was lying. Left it in a hell of a mess, but of course, they didn't find anything. And then they... then he... he said he was going to take Bethany."

"She was forced to go with them?"

"I thought I could stop him," Patsy wails. "I thought—or I wasn't thinking. I thought he'd leave her with me. I've just lost a son, I couldn't risk losing my daughter."

I stiffen. I notice Beef has too. It's Thunder who asks, "What did you do?"

Patsy swallows. "I told them the Satan's Devils MC had taken them."

Jesus H Christ she's dropped us right in it.

"But he took her anyway?" Of course, he did. It's why she's here.

"Yes." She's sobbing now. "He said she'd be staying with him until he gets his drugs back. I'm sorry…"

But who can blame her? I'd just told her, her son was dead. She was a mother doing anything she could to protect her only remaining child.

Beef, Thunder and I exchange glances while she quietly weeps. Behind us the door opens and the prez comes in. His eyes take in the distraught woman and then go to Beef with a raised eyebrow.

Beef sums it up succinctly, "Phil Foster has kidnapped Beth. He'll release her when he gets his drugs back." My eyes flick to Patsy and then back to the prez. "Phil knows we've got them."

"Fuck." Demon pushes back his hair with both hands. "Dirt?"

"Unharmed but overpowered. Seemed he couldn't do anything. Phil came mobbed up."

"He had instructions to call us—"

Beef shrugs. Guess Dirt's going to have to come up with an explanation for us. Can't see him getting his patch unless it's good.

Demon turns and smashes his fist against the wall. It's not hard to know what he's thinking. Satan's Devils have been pulled into this mess. Our brother Ink asked for one thing and one thing only, to protect Beth. Now she's been kidnapped, and if we give up the drugs to save her, there goes our leverage to get Ink released.

"Thunder? Get Rusty." Prez eyes are full of concern for Patsy. She's a complete mess, doubled over and crying unconsolably, now having given into that breakdown I'd been certain was coming.

Demon taps his VP on his shoulder, and when he stands up, takes his place on the chair in front of Beth's mother. "Patsy," he starts, his voice quiet. Then it sharpens when he repeats her name. The third time gets her looking up. "Will you listen very carefully to what I have to say?"

She makes a visible effort to pull herself together. Beef's produced some tissues from somewhere, and he passes them to her. After blowing her nose loudly and mopping at her tears, she raises her eyes to Demon. "I'll do anything. I can't lose both my children in one day. Look, I don't know what you took the drugs for. I know they're worth a lot. Maybe I can buy them back off you? I'll sell my house, do anything…"

"Fuck woman!" Demon roars. "I don't want your money. We didn't take the drugs to sell them. What the hell do you think we are?"

"I don't know," wails Patsy. "I just know Phil's got my daughter, and I want her back. The fastest way is to give him what he wants." Her eyes close then open again. "He's a psychopath, with no emotion. He'd hurt her without a second thought."

"And what happens then?" Demon challenges. "We give the drugs back. Do you think he'll simply let Beth come home? You know too much, what's to stop you going to the cops? He hasn't been busted for drug dealing, he'll want to keep it that way. I know you don't want to hear this, but it won't stop with a simple exchange."

I'm immediately on Demon's wavelength. Giving into Phil's demands won't solve anything. Beth and Patsy know far too much, I doubt Beth would be coming home. And Patsy? Well, she might be controlled over threats to her daughter, or more likely, she'll meet with a fatal accident of some sort. Even we'll not be safe. If we roll over and give Phil his H back, he could try and turn us into his bitches, threaten to take us down unless we work for him. Now it's my turn to smash my fist against the wall. *Fuck. What a mess. Ink, I'm so fucking sorry. I failed you in the one thing you asked.*

"We go to Denver. Face him head on," I suggest.

"What's the size of his organisation, Patsy? Anything you

know could help." Demon's voice and my proposal have Patsy straightening her spine.

She, in turn, ignores Demon and addresses me, "You'd get her back?"

"Patsy," Demon shoots me a threatening look as he gets her attention again. "We'll do everything we possibly can to bring her home but racing off blindly isn't going to help anyone. Tell us everything you know."

"Thank you," she says, but I notice she's trembling. "I don't know much at all. His brother-in-law, Alder, used to be his business partner years back. He said he had a falling out with him, but I don't believe that's the truth. He said it was Alder who'd hurt Connor. Oh my God, Connor," she wails his name as her double loss comes back to her.

I hold my breath, wondering whether Prez will ease her mind and tell her, her son is alive. In the state she's in now, I don't know if that will make anything better or worse, or whether she'd be able to deal with the knowledge rationally. She could rush out and shout his survival to the world, which would cause his death.

"I'm sorry about your son." Demon sounds genuinely sympathetic, and he probably is because he's keeping back information she should know. "But I promise you this. We will get Beth back."

She might not know the reason, but Prez has just made a vow. One we'll keep. For Ink.

CHAPTER THIRTY-TWO

Ink

I raise a questioning eyebrow at Sykes seated beside me. He gives an almost imperceptible shake of his head. Neither he nor I have any idea why the detectives want to talk to me this morning. More of the same, I expect. A repeat of the same line of questioning, wanting to trip me up so the prosecutor can build a strong case.

I'd spent the night trying to come to terms with the idea I wouldn't ever have my freedom again, would never watch the pavement rushing past under my wheels, or feel the wind in my face as I rode.

I thought I'd accepted that the first night but must still have had a kernel of hope. It hadn't come as a surprise that bail had been denied. Anyone who wears a cut of an outlaw MC can expect no mercy once they're in the clutches of the law. But for my sanity I'd held onto the notion that I could have some time to ride my bike, and to give Beth a fucking she'd remember forever before I went inside for the best part of my life. That I wasn't even going to be able to say goodbye properly had hit me hard.

I'm a hardened biker, a veteran, but last night I'd had to wipe tears from my eyes. If I'd deserved such a punishment, maybe it wouldn't be so difficult to accept. *I'm doing it for Beth.*

Does she deserve it?

Yeah. She does. I might not know the ins and outs of it, but she wouldn't have been there that night without good reason. I'd already known it in my gut. Demon's message via Sykes had only confirmed it. I'd feel worse if I was the one on the outside, and she was locked up.

Have I really claimed her as my old lady? Seems like I have. A small smile curves my lips as I dream about a future I'll never have with the tall woman who it seems I've become fonder of while we've been apart. Outside, I'd never have allowed myself to think of a wife and a family. Now I no longer have a chance, that's all that I want, along with my bike and club, of course. Like I know the Satan's Devils are the brothers I want to ride with, the only woman I want by my side is Beth.

But I can't have her.

She thinks I hate her. Was I wrong to shut her out? Yes, because I miss her. No, because cutting her out of my life might keep her safe. Might. The rucksack and her connection to it has been going around and around my head.

My smile which had already slipped disappears completely as the door opens, and two men step inside. Detectives Barker and Hastings.

I sit back and fold my arms, preparing myself. Have they found more evidence they can twist and use to stitch me up?

Barker doesn't look as full of himself as he had two days ago. He sounds tired, when he states, "Fender Childs. What's your relationship with him, Mr McNeish?"

"I don't know the man. Never heard his name before you brought it up last time." Nope. They're not going to trip me up and make me contradict myself.

"Do you know this man?" He slides a photo across the desk.

I take it and study it, keeping any emotion from my face as my mind whirls fast wondering how much to admit. I decide to go with the truth. "It's Connor Foster," I say at last. "I'm pretty certain, though I only met him briefly once that time I went to

Beth's house." Staring at the photo I realise how similar the siblings are. Same height and same facial features, though Beth's are softer and more feminine.

"Was that the man you took the drugs from that night?" Barker asks.

I stare at the photo again. I have a moment of guilt before I speak next. He might not have been there, but it was his drugs in that bag. He deserves to be locked up far more than me or his sister. "It was dark," I begin. "I couldn't see his features. But from the build it's very likely. How tall is he? The man who was there was almost as tall as me. And slender. But I couldn't swear to it."

Barker looks down at his notes. "Foster is six foot three."

"Then quite possibly."

"There's a good chance?" he presses.

I shrug. "As I said, I didn't get a look at his face and might not be able to pick him out in a line-up, but it's not beyond the realm of possibility."

"But you definitely saw Connor Foster at Ms Foster's house?"

"I did."

The detectives exchange glances.

It's Sykes who makes the suggestion, "If Connor Foster was seen at Ms Foster's house, then he would have had the opportunity to take Ms Foster's rucksack."

They remain impassive, but what he's said makes sense.

"Fender Childs has been talking," Hastings suddenly speaks. "He's told us he was to pick up a package that had been in the possession of Connor Foster."

Fender's been spilling everything? That's music to my ears as he has nothing to implicate me or my brothers.

"I take it you've made a plea bargain with him?" Sykes question is also an explanation.

Again, they make no comment.

My lawyer, though, speaks, "Have you spoken to Mr

Foster?"

Barker presses his lips together. "Connor Foster is apparently dead. His death certificate, dated last Sunday, came up when we searched for his name."

"What?" The question's surprised out of me. *Beth will be in pieces.* Anyone would be, even if they were estranged. Losing a blood relative isn't easy. Her mom will be beside herself. Fuck that I can't be there to support them and help. "How?"

"He was beaten and stabbed. Died of his injuries."

Briefly I wonder whether the club had had a hand in it but dismiss that fast. If they'd tortured and killed him for a part he played in getting me arrested, no one would ever find his body.

I suppress a smile at how frustrated these detectives must be. They've made a bargain with Fender Childs, but the only person he's presumably fingered, has turned up dead. I'd laugh if I could get away with it. Then my mental amusement fades. *Connor dead?* Oh, Beth, you've lost so much. All I want to do is be there and hold her. But it's impossible. Fuck.

Sykes taps the table. "I can't see how you've got any case against my client. Any jury or judge would agree that it was more likely Connor Foster took the rucksack from his sister's house. He was the one who brought the bag to the drop, and Mr McNeish's story holds water. Mr McNeish scared Connor Foster off and was taking the bag and contents to the cops, having made the reasonable assumption that anything being brought to that location on that night was likely to be something the police would be very interested in, the police who I'll remind you, Mr McNeish was very aware of being close that night."

I know they are going to argue.

But they don't. Barker looks at Sykes rather than me. "We are not intending to proceed with bringing any charges against your client at this point in time."

What? I shake my head fast in case my ears need clearing.

"We may, however, wish to question Mr McNeish if our

inquiries show he might have something useful to offer. But for now, Mr McNeish is free to leave."

As the detectives pull their papers together, get up and go, I remain seated, unable to believe the words I've just heard.

"You going to just sit there?" Sykes is looking at me with something akin to amusement on his face.

"I can go?" It seems like a dream.

"You can go. You want a lift to the compound?"

I'm still trying to process how my fortunes have turned around. Yes, the clubhouse first, see my brothers, pick up my bike. Then I'll go see Beth and commiserate about the death of her brother, then when she's in a better head space, find out how she'd feel about becoming my old lady.

"Too fuckin' right I'd like a lift," I tell him, a grin now splitting my face.

I have to go through the formalities, first signing the forms to regain my possessions, carrying my cut as I'll be leaving in a cage. I experience an incredible sense of relief when I'm on the right side of the steel door and security gates. It's not until I'm out in the open that I start to relax and begin to lose the feeling someone's going to run out from behind me and say letting me go was a mistake.

The skies are grey and there's a cold winter drizzle falling, but it doesn't prevent me raising my head and just staring at the open expanse of sky above me. Only minutes ago, I hadn't thought to see such a sight again, or not when it wasn't framed by prison walls.

"You coming?" Sykes is standing by his open door, unlike me, he seems to object to getting wet, as after his question he quickly slides into the driver's seat.

Yeah. I'm fucking coming. Don't want to stay here any longer than necessary. As I turn and walk smartly to the passenger side of his Lexus, I start to believe I really am free.

Sykes puts the car into gear. As he draws away, part of my mind wonders just how much we're paying him for him to be able to afford a high-end model car. But part thinks however much it is, it's worth it if he had anything to do with getting me out.

During the short journey, I try, not totally successfully, to rearrange my thoughts. I'd spent the last few days convincing myself I could cope with being locked up for the rest of what could be a short life. Bikers are in danger in the penitentiary. Now I'm apparently a free man.

A free man who's got a ball and chain. A man who's claimed an old lady. Well, as far as my brothers are concerned, I have. Beth, though, she's ignorant of my intentions. Guess I'll let her grieve some for Connor, then I better try to ease her back into a relationship that she thought I'd rather forget.

On the inside, there was some comfort in knowing everyone thought she was mine, a dream to cling onto. Now it's reality and I've got to face it. Is that still what I want? Now when I've got back my freedom, will I find my mind changing and our relationship disappearing like smoke?

I want to fuck her again, no doubt about that. My dick's already stirring in anticipation. But live with her?

Could we make it work?

Do I even want to try?

What if someone's let slip that I claimed her? What if she knows and she's all starry-eyed because she's got what she wanted, a biker of her own like Mel snagged Ro. What if she clings if I don't want to make a go of it? What if she holds me to promises I made inside?

I'd done it to give her protection. Had my brothers known it was a sham? Would they be let down if I unclaimed her just as fast as I'd told them she was mine?

And what if I did? Judge had been sniffing around her, Sparky too. As a woman with no patch on her, someone as beautiful and sexy as her would be fair game and wouldn't be on her own for too long.

"You okay?" Sykes gives me a strange look. "I swear you just growled."

But I'm saved from giving an answer. Karl opens the gates, his eyes widening as he recognises me sitting next to my lawyer, but like any good prospect, doesn't ask anything to satisfy his curiosity. All he does is give me a chin lift, accompanied by a wide grin.

"You coming in?" I ask Sykes.

"No. Just tell Demon he'll get my bill in good time."

I hold out my hand, he does likewise and shakes it. "Thank you for everything you've done."

"Cops have your number now. Stay out of trouble, Ink."

"You can bet on it." I never want to go through the last few days again.

Then I'm out of the car and opening the door to the clubhouse as Sykes does a three-point turn and heads out the gate.

I expect the clubhouse to be fairly quiet, it's Tuesday night after all, and not a day we'd have a party. Of course, there'll be club girls around doing what they're there for, brothers drinking or playing pool, but those who live off the compound will probably have gone home. I'm just looking forward to seeing any friendly face, have had it up to the back teeth with drunks or the police. But when I step inside, I'm surprised to find it's crowded, and noisy. Well, until people turn to see who's come in the door. Then silence descends like a switch being thrown.

I stand, hold my hands out to my sides, and grin widely. "Hey, honey, I'm home," I call out loudly, then chuckle at my own joke. It's only seconds before I realise nobody's laughing.

"Hey, I didn't bust out. They let me go," I say, wondering why no one's rushing up to greet me.

"Ink." Mace moves at last, coming forward and pausing, then his arms come around me in the bear hug I'd expected to be the first of many. But as we exchange back slaps, he doesn't say how good it is to have me back. Instead he tells me, "I'm so fuckin' sorry."

Pushing him away, I hold him at arm's length. "What the fuck you talking about?" I go to the only explanation for his behaviour that I can think of. "Who's fuckin' died?" I already know about Connor, but even so, can't think Beth's brother would cause my brothers' sorrow. They didn't know the man, unless, Beth's too distressed.

"Beth…" he starts.

Beth's dead? She can't be.

"What's happened?" I ask, at first quietly. Then start shouting, "What the fuck's happened to Beth?" Beth can't be dead. We never had a chance to find out what we were to each other. Pain slams into me at the thought I'm free, but it sounds like she's still lost to me. "What the fuck is going on?"

"Beth's been taken…"

"She's not dead?" I ask hurriedly, wondering if my interpretation's wishful thinking.

The VP comes up and pushes Mace to one side as if realising he's making a mess of telling me what's going on. "She's been taken by her father. He wants to exchange her for the drugs."

"What drugs? What the fuck is going on, Beef?"

Nothing makes sense. Beth doesn't have anything to do with her father. And what the fuck is all this about drugs? The police had gotten what she was carrying that night.

"I left her under your protection, Beef." My voice is growing louder. "What the fuck do you mean she was kidnapped? When? Where fuckin' from? Who do I kill as they didn't protect her?"

"I'm sorry…" he starts.

I interrupt. "Sorry? Fuckin' sorry?" My hand slashes through the air as all everyone seems to be doing is apologising. "What are you fuckin' doing about finding my ol' lady?"

"We're just about to meet about that," the prez's voice says, sharply and loudly. "Welcome home, Ink." He draws closer, clasping my hand and pulling me to him. "So fuckin' glad to have you back. I'm just sorry you've got out only to have to deal with this."

CHAPTER THIRTY-THREE

Beth

Sandwiched between my sperm donor's two henchman does not make for a comfortable two-hour journey. They're big and muscular, and I'm not a small person, being so squashed, the invasion of my personal space is claustrophobic.

My father isn't even in the same car, so I can't appeal to him. Instead, another of his men is driving, and a fourth is in the front passenger seat.

I keep quiet. I have no expectation that anything I could say might appeal to any better nature they may, or probably may not, possess. It's my father who's in charge of the purse strings, he's the one paying them. I've nothing to offer, except the one thing I couldn't even bring myself to suggest. It's not lost on me that the man next to the driver was the one who'd already made lewd comments and said things which made my blood run cold. When he glances over his shoulder and views me up and down carefully, the whole time leering, I want to shrink and disappear. *Phil would never let his men touch me.* Or would he? What do I know of the man who hasn't cared he had a daughter for eighteen years?

He said he'd exchange me for eight kilos of heroin. He didn't promise to give me back unharmed or unmolested.

Phil scares me, and with good reason. I had made myself believe Connor was still alive and breathing, the fact that Phil has come after me instead, means my optimism was for nothing. If he was convinced Connor wasn't dead, it would be him he'd be going after. That he knew what had happened to my brother strongly suggests he had a hand in it. Condoned it? Quite possibly.

What will Mom do? I run through her options. *Go to the police?* And say what? That I'm with my father? I'm twenty-seven, not a kid, and Phil would probably say I'd gone willingly. To give all the background would drop all of us in it. *Go to the Satan's Devils?* But she's put them in Phil's sights. How I wish Mom had kept her mouth shut, but I know she was only trying to keep me safe, taking a gamble which hadn't paid off.

Maybe the Devils will just hand the heroin over. The only problem with that is they might have destroyed them already. I feel myself pale. If there are no drugs, what would happen to me and the Devils then? I'm not naïve, I can guess how much money those drugs were worth. Maybe not put a precise value on them, but it has to be one heck of a lot. More than I've got or am likely to ever possess.

Phil's got at least five rough-fighting men working for him. I have no doubt he's got more, or even a small army. Would he go after them for revenge, the Devils and my friends, their old ladies? Mel's already lost so much, oh God, I hope no more harm or worry is heading her way. Heaven forbid she loses the baby she's carrying. They're Ink's family. I've taken his freedom from him. If Phil starts a war, I could be taking his family as well.

How the hell has it come to this, me being abducted by my own father? I didn't need Mom to spell out that he lacks empathy, he didn't so much as turn a hair at his son being dead. No, his only concern is the drugs and therefore the money he's lost.

I thought Ink being in jail and Connor dead was enough punishment inflicted on me. Now more people might die or be hurt because of the wrong decisions I made. Everything I touch seems to turn sour.

Maybe it's best Ink's locked up. Free, he might have tried to save me, and could have ended up killed instead.

The car rolls on. The men discuss a game they plan to watch at the weekend. Then, purposefully to unnerve me, they discuss their favourite sexual positions. I try to ignore their talk about women taking it in the ass. When I'm asked if I've tried it, I pay them no attention, focusing instead on my memory of Ink suggesting the very same thing. I hope, if I'm ever brave enough to try, it would be with the man who'd treat me carefully. I've no doubt I'd be forced if Phil lets his men have me. *He wouldn't, would he?* He's my father.

I close my eyes, trying to block out everything except thoughts of Ink. Wondering what would have happened if Connor had never left those drugs in our house. Would we have continued our relationship? Would there have ever been a chance he'd have made me his old lady? It's an impossible dream, but better to cling onto than consider the reality that's facing me now. I hope he really does hate me, then he wouldn't get upset when he finds out I'm gone.

Mom. I've tried to ignore the thought that she must be going crazy. She's supposed to be burying her son, now she's lost her daughter as well.

The journey seems to go on forever and the men won't stop talking. I want to scream, *Shut up*. I don't want to hear any more lack of respect for women. I don't want to know what it's like to force your cock into an unwilling partner. But I stay silent, knowing they're only trying to taunt me.

It's not even a relief when we finally draw up to some gates which seem to slide open automatically. Phil's lair, I suppose. I have a sense of being about to jump out of the frying pan and into the fire. All I can hope is that I don't get burned too badly.

My father has arrived before us. I'm shown into a pleasantly furnished room. He's standing in front of a fireplace holding a glass of something which is either whiskey or brandy, but I don't get to know as he offers nothing to me. One of the men who'd brought me in, closes the door with himself this side of it, as if emphasising I can't escape.

My father takes a sip of his drink and then waves the glass toward me. "What's your relationship with the Satan's Devils?"

"My boyfriend rides with them." He knows that already. "Other than that, I have none."

His eyes narrow. "Why the fuck did you give eight kilos of heroin to them? Heroin that was mine."

I shrug. "They just came and took them. I wasn't at home." Again, the truth.

Suddenly he puts down his glass and strides toward me. "Who told them where they were? You?"

My brother's dead, there's nothing more Phil can do to him. He might as well take the blame. "I don't know, Connor perhaps? Maybe Connor had worked out a deal with them?"

"Connor wouldn't have been so stupid," he spits into my face. "He knows the Devils don't deal in drugs." His hands twitch at his sides, and for a second, I fear he's going to hit me. Then, as if making an effort to control himself, he turns and says, as if he's voicing an idea, "I suppose anyone can change their views for that amount of money." He's quiet for a moment, then accuses, "I think you know a lot more than you're saying."

In truth, I don't. The Devils took the drugs because I told them they were there, and we wanted them out of the house. What they did with them, or plan to do with them is a mystery. I tell him a version of that. "I don't care what happened to the illegal substances. Had Connor told us what was there, we wouldn't have allowed him to leave it."

"Don't fucking care about something with a street value close to a million dollars?" His eyes widen in disbelief, and his jaw clenches betraying his anger.

I shrug. "Heroin kills people."

He snorts. "It kills people, whoever distributes it. I assure you, my naïve *daughter,* whoever took it will sell it and walk away with *my* money."

He's right. Most people would. But I know in my gut the Devils wouldn't.

"What are you going to do if the Devils don't give the drugs back?"

He stares at me as if I'm stupid. "You better fucking hope they do." His eyes flash me a warning. "But if they don't? I'll take them, of course. They can't have shifted that volume already. No one gets away with crossing me. But what am I going to do about you either way is another question." He eyes me in a manner I don't like, then goes back and picks up his glass, saying over his shoulder, "Don't think for a moment this is a fond family reunion, and don't bother playing on our relation-ship. I already got burned when I took your brother under my wing. I left you when you were a kid, never wanted to know about you. Thought Connor might have been useful, but he fucked up. I don't think of either of you as family. You got that, Bethany?"

It's hard to hear, but I'd already guessed there was nothing humane in him to appeal to. I nod.

"So you think on that. If you know more than you're telling me, if this was some plot you and your brother cooked up with the Satan's Devils to steal from me, my men will get it out of you. If you don't have anything useful to offer, then you're going to wish you had."

There's a chuckle from the man standing behind me.

I go cold as I read between the lines.

"But tonight, I'll see what Patsy gets up to. I'll give her a chance to get my drugs back." A twisted grin comes onto his face. "Straitlaced Patsy will have to walk into an outlaw MC if she wants her daughter back. Whether she'll walk out alive is another matter entirely. Men like that," he shakes his head, "don't care who they step on. And don't get your hopes up, a million dollars is a fucking lot of money. They won't give it up for a woman, I can tell you that. But if she hasn't contacted them already, I may need to send her a finger to prompt her. George, show her to the guest room, will you?"

The casual mention of cutting off one of my fingers is terrifying. He doesn't care about the danger he thinks he's put my mom in, forcing her to ask favours of an MC. I didn't know men as evil as him existed.

"Want me to keep her company?"

My father looks over my shoulder for a moment while I forget to breathe. Surely, he wouldn't let his men rape me?

But he seems to give it some consideration. "Not tonight. Time for that later. Let's see if the Devils make contact. We might need her… undamaged… to tempt them to hand the drugs over. Unlikely, but possible."

"Shame," I hear from behind.

There's another man waiting outside in the hallway with what I can only describe is a look of anticipation on his face. George gives a rueful shake of his head in his direction, then points me to the stairs and follows me as I ascend.

Like the rest of the house the room I'm shown into is clean, tidy and well-furnished. The windows though are locked securely, I know as George checked and pocketed the key. There's an en-suite bathroom, and a bed which would look comfortable in any other situation. All I see when I look at it though is George and/or another man forcing me down on it and me being raped.

George sees me staring down at the comforter and palms his crotch. As I look up in horror, he mouths, 'Soon', then, thank goodness, he disappears out of the door. I'm not surprised to hear a key turn in the lock.

As soon as the door closes behind him, instead of relief, my body starts to betray me. My eyes lose focus, a wave of heat floods through me making me sweat. I feel nauseous and dizzy, as though I'm about to faint. My breath comes in fast pants and my heart races.

I sink to the bed before I fall to the floor and, with my head in my hands, try to force myself to slow my breathing. I fight with the feeling that I'm dying, one half of my brain trying to rationally explain that I'm not, the other half swearing I am.

In, out, I breathe. *Slow, slow,* I tell myself. Making my lungs expand and deflate to a regular rhythm instructed by the sane side of my brain.

Gradually, my panic begins to subside, and then the tears start. Everything is overwhelming me. One minute I was enjoying life with my new boyfriend, looking forward to seeing him again. Then, because of my vain attempt to save my brother, he was arrested, and Connor died despite my efforts to keep him alive. Now I've been kidnapped, and I'm beginning to realise, even if the drugs are returned to him, Phil won't let me go. Everything with him is about making a profit, and I hate to think how he could make one from me.

Will I ever see my home and Mom again?

Will George get his chance to carry out his threat?

No, no. I can't think of that.

My body, if not my mind, calmer, I view my prison. The only upside is it's probably more pleasant than the one where Ink is detained, but four walls you can't escape from means I'm as much a prisoner as he is. The thought crosses my mind that I might have had a more pleasant future if I'd turned myself into the police. At least there'd be some authority I could appeal to if I was mistreated. Here there is none.

I lie on the bed. To say I spend the night with one eye open is an understatement. In fact, I have both. I stay fully clothed, wanting nothing to make me feel more vulnerable than I already am. There's nothing I can use as a weapon conveniently left lying around, and even if there was, I don't think it would be something I'd use. There're easily enough men here who could overpower me and taking them on would only end up with me being hurt. From what I've seen, the men here would love the chance to manhandle me. I'll have to use my brains to escape, not the brawn I don't have. *Why do I run and not work out?* Sure, my legs are strong, but I've no impressive muscles anywhere else.

When dawn breaks, I use the facilities but do little more than splash my face, wash my hands and clean my teeth with the toiletries provided. I'd love a shower, but I'm not getting naked when there's no lock on the bathroom door.

A short while after I'm ready for the day, I hear a key turning and the catch on the door opening. Trepidation floods through me, though it's not one of the men. I notice with relief, it's a pretty Hispanic girl. She looks like she's in her late teens or early twenties.

Would she help? Perhaps.

"Can you get a message to someone for me?" I ask quickly as she crosses the room and places a breakfast tray on the table by the window.

"*No hablo inglés*," she tells me. Then repeats so there can be no mistake, "No English."

And I don't speak Spanish. Well, I suppose that would have been too easy. She was probably chosen as the person to deliver my food on purpose so there would be no chance for communication.

She leaves, I don't stop her. For want of anything other to do, I go to the tray. There are pancakes, bacon, eggs, and sausage links, together with syrup and a variety of sauces and condiments. There's orange juice and a pot of coffee. It looks like a breakfast for the condemned man or woman for that matter.

I've no appetite, but unsure when I'll be able to eat again, I nibble on a pancake. I eye the orange juice and sniff it. Then scoff at myself. Why would Phil drug me if he wants me to talk? *But what if he can get his hands on a truth serum?* Oh, for goodness' sake. All the films I've seen suggest that has to be injected.

As I eat, I stare out the window. Phil's done well for himself with his ill-gotten gains. The grounds of this place are spectacular. A man comes into view pushing a wheelbarrow. He's another Hispanic. Somehow, I suspect Phil's workers aren't legal and probably paid far less than minimum wage.

I have no watch, no phone. There's no television in the room. I have no idea of the time, but it seems disproportionately long before the door opens. Again, it's George.

I'm not going to cower or show my fear, though inside I'm trembling.

"Back on escort duty?" I ask snidely. "Haven't you got a proper job to do?"

He grabs hold of my hair as I go to walk past him, yanking on it hard. "I suggest you keep a civil tongue in your head. Otherwise, you'll find something between your lips which will mean you won't be able to talk."

I smile sweetly. "Put that cock near my mouth and I'll bite it off." I give him my back and make my own way to the stairs, hoping he's never heard of a dental gag—something I'd read about in a book. But I doubt George is one for reading.

"This way," he corrects as I head for the room I'd met my father in the night before.

CHAPTER THIRTY-FOUR

Ink

"I want to fuckin' go now. Hit them under the cover of darkness." I slam my fisted hand down onto the table. I've been a free man for an hour now and already I'm sick to death of just hanging around.

I'd had no idea what I was going to say when I first saw Beth. Clearly my reaction would depend on her own. What I wanted to do was dispense with words and simply pull her close and take her mouth while pulling her ass against my pelvis, leaving her in no doubt of my physical feelings toward her. Then, I'd comfort her about the death of her brother, and, in time, tell her she was mine. My only worry had been her reaction. Would she push me away as she thinks I hate her? Or, would she understand?

I didn't expect I'd not even have the chance to see her, let alone touch her.

I thought I'd hit rock bottom when I was arrested for something I hadn't done. Now I've reached a new low. My fear for Beth consumes me and hasn't gotten easier while I tried to catch up with what's been going down. Quite rightly, they've not wasted time walking me through everything, so I've had to get up to speed via piecing together the patches of information I'm hearing. One thing for sure, Phil's bad news. He condoned the beating and death of his son. Now his daughter's in his hands, I'm fucking terrified.

I'm a man of action. I can barely sit still, let alone waste time going over old ground.

As he's already done a time or two during this meeting, Demon heaves a sigh, but keeps his calm. "Ink, I know you're fuckin' worried out of your mind. I've been where you are, remember? But we've got to come up with a foolproof plan. This is Phil Foster we're talking about. We don't know the lay of the land, who he's got working for him, or how well he's protected. We need information before we can move."

Cad nods across at me. "I've got messages out to all my contacts. If they've got any info that can help, I should start getting it anytime now."

"Beef's gone to talk to Connor," Thunder tells me. "He'll give us what he can."

I stare at Thunder in confusion, but Pal makes a suggestion before I can query his statement.

"If we wait for daylight, we can use the drone."

Drone? My eyes crease as I know nothing about what he's talking about. I've gathered some of the details of what went down over the weekend but had clearly missed a lot of shit. And why's Beef off communing with the fucking dead? "Connor's dead," I spit out. "How the fuck…"

"He's not dead. Who told you he was?" Prez says sharply.

"The fuckin' cops."

That causes laughter to go around the table.

"They believed it?" Demon asks.

"Yes, they fuckin' believed it. Part of the reason they let me off. I identified him as the man who I'd taken the bag from on Saturday. Gets me off the hook and Beth in the clear." I think for a moment trying to process this new information. "Patsy and Beth know he's alive?"

"No, they think he's dead."

My eyes widen. Christ. Patsy must be in pieces. One child she believes she'll be burying and the other… Well, what could be happening to Beth doesn't bear thinking about. And Beth thinks she's lost her brother? She must be out of her head with grief.

"Where's Patsy now?"

"Here at the compound. Vi's with her." Demon's sharp eyes meet mine. "You can't tell her, Ink. She's got to believe he's dead. Don't want to rehash the reasons while Beth's freedom's at stake, but just accept they're good ones."

My club wouldn't decide to mentally torture two women if there weren't. I raise my chin, not liking it, but agreeing.

I lower my head into my hands. I'll have to go and see Patsy, but what can I say to her? Fuck all. I feel some responsibility toward her. I like the woman, and if everything works out how I want it, she's likely to be my mother-in-law after all.

"Are we ever going to tell them the truth?"

Demon's shoulders rise and fall. "First thing is getting Beth back. Worrying about sorting Connor's mess can come later."

It certainly sounds like a fucked-up situation. But I'm happy Beth's situation takes priority for now.

"What if we do nothing?" Hellfire suggests. "What's Beth to us? Worth risking our lives for? I mean, she got you arrested, Ink."

In one split second I'm standing, leaning over the table and snarling at Hell. "I'll remind you, that's my ol' lady you're talking about." I'm about as angry as I've ever been. "If you lot want to sit on your hands, then I'll go fuckin' rescue her by myself." Never did I think they'd just abandon her, but when I turn to glare at the ex-prez, I notice a strange, almost twinkle, in his eye.

"That's the way of it, is it?" Pyro asks. "I wondered." He looks at Thunder and holds out his hand. Thunder slides a twenty into it.

My eyes narrow. "What the fuck?"

"We were fifty-fifty whether you'd keep up the charade when you came out."

"Claimin' Beth is not a fuckin' charade and this is no joking matter." My hands clench and unclench, then fist again. Maybe it's because I've been cooped up in a cell, but I'm itching to take action.

"Phil already knows we've got his drugs." Bomber gets back on topic. "Even if we wanted to, can't see how we can sit this one out."

My curiosity had been satisfied one thing at least, how Beth had come into possession of drugs, though I had been horrified to learn Connor had left such a large amount of heroin in Beth and Patsy's home. I'd wanted to kill him myself at that point.

The door is opened and then shut as Beef joins us. He chucks a diagram on the table. "Right," he starts as he sits. "House is in a fuckin' gated compound. Armed guards on the gate. Man's got his own private fuckin' army. Twenty guards on rotation, at least ten there at any time. Phil's fanatical about his safety. He's been threatened more than once."

"Connor have any suggestions?"

Beef nods. "Yes, actually. He's willing to come back from the dead and exchange himself for Beth."

"Give the H back to Phil?"

Now Beef's head moves side to side as he again answers the prez, "That's where his plan falls apart. The smack is his get-out-of-jail card. He loses that? Agent Caruso will throw the book at him."

"If he's still alive to feel the pages hit. Reckon he won't last long if Phil gets his hands on him," Bomber observes. "Kid must know what's likely to happen to him."

I'm still trying to get my head around the fact Connor's breathing. But I point out, "Connor put Beth in a fuckin' dangerous situation on Saturday, where's this new brotherly concern coming from?"

Beef gives me a measured look. "I've spent a bit of time with

Connor. He didn't have any idea SWAT was waiting, and why would he? He had no notion he was sending her into danger. But it's something else when it comes to Phil. Connor got wind daddy dearest traffics people over the border, immigrants in, others out. Seems a girl like Beth might make him money. Connor's adamant we have to get her back, and if he has to sacrifice himself, that's what he'll do."

I inhale sharply.

"Pretty girls go missing from Denver, find themselves over the border and sold," Beef's eyes have gone dark as he finishes.

I can barely think through the rage that floods my mind, so I restrict myself to, "Phil's got to die."

"I hear you, Ink. Man like that is a waste of air." Thunder nods.

Bomber spells it out, "If we don't hit him hard, Ink may never get his old lady back, whether or not he's thinking of putting a ring on her finger."

Just the thought I might not have a chance to explore a relationship with Beth is enough to give me chills. I'm getting her back. At least it sounds like I'll have my brothers by my side when I do it.

Prez bangs the table. "The more I hear about Phil the less I like him breathing. So how do we do this? Ideas?"

"He contacted you about the drugs, Prez?"

Demon shakes his head. "It appears he's leaving the ball in our court. Maybe trying to figure out what sway Patsy has over us."

"How are you going to play it?"

Prez looks around. "Depends on what we come up with, VP. Timing might be vital to cause a distraction, so I won't be rushing to pick up the phone. Don't want to show our hand too early. If he thinks Beth means something to us, he may up the ante and demand more."

"More?" I'm seething at the delay.

"He could want us to work for him or step back and let him

take over our locations for his dealing at the least," Mace enlightens me, clearly having given this some thought.

Right now, I'd sell my soul to have her back. To hell with the implications. "He'll think we don't give a damn about Beth." On my part, I want Demon to call him this very moment and threaten the wrath of the Devils should Phil harm a hair on her head.

Mace stares across the table at me. "Tip our hand she means something to us then he may up the stakes. He won't harm the ace he's holding, not until he knows what we're going to do."

"Beth will be expecting us to rush to her rescue." I hate to think what she's going through now.

But Mace contradicts, his eyes filling with guilt. "Nah, Brother. She'll have doubts. We didn't believe her fuckin' story about Connor, all we knew was what she did put you behind bars. We blamed her, she was only too aware of that."

"You voted her in as my ol' lady…"

But Prez is shaking his head. "Sorry, Brother. Agreed to give her protection, such that we could, but that vote's in abeyance until we saw how things worked out. Couldn't let you put your patch on a woman no one could trust."

My stare roams the table, my eyes widening. "So, she's left hanging thinking no one gives a fuckin' damn about her?" It's my turn for my head to move side to side. "She doesn't fuckin' know I'm free, and you haven't done the one thing I asked for."

Prez bangs the gavel loudly, the flare in his eyes shows he's fast losing patience with me. "What was done was done for fuckin' good reasons, Ink. I'll be the first to admit that I had my concerns about Beth. But we now know she was pressured into doing what she did. Even if we didn't, I assure you that we do give a fuckin' damn. Women shouldn't be used as pawns."

"I got out, Prez." I'm angry that they blamed Beth and didn't believe her reasons. If I, the injured party, could forgive her, they should have done.

"For fuck's sake, Ink. How could you for one minute think

we'd leave Beth with that monster? Don't forget, we've got the Mexican Horse in our stable, and it's more than just her at stake. We're fuckin' heading for a war and need to win it." Thunder lets me have it.

I purse my lips, partly to stop myself saying anything else. I'd been so focused on Beth, I hadn't thought of the ramifications. This isn't just Beth. It's us, our old ladies, and Demon must be thinking of his kid.

"It's not just a rescue mission," Prez explains slowly, his eyes focused on my face. "We've got to hit him hard, so he doesn't come after us. We've got to take him out."

"There's one thing in our favour which buys us some time," Beef butts in. "If he's thinking of making a profit by selling his daughter, he'll want to keep her unmarked."

He's right, but just the thought of her being smuggled over the border and sold turns my stomach.

Having given me one last stern look, Demon at last says the words I want to hear, "Right, Brothers. How are we going to do this?"

"I like Pal's idea of using the drone." Sparky raises his fingers to get our attention. "Means we can see what we're dealing with."

I keep my mouth shut about the drone that's still a mystery to me, not wanting anymore delays.

"Agreed," Demon says fast. "How are you fixed, Ro?"

"Prez, I've got enough C4 to blow that fuckin' place to smithereens. Grenades, rocket launcher, you name it, I can get my hands on it."

"That's my fuckin' ol' lady in there," I snarl.

Prez sends a fiery look my way. "I think we're only too well aware of that, Brother." His glare stays on me until I lower my eyes.

"His compound is guarded. We're talking about a business worth millions." The VP seems to be musing aloud. "Not sure how successful we'd be if we tried to attack. We couldn't ensure

Beth wouldn't be right in the firing line, or that he'd shoot her himself."

"Our ace is that neither she, nor he, knows she's important to us."

"In which case, Prez," Wills speaks up, "he might think we're sitting on our hands and laughing, with his cool million sitting in the bank. What's to stop him coming for us and taking it?"

If that's the way Phil's thinking of playing it, Beth has no value as an exchange. The chills that assailed me earlier return with a vengeance. "We've got to move fast, Prez," I plead.

"Bring the fight here, to the compound."

Everyone looks at Bomber as though he's gone mad.

Demon groans. "We've not long fixed the place up after the Mafia hit." His head drops into his hands, then he looks up. "But fuck me, I think you've got the makings of a good suggestion." His fingers rap on the table. "I don't want the fight here, but if we're going to meet Phil, we'll do it on our home ground. I'll call him, tell him we've got his shit and want the girl back."

"Think he'll bring her?" Sounds too fucking easy to me.

Prez focuses on me. "Hear me out, Ink. We'll attack this two ways. One, the bulk of us will remain here to protect the compound. If Phil brings your ol' lady, all to the good. If he doesn't…"

Despite his warning, I open my mouth.

"Shut the fuck up!" Demon roars before I get a word out. Then, when he sees I'm sulking but silent, he continues, "We'll act like we don't give a damn about her, just didn't want a fight we couldn't win." Now he has to glare at everyone else who are contradicting him. "Christ! Will you let me fuckin' finish?" His eyes seem to grow darker. "Bringing him here draws his attention away from his compound. Ink, Pal and…" he looks around, "Cad will go to Denver. If, as Connor has suggested, he might have other plans for Beth and leaves her there, well, you'll be in place to launch a surprise attack and get Beth out."

My sulk disappears, and I grin. I like that plan.

"Prefer Ink here," says Mace.

Pyro shakes his head, and points to me. "Apart from me, Ink is the best with explosives. He needs to go to Denver if I'm staying here. Phil's bound to bring his best men with him, that's what I'd do, but he won't leave his base unguarded. Best way to rescue a hostage is to cause a distraction. My go-to would be an incendiary bomb at the opposite side of the building from where Beth's being held."

"How the fuck will we know where she is?" Christ, there's a fuckload of holes in his plan.

Pal says flatly, as if he's explaining to a kid, "We'll know that from the drone."

Oh. That part now falls into place. But something else worries me. "Hang on, what are you thinking, Prez? You're seriously going to give him his H? I thought we wanted that shit destroyed, not sold."

Beef taps the side of his nose. "Got a plan for that, Brother. Don't forget, even if we give him his Horse, he'll still want to hit us where it hurts. Taking it in the first place shows disrespect, and he won't allow that to stand. But my guess is we'll avoid a fight until after he got what he came for. He'll be back to take us out."

Hellfire's raising and dipping his head in agreement. "He'll have a million dollars' worth of shit on him, he won't risk a fight until he's got that locked down. I'd bet once he's got what he came for, he'll leave town. For now."

It sounds like the plan does give me a chance of having my old lady back in my arms. Either she'll be brought to the compound, or I'll rescue her myself. Then I'll make plans how to kill Phil on my own if no one else is going to do it.

Demon raps the table. "Decision made. You'll need daylight to get the best from the drone, so we'll do this tomorrow. Ink, can it. I know what you're going to say, but if we don't do this properly, we'll fail."

I hate the thought that Beth will stay with her cunt of a father one more second than necessary. But Demon's right. There's a lot at risk, possession of the H being the least of it. We're risking our home and our lives.

"So, Ink, Cad and Pal know what they're doing. Now onto the rest of us." Prez pinches his nose. "We need him to come and leave peacefully. I hear what you say, but how about we negate the risk and head off a fight?"

"How?" Rusty asks what we're all thinking.

"He won't expect us to simply hand it over because we're intimidated, even he must know Satan's Devils don't roll that way. But if there's something in it for us, it will allay his suspicions. We give him his H *and* we offer him our premises to deal in. For a sum to be agreed, of course."

A thunderous roar goes around. Fuck noes, and nevers come from all sides. But Beef's chuckling, and Prez is joining in. My eyes narrow suspiciously.

Pyro's seems to have cottoned on quick as he's staring at Beef. "What exactly is your plan, VP? I take it, it involves me?"

"Yeah." Beef grins. "Ro, can you make up some bombs? Sacrifice some of the brown powder so if he opens them up, he won't suspect?"

"I can do that," says Pyro, his brow furrowing. "They'll need to be the right size and weight and packaged the same way. Will take me some time, but I've got all night."

"So, if he actually follows through, brings Beth with him, you'll let him take his Horse and ride out of town." Hell's mouth is curving up.

"And then dispatch him to meet Satan in fuckin' pieces. Once he's out of the residential areas of course." Bomber's hand bangs the table in appreciation.

I like that plan. Like it a lot.

"Beef, you work on getting our snipers in position, guns readied, and traps set, in case they come in guns blazing."

The VP jerks his chin in agreement.

"Women?" Hellfire offers. "Want Mo to have company tomorrow?"

I try to hide my grin. They need to be off the compound but doubt the ex-prez's wife will be happy with a house full of sweet butts though she won't mind the old ladies.

"Yeah, Hell. Thanks."

"I can organise the whores."

"Sure you can, Brother." Liz winks at Judge.

Prez relaxes back into his chair. "Pal, Cad and Ink will set off first thing in the morning. We give them enough time to get into position, then I'll give Phil a call. Tell him we've got his stash, and we're offering it in exchange for Beth."

"If I get the drone in place before you make that call, we'll be able to see if he's bringing her along."

Demon nods at Pal. "We'll keep in contact. Be useful for any info about how many men he's bringing along so we can be prepared. Everyone know what they're doing? Okay then, church dismissed."

I sit for a moment while the others get up and leave. What a homecoming this has been. I'd been bored out of my head in the prison cell, worried what my future might look like, and whether I could cope behind bars.

I never dreamed anything other than Beth was safe at home. It's been devastating to learn she's anything but.

Have we got time? Would Phil keep her unharmed, or will she be shipped over the border tonight? If he's no intention of handing her over, he might.

Then I'll follow her and find her. Not letting her out of my life now. Every obstacle put between us just makes me more determined that I'm right. Beth belongs to me. Now and forever.

"You alright?"

It's a superfluous question, I don't even bother giving a negative reaction.

"Beth's strong, Brother." Mace kicks out a chair and sits beside me. "She thinks fast. Deep down she'll know we'll be coming for her. She'll know Patsy will have persuaded us to help. I'm sure she will."

"Will she?" I turn my incredulous eyes on him. "You don't think she's sitting there worried the fuck out of her mind as she doesn't think anyone cares? I asked you to do one thing, *Brother.* I claimed Beth so you'd protect her. Instead you, what? Send untried hangarounds to babysit her. Not their fault they fucked up. No, it was your fault. You threw her to the wolves as you blamed her for putting me inside."

"It wasn't like that…"

"No? Tell me what it was fuckin' like then?" I stand, pushing my chair angrily back under the table. When I turn, I raise an eyebrow at him.

Mace's face looks shuttered, then pained as though I've punched him in the gut. I offer no comfort. Then he, too, stands. "You could be right. We could have done things differently. Yeah, we fucked up. But we'll make it right, Brother. I promise you that."

CHAPTER THIRTY-FIVE

Beth

"Who gave my H to the Devils?"

We've been at this for the past half-hour. Him firing off questions, me giving what responses I can. Inside I'm crying out for someone to save me but know that I'm on my own. I want to curl up and magically wake up at home to find this is all a bad dream, but I can't. It's real and I'm here.

Phil's a strong willful man, with no empathy to appeal to. If I show weakness, I won't have a chance. I have to act strong and stand my ground, when I'd prefer to retreat. I know my responses are annoying him, but I can't afford to give a damn. Going head to head with him is, I'm certain, the best plan.

"Connor."

"Connor's fuckin' dead."

"I'm well aware my brother, your *son* is dead," I spit back at the man who sired me. "Beaten so badly…" I choke up. "You don't think whoever did that tortured the information out of him? That they were in league with the Devils?"

He doesn't look upset. Which gives me the clue. "You did it, didn't you? You hurt your son so badly he's dead."

"I didn't," he refutes.

"But you know who did."

A sly expression comes into his face. "Yes," he admits, as if me knowing my brother was killed with his knowledge and clearly no regret is of no consequence at all. "But I know if Alder's men got information out of him, they'd have come to me with it."

"Would they?" I challenge. "You told me the heroin was worth a million dollars. Wouldn't your men like a share of that?"

The first look of distrust appears in his eyes, then he quickly recovers. "No, they would not. My men are loyal."

"But what about Alder's?"

"Alder and I work together."

"So Alder's men are your men?" He's just admitted not only did he know about it, he was responsible for Connor's death.

He realises it too, as the backhand across my cheek warns me. He leans in. "You're a mouthy bitch. Problem we've got is that nothing coming out of your mouth is what I want to hear. You think you can catch me out? Well, I've got ways of making sure you tell me the truth. Ways you won't fuckin' like."

"Boss? Phone call for you. Think you might want to take this."

He nods. Then backs off. "While I'm gone, George can soften you up." As he walks past him, he murmurs something in George's ear.

I have absolutely no desire to find out what.

I've decided I'll take the secret of the Devils' involvement to the grave with me, not prepared to allow hurt to come to any of their members again. If I admit I used to be friends with them, he'll know at the very least I'll be able to describe the compound and the number of members they have, making it easier for him to take them on. I suspect no one gets away with crossing Phil Foster, and taking his drugs, in his mind, is a serious crime.

George comes over. I stand up. It forces him to look up at me, something he doesn't appreciate doing at all.

"Sit," he snarls.

"Make me," I snarl back.

"Bitch."

"Asshole."

Okay. So we could trade insults all day.

"Oomph." Or maybe we won't, I can't breathe for a second, and bend double with the pain caused by his fist to my stomach. A hand on my shoulder pushes me down, I miss the chair and land on the ground.

George's short, but muscular body covers mine pushing me back until I lie prone. While I'm still trying to recover, he's trapped both my hands in his and has them over my head.

I buck and kick, but he's mad enough to lower his face to mine. His breath smells putrid.

As he tries to forcibly kiss me, I bite his lip. Hard.

"Fucking freak." He lets go of my hands to wipe the blood, I place my thumbs in his eyes.

He grabs my wrists and pulls them out to the side, it creates enough of a gap between us that I'm able to jerk my knee up straight into his balls.

The door opens, and my father returns in time to see George groaning, curled up in a foetal position, and me with a smug smile on my face. *Round one to me.* I've surprised myself, I hadn't known I had such fight in me. Though I may have won this one, I have no doubt there'll be a round two. I won't be let off that easily.

Unfortunately, my fight had reminded me of Ink, and what the difference had been. That night, while I hadn't wanted Ink to overpower me, I hadn't tried to seriously hurt him. With George, all bets had been off. If I've permanently damaged his manhood, he deserves it.

"Christ." It seems Phil has no sympathy for his man at all. "Get to your fucking feet." Then to me. "The Satan's Devils want to give me my heroin back."

I feel several emotions. Surprise, first and foremost, disgust they've given into his demands, then a glimmer of hope that I might soon be free. "You're making the exchange? The drugs for me?"

He actually laughs. "I always win, Bethany, and I win big. I don't need to use you to get my drugs back. The president of the MC has an interesting proposal for me. Money talks, my dearest daughter, money talks. You, though, mean nothing. Not to me, and not to him."

The Devils are making a deal with my father? How could I have been so wrong about them? I don't understand, but the brief glimpse of freedom fast disappears.

He chuckles again at the horror clearly written on my face. "Right. I've got some shit to collect from Pueblo. George, take her back to her room and make sure she stays there."

"Shall I keep her amused while you're gone?" George's voice sounds higher than normal.

Phil's incredulous eyes fall on his man who's still cupping his balls. "Think you might need some time to recover," he tells him. "No. Leave her to stew. Oh, and get her name down on the transport list, okay?"

That does not sound good.

"What transport?" I ask George as he limps up the stairs.

But the smirk he tosses at me suggests I'd rather not know.

In my room I flop onto the bed, once again fighting back tears. I've cried more in the last few days than I have before in my whole life, and not one tear drop has helped. Do the Devils really not care what happens to me? Are they actually going to do business with Phil? Why else would they have a proposition for him? Did the huge quantity of drugs tempt them into his line of work?

Maybe it's a ruse.

No, I tell myself. I can't expect knights on motorcycles to ride in to rescue me.

But what other hope have I got to hold on to?

Oh Ink, if only you were free. But even then, would he care? He told me via his lawyer our relationship was over. *He hates me.*

The facts are that Phil has gone to Pueblo, and sometime soon I'll be going on some kind of transport to God knows where.

Let's face it. No one is coming for me. I've only myself to rely on. Unless I can get free, I'll have to resign myself to an uncertain and unpleasant future.

I cross to the window and look out at the freedom that's so close, yet so unobtainable. I run my hands over the frame, it's solid and unmoveable, and the plaster around it is firm. Looking down I see my breakfast tray has gone, and so has the handy knife I'd forgotten to pilfer. My fingernails don't even make a mark on the plasterwork. All I do is break them, though I try until I make them bleed.

Giving up, I stare out across the grounds and out toward the wall of the compound. If I could get out, I could cover the distance in seconds.

Something glints in the sun. I lean closer to the window to take a look, tilting my head. *Is that a remote-controlled plane?* Are Phil's guards playing with a toy?

I tilt my head to one side as it starts to draw closer. What the hell...? Is it a... It's a drone. Is Phil using tech to keep an eye on me?

I jump back from the window fast. Christ, they must think I'm resourceful if they think they need to guard me from the sky. Or, I realise as I pull myself out of sight and stand with my back to the wall, they're creeps who hope to watch me getting undressed.

Perhaps it's not being controlled by Phil's men. *Could it be the cops? The FBI?* Sounds like something they might do. And Phil's a man they'd likely investigate. Quickly glancing around the room, I wonder if there's a convenient paper and pen. If it's the cops, I could write a message that I'm a prisoner, and hope they could see it. If it's Phil, well, he already knows.

But of course, there's nothing I can use to write on or with.

Wondering if I could mime being held against my will and

whether I could get my point across, I return to the window, but the drone, or whatever it was, has gone.

Feeling I've lost the only chance I might have had, I turn my back.

Boom!

Christ? What the hell was that? Automatically I've dropped to the floor, hunched over and put my hands protectively over my head. *Was that an explosion?* Before I can answer my mental question, fire alarms are going off all over the house. Footsteps run past my door but don't stop.

"Hey!" I run to the door and try and turn the knob. It's locked, of course.

Is it my imagination, or do I already smell smoke?

Hell, have they left me here to burn to death?

Now there are gunshots and screams. *Oh my God. What's going on?*

I rattle the door handle and pull on it, but it doesn't budge. Regretting lock-picking is not one of my skills, I wonder if I can kick it down, at least I've got strength in my legs, but it opens inward, and that wood looks too thick. And maybe, if the house is filling with smoke, and there's a gun battle going on, I'm safer this side. What if I get out and am shot?

My hand is still on the handle when I feel it moving. Someone's trying it from the other side.

Friend or foe? In this house there's little hope of it being the former.

I slowly back away, wishing there was somewhere to hide. In the bathroom, perhaps? No, it's too small, no room to manoeuvre. If it's George coming in, he's going to feel my knee in his balls again.

"Stand back!" a voice demands. It's a voice I recognise.

Shit. I'm hallucinating now. I thought I heard Ink.

Have I fallen asleep? Is this some nightmare I'm living?

The door flies open, bouncing back against the wall and almost closing again before revealing the man, not of my nightmares, but of my dreams. Convincing me my subconscious has conjured him up.

"Ink?"

"Babe. Stop staring and come with me. Phil might be on his way back with reinforcements."

He's got a phone in one hand and proceeds to talk both to me and the person at the end of the line.

"Yeah, Prez, I got her. Getting out now. I don't know if one of his men managed to get a message off. If they did, I don't know what he cares most about, his compound or drugs… Yeah, man. I hear you."

"For fuck's sake, Beth. Do I have to put you over my shoulder and carry you out? We haven't got much time."

The smoke wafting through the door confirms what he's saying.

I can't make my feet move. He grabs my hand.

"Move, Beth," he instructs using his dominant tone. At last my body unfreezes.

How? Why? runs through my head, though this isn't the time to ask. We tear down the stairs, and Ink stops so fast, I run straight into his back. George and Marcus, instead of running away from the flames, are trying to open a door that I hadn't noticed before.

Ink raises his gun.

"Got to get them out…" Marcus ignores him and rounds on George. "Kick it down."

"I'll find the key."

"There's no fucking time," Marcus spits back.

"What's down there?" Ink snaps.

"Merchandise."

Cad appears, his gun aimed at the two men. "Let the drugs burn."

"Not drugs man, the breathing kind."

"Fuck," Ink breathes out. "Kick that fucker down."

The heavyweight door at last splinters and falls in. It must have been soundproofed. Now it's opened, it's possible to hear screams and cries.

"Go bring 'em up." Ink waves his gun toward George and Marcus.

Marcus pushes George down the stairs, then follows him. There's a loud crack as if a timber has fallen, and the screams start again. Then, two young women appear, a girl in her late teens, and one even younger. Their faces are white with shock.

"Beth?"

I'm there. "You've got to get out. Come with me." I herd them toward the front door, sparing only a moment to ask Cad. "Is it safe out there?" I don't want to run into my father's men.

"Yeah, just don't look around too much."

"Hey what are you doing? Don't let them escape! They're worth money," Marcus shouts, trying to grab one of the women's arms.

Ink raises his gun and a perfect circle appears on Phil's man's forehead.

As his teammate falls to the ground, George raises his arms. "Hey, man. I was just saving them. Let them go, I don't..."

He now has also fallen and staring up with wide dulling eyes.

"Out, Beth. Now!"

Ink draws my shocked attention back to the smoke-filled hallway, flames clearly visible through the open door of Phil's sitting room.

The women have already run out but have stopped dead fearing Pal who's standing guard over the man I recognise as the gardener and the maid who'd brought me my breakfast what seems like a lifetime ago. I run over to the group, almost tripping on a severed arm. Now I heed Cad's earlier warning and keep my eyes focused on people standing. I yell at Pal when it looks like he's reaching into his belt.

"They're nothing," I shout at him. "Don't harm them."

"Sort of gathered that," he says. Then turns to the maid rattling off some Spanish.

"Si, Signor," is her response. "No," and shakes her head.

Ink's close behind me. "Tell them they can go," he tells Pal.

What Pal had been reaching for was a wad of dollars, he divides it in two then presses half into each of the Hispanics' hands. "Lay low," he tells them.

They don't need telling twice. With a stunned but grateful look, their fingers curl tightly around the money, and then they run off.

"You two," Ink addresses the shocked women who came up from the basement. "You got family close by?"

They still, hardly daring to breathe. "You're letting us go?"

"We're not going to be sold?" one asks wide-eyed.

Ink looks surprised it was ever in question. "Of course, you're fuckin' not. If you've got a place to go, then yeah, we won't stop you leaving."

The young teenager holds up her hand. "My family is in Denver."

"We haven't got family," the older woman says. "But we'll find our way on the streets."

Ink closes his eyes for a moment. "We'll get you back to your family," he tells the younger girl, then regards the other two. "Finding your way on the streets is probably what got you into Phil's clutches. Look, we're from Pueblo. You can come back with us if you want. We can get you to safety. Sort you out while you find somewhere to go."

The two women look at each other, then at me, then spy the house burning down behind us.

I see their reluctance. Remembering Ink's words on the phone, I tell them, "No pressure, but we've got to get going. Phil, the man who was holding you, well, he might be on his way back."

They put their heads together, then the older one who seems to be the spokesperson says hesitantly eyeing me, "Do you trust these men?" When I give a heartfelt yes. *They'd come for me.* She adds, "Getting out of town sounds like the best idea. We'll go to Pueblo."

Cad's on his phone now, but only for a moment. Almost as soon as he's ended the call a truck is driving up with the prospect Karl at the wheel.

"Sorry, ladies. Gonna be a bit of a squash until we get back to the bikes," Cad explains, bundling the women into the back. Ink, Cad and Pal indicate they'll go into the rear compartment normally reserved for transporting motorcycles. I go to squeeze in with the women, but Karl waves to the passenger seat.

"Thought it would be easier than folding yourself up in the back." I appreciate his thoughtfulness.

They discuss the women for a second, and Karl agrees to drop the teenager home before heading back to Pueblo. Ink, Cad and Pal will be left to come back on their bikes.

I sit during the short journey, trying to process my swiftly changing fate. Trying to work out how Ink is here and free, wondering if he's got a twin brother I hadn't known about who was here instead, then dismiss that. There's no doubt it was Ink. Which begs further questions. *How the fuck is he here? Did he get bail after all? Were the charges dropped?* And, most important, *what does that mean for him and for me?*

CHAPTER THIRTY-SIX

Ink

Yesterday I'd gone through the best and worst of times. My release from jail is about up there with one of the happiest moments of my life, but I'd crashed down to earth when I found out Beth was gone. When I'd seen her on that drone camera footage, looking unharmed, I'd felt relief, but urgency to get this job done and bring her home safe.

There had been a propane tank around the opposite side of the house. I'd fired the rocket launcher with an incendiary head straight at it, the explosion had taken out half of the building, and the fire spread faster than expected. We'd wasted no time approaching and picking off the men who'd come running out, more intent on saving themselves than anything or anyone inside.

I've found Beth. The relief that sweeps through me is overwhelming. There had been moments when I doubted ever seeing her again, in jail, of course, but even after I was released.

In the rush to get out alive, including those poor bitches kept imprisoned in a burning basement, then all of us away and safe, I hadn't had a moment to talk to her, nor even a second to read the expressions on her face.

She's safe. Alive. Unwilling to spend another minute apart, I'm determined I'm going to be feeling her arms around my waist as I ride back to Pueblo. In the back of the truck, I thank fuck I'd put that double seat on my bike before I'd gone inside.

The moment I'd seen her again, I knew I'd not exaggerated my feelings for her. If I have my way, from now on, she'll never be out of my sight.

If she's got doubts, if she doesn't want to commit, I'll just have to tie her to my bed and fuck her until she admits I'm the man she wants for the rest of her life. Maybe, if she's willing, put my baby inside her. I'll use every trick in the book to tie her to me. She's mine now, she's going to have to accept it.

Hey, if nothing else works, I'll play on her guilt. I could have gone inside for thirty years of my life, she should be prepared to give me thirty of hers.

Yeah, I'll find some sneaky darn ways to make her see sense. As long as she ends up agreeing to be my old lady, I don't care what the fuck I have to do to get that result.

Pal and Cad are talking, Pal nestling that fucking drone in his arms, the technology that had so impressed me and enabled us to carry out our mission successfully. As the two men discuss its performance, I tune them out. It's not long before we pull up to where our bikes have been parked, a relieved Beaver standing guard.

"Mission accomplished?"

Having jumped out of the back, I nod at him. Then go to the passenger side of the truck and pull open the door. Reaching over her, I undo Beth's seatbelt.

At her wide eyes, I explain, "You're coming with me." Then I grab hold of her hand, firmly, so she has no choice.

Glancing around, she sees there's no other mode of transport. "On your bike?"

"Want you close, babe." I rest my forehead against hers. "Missed you like fuck. Didn't expect to see you again…"

"They said you hated me. That you didn't want to see me. I don't understand, Ink."

Four days. Surely not enough time for her to have grieved and moved on? I sigh deeply. If her feelings hadn't the depth of mine, maybe that had been enough. "I had to cut you loose, babe. Couldn't have you dragged into it. Couldn't have had you trying to see me. The cops had to believe there was nothing between us."

"There wasn't, was there?"

Again, I exhale. "Oh, babe." Here, at the roadside, I really don't know what to say. How can I explain my feelings toward her?

She bites her lip. "I told the cops you were just my fuck buddy."

She did? That makes me chuckle softly. "I said the same." Then, I nuzzle the top of her hair with my lips and lower my mouth so it's against her ear and add, "I lied."

"Lied?" Her eyes widen once more.

"Yeah. You're more to me than that." I stare into her face, but she makes no reciprocal comment. Maybe the tying to my bed idea will have to be deployed.

"How did you get out?"

I don't answer as my back gets a hefty slap on it, causing me to raise my head and swear.

"Ink, Beth. Save the happy reunion until we're out of Denver, yeah?" Cad snipes. "I want to get as far away as possible in case Phil's coming back. Hey, Karl, we'll meet you at the waypoint."

"What fuckin' waypoint?" I ask.

"Weren't you listening to a fuckin' word in the truck?"

Pal nudges Cad. "He was thinking about fucking. Saw him adjusting himself."

His words make me look down. No, I'm not sporting a fucking hard-on. Though with Beth up behind me, I might well be by the time we get to Pueblo.

Beth, my old lady, who's currently tugging at my sleeve. "I think I should go back with the prospects," she says. "I've never ridden before."

"Here, have this." Karl's walked over and has passed her his thick leather jacket he must have had in the back of the truck. I thank him. As I hold it out, she automatically threads her arms through the sleeves while still protesting.

But the truck's engine has already started, and I give the dismissive signal that makes Karl pull away.

Opening my saddlebag, I take out a helmet and place it on her head. "You're coming with me. Sooner we get to Pueblo, sooner we can have that conversation we need to have." I then extract my spare bandana and show her how to wrap it around her face.

I get on the bike. She huffs, looks at me, then at Cad and Pal who are waiting for us, Pal looking amused, Cad looking impatient. Then, gingerly, she throws her leg over the saddle and climbs up behind me. I swear, as soon as her hands go around my waist, it feels like I've really come home.

I'm conscious no one's ever ridden behind me before. I tug on her hands to pull them around me more securely, then give her the instructions all new riders need. She carefully places her feet on the pegs and looks down at the exhaust I'd warned her about in consternation.

"Here," I pass her Karl's gloves he'd also given to me before he left, "put these on. It's going to get cold." I wish the weather was warmer for her first ride, but my body should shield her from the worst of the wind which will become biting when we pick up speed. I know I'm being selfish, but I meant it when I vowed not to let her out of my sight. At least not yet.

"Huh," she huffs in protest. "I should have gone in the truck." But then her arms tighten around me and she rests her head on my shoulder for a moment, allowing me to feel her warm breath against my neck. I swear she inhales as if reminding herself of my natural scent.

Cad and Pal start their engines, I follow a moment later, taking a few seconds to allow myself to believe she's really here.

Then I press the start button, kick down into first, let out the clutch and we're off. At first her arms have a death grip on me, but my new seat has a sissy bar attached and after only a few minutes, her hold starts to relax as she realises there's no way she can slide off and land on her ass on the road.

Still, when we come to a red light, I throw the question back over my shoulder, "You doing alright?"

"Fine."

I allow myself to believe, in this instance, when she says fine, she really means it.

As we head out of the city and onto the open road, I'm congratulating myself that I've found a natural. She moves with me as though she's been doing it all her life and this isn't her first ride. She's not unbalancing the bike at all, even though I'm also a virgin when it comes to having someone riding behind.

It's a two-hour ride give or take, and I just want to get her home. I take the lead then open the throttle and pick up the speed, Cad and Pal easily keep up. We're about half-an-hour from the compound when we reach the arranged waypoint, not having to wait long for Karl to catch up. He collects what we need from the back, and quickly I slide into my cut, welcoming its weight on my shoulders again.

"Drop the kid off okay?"

"Yeah, no problem. Saw her being hugged at the front door and took off," Karl reports.

Then, due to the decided chill in the air, we get straight back on our bikes. Soon after, I'm forced to slow. Red and blue flashing lights ahead warning me there's been an incident or accident.

Well, fuck me. Cars are queued up on the road and they're not moving. Being on bikes I cockily wave at Karl as we go past the truck and the rest of the cars and make our way to the front. A firefighter approaches us.

"Can we get past?" I can understand why they'd stop cars, but it looks like there's room for bikes to pass. "Fuckin' cold to hang around."

The firefighter views us carefully, and I swear it probably helps having a shivering bitch on the back as he appears sympathetic. "There's been an explosion. There's some sort of chemical on the road." I realise the mask he's wearing isn't to protect him from the cold. "We don't know what it is yet, probably not dangerous but there's always a risk. Keep your nose and mouths covered and don't hang around to gawk." Then he stands back and, *thank fuck* waves us past.

I spare a grin for the cars waiting who haven't been so lucky.

Of course, I look. There're two trucks, or what's left of them. The one in front has disintegrated entirely, looks like some kind of explosion to me. The one behind burned out on its side, the front smashed in as though it couldn't stop and drove into the first.

There are firefighters hosing down the road with some sort of foam, and a dust still blowing in the air.

What the fuck is it?

But I heed the firefighter's advice and pick up my speed, leaving the clearly fatal accident site in my rearview. An idea is forming in my mind, and I only hope that I'm right. An idea that's confirmed when we reach a turn off and two bikes come down from the hillside and join us.

Pyro raises his hand in a confident salute as he falls in by my side, allowing me to know while Beth doesn't know it, but she's just ridden past the remains of her dad.

When we reach the compound, she's still unaware of the implications. I tap her leg, then turn. "Off, babe. Then I'll park."

She puts a hand on my shoulder, then stiffly eases herself off. Having cut the engine, I hear her groan, and she balances herself on me for a second. When she lets go, I waste no time paddling my bike back into my space.

She's shivering, so I wrap my arm around her, and lead her straight into the clubhouse as fast as I can. Which is slower than normal.

"My legs have seized up. And my ass is numb," she hisses. "I can't feel my fingers or my nose."

I slide down her bandana, her nose is such a delightful red, I can't resist leaning forward and kissing it. Then quickly I take her hands and start rubbing them vigorously.

"You're as cold as me," she complains, pulling away, and briskly brushing one palm against her other.

"Bethany!" Patsy's voice sounds shrill and more than half-disbelieving as she comes running over. "Oh, Bethany. Are you okay?" Her arms go around Beth's waist, and Beth bends to cuddle her mother. For a moment there's silence, then Patsy pulls away. "You're a block of ice," she says, her accusing eyes coming my way.

I'm unrepentant. I've had my old lady up behind me. Wasn't going to let her come back with anyone else.

"Mom, I'm fine. I survived Phil and the ride." Her eyes, I notice, are shining with excitement. "Yes, I'm cold." She nudges me so hard I stumble. "But it was great."

"What did Phil do? Did he hurt you?" Patsy's concerned questions come fast.

I lean in anxious to know myself but have only time to hear Beth answer that she really is okay, when my name is called.

"Ink!" Demon's loud shout interrupts us. "Church, now." I notice Pyro and Lizard are already heading that way.

Damn. Can't get out of church and I think Demon might notice if I took her in and sat through the meeting with her on my lap. *Think my cock would too.* I'm reluctant, but I've no choice about it. Fucking vowed not to spend one moment without her and breaking it already.

"Babe…"

She catches my eye. "We'll talk later. You go do your stuff. I'll stay with Mom."

"Don't go anywhere," I warn, but it comes out almost pleadingly.

"I won't."

I curl my hand around her neck. "I shouldn't be long. Get warmed up and visit with your mother. Oh, and when Karl gets here with those women, can you watch them for a bit?"

"I'll speak to Vi or Jeannie. Whoever's here."

"You'll stay? I want, need to talk to you."

"I know." She bites her lips again. Christ, I've never wanted to get out of a meeting as much as I want to do now. "I promise I'll stay. And I'll make sure the women are made to feel comfortable." Her face falls, and her voice drops to a whisper. "If you hadn't have come…" As her voice trails away, I guess she knows what was ahead for the women would also have been her fate.

Patsy doesn't seem able to take her eyes off her daughter. I don't think she knows tears are flowing freely down her face. "Bethany, I was so worried. I thought I'd lost you, as well as Connor. I couldn't take that." I realise how much effort it had taken for Patsy to keep herself together. It's now she seems about to break, now knowing her daughter has come back to her.

Beth understands her mother's concern. "Mom. I'm fine. I'm safe. I'm…" her voice breaks off as she looks at me, and there's a hundred questions in her expression, mirrored in mine I suspect. "I'm home," she finally finishes.

Yes, she is, and here is where she's going to stay. Even if she and I currently have a different understanding of where her home is.

I catch her eye, and before walking away, say once again, "We'll talk later."

I take my seat in church, a whole different feeling than when I was last here. Last time I was battling with elation at my freedom and bone-chilling horror my old lady had disappeared. Today? Well, Beth's back. I frown. I've just got to convince her that this is where she's staying. Patsy will have to get used to living alone.

"Ro?"

Demon's banged the gavel and looking to Pyro for an update.

"Worked like a fuckin' charm." The man in question grins.

"Back up." I raise my hand. "What happened here? Any problems?"

Prez nods at me and raises his chin to the others also looking his way. "So, Pyro came to me and the VP late last night with an updated plan. We adjusted the details as we went along. Didn't let anyone know in case anything was given away."

"And?" Hell prompts, looking as confused as me.

"You know Mel bakes?" Pyro says, rather unnecessarily. We all do. The shit she keeps the clubhouse stocked with is good stuff. Even if it tends to add inches to our waistlines.

"What's that got to fuckin' do with it?" growls Bomber.

"Brown flour," Pyro says. "I remember she was experimenting with it."

For a moment I'm lost, then my lips start to curve as I realise where he might be going with this.

"Yeah, well, it took all night, that stuff's fucking hard to handle, but I managed to get it into the bricks so they looked identical to the Mexican Horse, Phil was expecting. Of course, I also had to add in a detonator and explosive, but it was easy enough to adjust the weight for that."

"Saw the results," I tell them, miming pointing a gun and pulling a trigger.

Rusty slams his hand down on the table. "So that's why you capitulated and just handed that shit over. Thought you'd gone out of your fuckin' head."

"You knew I was going to blow it up," Pyro reminds him.

"Yeah, but a brick or so to keep him happy. Not the whole fuckin' lot. Thought it was needed to keep Connor out of jail."

"It is. And can be," Demon explains. "Pyro blew up eight kilos of fuckin' baking flour."

It's probably a release of tension, but we're all cracking up. Suddenly I let out a loud barking laugh. "Firefighters were trying to clean up the shit, was worried it was some sort of chemical. Can't wait to see their faces when they find out what it really is."

"You ran a risk." I frown. "What if Phil had been suspicious and tested it?"

"Yeah, well, we brought one brick down and had it ready in case he wanted to open it. Luckily, he didn't."

"The good news," Beef says, "is that there aren't eight kilos of Mexican Horse literally blowing around Pueblo. When the cops find out Phil Foster was in that car, I doubt they'll come looking for us. There could be any number of people looking to take him out, and cops will probably be pleased someone's put him away for good."

"Yeah," Prez takes over, "there's nothing to link him to us."

I'm still chuckling to myself, wondering what the cops will make of a highway closed because of Mel's baking flour. Then I frown. "Really wanted to make him hurt, Prez. He was going to sell Beth."

Prez has sympathy in his eyes. "I knew we had to protect the club. Fastest way of doing that was to take him out clean."

"Dead is dead, Brother," the VP says. I suppose he's right. Now Beth won't need to keep looking over her shoulder.

"Ink. What's your update?"

"Got the propane tank in one hit, Prez. Must have been full, it exploded, set the house on fire."

"You risked burning your old lady?" Judge's eyes are wide.

"What the fuck do you take me for? Pal's drone worked like a charm. Showed us exactly where she was, in the opposite side of the house."

"Casualties?"

"We made sure of it. All the men Phil had left are dead." My face hardens. "We found something else there. Phil was keeping women in his basement. A teenage girl, who the prospect dropped back at her home in Denver, and two women with nowhere to go. I, er, well, Karl's on his way back with them now."

"The girl. She know who we are?"

I shake my head. "No. We weren't wearing our cuts and didn't offer any information."

"So we've got strangers coming to the compound?"

"Sorry, Prez. Couldn't think what else to do with them."

"Nah, you did okay. We'll sort it out." Just one more problem dumped in his lap to solve, but like everything, Prez just takes it in his stride.

"There's a women's refuge in town," Cad puts in. "I agreed with Ink. We couldn't do anything else. Oh, and there were some of Phil's staff, illegal immigrants I suspect."

"Yeah, your Spanish came in useful, Pal." Credit where credit's due. He's done well today with that and the drone.

Pal just shrugs.

Demon drums his fingers on the table. "The only loose end, as I see it, is Connor. When is this Agent Caruso back in town?"

"Saturday. Connor's getting twitchy staying in his room, but we can't let him loose while Beth and Patsy are here. I'm presuming Ink will want Beth to stay around. I was thinking he could go to the cabin?" Beef raises a brow at me.

I give him a *what do you fuckin' think?* look back. Then ask, "He still dead, now that Phil's gone?"

Beef thinks for a moment, and exchanges gestures and facial expressions with Demon, then speaks his mind. "I think so. Phil's gone, as you said, but Alder's still around."

Christ. I'd forgotten about him. "You think he'll come sniffing around?"

"Hopefully not. But it's best if Connor stays underground." Prez looks at Beef. "I understand why you said the cabin, but Connor probably still needs care. Beth and Patsy have had enough to go through, why not tell them the truth? Let him have some time with his mom and sister, before he has to disappear."

"You trust them to keep their mouths shut?" Hell doesn't look so sure himself.

"Beth will," I tell them. "And I think Patsy would too.

Wouldn't you rather know your son was alive, even if you had no contact?"

"Went through this with Steph," Beef puts in. "Her family missed her like hell, but they stayed clear knowing it was her life at risk. It was hard for her, but she made it work, as we all know. I've spent time with Connor. Once he knew what Phil was into, he wanted out, just couldn't get out of his clutches. A fresh start is what he needs. If we can trust Patsy and Beth, I think they'll see this is the best opportunity he could be given."

"You wanted them to arrange a funeral and be able to act genuine in case Phil turned up to watch. Phil's gone now." I'd been filled in on the details last night.

"Funeral still needs to go ahead. Want Connor's body burned and destroyed. That will get Alder off his back too if the official records have everything straight." Demon pinches the bridge of his nose. "Okay. We'll resurrect him from the dead, for now. As long as they understand it's not safe for him to remain local, and as far as anyone else knows, Connor is dead and gone."

I just hope Beth and her mom won't die of shock when they see a ghost alive and breathing.

CHAPTER THIRTY-SEVEN

Beth

By the time Ink emerges from church, I've just about thawed out from the cold journey home. I might have given him shit about it, but I wouldn't have preferred travelling any other way. I'm not going to give up the chance to have my arms around the man who I want.

Ink's giving me signals I can't quite compute. Having accepted whatever he might have started feeling for me had been killed stone dead when he'd gotten arrested that night, I can't understand why he's so concerned and friendly now. I wasn't surprised once I got over my shock at seeing him out of jail, that it had been him to come rescue me. I'd known he was an honourable man, whatever his feelings toward me were.

But to want me behind him on his bike? That's surely not the sign of someone wanting to part ways.

Then there's the not so small question of how he's free, and whether he's going to stay that way. Perhaps he's just out on bail.

Neither Mom nor the other women could satisfy my curiosity in that regard. Mom had been too distraught over Phil kidnapping me to take notice of what was going on around her, and Vi told me that there's been a lot of to-ing and fro-ing and club business going on. From what she'd picked up though, she thought he was home to stay. *I hope she's right.* I found out, also under the heading of club business, that the women and sweet butts had spent most of the morning at Mo's house and had only returned an hour or so ago.

It makes me wonder how they can live this way, being kept in the dark and never knowing anything. *I don't think I could do it.*

I'll probably not have a chance. Ink was just pleased to see me safe. He'd left me with those awful words hanging in the air, *we'll talk later.* Every woman and every man alive knows that normally preludes something they don't want to hear said.

He'd given me a message he didn't want to see me again. Though he had given a quick explanation it was to keep the police away from me, surely he could have softened it? Explained it was only for now, or as long as he was sent away? The words that had been given to me sounded so final. Now seeing him has resurrected my hopes. I don't know what he's going to say. *The waiting is driving me crazy.*

"Beth, Patsy? Could you come speak to Prez?"

I glance up to see Ink standing outside his prez's office, a serious look on his face. Mom and I exchange glances, both wondering what it is that Demon will have to say.

"Karl's not back with the women yet," I tell Ink as I walk past.

Surprisingly his mouth quirks and his eyes sparkle. "He'll probably still be held up behind that accident."

Yes, that will be it. But what is it about an obviously fatal crash that's amusing? Or is Ink just laughing as Karl's stuck waiting in what Ink calls a cage. I narrow my eyes as I pass him, failing to understand the joke.

The small office just about accommodates me, Mom, and Beef seated on chairs in front of the desk with Demon sitting behind it. Ink remains standing, leaning up against the door.

"Patsy, Beth," Demon starts by acknowledging us. "You've heard the term, club business?"

I snort. "Yeah."

"There's good reason behind it," Beef tries to explain. "What you don't know can't hurt you. It's not that we don't trust our women, but we keep some shit quiet, so it can't inadvertently be given away, or we have to ask people to play dumb or even lie if someone asks questions."

Demon takes over, "There are times when we need to share info that we'd otherwise not. This is one of those times. But I need both of you to give me your word you won't talk about the first thing until it's common knowledge."

He's got me intrigued. It's Mom who voices her reservations, "I'll reserve judgement until I hear what you're going to tell me."

"Fair," says Demon. "The first thing is to put your minds at rest. I'm not telling you how, who, or why, but I've received information that Phil Foster is dead. That news is not to leave this room."

I sit forward. Phil might have been my father, but that was only because of his sperm. He killed my brother or condoned his death and was going to consign me to a living hell because he preferred money to his kids. It's the best news I could have heard. "You're certain? Who? When? He left this morning… he said he had a meeting with you."

"Beth," Ink's voice chides from behind me. "Prez has just told you there are some things he can't share. We're only telling you now so you can relax. And act fuckin' surprised when you hear officially."

I glance at Mom, wondering how she's taking it, she was once married to the man after all. "Phil was behind Connor's death," she spits out. "He got what he deserved, I'm glad he's gone."

"About that." Demon looks awkward. Then he sits forward. "We're now entering the territory of shit that can never be spoken about. I won't ask for your word, because it will all become clear and you'll know why." He's about as serious as I've ever seen him, an MC prez for sure, as he starts talking again, "Your son, as you know, got involved with his father. Phil got him into some shady shit."

"We know that. Running drugs for him…"

Demon shakes his head. "You're wrong."

Mom's mouth snaps shut, mine opens and my eyes roll. "Ten kilos of heroin left in our house is a fair indication."

"Connor stole those to get them away from Phil."

I shake my head, disbelieving what he's saying. "But why? Was he going to sell them himself?"

"No," Beef says. "Look. We need to backtrack a little. Connor got himself arrested while working on Phil's protection racket. He was offered a chance to stay out of jail, he took it. He's been working with the feds. Connor had the opportunity to spirit the heroin away and took it. Only problem was, his contact was taking three weeks off. Hence he had to store them somewhere until he returned."

"He had no other contact?"

"No. Or none that he trusted."

Something starts to make sense. "So that's why he was beaten. Because he'd stolen from Phil and Alder."

"Yes. As you know, when Connor called you Beth, he was telling the truth. He was being hurt and feared for his life."

"You also know," Beef again takes over from Demon, "we managed to track down where that call had come from and that we'd gone to see if we could find him. At the time, Ink was sitting in jail, and we were desperate to find anything that could help get him out. Well we did. We found Connor."

I notice Beef's voice has deepened, and his delivery slowed, as if what he's saying carries merit. I close my eyes, not wanting to hear any more details about how they found Connor dead, Mace had told me enough of the suffering my baby brother had gone through. Mom reaches out and clasps my hand, and I don't know whether it's for my benefit or hers.

"We found Connor. Well, at first we didn't know it was a man, it was a bloody heap of rags, skin and bone."

Mom gasps and covers her face with her hand.

Beef relentlessly continues, "Until it groaned."

"He was alive?" Mom asks, her voice breaking.

"We brought him back. Arranged for a doctor who's friendly to the club to treat him. He produced a death certificate in his name."

Treated him? "You don't treat a corpse and give them a death certificate." I thought I'd just thought that, not voiced it aloud.

"Connor Foster is dead. Dan Forster is alive and getting well."

"My son?" Mom's voice is hesitant and filled with cautious hope. "Are you telling me my son is alive? Don't give a damn what he's calling himself now. But he's *alive*?"

"He is." Demon leans forward. I always wondered how he got his name. I stop wondering now as gold flecks glow in his eyes making him resemble his namesake. "But he'll only stay that way if you don't let that information leak out of this club-house. No one, apart from my members who I trust, know Connor's real identity. No one else must know his real name."

"Got to be clear here, Beth." One of Ink's hands lands on my shoulder, and his other on my mom's. "Patsy. We're hoping to make the deal with Agent Caruso, his handler. Alder's still around though Phil has gone. Connor—*Dan*—will leave Colorado and start a new life under his new name."

"Witness Protection?" Mom asks.

"That's what we hope. If the FBI doesn't come through, if eight kilos of heroin and certain knowledge that your son has in his possession don't persuade him to help, then we'll spirit Dan away and set him up on our own."

"Will we know where he is?"

As Ink's fingers press into my shoulder, I realise his tactile support is confirming that we won't. I squeeze Mom's hand. "It's better knowing he's somewhere out there alive than thinking he's dead, Mom."

She's quiet. Everyone gives her time. Then, slowly, she nods. "I've been through hell thinking he was gone. Thinking I'd failed him by not protesting harder when he left to live with his father. Though short of locking him up, I don't know what more I could have done. He's not dead, but he could have died had you not found him when you did. You're right, he can't stay in Colorado, and can't come home. I don't want to resurrect him only to bury him for real. I hate it, but if this is a chance for him to turn his life around, he should take it."

"You'll have to continue with the funeral arrangements," Demon says.

Mom and I exchange looks. I hadn't thought about that. I squeeze her hand again as she says, "We can do that."

As Mom agrees, I reckon we'll be crying hard enough to convince anyone. Connor might not be dead, but from what Demon has said, once he leaves Pueblo, we'll never see him again. As estranged as he might have been, he's still family.

"You can have some time with him before you have to say goodbye," says Demon. He takes out his phone and checks it. "I take it you want to go see him now." He glances at Ink and adds, "Skull's old room."

"I do want to see him." Mom stands.

"Patsy? He's a family friend, okay? That's all anyone here except the members know."

"Anyone seeing him will notice the family resemblance. He looks like me," I tell him straight.

"Not at the moment he doesn't," Demon replies enigmatically. Unless he's talking about my blue hair, I have no idea what he means.

A few minutes later Ink pushes a door open. It's a room laid out similar to Ink's. There, sitting on the bed, is a man. A man who, as Demon said, barely resembles me at all. One eye is swollen shut, the other open a slit. There's a big cut down the side of a nose that's also twice the size it should be. Same with his lips. As he turns his head to check who's entered, the whole of the upper half of his body moves with it, as though he's stiff as a board.

One arm is in a sling.

"Oh, Connor!" Mom runs over, then stops. Yeah, how could she hug him so it doesn't hurt? There doesn't look like any part of him that's unharmed.

"Dan." He looks up. His expression doesn't change, but I can hear some of the cockiness in his voice. "I'm Dan Forster. Nice to meet you." His one working eye closes and opens again, so I reckon he's tried a wink.

He looks past Mom and views me. "Beth, I'm so fuckin' sorry."

"Don't apologise to me." I can't keep the ire out of my voice. "Apologise to Ink." I gesture to the man behind me.

"No matter," Ink tells him. "I think we're even. I stitched you up and identified you as the one I took the drugs from that night. Fender Childs had already named you as who he'd been expecting, so I just confirmed it."

"Fender gave me up?"

"Plea deal," Ink explains. "Since you're 'dead', the cops had nothing to go on."

"Fender was one of Phil's trusted men."

"He was looking at thirty-plus years inside. You turned on Phil for less," Ink reminds him.

"You really going to make a fresh start?" Mom asks.

Again, he does that full body turn. "When I went to live with Phil, I knew he was wheeling and dealing. But it was a buzz, you know? I couldn't see what was wrong with what he was doing. But then it came about I could no longer turn a blind eye. He got me collecting loan repayments, and some of those people were addicts. I then found out that he was the one dealing to them or supplying the dealers to be exact. Then, worse…

"You found out about the trafficking," Ink's voice booms out.

Connor tries to shake his head and winces. "I can't believe how stupid I was. Phil kept me out of the house when he was bringing women in and out. The basement was soundproofed, until someone went down and left the door ajar." This time when his face twists, it's not with physical pain. "I confronted him, he said he was branching out his business. When I got arrested, it was almost a relief."

"You were going to give up Phil for a chance to start afresh?"

"Exactly." Connor's open eye meet's Ink's gratefully. Then he groans and holds a hand to his head.

"You need rest," says Mom, getting up and going over to rearrange his pillows and settle him back. "Sleep, now. I'll be here. I'll spend all the time I can with you while I still have you."

"And I," Ink says, his tone unreadable, "need to have a talk with your sister."

Going over to the bed I lean down and place the gentlest of kisses to my brother's head. It's hard to believe he's come back to life only for me to lose him again.

"Patsy?"

"Yes, Ink?"

"Don't forget you've got to arrange that funeral. It will be interesting to see who turns up."

CHAPTER THIRTY-EIGHT

Ink

As we exit the room leaving Connor and Patsy alone, I place my hand on the small of Beth's back and guide her to my own. Opening the door, I gently push her inside.

Apart from the ride back from Denver which had allowed no conversation at all, this is the first time we've been alone together since before I was arrested. I'd let her know I never wanted to see her again, while conversely telling my brothers I was claiming her. The latter at first only to make sure my club kept her safe.

We've known each other less than three weeks, and many people would say it was far too soon to know I could commit to her forever. But the nineteen days since I'd met her had been packed full of more than in the majority of most other people's whole time on earth. I'd lived through so much, things I wanted to experience forever, like how good it felt to be in her cunt, and shit I never wanted to go through again. When I thought I'd lost her for good, it had concreted my views. If I had another chance, this time, I'd keep her. I'd never met anyone like her before, I'd be a fool not to snap her up and tie her to me. People talk about finding the other half of their soul. Well, corny as it sounds, Beth is mine.

She's taken a few steps into my room and slowly turns to face me. For a second our eyes meet, then she looks away.

"Ink…" she starts.

Suddenly I don't want to hear what she has to say. I close the gap between us and pull her to me tightly. "Shush. I just want to hold you for now." I might have my own views on where I want us to go from here, but if she doesn't agree, this could be the last time I have her in my arms. Fuck I hope not. If she went, there'd be a fucking great hole in my life.

"Hey, what's up?" In my arms, she's gently shaking, crying quietly. Pulling back a little, I see tears leaking from her eyes.

"So much has happened, Ink. I feel like I've been trapped in a whirlwind, and now it's suddenly stopped," she sobs.

She doesn't have to explain, I feel much the same. "It's over now, sweetheart. Phil's not a threat anymore. Connor, or Dan, I suppose we should call him now, has a chance at a new life. It's all over now."

Her hands have been clutching at my cut, now she lets me go. "You're right, it's over." Pulling away from me, she walks to the wall, stands facing it and wraps her arms around her body.

Is this a sign that she thinks there's no future between us?

"I'm sorry, Ink," she starts, seeming to confirm my suspicions. She rises on her toes and back down as if she doesn't know what to do with herself. "I'm so sorry. I did everything wrong. And you, you ended up in jail. No wonder you hated, *hate* me." She stills. "Are you out for good?"

"I'm out for good." Unless the cops think they've got something else on me, but as I'd been telling almost the whole truth, there's little they can disprove. But I keep any residual concern to myself. "And hate you? Why the fuck should I hate you?" Didn't riding behind me all the way from Denver give her some type of clue to how I felt? Once again, it's me who steps closer. "Darlin'," I put my hand on her shoulder, still turned away, "what I feel for you is so fuckin' far from that it's a joke."

"But I got you locked up, Ink. I..," her voice breaks. "You could have gone away for years."

"I didn't." Something else I don't admit, how much I'd been convinced that was going to be the result.

Suddenly she turns. "Why did you do it, Ink? Why? When you knew the cops were waiting? You must have known what was likely to happen? Why?"

Why? The million-dollar question. "I've asked that myself," I admit.

Her face tightens.

I squeeze my fingers, anchoring her to me. "In one split second I knew you'd be walking into a trap and knew I had to stop you. One split second, but time for a myriad of thoughts. How I couldn't bear it if you went inside, even if there was a valid excuse for you being there? Hell, there was a SWAT team waiting, darlin'. You could have been walking into a bullet."

Now she gasps. "You knew all that? That you could have been *killed?*"

My hand moves from her shoulder around the back of her head. I grasp hold of her hair which has now faded to a much lighter shade of blue. "Yeah. I knew all that. And I'd do it all over again if I had to."

"Why?" She tries to shake her head, but my hold is tight, controlling.

"Because in that moment, I knew what you meant to me Beth. You staying safe was worth more than my freedom."

"But we hardly know each other."

I raise an eyebrow. "Know? Got a lifetime to find out our likes and dislikes. I do know we're compatible in bed, and since I met you, I don't need any other woman, and I doubt I ever will. The thought of any man touching you makes me want to kill whoever it is stone cold dead. Even if it's one of my brothers."

"But you told me to leave you alone. That you didn't want to see me."

"Yeah. And that's another thing I'd do all over again." I fist my hand tighter in her hair and tilt it back enough I can look down into her eyes. "I couldn't see how I wasn't looking at the next thirty or so years in the penitentiary, Beth. It wouldn't have been right to ask you to wait. Or hang around hoping I'd get out early on parole. You had to be free to get on with your own life. Fuckin' killed me, babe, but it had to be done. Could I stand the thought of you with another man? No, I fuckin' couldn't. But I knew you would find someone, knew some fucker would sweep you up, and it wouldn't be fair to hold you back." She goes to speak, I put my free hand over her mouth. "Wanted you to have the freedom which I hadn't. Wanted you to move on without feeling guilt. And last, but not fuckin' least, didn't want the cops to sniff out a connection between us. Could I stand being locked up? Wouldn't have been easy, but yeah, I'd have survived it. Could I have stood knowing you were in jail? Fuck, no. I couldn't."

Her eyes have widened. Her pupils are dilated. Whether it's my words or my tight hold on her hair, I've no idea.

My cock is swelling. He wants to be done with this conversation and right now, I don't blame him. "You were mine," I tell her. "Even though the words you were told were to stay away and that we were over. But my brothers knew different. I told them I'd claimed you."

"You claimed me?" Her head tilts to the side, and her brow creases.

"Claiming you gave me the comfort of knowing you had family watching out for you." I bow my forehead to touch hers. "Not that they did a good job of it."

"They tried," she says fast.

"Sure. They sent hangarounds…"

"Ink, they couldn't send anyone else. Else the cops would have sniffed out a connection between us or more than the one we admitted."

"You're not just a fuck buddy to me," I tell her. Hoping this time she'll say the words back. She doesn't, she seems at a loss for words. If she won't say it to me, perhaps I'll spell it out to her. "I told my brothers I'd claimed you, and that's what I want. But I need to know you're with me." I hardly dare breathe as I start asking questions to which I might not want to hear the answers. "Do you want to be claimed, Beth? Do you want to be the only girl who's ever ridden behind me on my bike and know it will only ever be you there? Do you want to wear my patch showing I own you, as you, in return, own me? Do you want to spend the rest of your days in my bed and in my life? Because that's what I want, sweetheart."

Her eyes stare into mine, disbelieving as she tries to process what I've said. "We've only just met."

"Why waste time? I don't need longer, fuck, I've had more than enough time to think. Sitting in the jail cell, all I could think of were the chances I'd lost. Now I'm a free man, I don't want to wait any longer. I'm ready to be all-in, babe."

It's now her hand touching my cheek. "I feel the same way, Ink. Losing you hurt more than it should. I couldn't stop thinking about you, even when you told me it was over. Now you're saying everything I wanted you to say, but I can't believe it. I must be dreaming."

I chuckle with relief. "I'll pinch you if you like."

"Kiss me." It's almost a challenge.

A challenge I'm more than happy to rise to. Without hesitation I lower my head, taking her lips gently at first, then applying more pressure, sweeping my tongue inside her mouth. That taste, it's like home. My pelvis leans forward, my hardness grinds against her. After a few minutes when I pull back, her face is flushed.

"You sure it isn't just sex?" she asks, having realised my state of arousal.

"After everything I've said, Beth? After I've laid my soul bare?" I go to say more, but now it's her putting her fingers over my lips.

"My turn." She looks away, then back. "I didn't understand

how quickly you'd wormed your way into my heart until I thought I'd lost you forever, or for a good long time anyway. I didn't want anyone else, Ink. I would have waited."

"You'd have forgotten me soon enough." I smile to soften my words. I wouldn't have blamed her.

"Forgotten you? There's never been another man like you, Ink. You take, you don't ask. Yet you never ask more of me than I'm prepared to give, except for your request which I only heard second hand, to stay away from you. But I'd have done that, if I'd thought that was really what you wanted. Now you say you already claimed me?"

"I wanted you to have protection."

"Your club hated, *hates* me, with good reason."

"My club doesn't hate you. They didn't trust you, but when they found Connor, they knew you'd been telling the truth." I don't tell her they treated her as my old lady with a caveat, a caveat that no longer exists. They've still to officially vote her in, but I'm sure there won't be a problem with that.

She's staring past me at a point on the opposite wall. I'd felt we were making headway, now I'm not sure at all. Cupping my hand under her chin, I turn her to face me again. "What is it, Beth?"

"It's stupid… but you mean everything to me, Ink. It was only ever you. I saw you at Mel's wedding and didn't want anyone else. Yes, I came onto Mace, but only to get a reaction from you. I'd never have gone with him. If you'd turned me down…"

"I didn't," I tell her. "Even then I didn't want you with anyone else."

"Ink, you knew what you were doing, you were prepared to give up your freedom for me, well, I wanted to give up mine for you. I wanted to go to the cops, but Demon and Mom told me it wouldn't make any difference. If it had meant you'd have gotten out, I'd have done it."

Again, I chuckle. "Two martyrs, yeah?"

She smiles back. "Seems it would be a waste not to give whatever's between us a chance."

"I want everything, Beth," I warn her, laying out what I want to happen. "I want you with me, living with me, sharing my life. If we're going to make a go of this, I want the whole damn package."

"Live, here?" She looks around my room. It's not much to offer her, I know that.

"We'll buy a house, Beth. Choose somewhere together. But yeah, for now, here will do."

She glances around again, and once more her lips curve. "Well, you do have a well-equipped bed."

I move closer, putting my mouth to her ear. "I'm ready to show you just how well equipped it is." More than fucking ready. It's time I physically claimed her.

Her hands wrap around me pulling my body into hers. "I don't mind if you do."

I can't wait any longer. "Strip."

This time I don't turn away. This time I keep my eyes on hers. When she removes her tee, I remove my cut. Her bra goes, so does my shirt. In unison our hands go to our hips, our jeans pushed down as though in a choreographed dance.

"On the bed," I instruct when all our clothes have disappeared. I'll take my time with her later, but now I want to do what I've been dreaming about, slide inside her perfect cunt.

She's on her back, but not lying flat, she's propped up on her elbows. Her teeth are biting her lip, and her tongue comes out to soothe the slight hurt. I doubt she knows she's doing it, but each action is turning me on more.

"Bend your legs and spread those thighs. Give me some room to work." Christ, I can smell her arousal as I place one knee then the other on the bed, and stalk toward her.

She's obeyed me. Oh, I doubt she'll always be so compliant, but for now I'm sure she's feeling the same as me, wanting to be joined as close as humanly possible. First though, I want a taste of her. Want her essence on my tongue, want her screaming out to the world.

I groan as my tongue meets her cream, she moans, and her hands clasp the sheets as I get to work. I've already learned her and now remember just the pressure she likes. I'm thoroughly enjoying myself, her taste messing with my brain, sending endorphins through me, making my spine tingle and my balls throb. Soon, though, her hips close around me, her stomach muscles ripple and she's screaming her orgasm out loud.

Reaching to the bedside table I take out the condoms that are always there, stocked up as one of the duties of the prospects. I slide one on, longing for the day when I'll take her bare. Put a baby inside her. Too early yet, but one day.

She feels unbelievably fantastic. Her cunt grips my cock just right, her reactions couldn't be more perfect. When I'd fucked other women before, there was always something missing, something elusive I couldn't find. As I thrust inside her, I realise what it is, that however intense our sessions will become, I won't be just fuckin', I'll always be making love to my old lady.

Knowing I won't be able to last long, I swivel my hips, making my ass muscles flex so I'm hitting that all important place inside her. Using my fingers on her clit, when she starts coming, I'm right there with her, this time, my roar mingles with her screaming.

I stay, relishing the feeling of our two bodies being joined, something not even a day ago I thought I'd ever feel again. Eventually my cock softens, and I lose contact with her. I move so I'm lying on my side, and pull her into my arms, holding her like I never want to let her go.

"I'm sorry," she whispers, softly. "I should have come to you, told you."

"Beth, I'm going to say this once, and then we'll move past it, okay? Sure, I had a few days in jail, and more than a few moments when I thought life as I knew it was over, but I'm out, I'm free. Yeah, if we were then where we are now, then I'd spank your ass if I wasn't the first person you came with any worries you had, major or minor. But we were. I couldn't have said I do *anything* for you, it took that sight of you walking into danger to show me what I hadn't known I already felt." I pull myself up on one elbow, looking down at her. "You hear me? From now on, you always come to me, or one of my brothers if I'm not around. Promise me, Beth."

There's no hesitation in her response, "I promise."

I believe her. The corners of my mouth turn up. "So," I toy with her hair, twirling it around my finger, "what have you been doing while I've been away? Hmm? I wonder how many transgressions I can count?"

She stills in my arms. "I've been good."

"Good? Hmm, I doubt that little girl. Somehow, I think your ass is going to be very sore later."

"Yeah?"

"Yeah. One for sure. You haven't sucked me off yet. Don't you think you should greet your man properly?"

"Oh. How remiss of me." Her face splits into a wide grin. "Will you go easy on me if I correct that now?"

"Depends how good it is," I tell her, having difficulty keeping the laughter from my voice. "You're going to have to try really hard."

Of course, with Beth, it's very good.

CHAPTER THIRTY-NINE

Beth

I'm amazingly going to have a lifetime to learn everything about Ink, but fast I find, once having determined something, he doesn't let the grass grow under his feet.

That night after I'd been rescued, I'd slept in his room, and he all but had me moved in from that point. A lot of my clothes have already been bought back from the house, and I admit to getting a pang of pleasure when seeing them hanging alongside his in his wardrobe. I've not slept in my own bed either. For a man who once told me he didn't spend the night with bitches, now he doesn't seem to want to spend even one alone.

I've no experience of living with someone other than my mother but am quickly getting addicted to going to bed with a man and waking with him beside me. The hours in between, well, as can be expected, we spend many making love.

Suddenly I hear him clearing his throat behind me, the sound breaking into my thoughts. "Hey, babe. I was a Marine, remember. I don't expect you to do that shit for me." I swing around to where he's lying back on the bed, watching me folding some clothes I'd just put through the laundry.

I peer at him and shrug. "Mine needed doing, no bother to throw yours in. You can return the favour another day." I'm discovering more each day about the man who's claimed me, and so far, everything I like.

There's a knock on the door. "You decent in there?"

I roll my eyes. "Yeah, come in, Mom."

"What is it?" Ink says fast, sitting up.

I'd also picked up a vibe when Mom walked in, something is most definitely on her mind. "Is Con… Dan, okay?"

Her lips purse for a second. She waves toward the seat where Ink had once spanked me and hopefully will soon do so again. I suppress a grin at the memory as Ink says, "Help yourself."

"Dan's doing fine, but he is what I wanted to talk to you about."

We're both quiet while she draws her thoughts together. I shoot Ink a concerned look, and he sends one back to me.

"I need you both to answer a question. Is this serious between you two?" She looks at Ink.

Ink huffs a laugh. "Are you asking me what my intentions are?" At her small nod, he holds out his hand to me, and I put the last of the folded clothes down and walk over to join him. "It's as serious as a fuckin' heart attack, on my part at least. Beth's it for me." He pulls me down to sit beside him and kisses me sweetly.

I hold the eyes of my mom. "I'm serious about Ink. I love him, Mom." I realise I haven't actually told him, but we've expressed our emotions in other ways instead. When I glance at him, he mouths back, *I love you too, Beth.*

Mom seems to need convincing for some reason. "You'll always look after her?"

Ink's brow creases. "Of course I will. I love Beth. Not only has she got me, she's got my brothers."

"A family." Mom smiles. "I may have been speaking to Mel. She's explained how it works."

There's still a little residual awkwardness between me and some of Ink's brothers. Not that they still blame me, now they feel guilty for not believing my version of events. But things are getting easier, and I think we'll get to the place where I'm accepted in the same way as my friend. That's what I want. It's mismatched and not perfect, but it's just as Mom's said Mel described it. The club is a family.

"Connor will be alone," she states.

"It's how it has to be," replies Ink quickly. A worried look my way. It's the only way to keep Connor out of the clutches of Alder. I, too, hope she's not going to be difficult. "You know this, Patsy. If anyone thinks he might not be dead, they'll be watching you and watching Beth."

But that doesn't seem to be what she has on her mind. "I know that Ink. I'm not going to do anything to jeopardise his future. But that doesn't mean I can't work something out. I'm not tied here, I can work anywhere. And Beth, you've got Ink and his family."

"You're going with him?" Ink's quicker on the uptake than me. His hand rests on my arm, as if telling me to consider it and not dismiss the suggestion immediately.

I do take a moment. "Mom, have you really thought about this? If you do. It will be hard, impossible even, for us to stay in contact." I'll lose my mom? I didn't expect her to suggest that. My first thought is panic, what will I do without her? I've lived with her all my life. She's been there every day, my rock.

Ink's hand starts caressing my arm, the gesture, as it's meant to be, is calming. "Think of your brother, babe," he says carefully. "He'll be on his own. He's younger, hell, he's only just old enough to buy himself a drink, and he's not had the best influence for the past few years. He needs love, support and stability, else he might end up throwing this chance away. You've got me. This might not be forever, once Connor's settled into a new life, has new friends, maybe a girl of his own, maybe your mom can come back home."

"Might be years." I bite my lip. *Might be forever.* Am I selfish wanting her to myself? Until Ink, I haven't really considered moving away from home. Of course, I'd been toying with the idea sometime in the future, but never for one minute did I think she'd be the one to move out. I've had a comfortable existence. But Connor, I can see how he could need her. Much more than I do myself.

"Ink's on the right track. I am worried Connor might fall in with the wrong crowd if he's left to his own devices," Mom says. "I don't want to leave you Bethany, you're more than my daughter, you're my best friend and I won't deny I'll miss you. But Connor's my son. We've been doing some soul searching these past few days, and he'd like to go to college and make something of himself. I fear he'll find it hard on his own."

"What about the house?" The home where I've lived all the life I remember. The house with the beautiful yard.

"I'm sorry, Beth, but I'll have to sell it." That she's replied so quickly shows how seriously she's been thinking about this.

"Sell it to us," Ink says fast. *What?* I turn to him. "That's if Beth's agreeable, of course."

"It's got a big yard," Mom says. "Needs upkeep and maintenance."

Ink isn't put off. "That's what prospects are for."

My mouth drops open. He shrugs, unrepentant. Seems like this life might have benefits I hadn't realised I'd signed up for.

"It's a big house. A family house." Mom seems to want to make sure Ink understands what he might be taking on.

But he just shrugs. "We'll have to have a big family then."

Kids? Again, I turn to him in surprise.

But he simply says, "Told you I wanted everything, babe."

I think it was that statement that convinced Mom she'd be leaving me in safe hands. I put on a brave face, but it was the hardest thing I'd ever done to try to be positive about her leaving my life. My problem is, I'm twenty-seven years old, Connor just twenty-two, and his knowledge of adult life tainted by living with Phil. He's no idea of how to fend for himself, and I share Mom's worries, that left to his own devices, he might take the easiest path which isn't necessarily the right one.

When I'd told him I knew of their plans, his face had brightened when I gave him no other indication than I was fine with the idea. There's no doubt the fear of him starting afresh had eased once he knew he wouldn't be alone. That had given him a new confidence.

A day later, the clubhouse is on its best behaviour when Agent Caruso comes calling. Of course, us women weren't supposed to know what was going on, but Connor had been so worried about what might happen, he'd needed someone to confide in, and naturally that was Mom and myself.

Ink had later enlightened me simply that it had all gone as planned. Connor has wiped his slate clean as Caruso would be getting a pat on his back for getting eight kilos of heroin off the street. While at first he was annoyed that he'd returned to find Phil Foster dead, when Connor was able to offer up Alder and what he'd learned about how the drugs came in from Mexico, he agreed Connor had done enough. As a result, the feds are going to help him get settled with his new identity in a new town. I was relieved that his new papers would be officially prepared. While the Satan's Devils had suggested they'd sort out his new identity themselves, I didn't really know Cad's skills or connections, and had worried there'd be a chance his new identity might not stand up to scrutiny.

Of course, Mom would have to change her name as well, but she was keeping her first name, and just changing the last to Forster. They'd agreed to use the name Connor had already become.

The next few days pass in a whirlwind. Ink and I spend a lot of time at my house, packing up bits Mom wants to take. There wasn't a lot apart from her clothes and her sewing machine of course. Steph, with her knowledge of Wit Sec had advised her to leave personal possessions behind, anything that might connect her with her old life. So, I became the custodian of the family photographs. I found myself not envying her.

Of course, we also attend the funeral that we'd somehow found time to arrange.

It might not have been my brother in that box being solemnly carried into the crematorium, but I am in mourning.

This is the last formality before Connor and Mom leave for pastures unknown, and this is the first occasion since the decision had been made that I've allowed myself to think how much I'll be losing. I'm going to miss them both. Over the past few days, I reconnected with my brother and have regained more of the relationship we had when we were younger. As for Mom, she's been there all my life, and what's a girl supposed to do without her mother? She won't even be at the end of the phone. All contact is prohibited.

The coffin is symbolic of the loss that's about to happen in my life, and I'm not acting as tears start to fall as I listen to the brief service. The officiant talks about my brother's life, a complete fiction about a young man with so much promise taken from us all too soon. Mom sits beside me, squeezing my hand as if she too is sad for how her life will be changing.

Ink's sitting beside me and stands with everyone else as we watch the coffin soundlessly slide away until it's hidden from our view. Mom turns to me with tears in her eyes. Then we're in each other's arms and weeping.

"My sincere condolences."

The deep voice makes us jump, and I feel myself tense as mom turns.

"You've never been sincere about anything. I doubt you're starting now." Mom steps back from me and rounds on the speaker, quietly hissing, "What the hell are you doing here, Alder?"

I'm proud of her in that moment, she might be small, but she's standing up to the man. I look around for Ink, but he's no longer here.

Mom continues, pausing only to dab a tissue at her eyes, "Have you any idea who did this to my son?" She waves to where the coffin is now hidden behind curtains. In a moment, or perhaps when we're gone, it will enter the furnace and whoever's body is inside would be gone forever.

"I don't know." My attention snaps back to Alder, his deep voice sounding chilled. "But I'll do what I can to find out." He too stares at where the coffin has disappeared. "It's a fucking shame Phil couldn't be here. He was close to Connor."

So close he condoned him being beaten and killed. And Alder need look no further than a mirror to see who was responsible for the supposed death of my brother.

"Any news on Phil's accident?" Mom asks politely, her tone suggesting as he'd lived on the wrong side of the law, his death was predictable and while she could cry an ocean of tears for her son, she wasn't going to waste any on her dead ex.

Alder appears slightly more interested in who caused Phil's death, than Connor's. "It was no accident," he growls. "Someone took him out and cost me a fucking fortune when he did it. I'll find out who's responsible, eventually. I always do." It sounds like a half promise, or a half warning. "He, or they, stole from us."

I start to feel uneasy, and look around for Ink, but he's still nowhere to be seen. Has he made himself scarce, so Alder doesn't notice him? I've no proof, but I'll always wonder if the Satan's Devils had a hand in Phil's death. At times like this, maybe keeping club business from old ladies makes sense, I'd rather not know. The bigger worry is whether Alder knew the Satan's Devils had the drugs Connor had stolen from him, but so far, there had been no indication whether he does or not. Phil's dead, and his close confidants died along with him. It's quite possible he doesn't know, but of course, still a risk. I hope Caruso is able to arrest him soon.

Alder's staring at the closed curtains, his eyes narrowed suspiciously, then he turns back to us. "Well, it's been nice getting reacquainted Patsy. Unless you hear from the dead, I doubt we'll cross paths again." He moves forward and threatens in a low voice, "No one gets away with stealing from me, not even a ghost."

"Hey, babe, sorry about that." Ink comes up and puts his arm around me. "Needed a piss. Friend of the family?" He nods toward Alder, seeming unconcerned.

"No friend of mine," Mom says.

Alder raises an eyebrow, then, with a smirk, walks smartly away.

"Where have you been?" I turn to Ink. "Pissing, really? That was *Alder.*" I emphasise his name, stressing it was a bad time for him to make himself scarce.

He leans in and speaks into my ear, "I know who he is. That Alder's here suggests he's suspicious. Must admit some bucks just changed hands, and the coffin is in the cremator now."

"Don't they always burn them immediately?"

"Just wanted to make sure, Beth. Didn't want to take a chance of Alder having the opportunity to examine it. Now, though, he can't."

That had been quick thinking by Ink. Now the body has been destroyed, Alder has no proof Connor is alive.

"Just who did we cremate today?" I ask as we get into the car. "I feel so bad that we might have taken someone away from family."

"Nah," Ink turns before he starts the engine, "he was a homeless man who was killed by a car when he stumbled drunk across the road. No living relatives found. Look at it this way, he got a send-off he didn't expect, tears shed for him, nice words said. Probably more than he expected or deserved."

"Are you worried about Alder?"

He shoots me a glance. "Why would I be, Beth? Neither I, nor the club, have anything to do with the man."

CHAPTER FORTY

Beth

Things happen fast after the funeral. Whether it was that Alder had turned up, or whether there was no point in delay, the final arrangements are quickly made for Mom and Connor to relocate.

I have no idea where, if either of them knows, they keep it to themselves.

I force myself to be strong, joking with Mom that I'll be jealous if they're heading into sunshine, as here winter seems in no hurry to give way to spring. It hits me hard after I spend a while talking to Mom, telling her I'll watch out for her new designs on the internet, with some hints about the type of clothes I'll want designed. When I realise I'll be buying online from now on and not just popping upstairs to her sewing room, I have to leave the room to pull myself together.

I realise while she's upset, Mom's also excited. She's given the best years of her life to raising her children, and now she's got the chance to go somewhere new and start afresh. While I'm also beginning a new life with Ink, I can't help but be a little envious that I won't be the one sharing her adventure with her.

But again, I let none of this show. I force myself to pretend I'm completely okay with their move.

I keep a smile on my face as the car is packed and then tell them to take care.

When Karl slides the gate open and the car turns out into the road, Ink holds me to him tightly as though fearing I'm going to run after it.

"It's for the best," I turn to tell him, still with my lips curved upward. "Connor will have a fresh start. Mom too. She's still young enough to start a new life. Perhaps she'll find a man of her own."

He doesn't buy my fake pleasure. "They'll be fine, Beth."

"I know they will," I reply. But I can't stop my head turning back in the direction where the car had driven away.

"It's okay to be upset, babe." Ink's hand is caressing my back.

"I'm not upset. I'm happy for Connor and Mom. Connor will be safe."

Ink gives me one of his intense stares, then his lips thin. "Come on. There's a matter that needs to be resolved between us."

What? My confusion must show as he takes a firm hold of my hand and leads me back into the clubhouse, across the main room, up those industrial metal stairs, and into his room. He locks the door, then turns with an eyebrow raised.

"Get naked."

For probably the first time that I've met him, I'm not feeling aroused. I've kept my despair deeply buried, hoping he doesn't know how empty I'm feeling having watched my family drive off. Them leaving was the right thing to do, it's just going to be awhile before I can accept it. But I don't want that to show. I have to be strong, the woman Ink expects me to be.

"Babe, take your clothes off."

"Ink. I'm not..."

He pushes away from the door against which he'd been leaning. He comes into my personal space. "Trust me," he says, softly. His hands go to the bottom of my sweater. "Lift your arms." As he uses that commanding voice, I obey automatically, though doubting however skilled he is as a lover, that today I will be able to respond.

I stand, only helping as far as I lift my feet when he asks. Soon all my clothes are lying on the ground, and he's fully clothed. My mind's miles away, already thinking of everything I hadn't said to my mom. And now I've lost my chance, maybe forever.

I don't object as he takes my hand and leads me to the chair, but when he pats his lap, my eyes widen in horror and I shake my head. "No."

My reaction doesn't seem to take him by surprise. Pulling me down like he had once before, he traps me with his strong muscular legs. I struggle, but within seconds there's a sharp sting on my right ass cheek, followed by one to my left.

"Stop," I cry out. "Ink, no."

But he doesn't stop.

It's not erotic. It hurts. He continues. There's no getting away from this, I go limp, and then the tears start.

"That's it," Ink murmurs, rubbing my sore ass. "Babe, you needed to cry. You're keeping everything bottled up and that's not good. I've watched you holding it together for days, but you don't need to keep it up. Just let it out. Give it to me, let me help you with your pain."

He stops the spanking, pulls me up and holds me tight in his arms, his hands now smoothing up and down my back. I'm ugly crying, letting out everything that I've held back, covering his shirt with snot and tears, snorting and hiccupping, but he doesn't seem to mind.

"Cry, babe. Cry. That's it, that's good."

The sobs keep coming as though they'll never stop. Then I'm wailing, "Why did she choose, Connor? I need my mom."

"She didn't choose Connor because she wanted to, Beth. You're strong, you're in a good place. She respects you, respects the choices you make. Connor? Well he's shown he needs a guiding hand."

I hadn't even understood how much I felt her leaving was desertion, but Ink's more patient than I would have thought, and takes time to help me break things down and put them back together in a way that's not so painful. Slowly his words change, and he's painting a picture of a future we can build together. Letting me see that I can branch out on my own, and while I won't be able to see or talk to her, my mom will always be there, out there, somewhere, supporting me.

I don't know how long I cry, but slowly Ink's supportive words get through. Eventually my tears dry, and I use several tissues to try to clear my blocked nose. When he sees I've calmed, he lifts me up and carries me to the bed. It's then I notice the sky has darkened outside. I must have been weeping for hours.

I'm tired, exhausted, and thankful Ink had been so patient with me. I hadn't known how much I need to face all the emotions locked inside head on. It wasn't just only the loss of my mom, but everything that's happened over the past couple of weeks. Something needed to break, that Ink had seen that was just another good reason to love him.

As I watch him make himself ready for bed, the sight causes a kernel of arousal to start growing inside as he reveals his muscular inkless body to me.

Seeing me watching, he smirks.

"That was extreme," I tell him.

He doesn't pretend not to know what I'm talking about. "Extreme times call for extreme measures, babe." Naked, he perches on my side of the bed, his hand brushing back my hair from my face. "We're going to be okay, Beth. You're not alone. I'm going nowhere, okay? Any choice to be made, I'll always choose you."

"Are you coming to bed?"

He chuckles softly. "I am."

That night, Ink takes his time. No ropes or cuffs, no more

spanking, erotic or otherwise, he just does everything he can to show how much he feels for me.

With my mind now accepting how things have turned out, even though I regret it had to happen, I fall into a dreamless sleep. I could have sworn I've only been resting a few minutes, when I'm woken.

"Come off it." I roll over in bed, squinting as he pulls up the blind and lets daylight flood into the room. "What's the time?"

"Time you got out of fuckin' bed." He laughs down at me.

I am so not amused. "Thought you knew me by now. I need coffee to function, babe."

He raises his eyebrow and points to the cup sitting steaming beside me. I throw out my hand but it's too far away.

"You really aren't a morning person, are you?" He chuckles again, comes over, sits and places an arm around me helping me to sit up. Then he lifts and hands my coffee to me.

"When I'm not planning on going for a run, I'm not," I admit. "And why have you woken me so goddamn early on a Saturday?" When I've now got to face the reality that I no longer have my blood family around me, I frown slightly, wondering where Mom and Connor are, and what they are doing today. Is it exciting for them? Or scary. A bit of both I expect.

His finger comes under my chin. "Hey, doll. Why the frown?"

I shrug.

"Your mom and brother will be okay."

But he can't know that.

Or maybe he can, I realise, as he goes on to say, "When I was getting you that," he points to my drink, "Demon came in. He's heard from Lost, the San Diego prez, and apparently, they arrived okay. The feds have got them a house they can move into temporarily."

"What? How the hell do you know…"

"We might have suggested to Connor that he ask to go to San Diego."

"And Caruso went along with that?"

"Sure. It's far enough away, and location didn't matter to him. As we've got a chapter there, our brothers can watch out for them without them knowing..." he breaks off and winks. "May even be able to tell you if Connor finds a nice bronzed California girl, or Patsy her own surfer."

"I'll get updates? Why didn't you tell me before?" I sit up, excited. "Can I visit?"

"No," he says sharply. "And the Devils won't be involved. Look, Beth, Wit Sec is pretty damn good. Mostly, they only lose people when they bring themselves out of hiding. But Steph went through some shit, so we wanted to do what we could to make sure it all turned out right. You're mine now, and part of that is looking out for family."

"You sure you're not bringing danger to them if they're linked back to the Satan's Devils?"

"Won't be a link. Lost and the boys down south know how to fly under the radar and anyway," he takes my now empty cup from me. "How's about you get up and showered and we get on with our day?"

He's excited about something I can tell. Normally he'd wake me with his cock, or his mouth, but not today. But he's bouncing on his feet with impatience. Must be important if it's replaced sex as the first thing on his mind.

"Okay, okay," I say, still grumpy. "I'll get ready. But I expect my morning sex later."

His hand curls around my neck in that possessive way I love. "You can use my cock any time you like, babe. I'll sacrifice my own comfort to keep my woman happy."

I grin. "Sacrifice, eh? But why not now?"

"Because, we've got places to be."

Have we indeed? But my glare doesn't work on him and he doesn't enlighten me. He has got me intrigued. Enough so that I have a quick shower, blow drying my hair in record time, making a note to make a hair appointment to have my hair dyed again soon as it's faded so much.

Once I'm ready, I comment I'm hungry, so we go straight to the kitchen. I follow Ink in, then come to an abrupt halt. Whatever's going on must involve the whole club, I hadn't expected this many people to be around.

"Beth, hi. I made cinnamon buns. You want one?"

The question distracts me from wondering why it looks like everyone's here. Mel gets her answer by way of a gimme gesture, and soon I'm filling my mouth with the deliciousness she's baked. I manage a 'mmm-mmm' by way of thanks and to show my appreciation.

Already showing how quickly he's learned about me, Ink's refilling my cup and passing another cup of coffee my way.

"Ready for your big day?" Ro's voice suddenly booms. Then when Ink glares at him, he holds up his hands and says, "Forget I said anything." Mel bats at his arm.

Big day? What's going on? Quickly, I finish my impromptu breakfast by sucking my fingers into my mouth and licking the sugar off carefully, not missing Ink turning away and looking like he's adjusting his jeans. Then I say, "Okay, tell me. What's going on?"

"Here." Ink passes a leather jacket over. It's new. Soft and lined. "I didn't have time to get my patch on it, but we'll do that in time."

"We going for a ride?" Glancing outside I see it's probably a cold, but dry day.

Ink chuckles. "Not exactly."

"Oh, come on. Let's get on with it." Mace looks impatient. There's a look on his face which I don't quite trust.

CHAPTER FORTY-ONE

Ink

I toss a glare in Mace's direction. Then give one in Pyro's. Trust him for not keeping his mouth shut. Under the guise of them wanting to give my old lady support, I know they're really here to see whether she's going to crash or put a scratch on Beaver's Sportster. I've far too much confidence in her for that, but it won't help having darn near the whole club watching her, but once Liz had overheard me getting the keys from the prospect last night, word had gone around.

I know the Tucson chapter have a couple of bike-riding old ladies, but this is breaking new ground for us. Lizard seemed surprised I wasn't concerned about the thought of my old lady having her own motorcycle as though it might be a challenge to my manhood, but I'm not at all. Instead, I hope she likes it. I can't wait until we're heading out onto the highway.

I'd organised this as a distraction for her after Patsy and Connor had disappeared into the sunset, so to speak. I knew she was devastated but had admiration for the way she was trying to hide it. I hoped making one of her dreams come true might make her acceptance of her new life a little easier, replace the normality she'd lost with something new.

Right now, I'm grinning at her confusion and suspicion, and can't wait to show her the reason why everyone's around.

"Come on." Again, placing my hand against the small of her back, I lead her out the main door of the clubhouse. The front parking lot has been emptied, to give her the space she needs the brothers had moved their bikes around the back.

Her eyes first look at me in confusion, then at the men crowding out behind her. She clearly expected to be on the back of my Fat Bob, which isn't out here. Instead, there's just one bike looking forlorn without its companion.

Taking her hand, I put something in it. She looks down, squints at the object, then quizzically glances at me.

I nod toward Beaver's ride.

He's clearly cleaned it for her. Every bit of chrome sparkles where the weak winter sun hits it. The cherry red paint is shiny and bright.

"My riding lesson?" She turns and looks behind her, her eyes narrowing in on Mace. "So that's what you're here for so early on a Saturday." Her gaze goes over every man and old lady in the club who have followed us outside. "You all expect me to fall off, don't you?"

"Nah," Mace contradicts, having looked around and taken on the role of spokesman. "We're just here to cheer you on."

"Yeah, show us how it's done!" shouts Liz. Then I hear him mumble, "This I had to see. A bitch learning to ride." He gets treated to one of my glares too. So much so, that he takes a step behind Pyro.

"Ignore them," I tell her, and lead her over to the bike.

As I'd expected when the idea of her riding first came up, her height gives her a clear advantage and she has no trouble at all standing astride that Harley, and with both feet firmly balanced on the ground, pulls it upright, easily handling the weight.

"Hey, Ink. Hold up." Mace, comes over, frowning at me. "Think you ought to talk her through the basics."

My eyes crease. *Like what?* I can't actually remember not

being able to ride, to me it's just like breathing. If I had to give instruction how to draw air into my lungs, it would be as hard to describe it. As Mace starts to tell her shit like where the high and low beam is, and where the indicators are, I start to welcome his assistance.

Taking his cue, and not to be left out, I explain the front brake on the handlebars, and the rear operated by her right foot. Truth is, without his reminder, I'd have overlooked all that.

"Okay," she says, her teeth biting her lip, then giving me a cocky grin. "I know how to stop. How do I start?" I notice her eyes gleaming with excitement. Unable to resist, I lean over and take her lips with mine.

"Get on with it. We haven't got all day," I hear Beef call out.

"Thought she was going to ride the fuckin' bike, not that we were going to watch you ride her," Pyro shouts.

"I wouldn't object to a show," shouts Liz. His comment is followed by an ouch, and I make a note to find out who punched him later and thank them.

"You ever driven a stick shift, darlin'?" Mace asks, while I'm still glaring at my brothers. I turn back in time to see her nod, and Mace continues, "You've got your clutch there," he points the lever out, "and your left foot works the gears. Where you are now is neutral. When you start the engine, pull in the clutch and nudge down to select first. You've got five gears. To select second, pull in the clutch, come back to neutral, and kick up to second, then clutch, then up to third."

"Just up, up and up?"

"Yes," I re-enter the training session. "You just keep kicking up through those gears as necessary. Back down the same way."

"Just be gentle when you come back from first to neutral, kick too hard and you'll go into second. You'll get the hang of it after a while," Mace reassures her.

She's concentrating so hard she's forgotten she's got an audience. But she is getting impatient. "Can I just get going?"

Mace laughs, his eyes meeting mine. "Okay. You're going to

start the engine, put it into first, then very gently start letting out the clutch. The bike will begin to move. You're tall enough, you can slowly walk it forward. Just have a go, use the clutch, take it a few feet, pull the clutch in and stop."

She does. A huge smile spreading over her face when the bike starts to move.

"Hey." Beef's wandered over now. "Next time, sweetheart, you twist the throttle a little. Only a little, you hear me? Too much and you'll scare yourself and crash."

She nods at him. Selects first, lets the clutch find the sweet spot, then once the bike starts pulling forward, very, very, gently, twists the throttle. I run alongside her, proud as punch.

"Hand off the throttle, clutch in, and pull the front brake," I yell, loudly to be heard over the rumble of the engine.

"Can I do it again?" she asks, her eyes shining.

"Give it a go."

For the next half-hour she starts, stops, keeping to first and second gear while learning the confidence to raise her feet off the ground. When the skies darken and rain starts falling, I call it a day.

There's a round of applause as she walks into the clubhouse, and fuck me, I'm proud when she takes a bow. Beaver, now looking relieved, offers her a celebratory shot.

"What do I have to do to be able to ride on the road?" she asks, as she takes it.

I may have checked out the current rules. "You need to get M added to your driver's permit. You take a written test, pass a road skills test and that's it. You work at the government offices, ask the DMV department to arrange it."

"I will. Hey, Beaver. Your bike really up for sale? Can I buy it?"

Fuck, she's wasting no time. "For a good price," I growl, my eyes signalling Beaver a message. I'll give him what he wants, but she'll only be paying what she can afford.

"You did good." Mace comes over. "You're going to be a natural. Got a feel for it already, saw that."

I watch her, animatedly rehashing her lesson with Mace, happy how he and the other brothers have come to accept her now they know the truth, that she really had no part in me being taken in by the cops. I settle back against the bar, happy to let them talk, and me just listening. Mace and I have always been tight, and it's great to see him trying to make up for any awkwardness with Beth. He'd admitted he'd played the enforcer on her when he thought he might have needed to make her talk, but that's water under the bridge. I'd understood, I'd step up too to protect any of my brothers should I think there was a need. It looks like my best friend and old lady are going to be good friends now.

Me, with an old lady. Was it really only a few short weeks ago I'd met Beth for the first time?

Pyro and Mel's wedding. I hadn't had a clue how things were going to turn out. There I'd been, happily single, thinking there couldn't be anything better than having my choice of club girls to go with for the night. Sex without strings, then kicking them out of bed afterwards.

Once Beth had made a beeline for me, I'd fallen under her spell. Under normal circumstances, she'd still have ensnared me, but I'd have taken it slow, fought it kicking and screaming all the way. Having the chance taken away had focused my mind, made me see it was her I wanted with a clarity that might otherwise have taken months or even years.

I watch her again for a moment. Judge and Sparky are now giving her tips on what to do the next time she rides the bike. It makes me remember, if I hadn't had stepped up, one of them might have claimed her. Thank fuck I came to my senses in time.

Beth catches my eye, and winks.

Yeah. She's mine. I've got an old lady, and fuck me, am buying a house. A house Beth and I will visit later and see what we can do to make it our own. I don't want to remove the memory of her mother, but Patsy has lived in it forever, could do with some updating for sure.

In time, maybe we'll be setting up a nursery and filling that house with kids.

Sooner, though, when the weather warms up, I'm looking forward to setting up the grill and getting some burgers and brats on to cook for my brothers. Probably after a good long ride out with them and my old lady beside me on her own bike. Can life get any better?

A few weeks ago, I thought I had all I ever wanted.

I'd been wrong.

"Hey, Ink. Got a moment?"

I check Beth's still reliving her moment of triumph among her admiring fans, and turn to Mace, surprised to see Beef alongside him. "Sure."

"Want to show you something outside."

They seem relaxed, so unconcerned, I go along with them. We pass through the yard Beef had tidied and made safe for Steph, Theo and whatever other clubhouse children might come along and through the gate in the fence beyond which is the end of the flattened ground. Out here is another of the old steel mill buildings, disused and abandoned long ago.

I stand and stare, looking for what they've brought me here to see.

"Thought you'd have given us more time," Mace offers.

My brow creases.

"Yeah, we probably needed the full thirty years to get it done," Beef says moodily. "You sure about this, Mace?"

"Yeah. The building is structurally sound. Brick needs repointing in parts, and most of the wood has gone, but the fabric is there."

They've lost me. "There for what?"

For an answer, Mace turns fast and while he pulls his punch, it's still got enough force behind it to have me reeling back, sucking in air and bent double. He'd given me no time to tense my stomach muscles.

"See?" he says to Beef while I'm still gasping. "Going soft."

"I can see." The VP's laughing, the bastard.

"I'll give you fuckin' soft." I launch at the enforcer, only to be held back by Beef's strong arms.

"Hear him out."

"I would if he started to make fuckin' sense," I gasp out.

Mace waves his arms toward the falling down building. "Thought it was time we had us a gym."

"Mace was going to get it ready for when you came out of jail. But," Beef winks, "you fucked up his plans."

A gym? I turn and eye the building. It's certainly big enough. But I can't help messing with Mace. "You want me to go back inside so you can get on with it, Ground Pounder?"

His shoulder bumps hard into mine. "Nah, you fuckin' Leatherneck. Want you to stay right where you are, Brother. Working on it with me."

All jokes are put to one side as he turns and looks straight into my face. "You're fuckin' home."

I am. And fuck me. A gym of our own? "You brought this up in church?"

"Not officially. Didn't have a chance, but I know everyone's for it."

"Count me in," says Beef. "Need somewhere to work off Mel's fuckin' cupcakes."

I walk to the building, then eye the surroundings, then look back at the fence behind. "You know, we could do more than just have this for us. It could have its own access. Maybe start a new business venture on our own land."

"Now you're talking." Beef looks at the unpaved road that runs along the back of our property, an approach road for the mill at one time. "You know, you might just have an idea there, Ink."

I raise my chin at him. Of course, at the back of my mind is the thought that I'll be able to train with Beth under my watchful eye and won't have to deal with the worry of her being out of my site at that place she currently frequents.

Did I say I've got it bad for my old lady?

Well, I have.

Vanna

Being a single mom of a fourteen year old boy isn't easy. Now he's gotten on the wrong side of the law, I'm at the end of my tether. He has a dad, just one who denies his existence. But for my son's sake, I have to give it one last try to break the barriers down. Perhaps this time he'll step up and help.

Trouble is, he doesn't recognise me, let alone the boy he left ten years ago.

He's also the member of an outlaw MC, and nothing like the man I used to know.

Mace

Lizard had been right to worry about the girl wanting her 'Property of' tat removed from her back. Putting a patch on someone has meaning in our world and at the very least we need to know whose patch we're removing.

Then I find out about the kid she's brought with her, and the story she tells is heart-breaking. I didn't realise by offering mine, and my club's protection, not only was she going to break it, she was going to steal the heart of this confirmed bachelor as well.

That patch I have to ignore? Well, unless we tread carefully, that's going to bring trouble to the club.

Turning Wheels
Drummer's Beat
Slick Running
Targeting Dart
Heart Broken
Peg's Stand
Rock Bottom
Joker's Fool
Mouse Trapped

Paladin's Hell (Colorado Chapter #1)

Blade's Edge

Demon's Angel (Colorado Chapter #2)
Devil's Due (Colorado Chapter #3)

Truck Stopped

Devil's Dilemma (Colorado Chapter #4)
Amy's Santa (Next Generation #1)

Ink's Devil (Colorado Chapter #5)
Coming Soon
Devil's Spawn (Colorado Chapter #6)

Note 1:

Each book can be read as a standalone, but to get the best reading experience for the Satan's Devils, read the books in the order above.

Note 2:

While the Blood Brothers series is completely separate to the Satan's Devils series, there is some crossover. Turning Wheels continues the story of a minor character who appears in Second Changes, and some characters appear in both series.

OTHER WORKS BY MANDA MELLETT

*<u>Blood Brothers – A series about sexy dominant sheikhs and their
bodyguards</u>*

Stolen Lives (#1) Nijad and Cara

Close Protection (#2) Jon and Mia

Second Chances (#3) Kadar and Zoe

Identity Crisis (#4) Sean and Vanessa

Dark Horses (#5) Jasim and Janna

Hard Choices (#6) Aiza

<u>Satan's Devils MC - Arizona Chapter</u>

Turning Wheels (Blood Brothers #3.5, Satan's Devils #1) Wraith and Sophie

Drummer's Beat (#2) Drummer and Sam

Slick Running (#3) Slick and Ella

Targeting Dart (#4) Dart and Alex

Heart Broken (#5) Heart and Marc

Peg's Stand (#6) Peg and Darcy

Rock Bottom (#7) Rock and Becca

Joker's Fool (#8) Joker and Lady

Mouse Trapped (#9) Mouse and Mariana

Blade's Edge (#10) Blade and Tash

Truck Stopped (#11) Truck & Allie

<u>Satan's Devils MC - Colorado Chapter</u>

Paladin's Hell (#1) Paladin and Jayden

Demon's Angel (#2) Demon and Violet

Devil's Due (#3) Beef and Steph

Devil's Dilemma (#4) Pyro and Mel

Satan's Devils MC - Next Generation

Amy's Santa (#1) Wizard and Amy

ACKNOWLEDGMENTS

I enjoyed writing about Ink and Beth, loving their characters. But somehow, my vision in my head hadn't translated on to the page properly. Massive thanks must go to Danena and Maggie for reading the early draft and telling me where things weren't working. Hopefully they've helped me create a book which you've enjoyed reading.

A new person I have to thank is Sara, my tall friend, who gave me some ideas for Beth's story. I hope you like where I've taken it. Thank you, Sara – I've enjoyed our chats and learning about tall people's problems.

Another successful venture with Dar of Wicked Smart Designs for the cover. Thank you for being so responsive and helpful.

As always I have to thank Maggie Kern my editor who had to work hard on this one. You know I love you, woman.

Melanie has again done a stellar job on the proofreading. Thank you so much.

As normal, as well as Danena, I have to thank all my beta readers. Sheri, you always find something everyone else has missed. Alex, your input is invaluable. Same goes to all the team, Tami, Terra, Zoe, Nicole and of course, my husband, Steve (who's own habit of fainting at the sight of his own blood gave me the idea for Lizard's reaction).

As normal, special thanks to my PA, Tracy Wood. I can't thank her enough for everything she does to keep my social media running smoothly.

I have left the most important to last, all you readers who take a chance on buying my books, and then telling me how much you enjoy reading them. My whole day can be boosted by one message, one comment or one review. You may have no idea how much it spurs me to write more.

The best way of telling me is to leave a review on whatever platform you read on, or anywhere you can review. I read and appreciate every review good or bad. Reviews help authors make sales, sales allow authors to pay editors, models and photographers, cover designers etc, and put food on the table.

What's next? Devil's Spawn (Satan's Devils MC Colorado Chapter) will be my next book.

Love and peace
  Manda

ABOUT THE AUTHOR

Manda's life's always seemed a bit weird, starting with a childhood that even today she's still trying to make sense of, then losing her parents in the late teens. Going from the tragic to the bizarre, who else could be unlucky enough to have had two car accidents, neither her fault, one involving a nun, and another involving a police woman?

There isn't enough space to list everything that's happened to Manda, or what she's learned from it. But by using the rich fabric of her personal life, psychology degree, varied work experiences, and amazing characters she's met, Manda is able to populate her books with believable in-depth characters and enjoys pitting them against situations which challenge them. Her books are full of suspense, twists and turns and the unexpected.

Manda lives in the beautiful countryside of Essex in the UK, the area's claim to fame being the Wilkin's Jam Factory at nearby Tiptree. She can usually find jars of jam which remind her of home wherever she goes. As well as writing books and reading, Manda loves walking her dogs and keeping fit. She lives with her husband of over 30 years, who, along with her son, is her greatest fan and supporter.

Manda is thankful that one of the more unusual, and at the time unpleasant, turns her life took, now enables her to spend her time writing. Confirming, in her view, every cloud has a silver lining.

Photo by Carmel Jane Photography